If Alison had known I was here, she wouldn't have come back.

Catherine was glad for once that she had developed the talent of fading into the background. Even so, her heart was racing. She felt light-headed and hot, as if she had a fever. "It's just a girl you once knew, a girl you fell out with over a boy," she told herself. "It doesn't matter. Why should it matter now?" But Alison hadn't come back alone. She'd come back with two girls and a teenage son . . . and her husband.

Her husband. Catherine had never known what became of Alison and Marc.

Once again, her eyes swept the room, but this time she was looking for something different. The sight that stopped her heart was the back of a man's head, dark hair cut short into the nape of his neck. She was looking at her living, breathing past.

And then, as if he sensed the touch of her gaze on his skin, slowly and uncertainly the man turned around and looked right at her and recognized her.

Praise for *The Accidental Mother* by Rowan Coleman
"A disarmingly sweet tale of motherhood and reluctant love."
—*Publishers Weekly*

"Brilliant . . . moving and funny."
—*New Woman* magazine

"Fun, poignant."
—*OK* magazine

Also by Rowan Coleman

The Accidental Mother

Rowan Coleman

Another Mother's Life

Pocket Books

New York   London   Toronto   Sydney

Pocket Books
A Division of Simon & Schuster, Inc.
1230 Avenue of the Americas
New York, NY 10020

First Pocket Books trade paperback edition October 2008

POCKET and colophon are registered trademarks of Simon & Schuster, Inc.

For information about special discounts for bulk purchases, please contact Simon & Schuster Special Sales at 1-800-456-6798 or business@simonandschuster.com.

Manufactured in the United States of America

10 9 8 7 6 5 4 3

Library of Congress Cataloging-in-Publication Data

Coleman, Rowan.
    Another mother's life / Rowan Coleman
        p. cm.
    ISBN-13: 978-1-4165-8302-8
    ISBN-10:   1-4165-8302-5
    1. Motherhood—Fiction. 2. Domestic fiction. 3. England—Fiction. I. Title.
PR6103.O4426A85 2008
823'.92—dc22

                                                                2008002513

For my daughter, Lily, who is my sunshine.

Another
Mother's Life

One

Alison James found that her feet could not move.

"Good-bye fireplace, good-bye window, good-bye spider's web, good-bye doorknob . . ." Alison listened to her five-year-old daughter's litany of farewells and she knew that her husband would be in the car, his forefinger drumming against the steering wheel impatiently as he waited for her and Amy to come out and join the rest of the family on their trip to their new home, their new life. The moving van had left almost half an hour ago and Alison knew that Marc was horrified at the thought of his widescreen TV languishing on the damp front lawn while the movers waited for someone to let them in. What he didn't know was that despite all that had happened here, for two of the family, at least, it was hard to say good-bye.

The horn sounded from outside, three long bursts that made Amy jump in her skin.

"Come on then, sweetheart," Alison said, picking up her

daughter's hand. "It's time to go to our new home, it will be very exciting, won't it? A proper adventure."

Amy looked up at her mummy.

"But I haven't said good-bye stairs, good-bye loo, good-bye airing cupboard, good-bye . . ."

"How about you just say one big good-bye to the whole house?" Alison prompted, even though she would be perfectly happy to wait while Amy bid farewell to every brick and board. She knew exactly how her daughter felt about leaving their London home because she was just as reluctant to leave it, particularly considering where they were moving to. Everyone else thought they were starting afresh, beginning a new life and turning a clean page. Only Alison seemed to understand that they were traveling back into the past, specifically her past.

But the decision had been made and now it was impossible to turn back.

"Is Farmington nice, Mama?" Amy asked, closing her fingers tightly around Alison's. Alison felt an echoing clench of anxiety in her gut.

"Yes, darling, it's lovely. It's the place where Mummy grew up, remember? And the town where Granny and Grandpa live is only a few miles away. When they get back from their trip we'll see them all the time. Besides, Farmington has lots more room to play and not so much pollution. And the school will be great. You'll love it. Just think of all the new friends you'll make."

Alison looked down at Amy's small, quiet face. She could only guess at how terrifying this move must seem to the five-year-old.

What her husband didn't seem to be able to understand was that going home was nearly as terrifying for her.

"Good-bye house," Amy said on a heavy sigh. "Be happy with your new family."

Then, finally, Alison forced her leaden feet to move and,

leading Amy by the hand, she shut the door on her old life forever.

"Get a move on, love." Marc leaned out of the car window. "I'd like to get us all in before dark!"

Once in the car, Alison looked in the rearview mirror. Fifteen-year-old Dominic was slumped in the very rear, his arms crossed, his woollen hat pulled down over his brows so his black hair fanned into his eyes, his beloved electric guitar in its case on the seat next to him. He was plugged into his iPod with his eyes closed, shutting the world out, displaying his disapproval at what was happening with a silent if not peaceful protest. Her middle child, eight-year-old Gemma, was staring happily out the window, her legs drumming in anticipation of a new adventure, a new world to conquer and hundreds of new friends to make—possibly the only one in the whole family who was truly looking toward the future.

Only Amy, who had the flats of her palms pressed against the car window, kept looking back. Only Amy was still saying her good-byes even as they turned the corner and their old street was out of sight for good. Only Amy, who brushed away a tear, then put her thumb in her mouth and clung to her toy for dear life, seemed aware of exactly what they had left behind.

Only Amy and Alison, that is.

"Come on Alison, it's perfect, admit it." Marc had pressed her only six weeks earlier when he'd come home and told her he thought they should put the house on the market because he'd found them the perfect place to move to.

Alison had half looked at the details of the new house he had thrust under her nose the minute after he'd walked in the door. That was Marc. He was an all-or-nothing kind of man; things had to be done right away or not at all, and this, it seemed, was one of them. He had made a mistake and now he was taking decisive action to fix it, decisive and drastic. The house in the photo was certainly much bigger than their current house, set in some grounds at the end of what looked like a long driveway.

"There's no way we can afford a house like this near enough for you to be able to commute, and if you think that I'm going to be stuck out in the country while you're in town all week, then . . ."

"That's not it at all, Al," he said. "I've been thinking and, well, the dealership in Notting Hill runs itself more or less, it's established. There's no challenge for me there anymore and I think we all need a change, a proper fresh start for all of us." Alison looked at him and waited for the hard sell. Marc picked up her hand as he sat down next to her. "You need a change of scenery after everything that went on at Christmas, not to mention what's been going on with Dom. That's twice now he's been brought home by a policeman, Alison. He's been warned for riding in a stolen car. What will happen next? Will we find a knife in his school bag or have the next policeman turn up on our doorstep to tell us our son's been shot for looking at some kid the wrong way? You don't want that life for him, do you, Al? This is the perfect solution, and look at where the house is."

Alison had stopped looking at her husband the moment he mentioned Christmas. Only Marc could refer to something so painful and humiliating in passing, as if what had happened was merely an inconvenience that a good holiday could sort out. But when she looked at the address of the house, all thoughts of Christmas disappeared.

"This house is in Farmington," she said slowly, feeling suddenly chilled to the core. "We're not moving to Farmington."

"Why not Farmington?" Marc asked her. "We'll be much closer to your parents, once they get back from their grand tour. They only live a few miles away from Farmington and you know how much you'd like to be nearer your mum, especially now that you two get on so much better. You're the only one of us with any family, and I happen to think we should make the most of that, for your sake and the kids'. You spent too long separated from your family; this is a chance, maybe a last chance, for you to make up for those years." Marc paused, holding Alison's gaze. He sounded so persuasive, so rational. As if he wasn't asking her to go back to the place where her life had changed course forever, as if she was the mad one for not wanting to go back.

"Besides, you grew up there," Marc carried on. "It's the perfect place to bring the kids up, it's surrounded by countryside, it's got good schools and low crime rates . . . and look at what we'd get for our money over there compared to this place. So, why not Farmington?"

"You know why not Farmington," Alison said, redirecting her gaze at him. "Marc, you're incredible, you really are."

Marc stared at her wide-eyed for a moment or two as she waited for him to catch up.

"What? You mean because of . . . ? Oh, Al, don't be silly. That's all in the past now, long gone and forgotten. Nobody cares about that anymore, not even your parents!"

"I care!" Alison told him, fighting to temper her tone because the girls were in the next room and Dominic would be home soon. "Would you move back to Birmingham, to the place where your foster mother told you she didn't want you living with her anymore and that she was putting you back in a children's home?"

Marc removed his hand from hers and she felt the chill of its departure.

"I wouldn't move back to Birmingham because it's a shithole," he said, reacting angrily as he always did when Alison mentioned his childhood. "It's not the same and you know it. I got dragged up through foster care and children's homes, kicked about from pillar to post. You had everything you ever wanted. A nice safe life, in a nice safe town, with nice safe parents. Is it so wrong that I want to give that life to my children, and especially to Dom, before he messes up his life for good?"

"You don't give him enough credit," Alison protested. "If you could have seen him in the school show, you would have seen how talented he is. Maybe if you talked to him every now and again—"

"I have talked to him," Marc interrupted her impatiently. "I talked to him for hours after the car incident. I don't know, I look at him and I see myself, Al. The boy needs straightening out. I think living in Farmington could be the answer."

"Look, if you want to move from here then fine. I'm not thrilled to live here anymore either. But we don't have to go to Farmington. That is the last place we should have to go," Alison told him bleakly. "The night I left there with you I knew I was never going back, I never *could* go back."

"Who cares now about what happened back then? It was an age ago, Alison, it doesn't mean anything now."

"Not to you?"

"Of course not to me!" Marc exclaimed. "Al, the last couple of months have been hard on you, you're not thinking straight. If you were you'd see how perfect this is."

"Even so"—Alison looked up wearily at Marc—"it doesn't have to be Farmington. There are a hundred towns like Farmington, two hundred—a thousand even. Any one of those would give the children the kind of life you want them to have, but not this one, Marc. It doesn't have to be Farmington. Mum and Dad don't even live there anymore!"

Marc bowed his head, his hands folded in his lap as they sat side by side on the sofa. "When I came to Farmington I was a railway laborer," he said, beginning the story she already knew so well. "Working nights repairing the lines, sleeping all day in the park, drinking warm beer in the sun waiting for some girls to walk by, hoping they'd give me a second glance. I was twenty years old and I was already dead, my life was going nowhere. I looked around that town, and those people and those girls, and I knew that it was a world I couldn't ever belong to. I knew I'd go on drifting from one place to the next until the day I died. I didn't have anything, Alison, until I met you. I didn't even have myself. "

"That's not true," Alison said, trying to interrupt him.

"You turned my life around. And now I have you. God knows I don't deserve you, but I still have you and I want to keep you. I want to keep the family I love, with a successful business under my belt and another one in the pipeline. I want to go back to Farmington, Ali, I want to go back to the place that rejected me back then and I want to *own* it. Most of all I want to deserve *you*."

"Tell me," Alison said, feeling suddenly inexplicably sad as she looked into the same dark eyes that had beguiled her when she was only seventeen. "Is that any better a reason to go back than mine is to stay away?"

"We're going back for you," he whispered, moving his lips over hers, tucking a strand of her blond hair behind her ear. "Because that's the place where you and I started. It's the place where we belong, and all of the things you're worried about are long dead and buried. I promise you when we're there you and I will be happy again. You'll be happy and I'll be different. I'll have more time to spend with you and the kids. Everything will be different, it will be better."

He'd kissed her then, his hand sliding from her knee to her thigh, and because Alison had wanted so much for this to be the fresh start that Marc talked about, she'd let the discussion slide with it. It was one they would never have again, she knew. Once Marc had made up his mind about something he stuck to it like glue, which was something she supposed she ought to be grateful for. After all, he'd made up his mind to choose her sixteen years ago.

She just had to hope that he was right, that all her fears and misgivings about going back to Farmington were foolish and irrational. That once she got settled back in, it would feel as if she had never been away.

The only problem was, that eventuality was what terrified her the most.

Dusk had fallen by the time their car finally rolled into the driveway of their new home. Amy and Gemma were both asleep in the backseat and Dominic was still nodding his head to some barely heard beat.

"Leave them for a second," Marc whispered. "I've got something I want you to see."

Glancing back at her children, Alison got out of the car and waited as Marc asked the moving men to give him another few minutes. Alison found herself smiling, suddenly engulfed in the warmth of nostalgia. In this light, in his jeans and jacket, he looked just like the dark-haired, olive-skinned boy she'd first fallen for, the boy she had sworn to do anything for.

"Come on." Marc held out a hand to her. "Hopefully if all of my plans have worked, then . . ."

Alison walked into the cavernous hallway just as Marc switched on the lights, and she saw that it was filled with bouquets of red roses. Twelve of them, Alison counted as she looked around, arranged on the marble tiled floor in the shape of a love heart, their sweet scent struggling against that of the new paint, but their color vibrant and bloody against the magnolia walls. It was a dramatic gesture. It was typical Marc.

"Happy Valentine's Day, my beautiful blond bombshell wife," Marc said, wrapping his arms around her from behind.

"And welcome home."

Alison couldn't help but smile as she bent over and picked up one of the bouquets. Suddenly she heard a noise—a sharp yelp and a whimper coming from somewhere deeper in the house.

"What was that?" she asked Marc, wide-eyed. "Rats?"

Marc laughed. "As far as I know rats don't bark. That, if everything has gone according to plan, is the other part of my surprise. Only this part is mainly for the kids, to help them settle in. Follow me."

"Marc, what have you done?" Alison asked ominously as she followed him into her brand-new kitchen.

"Well, they've been asking and asking for years, and it turns out that one of my new clients is a breeder, so I did her a deal and this was part of it." Marc gestured to a pen that had been set up in the corner of the kitchen, a pen that was inhabited by a small chocolate brown Labrador puppy. "Meet Rosie, our new dog."

Alison's jaw dropped as she watched the puppy climb up the sides of its pen, yapping excitedly, its whole body waggling in greeting.

"It's peed on the floor," she said.

"So she has," Marc said. "But the breeder says it should only take you a couple of weeks to house-train her. You'll be fine."

"*Me? I'll* be fine?" Alison exclaimed. "Marc, no way. We are not getting a dog. The puppy has to . . ."

"A puppy!" Gemma shrieked as she raced into the kitchen. "A puppy! Daddy's got a puppy, she's soooooo cute!" Immediately Gemma went over to the young dog and hefted the animal up into her arms, giggling as the puppy licked her face.

"He's kissing me!"

"He's so lovely," Amy said, wide-eyed, stroking the dog's back as Gemma held it. "Let me hold him now, Gemma."

Alison had to concede that as Gemma handed the dog over to

her sister, it was the first genuine smile she had seen on Amy's face all day.

"Actually," Marc told them, "she's a girl. Her name's Rosie, but look, don't get too attached to her. Mummy's not sure that having a dog is the best thing, and I expect that Mummy is right. We might have to give her back . . ."

"Mummy, no!" Gemma was horrified.

"Please, Mummy, don't make us send Rosie back," Amy wailed, clutching the dog tighter to her chest.

Alison sighed, still holding her Valentine roses, as she realized that her husband had stitched her up.

"We can keep her . . ." Alison had to hold her hand up until the cheers stopped. "As long as I am not the only one walking her, cleaning up after her, or toilet-training her," she added, reaching out to stroke one of Rosie's soft ears. "She is quite sweet, I suppose."

Amy wrinkled up her nose. "And I think she just peed on my foot," she said.

"Oh well," Alison said, setting down her bouquet of flowers to look for the box with detergent in it. "Every rose has its thorn."

Two

*H*ow Catherine Ashley came to be spending Valentine's Day with her almost ex-husband was a story that pretty much summed up her life.

"You don't mind booking Jimmy, do you?" Lois, the PTA chairperson, had asked her at the last meeting, with her own special brand of tact. "It's not awkward at all booking your ex to play at the Valentine's Dance, is it? It's just that I know how you two get on still and he'll give you a reduced rate. You know that every penny counts if we're going to raise enough money to pay for the new computer suite."

Catherine had said she didn't mind, and mostly she didn't. It was a fact of life that Jimmy and his band were present at every wedding and christening, and even the odd funeral that she attended both before and since they had split up as a couple, playing for the locals in order to pay the bills while they waited for the stardom that had so far eluded them. Besides, for the last few months peace had broken out between her and Jimmy and he had become almost as much a part of her daily life as he had been when they were living together. Maybe even more so, because all the stress and tension between them had dissolved away now that she had stopped waiting for him to leave her and had kicked him out.

Her friend Kirsty said they were the happiest married couple she knew, and she attributed it to the fact that they'd been living apart for two years. Kirsty hadn't been there for the first year, those long and difficult months when Catherine and Jimmy had tried to find a way to be parents without ripping themselves or their children to shreds. But the second year had been okay, good even. Friendship had finally emerged from the ashes of what they had once had. Catherine knew that one day they'd get divorced properly, but until something happened to push either one of them in that direction, she was still officially Mrs. Jimmy Ashley. That's why booking her husband's band to play the Valentine's Dance was the least of her worries.

The gas bill, the hours her boss wanted her to work, whether or not she'd have the money to get Eloise what she really wanted for her birthday—those were the worries that kept Catherine up at night. But those were practical problems that Catherine could tackle and fight. What she had never been able to overcome was the utterly paralyzing fear of loving Jimmy the way he wanted her to love him, the way *she* often tried to love him, because doing so would expose her long-guarded vulnerability. That fear had stalked her throughout her marriage until one day Jimmy betrayed her, proving all her misgivings correct and making her thank God that she had never fully committed her heart to him, because the shock of what he had done to her and their family was hard enough to bear as it was.

It had taken her a long time to adjust her feelings for him, but she had done it for her girls, for Eloise and Leila, who she lived for, content to let her life orbit around them with the same ordered regularity with which the earth turns around the sun, letting their happiness and beauty warm her, because their love was all that she needed.

And manning the bar at the Valentine's Dance with her friend and neighbor while her ex-husband played his guitar, which looked like a mammoth outsized phallus, onstage was just one of those things. It was a Jimmy thing. Like talking endlessly about sex was a Kirsty thing.

"On reflection I think I *am* in love with my personal trainer," Kirsty said thoughtfully, for the fourth or fifth time since she had started this one-sided debate. She was holding a plastic cup full of wine and gazing contemplatively at one of the many red cardboard hearts that had been hung from the ceiling and stirred gently, wafted by warm air created by the dancing crowd below.

Catherine looked at her, crossing her arms.

"No, you are not in love with your personal trainer," she replied, also for about the fourth or fifth time. "How can you be in love with him? You hardly know him. You've seen him three or four times for an hour twice a week at most."

Catherine was grateful that Kirsty had offered to come with her to the dance as the only other single woman in town without a date, because Catherine wouldn't have come herself if she hadn't been on the committee. She had been volunteered to run the bar, so having Kirsty by her side took the edge off the whole Valentine theme and helped to make it almost bearable.

"So?" Kirsty was questioning her. "What do you think I should do? It's hard to pick up your personal trainer, you know, because whenever you see him you are fat and red and sweaty. How can you make a man want you when you are fat and red and sweaty? Particularly when based on the research I've done, the kind of women he likes are thin and blond and have massive tits. Any ideas?"

Catherine looked down at her friend. At six feet exactly, she towered over Kirsty by almost five inches.

"You are not in love with your trainer," she repeated firmly, as if she were telling her five-year-old Leila that no way was she staying up for the end of *Strictly Come Dancing*. "So you don't have to try and pick him up because you don't love him. You probably don't even fancy him, not really."

"I think you'll find I do," Kirsty avowed. "Have you seen his arms, his chest, his legs, his butt, his . . . oh God I'm having a hot flash and not on my neck."

"That's lust, Kirsty!" Catherine exclaimed, feeling her cheeks color. After a year of knowing Kirsty she was still not comfortable with the other woman's insistence on conducting full and frank discussions of a sexual nature in public places. "It's lust, lust is not love and love isn't even love—it's hormones."

"It's not lust." Kirsty was adamant. "It's so much more than that. We talk and laugh and he *listens* to me. Plus he is the only man in the whole wide world who knows exactly how much I weigh *exactly*. If that's not grounds for marriage, then I don't know what is."

"It's transference," Catherine went on. "Like when people fall for their psychiatrists. You are transferring your sexual urges onto the poor man. Remember, you pay him £59.95 an hour to train you. He doesn't turn up out of the goodness of his heart or just so he can get a look at you sweating. And anyway, like you said, he fancies blond eighteen-year-olds with breast implants."

"No, no, he *thinks* he fancies blond eighteen-year-olds with breast implants, but that's only because he hasn't met me yet. I mean he's met me, but he hasn't met *me*. Once he truly knows me, he'll see what love really is. Or else there's always plastic surgery."

Catherine took a much-needed sip of wine. "You are not in love with your trainer and he is not in love with you. He is probably in love with himself. Now get over it. Do me a favor and go and ask someone's husband to dance with you. I could do with a laugh."

Kirsty sighed but allowed the change of subject nevertheless.

"You don't just rush up to a couple and tap the woman on the shoulder and say please can I dance with your husband," she told Catherine. "There's no fun to be had there and besides, it never works; the married woman is a particularly fierce and protective creature.

"Why do you do all this PTA lark?" Kirsty asked. "You should chuck it all in and have a proper grown-up life. After all, you and me, mainly me—we are single women, we should be doing proper single-woman stuff, going on ill-advised dates with men who don't deserve us, setting a terrible example for children and falling out with our estranged ex-husbands, with the emphasis on *strange,* and not inviting them round to Sunday tea! That's what proper single women do."

"You haven't got an ex-husband," Catherine remarked.

"Well, there's no need to brag," Kirsty sighed. "I could be in the Three Bells Pub right now impressing my trainer with my all-natural if subtle cleavage. You could be with me; maybe he's got a friend, I don't know. The point is that you and I could be out on the town getting noticed."

Catherine raised a brow. At six feet tall with red hair, she had never had a problem getting noticed. She'd always tried to blend in, to stay out of the limelight. She always wore black trousers, a black top, and flat black boots or shoes. Usually she wore her long hair up, knotted on the top of her head, but she never dyed it and only cut it every other month with the kitchen scissors. Beauty was something that Catherine had never quite understood, but she was fairly certain she wasn't it. Most men were scared of her, and of the two men she had "known" in her life, the one she had married had been caught having sex with a groupie in the ladies' loos at the Goat Pub. And what's more, he'd been caught by Catherine. In the end she'd scared him off too. Getting noticed in any way at all was not at the top of Catherine's to-do list.

She watched the crowd dancing for a minute or two and suddenly found herself remembering the last Valentine's Dance she had been to. It was a bittersweet memory, tinged with sadness, but this was true of all her memories before she had gotten together with Jimmy. Recalling any of them required her to pay a certain price.

Catherine had been fifteen and she had planned a daring escape for the night, telling her parents she was going to a rehearsal for the school public speaking team so that she could go to the school disco with Alison.

She and Alison had met outside the church on High Street and got changed together in the public loos outside the supermarket, putting on lipstick haphazardly as they peered into the scratched mirrors that were screwed to the walls. Alison had brought Catherine a skirt to wear and she tied a piece of black lace into her red hair. She must have looked a sight, but Catherine didn't care. When she was with Alison she felt invincible.

Of course none of the boys had asked Catherine to dance, but she was glad of it. She couldn't think of anything worse than turning in a slow deathly circle to "Love Is All Around" with some boy's hand on her bottom and his nose in her cleavage. Alison had refused to dance with any of the many boys that kept asking her, telling all of them she wanted to dance with Catherine instead.

When Lee Britton accused her of being a lesbian, Alison had grabbed Catherine's hand and kissed it, winking at him.

"You've got that dead right, Lee," she'd said. "Imagine that when you're tossing off in bed tonight!" And she had spun Catherine around and around in a circle until the pair of them, dizzy with laughter from the look on Lee's face, had collapsed on the floor.

On the way home that night the two of them had stopped once again in the loos outside the supermarket and changed back into jeans and sweaters. Alison too, even though her parents knew she'd been going to the disco and all she had to hide from them was makeup.

"Your parents are weirdos, babe," Alison had said as she wiped the lipstick off of Catherine's mouth, holding her chin between her thumb and forefinger.

"It's just their way," Catherine had tried to explain, although the older she got the harder she found it to understand them herself. "They were old when they had me. They still haven't got used to having a kid around."

"Well, you might not be able to choose your family, but at least you've got me, right? And that makes you lucky."

They had hugged each other before going their separate ways. And for a long time, Catherine had thought that Alison was right, she was the luckiest girl in the world to have Alison as her best friend, her protector, and her confidante. It had seemed like the kind of friendship that would last forever.

"This dance sucks," Kirsty said, snapping Catherine back into the present. "I thought all the best men were supposed to be married. Why are none of them here?"

"I'm sorry, Kirsty, I should have told you that the school PTA Valentine's Dance would be no place to meet a man."

"And *that* is why you are alone," Kirsty lectured her. "Everywhere is a place to meet a man if you look hard enough, a pub, a club, the gym, the supermarket, even the optician's . . ."

"The optician's?" Catherine asked.

"Long story," Kirsty said. "What I'm saying is if you really want to meet a man, then you have to try a bit harder."

"I'm not trying to meet a man," Catherine said. "I don't want to meet a man, I'm a happily nearly divorced married woman."

"Your trouble is that you don't realize what a fox you are. Men would queue up to go out with you if you weren't so uptight and always slightly scary looking. You know, plucking your eyebrows would make you seem a lot less frowny—I'm just saying."

"I'm not uptight," Catherine replied mildly. "I just don't want to do it again."

"Do you mean you don't want to have a relationship again or do you mean you don't want to do *it* again? Because if you are telling me you never want to have sex again, I refuse to believe it. You're thirty-two, Catherine. You are at your sexual peak. Why on earth wouldn't you want sex in your life again? Preferably with an eighteen-year-old, I've heard that's the perfect match sexual peak–wise."

Catherine looked at Kirsty and wondered how to answer that question. By the time she went to bed with Jimmy, she'd more or less qualified as a virgin again, such was the length of time that had passed between her first sexual experience and her second. It had been clumsy and difficult and she had been embarrassed and awkward, but to her surprise and relief Jimmy hadn't run away afterward. He's treated her sweetly and gently and gradually the two of them began to work together well, becoming easy and familiar lovers. For a while they brought out the best in each other. Catherine inspired Jimmy's tender and protective side and he made her laugh and relax. She was able to stand tall in a crowd, happy in the knowledge that the man she was holding hands with was two inches taller than her. But although she had cared for him, needed him, she had never fallen in love with him the way he always told her she would do. In all the years they had been married she had never found the courage to let herself go until the night she found him having sex with Donna Clarke in the ladies' loos of the Goat Pub. Ironic, really, that the peak of her passion for Jimmy had manifested itself on the day he decided to cheat on her, the day she knew she would never be able to trust him again.

It was only when Jimmy tried to explain to her why he'd been having sex with a total stranger that she understood why their marriage was over.

"It's not that I don't love you," Jimmy told her, holding both her wrists so that she wouldn't punch him anymore. "But you don't . . . you don't . . ."

"Don't what—excite you? Is that it? Have you finally realized after making me marry you, after making me trust you and rely on you, after persuading me to build my life with you and have your children, that I'm not good enough for you?" Catherine had shrieked at him.

"No!" Jimmy protested, letting go of her wrists so that she sprang forward and pushed him to the tile wall with a thud. "No," he repeated as she stepped back, hanging her head, her shoulders heaving. "You don't love me, not really, you can't. You're still waiting for the man you can love to walk into your life. I'm never going to be that person, Cat. I'm never going to change into the kind of man you need."

"The kind of man I need?" Catherine asked him furiously. "Tell me, Jimmy, what is the kind of man I need?"

"Someone you can let yourself go with again. I've spent years trying to make you love me, and it hasn't worked. And why should you love me? Look at what a shit I am . . ." Jimmy paused and took a breath as Catherine studied his face. "Tonight has proved it to you and it's proved it to me. I don't deserve you, Catherine, and I can't stand seeing the disappointment in your eyes anymore, just like I can't stand loving a woman who doesn't feel the same way about me. I'm worn out. I can't do it anymore."

"But . . ." For a moment Catherine was lost for words, acutely aware that she hadn't denied his charge. "Why didn't you just tell me, why do *this*?"

"I didn't plan this, I never plan anything, you know I don't. I didn't tell you how I was feeling because I didn't have the guts," Jimmy said levelly.

It had taken Catherine a long time to stop being angry about that.

Now, at last, Catherine's life was a calm ocean and she had some peace. There was no way she could explain to someone as restless and as searching as Kirsty how important peace was in her life and that she'd take order and regularity over excitement and change any day of the week. So she decided not to.

"Look"—she nudged Kirsty in the ribs—"Lois's husband has been separated from the pack. Go in for the kill now, while he's weak and vulnerable."

"Right you are," Kirsty said, her automatic vixen mode revving up, and then she was gone.

Catherine couldn't decide what was funnier, Lois's indignation at her husband doing the tango with Kirsty or Mr. Lois's bright red cheeks and sweaty brow as Kirsty twirled him around the school hall as if they were in Argentina. Either way she kept her mirth to herself, watching with the same implacable mask she always wore to these functions.

The music changed tempo and Catherine realized that Jimmy's band was taking a break. They put a mix tape on and the floor filled instantly to the opening strains of "Dancing Queen."

As Catherine scanned the crowd, she spotted Jimmy fending off one of his groupies, who hung around his neck in a swoon, clearly dying to be kissed. In his well-meaning attempt not to embarrass his wife in front of the whole school, Jimmy untangled himself from the girl's advances and smiled at her as she attempted to lunge at him again.

Catherine looked down at the table and counted to twenty in the hopes that when she looked up again the girl would have stopped pursuing him. It wasn't jealousy she felt. It was more embarrassment and discomfort in knowing that everybody else in the room who saw him would be thinking the same thing—"Poor Catherine, poor old Catherine, all on her own and heartbroken"—while her husband snogged another floozy in front of her very eyes.

When she stopped counting and looked up, Jimmy was standing right in front her.

"Hey, babe," he said, pushing the shades he regularly wore in February up into his long, dark brown hair. "Any chance of a beer?"

"I've got white wine, red wine, or juice," Catherine said with a smile. "I could probably rustle up some juice for your girlfriend over there."

"Ha, funny," Jimmy said with an easy grin. "I'll have two wines then, don't care which color. You look nice, by the way."

"I look the same and you know it," Catherine replied as she handed him a glass.

The girlfriend was loitering a few feet away, uncertain about whether to come over, probably intimidated by the Amazonian ex-wife, Catherine thought with some small satisfaction. She did tend to scare his groupies whenever she was around. Probably due to the rumor that Catherine had punched Donna Clarke so hard she broke her nose in the ladies' loos of the Goat. The truth was far more seedy and mundane. Donna Clarke had been so drunk that in her hurry to exit the crime scene she had careered into the door, catching herself right between the eyes.

"She looks nice," Catherine said, nodding at the girl. "Very . . . firm. What's her name?"

Jimmy shrugged. "Suzie . . . she is a nice girl but not for me, you know. Nothing much in common."

"Except for a mutual love of you," Catherine teased.

"Well, yes, but I have that in common with all women," Jimmy replied with a grin.

"Are you playing another set?" Catherine asked.

"Yeah, some power ballads to get them going. I was thinking of 'The Power of Love' followed by 'Move Closer.' What do you think?"

"I think good." Catherine nodded. "If you can play any Celine Dion, then you're laughing."

Jimmy smiled. "What will you do the rest of the weekend?" he asked. "Maybe a trip to Paris? Maybe find some handsome Frenchman to French kiss you under the Eiffel tower?"

"I'm planting the vegetable patch in the back garden," Catherine said. "We're nearly self-sustainable now, you know. There'll be enough for you too, if you want it."

"Free veg," Jimmy said, smiling as he watched Catherine realigning the glasses she had just polished. "Radical."

"Hey, mate!" Gazza, the band's bassist, beckoned Jimmy back to the stage. "We're on!"

"I can drop you home later if you like, I'm the designated driver tonight," Jimmy said with an offhand shrug. "I've got the van until tomorrow and I'm going that way after all."

Catherine smiled at her husband. "Aren't you forgetting something?" she asked.

"Just because we're separated doesn't mean I can't drive you places," Jimmy said defensively. "I worry about you out on the street at all hours."

"No, I meant your girlfriend, idiot," Catherine told him mildly.

"Hadn't you better drop her home or take her somewhere and do whatever it is you do with them?"

"Oh yeah," Jimmy said as he glanced back at Suzie.

"I might pop round tomorrow then," he said casually. "See how you're getting on."

" 'Bout lunchtime-ish?" Catherine asked.

"Why, are you cooking?" Jimmy said.

"You know I am," Catherine said. "And you know you're welcome."

"Cool," Jimmy said, breaking into a happy grin. "I haven't eaten hot food in three days."

Three

Alison sat on her new bed in her new bedroom in her new house and considered crying. She couldn't allow herself the luxury, she decided. If she started now she'd never stop and then the house would look no better by the time her three children got home from school.

Besides, she wasn't unhappy *exactly*. She was just exhausted and stressed and it felt strange being in this literally new house with the scent of paint and new carpet still in the air. The enormity of how her life had changed stunned her, to such an extent that as she tried to come to terms with it she let Rosie chew unchecked on one of her favorite green Nine West pumps. And she was worried about the children and about how the three of them would get on with their first days at new schools.

It seemed surreal to Alison to be back in Farmington. Whenever she looked out of the windows of her bedroom and saw the gentle rise of the hills rolling behind the tree line, she suffered an immediate and unprecedented bout of agoraphobia. You knew where you stood in London, which was largely in the thick of it, shoulder to shoulder with the masses, each of you working through your daily lives trying to interact with as few people as possible.

The Farmington of her childhood could not have been more different than the Farmington she lived in today. It had been a small rural town where everybody knew everybody else and felt as if they had some form of ownership over the lives of others. That's why her mother especially had suffered so terribly when she and Marc ran away. It had taken Alison a long time, years actually, to see her parents' side of her unexpected departure. What she had never been able to explain to them was that it wasn't their fault that she had run away before she could take even one of the A levels she'd been studying for. Just as she couldn't make them see that there was nothing either one of them could have done or said differently that would have kept her at home to live the safe, loving life her parents had always planned for her.

The simple fact was that her love for Marc had eclipsed everything else. Even the fact that she had been pregnant with Dominic on the night she'd left with Marc had seemed incidental compared to the urgent need she'd felt to escape with him, to make him hers before anything could come between them. She hadn't told him she was pregnant until two weeks later on an evening when he was drunk and angry and she was tearful and desperate.

"I'm having your baby!" she had screamed at him. "Are you staying with me or what?" He'd decided to stay. That night Alison had been glad for the first time that she was pregnant, not because she wanted a baby but because she wanted to keep Marc.

At least six years had passed before her mother said something that had finally given Alison an insight into the devastation her parents had experienced when she'd left. She and Marc and Dominic had visited them in their new home, in a small village about twenty miles outside of Farmington.

"This is a nice village," Alison had said as she set out her mum's best china for tea, a sign that her parents had at last accepted her and Marc as a couple because the best china came out only for people her mum approved of.

"It is nice," her mother had said quietly. "It's nice living in a place where people don't know everything about you."

At that moment Alison realized how difficult it must have been for her parents to explain to their friends and neighbors what had happened to their daughter, why she had felt the need to run away from home for a life with a man she hardly knew. And now, sitting on her cellophane-covered mattress in her brand-new house after returning to the place where her name had once been the hot topic of gossip, her mother's simple sentence gained a new significance.

Alison had driven Dominic to school first, before the girls, negotiating her way gingerly around the familiar roads and streets as if she half expected her past to leap out from some dark corner and run her off the road. But the town was indifferently busy, caught up as it was in the midst of the school run, and Alison was able to relax as she realized her 4x4 was just one of many on the roads that morning. Although hers was perhaps the only one with a determinedly destructive puppy in the pack. Rosie, it seemed, could not be left alone in the house unless Alison was ready to sacrifice her real oak kitchen cupboards or specially carved banister rails. As large as the house was, Alison was fairly confident the puppy would be able to eat it in its entirety in just under a month.

As she drove the children along High Street, she even felt a surge of affection for the old place, still so pretty with its Victorian shop fronts and medieval church. There was a Costa coffee and a Chez Gerard in situ now instead of the All Day English Breakfast

Café and the Italian restaurant her parents had always taken her to on her birthdays for a gigantic ice cream sundae.

The grocers and the butchers had been replaced with several estate agents and nowadays there were a number of smart fashion boutiques that looked as if they were brimming with exactly the kind of clothes that Alison had far too many of, designer and expensive, the kind of top or dress that would only do for one season and then could never be seen in smart company again. The old co-op had been turned into an exclusive gym. Alison knew if she looked in the estate agents' windows, it would be difficult to find even a modest house priced under five hundred thousand pounds, which made it a place where it was almost impossible for those on an average income to live. It was an exclusive town now; you could see that by the cars parked along the side of the road. In how many other places on the planet could you see an Aston Martin, a Porsche, two Mercedes, and countless BMWs all lined up nose to tail? The town she had grown up in had been middle class, suburban, and staid, where respectability was treasured and flashiness frowned upon. Back then it was a fusty maiden aunt of a town, prim and proper. Now it was a showy trophy wife, with diamonds on its fingers, a pair of gold leather sling-backs on its feet and a year-round fake tan.

But Farmington's apparent face-lift offered Alison little comfort; this was not the town that she had once fled, that was true. But it was also not a place that she wanted to come back to. Gentrified or not, this was still the scene of Alison's darkest hour, the place where she had behaved in the most terrible way, leaving her parents in the middle of the night with only a note of explanation, and, worse still, betraying someone she had loved and who had trusted her.

And although she tried to believe Marc's all-too-rational comment that no one would care or even remember what had happened back then, from the moment Marc had begun to move their lives back here it had been hard not to believe that somewhere amid the coffee shops and boutiques, her past was still lying in wait for her.

While Alison had been putting on a brave face for the children and Amy had rallied, bravely stoical about the upheaval, Dom was openly disgusted. The thunderous expression on his face as she drove him to the school gates said it all. He was furious with his parents for bringing him here to this place he had already referred to as a dive and a dump on numerous occasions since they had moved in over the weekend.

"I used to go to this school when I was your age, can you believe," Alison said lightly as she pulled the car up to Dominic's new high school. She had had to cover the shock of emotion she felt at being confronted with the building that she spent so many pivotal moments of her life in, forcibly reminding herself that it was just a building. "It's a good school, Dom, you'll make new friends really quickly here. And there's Rock Club, don't forget. Once you've started there you'll be right at home."

Alison had been pinning all of her hopes of winning her son over on the flimsy promise of Rock Club. He was a dedicated guitarist, it was one of the few things he openly took pleasure in, and he had worked for two summers without complaint to earn half the two thousand pounds required to buy his dream guitar. When the head teacher had taken them on a tour of the school a couple of weeks before they had made the move, the news about Rock Club, run by a local music teacher, was the only thing he had shown any interest in despite his very best attempts to hide it.

"This sucks," he told Alison as he opened the car door reluctantly. "It really sucks that you are making me go through with this."

Alison knew he was resentful and possibly even a little bit

scared about what his new set of peers would think of him. But she also knew she couldn't reach out and put an arm around his shoulders to comfort him because he'd find that almost as distressing as getting out of the car and walking through the gates.

"Do you want me to come in with you?" she offered impulsively. He looked at her as if she were mentally ill.

"No," he said, getting out of the car and slamming the door shut behind him. "I'm not a kid."

Alison watched him for a few minutes as he walked away.

Once, they had been so close. They had always been side by side and hand in hand—in step with each other. It hadn't been the birth of his sister Gemma that had changed that, nor even his bumpy and painful ascent into manhood. It was the day he realized that Alison was weak and flawed and incapable of doing anything to change herself. Since then all he had ever seemed to be was angry with her.

"He looks like a right old grump," Gemma said, leaning forward in her seat to watch Dominic slouch away.

"Will he be all right, Mama?" Amy asked anxiously. "It looks like a big place to be in on your own. Is our school this big?"

"No, darling, it's little. Remember when you looked round, you said it looked like a doll's house? And anyway Dom won't be alone; he'll be making lots of new friends just like you will." Alison waited for him to go through the gate and head toward the main entrance; then she took her mobile out of her bag and phoned the school reception.

"Hello, it's Mrs. James here. I just want to check that my son is signing in with you like he's supposed to. It's his first day and you know how boys are. He won't let me come in with him to make sure he's okay."

"Yes, thank you, madam," the receptionist said in an even tone. "The delivery has arrived safely. We are dealing with it now."

"Thank you so much," Alison said warmly, grateful for the discretion.

"Not at all," the receptionist said.

It was about two minutes later that she got a text from Dominic saying "Stop checking up on me."

She was a little late getting the girls to St. Margaret's First School, but she didn't think it mattered on their first day because she had to go see the headmistress first anyway before they would be taken off to their classrooms.

Whereas Dominic's school was attended by all the children in the town who weren't privately educated, St. Margaret's was not; Alison had not gone there when she'd been her daughters' ages, and it was something of a relief to be in an unfamiliar and neutral environment. She only wished that both of her daughters felt the same way.

It was a sweet little school, built around an original Victorian schoolhouse, and what it lacked in playing fields because of its town center location it made up for in atmosphere. The thing that Alison had liked about it most was the sense of community in the school. The children all seemed to care about each other, the bigger ones looking out for the little ones. Alison thought that this was especially important for Amy.

Dear, precious, uncomplicated Gemma, who could have little idea how her self-confidence and adaptability kept her mother going, had been chatting happily to her teacher when she was taken off to her classroom to be introduced to her new classmates. Amy had not gone happily at all. She had cried and cried, clinging to Alison's skirts, begging her mummy to take her home with her. Eventually Alison had had to peel her daughter's fingers from the fabric, desperately trying not to cry herself, and physically hand her to the teacher.

"Come on, darling," Alison had said, holding her daughter's hand out to the teacher. "You go with Miss Pritchard now. You're going to have a lovely time and I bet you'll make a lot of friends, you'll see."

"Please, can Rosie come too?" Amy begged. "I'd feel better if Rosie could come in with me."

"Doggies aren't allowed in school," Alison explained.

"But I want to stay with Rosie!" Amy's sob had echoed all the way down the corridor.

When Alison had come out of school the playground was empty of parents and pupils and she had been relieved. She wasn't ready to meet anybody just yet, particularly after that dramatic farewell with Amy had left her on the verge of tears.

She had made the short drive back to her new house with a heavy heart, and once she had pulled into the drive she sat in the 4x4 and looked at the house for quite a long time. It was a huge house. Six bedrooms, third-floor guest suite, an open-plan hallway with a living room, dining room, and gigantic kitchen radiating off of it. It was twice as big as their London house and ten times as grand. Marc loved it. He loved buying this overstated and opulent palace. He loved the fact that it was brand spanking new and slightly tacky, with none of the grace and dignity of some of the other houses they had looked at, the Victorian villas that populated over half the town. He loved the remote-controlled electric gates, the faux regency pillars that stood proudly on either side of the double front doors, and he loved the fact that he was able to buy up the paddock at the back of the house that one day soon he'd promised would be occupied by a pony for the girls.

"This says we've arrived," he'd told Alison on the night they moved in, kissing her on the forehead. "Who'd have thought that you and I would have made it all the way here, hey? House, kids, dog—the works. We've beaten the odds, Al, we've proved them all wrong."

Which had made Alison wonder—who did they have to prove anything to now? Except themselves.

Still sitting immobilized on the bed, Alison looked around at her new bedroom, the cellophane of the mattress squeaking beneath her bottom as she twisted to survey the mountain of boxes that required unpacking.

And she decided she would cry after all. Just then, crying seemed about the only thing she was confident she could do.

Four

Catherine was out of breath when she hit the school gate at three fifteen because she had run the length of High Street from work in order to be there in time. Her job, working as an administrative manager at a local PR agency, Stratham and Shah, couldn't exactly be called a career, but the hours fit perfectly into the school day as long as she was prepared to sprint there and back every morning and afternoon. Aside from the vital if meager income it provided, it also gave her something to do outside of the house and apart from the girls. There wasn't much glamour in binding presentations or managing the online calendar for the practice, but Catherine was very good at it. She enjoyed bringing order to the often chaotic and capricious office and garnered quiet satisfaction from the frequency with which the word "indispensable" was used in connection with her name.

Eloise was already on the playground, hopping randomly, her head bowed in concentration as if each hop was being placed with precise care. Catherine stopped just inside the gate to catch her breath and watched her daughter in her one-legged endeavors, her red hair flying in all directions, her green eyes glittering with laughter.

"Mum!" Eloise spotted her and raced up to her at full pelt, using her mother's body to break her speed.

"Guess what, it's so exciting!" Eloise hopped on Catherine's toes. "I've got a new best friend! She started today and her name is Gemma and she's got a sister in Leila's class. She has just moved to Farmington from London and she has got a bedroom to herself and Mummy—guess what? She's got a brand-new puppy called Rosie! A real dog! Where is she? I wish she were here, Mummy, and you could meet her!"

Catherine looked at Eloise's face, her cheeks glowing hotly on her otherwise pale face and she felt her heart sink.

"A *puppy?*" she repeated. This was bad news. Her daughters begged her for a pet, any kind of pet, on a daily basis, frequently stating that even a gerbil would do. But Eloise's heart's desire, the one thing she longed for more than anything in the world, was a dog. And now here was a girl who was going to have her very own dog. Catherine would never hear the end of it.

"And," Eloise went on, tugging at Catherine's hand, "she says I can come round and see it whenever I like and walk it and play with it and groom it and everything," Eloise was almost shouting in her excitement. "So can I go over tonight, Mummy, can I? Can I? Can I, please?"

"I expect tonight is a little bit too soon," Catherine said. "They'll still be unpacking."

"But please can Gemma still come to tea one day soon?" Eloise begged. "Please!"

"Of course she can, one day," Catherine said, deliberately noncommittal. "Let's go round and pick up Leila and then when we get back we'll see Gemma and her mummy and we'll ask her, okay?"

"Yippee!" Eloise called out happily as she skipped along beside Catherine on their way round to Leila's class, catching Catherine's hand and swinging it back and forth.

"I knew eight was going to be my best age," she said happily.

"How did you know that?" Catherine smiled in anticipation. While her younger daughter, Leila, had the light hazel eyes and wavy dark brown hair of her father, she also had the staunch practicality of her mother, as well as, since starting at St. Margaret's First School, what appeared to be a quite sincere and devout belief in God.

Eloise, on the other hand, although a carbon copy of Catherine from the ends of her wild red hair to the tips of her long, skinny legs, was the dreamer and the rebel, like her father. Catherine couldn't wait to hear Eloise's theory on why eight was such a great age.

"Because one, two, three, four, five, six, and seven are baby years," Eloise said, gesturing as if she were presenting a news report on TV. "But eight is halfway to sixteen. Halfway to being grown up. When you're eight you start to count in the world, you're not a baby anymore."

"You'll always be my baby," Catherine said, putting her arms around Eloise and squeezing her tight on impulse.

"I won't, Mummy." Eloise wriggled free. "I'm growing up, you know!"

"I know you are," Catherine said, picking up a strand of her daughter's hair. She remembered the morning when Jimmy had put their firstborn in her arms. Her touch, her weight, her smell, and the joy of her tiny fingers enclosing around Catherine's fingers made the world seem so much brighter and so sharp, as if she was looking at her life through a new pair of eyes. "But I'll always love you and your sister just as much as I did from the moment you were born."

"And now I've met Gemma, and she's got a puppy and Leila's stopped snoring at night and well, things are getting better. They are starting to go the right way, aren't they, Mummy?"

Catherine paused and looked down at her daughter.

"Are they?" she asked her tentatively. Although it was Eloise who had suffered the most visibly during the pain and mess of the breakup, the first year after Jimmy had moved out had been raw, confusing, and difficult for them all. If Eloise was now beginning to see the separation in a better light, if the work that she and Jimmy had done to restore some stability to their daughters' lives was finally paying off, then Catherine could not have been happier. "How's that?"

"Well, now that you aren't so angry with Daddy anymore and he's stopped making you angry. Now you let him come round when he likes and have dinner and put us to bed. Things are nearly back to the way they were, aren't they, Mummy? It won't be long now."

"What won't?" Catherine asked, battling the sensation that she knew exactly what Eloise was going to say next.

"Well, soon Daddy will come home for good, won't he?"

Just at that second Leila came tearing out of her classroom, her coat attached to her only by its hood, which was hooked over her head, and her arms filled with several sheets of artwork and some junk models, leaving bits of toilet paper and empty yogurt cartons flying in her wake.

"Leila, put your coat on properly," Catherine said automatically, picking the coat off her daughter's head and holding it out for her to put on.

"Look!" Leila said, thrusting out a jumble of what had formerly been food containers of various descriptions. "It's great, isn't it?"

Catherine hazarded a guess. "It's an amazing . . . car."

"Is it a car?" Leila scrutinized the object. "I thought it was an octopus, but anyway it's good, isn't it?"

"Well?" Eloise asked Leila as she unburdened her sister of her treasure and Catherine helped her on with the coat.

"Well . . ." Leila looked thoughtful. "I learned about China today, Mummy. Did you know its flag is bright red and there are dragons there, but not real dragons because there aren't really dragons in this world. There are real dragons in Australia, though, and kangaroos, which are true animals because we saw them at the zoo, do you remember, and they went bounce . . . bounce . . . *bounce* . . . do you think there were kangaroos on the Ark, can we look it up when we get home?"

Leila bounced into her sister, dashing her model octopus/car to the ground, where it promptly exploded. Catherine bent down and began picking it up, stuffing its various components into her capacious bag.

"Not that, silly," Eloise said impatiently as Catherine, still on her knees, buttoned up Leila's coat. "I mean what about the new girl in your class? Have you made best friends with her? Has she told you she's got a puppy called Rosie?"

Leila's face looked blank.

"Did you meet the new little girl that started today?" Catherine interpreted. "Did you play with her?"

"Oh *well*," Leila said, instantly transforming herself into a world expert on the subject. "The new girl's name is Amy and she cried the *whole* time and Miss Pritchard didn't even shout at her or put on her sad face or anything and we were all nice to her, Ryan didn't even try to chase her, but she cried all day and didn't do any reading because she cried and said she wanted her mummy, which made Isabelle cry for her mummy and then Alfie did and then everyone was crying for a bit. I joined in too, but I only pretended because I quite like reading."

"Everyone in your class was crying?" Catherine asked her.

"Well, Amy and Alfie and Isabelle did," Leila said with a shrug. "And when Amy's mummy came to school to pick her up they had to go and talk to Mrs. Woodruff. About the crying I 'spect."

"Typical." Eloise sighed dramatically. "Can we wait for them to come out from Mrs. Woodruff's office, Mummy, can we, *please*?"

"No, we can't," Catherine said firmly, feeling some empathy for this unknown mother and her attempts to get her children settled in a new school. "We'll see her tomorrow, I expect, and I'll go and say hello to your new friends then."

"And you have to make best friends with Amy, okay? Even if she does cry all the time," Eloise ordered her sister urgently.

"Okay," Leila agreed as she fished a sawed-off plastic bottle from out of her mother's bag and looked at it. "Actually, it was a pony. It was a good pony model, wasn't it?"

"The best," Catherine said. But as she shepherded her daughters out of the school gate, she was only thinking one thing. What if by trying to make things better with Jimmy for her daughters, she had actually made them worse? How was she ever going to be able to explain to Eloise or Leila that their daddy was never coming home?

As the three of them walked down their street toward their terraced house, they could hear music from three houses away.

"Dad's home!" Leila exclaimed.

"And he's written a new song," Eloise said, listening as they approached the front door. "It's good, isn't it, Mum?"

Catherine listened for a moment to the wail of Jimmy's electric guitar, which was barely muted by the walls of the house.

"It sounds very interesting," she said diplomatically. This unscheduled appearance at home was exactly the kind of thing that was confusing the children. But it was also exactly the kind of thing that Catherine had encouraged over the last year. After all, it was still half Jimmy's house; he still paid the mortgage. And in order to be able to do that, he lived on a freezing-cold and leaky canal boat that his dead best friend had left him. And why shouldn't he be there when his children got home from school? She'd have to talk to him; they'd have to find a way to help the children understand the situation.

Just as Catherine opened the front door for the girls, Kirsty stepped out of hers.

"Any chance you could get him to either shut up or cheer up? Whichever one is likely to happen . . . sooner?" She stopped shouting as the girls ran in and Jimmy put down his guitar to greet his daughters.

"Thank the Lord," Kirsty said, briefly pressing her palms together in an expression of prayer.

"I'm sorry," Catherine said. "He says he can't really hear how it's going to sound unless he plays it loud. Count yourself lucky you didn't live next door when we were still together. Actually, that's probably why the neighbor moved . . ."

"So divorce him and then it will be all your house and you won't be a default wife anymore. I'd suggest taking him to the cleaners, but in his case I mean it literally. Look, I'm glad I caught you. I need you to come out with me on Friday night."

"Come out with you? What do you mean come out?" Catherine frowned.

"I mean you coming out of your house, that's the big thing with the bricks and the roof, by the way, and proceeding with me to the pub on Friday night for a drink. That's another brick thing with a roof on top, only it has a license to sell alcohol too. Now do you understand or would you like me to draw you a diagram?"

"I've told you I don't go to pubs . . ." Catherine started. "I'm not normally a pub person."

"You're not normally a normal person period, but you are

going to be one this Friday because the kids are going away with Bon Jovi in there, aren't they? And because I need you." Kirsty smiled like Leila in possession of a chocolate-filled doughnut and a DVD of *The Sound of Music*. "We're going to just *happen* to be in the pub where my trainer drinks. I worked it all out this morning while I was teaching the over-fifties pilates class. He hasn't fallen in love with me yet because he's never seen me at my finest, with my hair done and my push-up bra on and mascara. So I'm going to *coincidentally* go to the pub where he always is on Friday nights in my new turquoise crocheted dress with the cleavage and he's going to see me and think 'Wow' and fall in love with me on the spot for the kind and sensitive person I am. Do you *see*?"

"And you want *me* to come with you," Catherine said. "You don't want one of your other friends? You know, the friends who actually like people?"

"Of course I do," Kirsty sighed. "But the bastards all have someone. You are all I have left, it's the cross I have to bear. Besides, what you need most in the world is to be brought out of yourself a bit, and if me helping you do that also means that you are helping me in some tiny little way, then it's synergy, isn't it? It's cosmic forces in balance. Plus, I put up with your husband wailing his head off for hours on end when I'm supposed to be teaching Tantric meditation to Mrs. Evans so that she can bring herself to have sex with her husband, so you owe me."

"He's my *ex*-husband and you've got a student in there—where is she?" Catherine asked.

"Meditating, obviously. Now, what do you say? Yes or no?"

Catherine tried to imagine herself standing in a pub full of Friday night drinkers and couldn't. Then she tried to imagine herself successfully saying no to Kirsty and that seemed even more unlikely. Perhaps it would be better to just go and try to get the whole thing over and done with as quickly as possible.

"Okay," she relented. "I'll come for an hour tops, just long enough for you to pull him, then I'm going home."

"Of course you are," Kirsty said happily. "That's what I'm counting on."

Inside, Jimmy had thankfully unplugged his electric guitar in favor of his acoustic one and was now strumming his new song, singing to the girls, both of his feet up on the coffee table, an adoring daughter on either side of him on the sofa. Seeing the three of them together like that still gave Catherine a wrench; it was impossible not to imagine what their lives could have been like if she and Jimmy had been different people, or not even different but just the right people for each other. Jimmy glanced up at her and flashed her a grin as he played, reminding Catherine why so many women found him attractive. It wasn't just his height, or broad shoulders and strong arms that they adored, or even his hazel eyes or expressive mouth. Jimmy was a handsome man, everybody knew that. But what was irresistible about him, for so many, was his intensity when he played guitar. It was as if he was burning with energy, and you couldn't help but feel that if you picked up his hand in that second you'd feel the full force of the universe charging through your veins.

"The neighbors hate it when you play loudly," Catherine told him, dumping her assortment of bags, drawings, and cartons on the dining table, keen to disconnect Jimmy from the universe for a moment or two.

"Sorry, babe," Jimmy said, stopping his guitar by placing the flat of his palm against the vibrating strings, before handing it to Eloise and getting up to join Catherine in the kitchen. "We're laying down a new demo tomorrow and I needed to hear how it sounded on the electric. If I tried it on the boat I'd probably sink it."

"You know I don't mind—it's just that . . . well, if you could think about the volume now and again. I'm sure it doesn't have to be that loud."

"It's rock and roll, babe," Jimmy said, looking confused. "Of course it does."

He watched her for a few minutes as she crouched and peered in the fridge and began to take out the ingredients for dinner.

"So what are you doing now?" he asked her after a few minutes.

"Chopping an onion," Catherine said as she sliced into the vegetable.

"No, I don't mean now this second. I mean this evening, generally," Jimmy explained. "I mean do you mind if I hang out, have dinner with you and the girls? Put them to bed—that sort of thing?"

Catherine paused briefly. She needed to talk about what Eloise had said.

"Jimmy, do you ever think it's weird that we still see so much of each other?"

"No," Jimmy said firmly, pulling himself up into a seated position on the counter. "I think that after everything that happened, the fact we're able to put our children first and be friends means we're well adjusted and like, you know—cool."

"So why aren't we divorced yet?" Catherine asked him, lowering her voice.

Jimmy didn't answer her for a second or two and then said, "Because it costs a lot of money and we haven't got any right now."

"It's just sometimes I wonder . . ." Catherine trailed off.

"Wonder what?"

"Eloise told me today that she thinks you're going to move back in, that we're going to get back together. She's taking you and me getting on and you being here so much as a sign. We can't let them have false hope, Jimmy. We need to talk to them again. Get them to see that this is the way things are for good. "

Jimmy drummed the heels of his cowboy boots against the kitchen cupboards.

"I don't want to do that," he said.

Catherine turned around to look at him, onion tears standing in her eyes. "But why not, it's the truth."

Jimmy paused for a moment. "I know it's the truth, but I don't want to take away hope from an eight-year-old girl, let alone her kid sister. When you're a kid is practically the only time when hope seems like a real possibility. We might as well tell them Father Christmas isn't real and that it's been us they've been bankrupting and not the tooth fairy all this time. Next you'll be wanting to tell Leila that Jesus is no more than a historical figure and not the son of God."

"This is different, Jimmy, and you know it," Catherine said in a low voice. "We can't lie to them about *this*. It's their lives we're talking about."

"We're not lying, we're not doing anything," Jimmy corrected her. He hopped off the counter, put his hands on Catherine's shoulders, and looked into her eyes.

"Look, we hurt each other pretty badly. We tore each other up and those two were in the middle of it. And now you don't hate me anymore, and that's all right by me, and I'm not messed up by you anymore, and that's all right by you. Those two girls in there have had enough pain in their lives already. It just can't be wrong to let an eight-year-old have hope, it just can't."

"But it's false hope," Catherine persisted, wiping the back of her hand under her eyes and feeling an instant sting.

"All hope is false hope, that doesn't make it a bad thing," Jimmy said. "Look, if they ask me anything like 'When are you moving back in, Dad?' then I'll tell them I'm not and you'll do the same and in a few months they'll stop asking. In a year or two they won't even think about it anymore and the way we live will seem normal to them. The hope will fade all by itself, don't you worry."

"That sounds wrong coming from you, the eternal optimist," she said.

"Oh, don't get me wrong," Jimmy said, mustering a grin. "I'm still an optimist, it's just that I'm starting to realize eternity is a very long time. So what do you say—is that a plan?"

Catherine looked into the living room, where Eloise was picking out the riff from "Hotel California" on Jimmy's acoustic guitar, her head bent over the strings while Leila watched her fingers, trying to pick up the notes herself. At that moment her children seemed safe and happy, and it was a feeling that Catherine was as desperate to preserve as her husband was.

"Okay, we'll do that, then," she said. "We won't lie but we won't say anything either."

The two of them stood in silence for a moment in the small galley kitchen, sensing the unraveling of another thread of the lives they had once woven together so hopefully. Catherine still mourned the loss. Not because this relationship had once been right, but because she had wanted so much for it to be.

"So are you staying for dinner, then?" she asked him finally, breaking the thread.

Jimmy's smile was weary. "I thought you were never going to ask."

It was past eight when Catherine finally got the girls into bed. It was Jimmy's fault. After his quiet resolve in the kitchen, he'd returned to his tall-tale self by the time Catherine served dessert, regaling the girls with stories of what a wonderful life they were going to lead as soon as the band was discovered and he hit the big time—which would be sometime soon, now that they had the funds to make a new demo. Eloise asked for a pony and Jimmy told her she could have a fieldful if she wanted, and there was to be an unending supply of sweets for Leila, who planned to distribute them to the world's less privileged children.

Jimmy and the girls were still singing by the time Catherine finally managed to shepherd them up the stairs, and she did have to admit, as they hummed while brushing their teeth, that Jimmy's new song had a catchy tune. Jimmy was good at catchy tunes, but somehow they never seemed to fit into his rock-and-roll image. When you looked at Jimmy you saw a tall, long-haired, strong, purposeful-looking man. The sort of man who, if you didn't live in Farmington and didn't know Jimmy Ashley, you might be slightly threatened by. After all, Jimmy stood out in a crowd in his full-length leather coat. He should be writing songs about mayhem and seducing countless women, but it was always these softy lyrical love songs that he kept on producing. Jimmy might have a skull and crossbones tattooed on his right shoulder, but it was wreathed in roses, and once many years ago when Catherine had teased him about his rock credentials, he'd replied, "I'm a lover, not a fighter, babe."

He'd more than proved himself right since then.

When she came downstairs Jimmy was still there strumming on his guitar and humming the now familiar tune. He'd opened a bottle of wine and poured two glasses, which meant he wasn't planning on going back to the boat anytime soon, and Catherine realized that she was glad. They'd sit and talk about the girls, and her job and the PTA, and he'd entertain her with stories of the band's latest exploits or whichever kid he was teaching in Rock Club who had the most promise. What Catherine missed most about living with him was simply having him around on a week-night, sipping a glass of wine and talking. Loving each other had been a trick they had never quite pulled off, but even after everything that had happened, they still had a knack for liking each other.

"Do you mind?" Jimmy asked, nodding at the wine. "I'll go back to the boat in a mo, but the forecast said frost overnight. I could do with a drink to help keep the cold out."

"You need a proper home, really," Catherine said as she sat down, picking up her glass.

"I've got one," Jimmy said with a shrug. "It's just that I don't live in it anymore."

Catherine took a sip of wine. "I mean you need a proper home for yourself. You can't go on living in that boat. It's not even a proper boat, just some floating rust bucket that Billy cobbled together when he was half cut and off his face."

"Don't talk that way about Billy," Jimmy said mildly, referring to his oldest friend and one-time bandmate who had died from an alcohol and prescription drug overdose almost three years ago. "If anybody had a good reason to drink, it was him. He went from the brightest, best-looking, most talented bloke I've ever known to a shell of himself in less than five years. He could never let go of what he had once been, that's the worst tragedy of schizophrenia. Everyone stopped seeing him and only saw his illness, and yeah, it did make him pretty weird and hard to be around, what with him thinking he was being hunted by the FBI, but to me he was still Billy. He was still my best mate. But *he* knew he'd never have the life that everyone else would, never get married and have kids. So he loved that boat instead." Jimmy paused. "I miss him."

"I'm sorry," Catherine said. "I know you do. And it's a great boat, but it's not a home, not for you. If paying the mortgage on this place is stopping you from getting a flat or something, then we need to think again. I might be able to manage if we cut down a bit."

"Cut down on what?" Jimmy asked. "You haven't got anything to cut down on, Catherine. And it's not a rust bucket. Billy might have been a drunk, but he was a master craftsman."

"I just don't think it's fair that you should be freezing to death on a canal boat," Catherine said.

"It is fair," Jimmy said. "The girls need something constant in their lives. They've grown up here, Leila was born here while I played Clapton to her so it would be the first thing she ever heard. I want to keep this place for them. And besides, I'm moaning now but you wait, in the summer that boat's a little bit of paradise. The chicks really dig it."

Catherine found herself laughing.

"It's just that you're getting on now," she reminded Jimmy playfully. "You don't want to be getting arthritis in this weather."

"Hey, lady," Jimmy warned her with a grin. "I'm still young. I've still got it all ahead of me."

"Have you?" Catherine asked, skeptically.

" 'Course I have, and so have you."

"Have I?" Catherine said. "Sometimes I think I don't want anything new in my life. I think that just the way it is now is enough for me. I love the girls, and you and I are friends now, more or less. Everything's ordered and calm. If all I had in front of me was fifty more years of the same I'd be happy enough."

"Happy enough? Happy enough isn't enough. If it was, then Billy would have kept taking his medication and living half a life and I'd have given up my music years ago and become a postman. I've thought I'd quite like the early mornings and the uniform," Jimmy said, making Catherine smile just as he intended. "Everybody needs to be loved, everybody needs to love someone."

"And some people need to love everyone," Catherine added wryly.

"I don't, though," Jimmy said, tipping his head back on the sofa and looking at the ceiling. "I don't love anyone. Not since us. But I know I will love someone again and that someone will love me, because I need that to happen and so do you, it's what makes us human."

Catherine wanted to disagree with him but she couldn't quite bring herself to do it.

"I'd better get going," Jimmy said after a while, finishing his glass of wine. "If I don't get the stove lit now I'll be a block of ice in the morning and frozen corpses hardly ever have number one hits on iTunes. I'll leave the electric here if you don't mind. If the damp gets into her she'll be knackered."

He kissed Catherine briefly on the lips as she stood up to let him out, and then with his hand on the latch of the door he turned around and looked at her.

"Look, I don't know why I'm saying this—but try to remember the last time you were really in love, Catherine, the last time your heart burst out of your chest every time you thought about that person. The nights you spent awake just dreaming about what it would feel like to touch them, longing for their arms around you. He hurt you, I know he did, and she let you down and left you alone to cope with everything. But sometimes I think when you buried the hurt and the pain they left you with, you buried a bit of yourself as well. I know it's none of my business anymore, but I'm only saying you deserve to be loved, so try to remember what it felt like and then maybe, when the time comes, you'll be able to let it happen again. I want to see you happy."

Jimmy nodded once and then closed the door carefully behind him so as not to wake the girls.

Catherine tweaked back her curtains and watched him

hunched up against the cold as he marched stalwartly toward the canal, his hair whipped by the wind, clutching his guitar by its neck.

Despite everything, he was still the only person on the planet who really knew her, who understood her better than she understood herself.

Five

*I*t had been almost unbearably hot on the day she had met Marc James.

For most of the summer holiday Catherine had been required either to help her mother in the church bookshop she ran or to do a long list of chores at home that Catherine felt sure had been invented to stop her from leaving the house. But occasionally over the six-week break, there would come a day when Catherine could find a few hours for herself and Alison, whose weekend job at the supermarket gave her plenty of free time.

If it rained they'd sit in Alison's bedroom listening to her *Take That* CD over and over again, while Alison told elaborate stories of how one day the two of them would meet the band and be whisked off on a romantic world tour with them. Alison always got Robbie, Catherine could have her pick of the rest. But on a sunny day, like the day Catherine had met Marc James, they would go to the park so that Alison could work on her tan while she peered over the top of her sunglasses at any passing boys. Sometimes they'd see other girls from school who'd sit with them a while and gossip about who fancied whom, but that was only if Alison was there. If Catherine was alone the other girls would wave at her and shout hi, but they would never sit down. Catherine just didn't have that knack for friendship that Alison had, the easy ability to make people want to spend time with her. The older they got the more it puzzled Catherine that Alison wanted to invest so much time in her, maintaining their friendship when it would have been so much easier for her not to. But now that they had known each other so long it seemed foolish to ask. The two of them together, that was just the way it was. Catherine trusted in that.

One day Catherine had been waiting in the park for Alison to make an entrance into her life. When the two girls had reached the age of seventeen, it seemed Alison no longer arrived anywhere on time because she had learned that most people, especially boys, would wait for her almost indefinitely. And that summer, even though Alison had been nursing her own secret crush, she'd started to accumulate boyfriends. Not the kind she used to have—some fleeting romance that would begin at registration and be over by the afternoon break—but dates with real boys to the cinema, McDonald's, and sometimes even the pub, where Alison would sip a Cinzano Bianco and lemonade.

Catherine had laughed and listened, wide-eyed, to her friend's detailed descriptions of her first kiss, the first time a boy had put his hand up her top, and how it had taken David Jenkins ages to undo the hook of her bra because his hands had been shaking so much in excitement. It was a change in her friend's life that was as alien as it was fascinating to Catherine. Her imagination simply could not conceive what it would be like to touch a boy, kiss one, or even hold his hand, so limited was her experience of the oppo-site sex. All she knew was that ever since Alison had started going out with boys, her lateness increased and once or twice she hadn't shown at all.

The trouble was, Catherine remembered thinking on that day as she sat, her back against a tree, feeling its rough bark imprinting into her skin through the thin cotton of her dress, she often felt a little bit as if her life wasn't actually real when Alison wasn't in it. It was like that riddle about the falling tree in an empty forest and whether it made any sound as it crashed to the ground if no one was there to hear it. When Alison wasn't there to see her, Catherine felt entirely invisible.

She had closed her eyes briefly and pushed her sunglasses up her nose, tapping her feet as she hummed quietly to herself. And then the sunlight had dimmed behind her eyelids and the skin on her legs cooled as a shadow fell over them.

"Well, it's about time," she said easily, pushing her sunglasses into her hair, opening her eyes and expecting to find Alison, her vision momentarily dazzled by the bright light. The shape that loomed over her in the instant it took her to focus was male, it was a boy—no, not a boy. It was a young man.

Catherine judged that he was shorter than her, stocky with muscular arms and a bare chest, dark-haired, and olive-skinned. He was barefoot, holding his T-shirt in one hand and a can of beer in the other. And yet Catherine remembered quite clearly she hadn't felt intimidated by him. Not even then.

She sat up, pushing her hair off her shoulders, straightening her back a little. She waited.

"Sorry, I didn't mean to make you jump," he said as he sat down on the grass, even though Catherine hadn't jumped. "I'm just so tired. I work nights on the railway line, repairs and maintenance. I should be sleeping right now, but I can't. It's too nice outside. I wanted to come out and sit in the sun for a bit, but every time I relax I fall asleep and I can't do that. I'll turn the color of your hair and if I miss the start of my shift I'll get laid off. So I thought I'd talk to you for a bit, if that's all right. At least while you're waiting for your friend . . . boyfriend?" His dark eyes creased as he smiled at her.

"Friend," Catherine corrected him hastily. For once she was glad Alison was late, because she knew that if her golden friend had been here, this incredible-looking being would not be talking to her. He would not have even seen her.

He sat down on a patch of grass just beyond where the shade of the tree's canopy ended, the sunlight reflecting off his amber skin.

Catherine had never seen anything or anyone so beautiful in her whole life. The sight of him made her heart stop in anticipation. His dark hair was cut very short into the nape of his neck, his dark eyes set beneath strong, straight brows, and he had the kind of square jaw that Catherine thought only film stars and male models in razor advertisements had.

"My name's Marc," he said, leaning back on his arms so the muscles in his shoulders and biceps stood out in sharp relief. "I'm from Birmingham, I go where the work is and this month the work's here. That's pretty much my story. I don't have any hobbies or many friends. I don't read books or go to movies. I get up, I go to work, I go home—wherever home is that week. This week it's here." He smiled at her again and there was something in his smile Catherine recognized. As impossible as it seemed, he reminded her of herself, the outsider. "There's this postcard stuck to the bathroom wall in the rooming house I'm staying in of a girl floating in a river. I think she's supposed to be drowned actually."

"Ophelia," Catherine said. "It could be Ophelia, a character from *Hamlet*. She kills herself because loving Hamlet drives her mad. There's a famous painting of her by an artist called Millais, he made his model, Elizabeth Siddall, lie in the bath for hours at a time until she became so ill she almost died for real. She was only nineteen, not that much older than me."

"You know a lot, don't you?" Marc said, smiling. "You know all of that from me describing one postcard, and pretty badly at that. That's cool."

Catherine felt her cheeks color. "It's just something I'm interested in. I like art history. If I get to go to university, that's what I'm going to study."

Marc nodded. "You should. What I was trying to say was that you remind me of the girl in the painting. You've got the same incredible red hair and pale skin. She's a beautiful girl, especially considering she is meant to be dead!"

He laughed and Catherine found herself laughing too, glowing at what she thought was the first compliment she'd ever received from a man.

"Tell me more about you," Marc said, his voice low and gentle. "Tell me everything you know."

And at his bidding, quiet, shy, awkward Catherine, who up until that point had been unable to hold anything other than the most stilted and awkward conversations, except with Alison, started talking. It was as if by the simple act of noticing her, this handsome, attentive young man had burst a dam in her. Suddenly hundreds of words poured out of her, thoughts and ideas that must have been building pressure somewhere inside her for years. They talked about everything and nothing as she looked at him, drinking him in like a thirsty person stumbling across an oasis in the desert. The light in his eyes as he watched her, the slope of his back as she shifted position, the set of his chin, the line of his nose. She wasn't able to stop looking at him and talking to him, about everything: school, her parents, her home life, her favorite books, music, films, her hopes and dreams—things she hadn't even told Alison. And he listened. And not only could he hear her, he was seeing *her*. For the first time in her short life Catherine felt like her own person and not just Alison's friend or a neglected daughter. She experienced what it was like to be truly seen.

Jimmy had asked her to remember the last time she'd been in love. Looking back, Catherine realized that she had been in love with Marc before they had even known each other half an hour. It had taken less than thirty minutes to happen and how many years to shake off? Catherine wasn't sure she could answer that yet.

"So how about you, how have you ended up drifting from town to town?" she asked him at last, desperate to know more about him. "Why did you end up in Farmington?"

"You're here," he said to her, the roll of his Midlands accent washing over her. "That's a good reason to come here and it's a better reason than the one I've got. I follow the work. I've not got any skills, or degrees. I've not got a lot going for me."

"You have," Catherine retorted automatically. "I mean, you just probably don't know that you have."

Marc shifted his position once again, crossing his legs.

"I don't know," he said, with a one-sided smile. "I think the best thing I've got going for me at the moment is that you are talking to me. I like you, Catherine, you're different."

"I know," Catherine replied in dismay.

"It's a good thing," Marc told her. "Most girls I try and talk to either won't have anything to do with me, or if they like the look of me they turn themselves into idiots flirting and pouting and showing themselves off. I'm not saying I don't like it when a pretty girl flirts with me, but well . . . I don't know the last time I really talked to anyone, the last time anyone ever really cared about what I'm thinking or feeling."

"Me either," Catherine said, afraid to move in case she caused one second of the remaining time she had with him to fall away before she was ready.

Marc knelt and pulled his T-shirt on over his head, then walked over on his knees and stopped in front of her.

"I've got to go," he said. "Got to put my head down."

"Okay," Catherine replied.

"Will you be here tomorrow?" he asked, and Catherine felt as if lightning had just struck in the center of her chest, leaving a gaping, burning hole.

"Yes," she said, unable to manage any dissembling.

"Can I meet you here again tomorrow at the same time?" Marc asked as he reached out and picked up her right hand.

"Yes," she said again, her voice fading.

He pulled her gently toward his body until she was kneeling opposite him.

"Can I kiss you, Catherine?" he asked her, quietly, almost shyly.

"I . . ." Catherine froze for a moment, her lips felt numb and immovable. "I don't know . . . how to," she finished painfully, dropping her chin to her chest and closing her eyes.

The next thing she felt was the rough surface of Marc's palms against the skin of her cheek, drawing her face back up to look at him.

"I do," he said.

What she had felt first was the gentle pressure of his mouth on hers, the sensitive exploration of his tongue between her lips. And then she remembered his arms encircling her waist and the heat from his body radiating through the thin cotton of her sundress and penetrating her bones. Finally, as Catherine began to return his kiss, she realized that her arms had crept around his neck, the muscles of his shoulders contracting beneath her fingers as she held him.

Looking back, it wasn't a long kiss, or a particularly passionate one. But it was perfect. It was a perfect first kiss. A kiss that every other she might receive in her life would have to measure up to.

Afterward, with his arms still around her waist, Marc smiled into her eyes.

"I've never been with a girl like you," he said, almost regretfully. "And I'm guessing you've probably never been with someone like me. You're different, Catherine, fragile and . . . nice. And I'm nothing special, I'm not nice." He grinned at her. "I've made a lot of girls angry with me and I don't take things too seriously. I like you, I want to see you again, but I want to be straight with you, make sure you know what you're doing." Marc sat back on his heels, dropping his arms from her waist.

"I've got to go," he said. "If you don't want to come tomorrow, I get it."

"I'll be here tomorrow," she told him steadily, not certain at that second exactly how she was going to make that happen.

"Will you?" He watched her as he stood up, a faint frown between his brows. Catherine swallowed and took a breath. "Are you sure?" he said.

"You said I'm not like the girls you normally go with. You said I'm different, so if I'm different then maybe . . . this will be different. Maybe you'll be different and anyway . . ." She had to force every single tendon in her body to relax sufficiently to allow her to say what she had to. "I've never had anything like this before, that's mine, just for me. I just want to feel like this again—I don't care what happens."

Marc smiled. "Someday you'll learn not to wear your heart on your sleeve," he'd said, and then nodded. "I'll see you tomorrow, Catherine, same place, same time."

Later that night, while her parents were watching the ten o'clock news, Alison crept into Catherine's bedroom window as she had done every night she could get away with it since they were twelve years old.

"Are you mad at me?" Alison whispered, easing first one bare leg and then the other through the window. Catherine, who had been lying on her bed reliving every single moment of her afternoon, sat up on her elbows and shook her head.

"No, I'm not, you'll never . . ."

But Alison interrupted her. "When you hear what happened you'll understand."

Catherine sat up. Alison was so used to telling her stories, it would never cross her mind that Catherine might have one of her own to tell.

"Go on then, but be quick, Mum'll be up as soon as the news is finished to tell me to turn my light off."

"I was just leaving to meet you when *Aran Archer* rang me up and asked me if I wanted to watch a video at his house. Well, I had to go, didn't I? Samantha Redditch has been after him since Easter. I thought she'll die if she knows I bagged him."

"But I thought you like . . ."

"Yes, of course I like him, I *love* him, but he hasn't noticed me yet, so while I'm waiting why not go out with Aran Archer? He's upper sixth, so there'll be parties and I'll get to hang out with my true love more."

"If you say so," Catherine said, having learned never to question Alison's plans because Alison did what she wanted to do and worried about the consequences later.

"So I go round to Aran's and his mum is out, of course. He draws all the curtains in the living room, tells me to sit on the sofa, and gives me a drink of orange *squash*!" Alison shook her head. "What a loser! Of course the film had only been on five minutes before we were kissing. His tongue was down my throat straightaway and his hand was up my top, squeezing them like they were lemons."

Alison laughed, remembering to cover her mouth with her hand at the last second in case anyone heard her. "It was so not sexy," she said. "So I push him off me and he says, 'Oh go on, Alison, let me see them, please!'

"And I said to him, 'Are we going out or what?'

"And he says yeah we are, all sort of desperate and pathetic, so I said, 'Okay, then.'

"I couldn't get him off of me for the rest of the afternoon. He wanted to go further but I wasn't having any of that. I'm not losing it to him. Still he's quite sweet really when he's not with his mates. He said he's fancied me for ages."

"So you've chucked Ryan then?"

"Well, I will," Alison said, glancing at her watch. "What about you? What did you do? I would have phoned you here to tell you but I knew you'd rather get out than be stuck at home cleaning up after the wicked witch all afternoon."

Catherine thought about her kiss with Marc and how it would sound if she tried to explain it to Alison in the way Alison had just described her afternoon with Aran Archer to her. The moment was too precious for her to share with anyone, not even Alison. Especially not Alison, because once she knew she'd have questions like whose hand went where and what did it feel like and when could she meet him? Catherine had realized with a sudden lurch that she didn't want Alison to meet Marc. The afternoon she had spent with him, the talk they'd had, and the kiss were hers. Catherine wasn't ready to share them.

"We can do something tomorrow if you like," Alison said. "Aran will be begging me to see him but I don't think I should, do you? I'll be fighting him off again all afternoon and it's such a drag."

"Actually I can't tomorrow," Catherine said quickly. She had already told her mother that she had forgotten a summer study project she had to work on for school and she would have to be excused from the shop to go to the library. Her mother had not been pleased, not with her slapdash attitude to schoolwork or her absence from the shop. But she had agreed that Catherine could go because the only thing more important to her than keeping her daughter under control was keeping up appearances in the community, and having a child that did well at school was part of that. Catherine didn't care if her mother eventually found out she'd lied. She didn't care about anything except seeing Marc again.

"Really?" Alison looked disappointed. "The witch?"

Catherine nodded. "She's got me sorting out all the paperwork from the shop."

"Poor you." Alison gave her a sympathetic hug. "Just think, one more year and we'll be off to university in Leeds. I'll be studying English literature and writing my novel and you'll be doing art history and some hunky artistic type will fall in love with you and make you his muse."

Catherine smiled and thought about Elizabeth Siddall. She didn't suppose she would ever be Marc's muse.

"We'll sneak your application past your parents and once you've got your place you'll never have to see them again. One more year and you'll be free and so will I."

"*Your* parents are lovely," Catherine chided her.

"Yes, but they are so safe and careful, always saving. Always putting every penny aside for a rainy day. Do you know we can't even go on holiday this year?"

"Because they're saving money so you can go to college," Catherine reminded her. "If I ever get there I'll have to work about ten jobs to pay my way."

"You will get there, and so will I. We'll have the best time ever. Only one more year to go."

"Yes," Catherine said thoughtfully. "One more year."

They heard a footfall on the bottom stairs.

"I'll be back tomorrow," Alison hissed as she climbed out of the window. "Same time, same place, okay? Love you!"

Hastily Catherine pulled the window shut after her, and glimpsed the silhouette of her friend on the garage roof before scrambling back into bed.

"Lights out now," her mother said, opening the door.

"Yes, Mum."

Her mother paused for a moment looking at the window, the curtain a little askew.

"Have you had the window open?" she asked Catherine.

"Sorry," Catherine said.

"No windows open at night. Any madman could get in."

Her mother shut the door behind her, snapping the light switch off as she went. Catherine remembered lying back in her bed, stretching from the ends of her fingers to the tips of her toes, knowing that at last she had something to dream about.

Things would have been so different, Catherine thought as she finished her glass of wine, if Marc just hadn't turned up the next day.

She had told her mother she was going to study at the library, taking a big net bag of books and several pens to prove it.

Catherine remembered she deliberately walked along the canal toward the park in a bid to avoid meeting anyone she might know, including Alison, on High Street. The spot in the park where Marc had found her was out of the way, beyond the swings and climbing frame, under the canal bridge toward the back of the field where the park met the railway embankment and the grass was long. Catherine felt confident that once she was there she would not be spotted by Alison, her mother, or anyone.

Which was reassuring, because she hadn't expected Marc to

be there at all. She'd prepared herself for disappointment, relieved that she hadn't told Alison about him.

But as she made her way under the bridge she could see that Marc was already there waiting for her, leaning against the trunk of the tree they had met under, the August sun painting his bare chest with patches of gold as it danced through the tree's canopy.

Catherine stopped in her tracks and looked at him. She was seventeen, the most inexperienced girl in her class, if not the whole school. She was thin and flat-chested, with long, bony fingers and feet. What did Marc want with her? Because he could not want her like *that*. He couldn't look at her the way other boys looked at Alison and actually want her. Besides, he wasn't a mere boy. He was a man, more than three years older than her. His waiting there under the tree didn't make any kind of sense.

Instinctively Catherine knew that now was the time she should turn back, it was her chance to heed the warning he had given her yesterday and leave. But even as in her mind's eye she was rotating on her heel and scurrying away to the shelter of the library, her treacherous body carried her right to his side.

"I saw you watching me," he said, smiling up at her, blinking against the bright sunlight. "Having second thoughts?"

"No," Catherine said. He reached out, catching her hand, and pulled her down onto the grass. "It's just, I look at you and I . . . I don't know what you want with me."

Marc laughed. "Whatever it is, it must be something pretty strong, because after we said good-bye yesterday I swore blind to myself I wasn't coming here today. But here I am. And now that you're here I feel happy. I hardly ever feel happy. I brought you something." Easing himself up, Marc reached into his back pocket and produced a creased and dog-eared postcard. He handed it to her. "You were right, it is meant to be that character you said and

I think that's the name of the artist you told me. It's not much of a gift, but I thought you'd like it."

For a moment Catherine gazed down at the painting of Elizabeth Siddall floating in water, wearing a silver embroidered dress, her body wreathed in flowers as she portrayed the doomed Ophelia, and she smiled. "Thank you," she said, impossibly touched by the worn reproduction.

"Read the back," Marc urged her.

Holding her breath, Catherine turned the card over. Written on the back in large and loose handwriting were the words "To Catherine, more beautiful than Ophelia."

The two of them watched each other and the anticipation that he might kiss her again made Catherine's insides burn.

"So what do you want to do today?" Catherine asked him instead, still holding the card between her palms.

Applying very gentle pressure on her shoulders, Marc pushed her back into the long grass and lay alongside her, his head propped up on one elbow. "I want to lie here in the grass, talking and kissing you," he told her. And that was exactly what they did, while Marc wove buttercups and daisies into her hair to make, he whispered in her ear, his own masterpiece.

They met every chance they could, every free hour that Catherine could steal from her mother and explain away to Alison. She would have been content to lie in the long grass with Marc day after day, but one day Marc pulled her to her feet and said, "Let's go somewhere else."

"Where else?" Catherine was reluctant, afraid of who might see her and afraid to tell Marc that she felt that way, because she didn't want to hurt him.

"The movies," Marc told her, raising his eyebrows. "They've got a showing of that film *Ghost* on at the cinema. I've heard it's rubbish, but girls like it, right?"

"You're taking me to *Ghost*?" she said, repressing a laugh because it seemed like such a normal thing for a boy and a girl to do and exactly the sort of thing she thought she would never do, especially not with Marc.

"I'm doing better than that." He grinned, tugging at her hand. "Come on." '

Never in her life as the tallest, thinnest, most ginger-haired girl in school had Catherine ever felt as self-conscious as she did that afternoon, walking hand in hand with the shorter, compact, shirtless Marc through the town toward the Rex cinema. She was sure that this would be it, this would be the moment when one of her mother's friends or, worse still, her mother caught her in a lie and the daydream she had been living would be over. Amazingly her luck held, and as they approached the grand but shabby art deco building Catherine saw a small queue forming outside its doors.

"This way," Marc said, not leading her to the entrance but pulling her down a narrow alley that ran alongside the building.

"What are we doing?" Catherine asked him, giggling.

"I met this guy in the pub last night, works in the projection room." He pulled her into a doorway with a locked fire door that was marked "Fire Escape, Keep Clear!"

"Years ago this old heap was the go-to place for miles around, he reckons. Gold paint on the ceiling, velvet chairs, cocktails brought to your table."

"Yeah, I've heard that," Catherine said with an uncertain smile. "I've seen some of the old photos in the local history books. So?"

"*So*, there were boxes, just like you get in a theater for the really posh people to sit in. They don't use them now, except for storage, but they are still there . . ." He smiled at her and kissed her gently on the lips. "And the bloke said if I bought him a pint, he'd let us in the side entrance and we could watch the film in a box."

"Really?" Catherine gasped, delighted more that Marc had

been thinking of her when he came up with the plan than with the plan itself. *Ghost* was one of Alison's favorite films and they had seen it so many times she was fairly sure she knew the script better than Demi Moore did.

Marc nodded, looking pleased with himself as he banged several times on the door. After a while the door swung open and Marc and the projectionist exchanged a few words.

"Don't get up to anything too energetic in there," the projectionist told Marc as he pointed them toward the box, chuckling to himself.

"Do you mind," Marc said, smiling at Catherine as he held the door to the box open for her. "I'm with a real lady here."

They sat side by side on plush old velvet seats, Marc's arm around her shoulders.

"This film is crap," Marc said after about twenty minutes, making Catherine laugh.

"Do you want to leave?" she asked him.

"No," he said, looking into her eyes. "I want to make out."

Almost every night that she came back from seeing Marc, Catherine would hear Alison's latest exploits with Aran, the things he tried to do to her or make her do to him, the things she sometimes let him do and the things she sometimes did. But it was never like that with Marc, he never tried anything with her beyond kissing. They'd sit or lie in the long grass, out of sight of the passersby while he stroked her hair and told her about his life, how he'd grown up alone, pushed from one foster home to another. How he'd been kicked out of foster care at sixteen and had to look after himself, make the choice between getting a job and turning over the local off-license with some of the other boys from the home. He'd chosen laboring work because he knew what he was like, he knew he'd mess up and get caught and then his life would be over.

Then suddenly he'd stop talking and Catherine knew he was going to kiss her. She would feel his hand in her hair, or on her waist, but never anything more.

She felt safe when she was talking to him, telling him about her parents, who did not love each other, let alone her, and all the anger and resentment they hid behind the facade of a neat and respectable Christian family. It didn't seem so sad or so desperate anymore that she'd grown up in a house without any affection or compassion and that the nearest thing she had to a real family was the girl who lived down the road and climbed in through her bedroom window nearly every night.

Then on the ninth day something changed. Marc was kissing her, just as it seemed he always did, when suddenly without warning something shifted inside her. Catherine found her arms snaking their way around his neck, and she pulled his body hard into hers as she kissed him back, arching the small of her back so that their hips met. Marc stopped kissing her.

"Whoa," he said, breathless.

"What?" Catherine asked him. "Did I do something wrong?

"Yes, I mean no, not wrong but . . ." Marc looked at her. "I don't think you're ready to . . ."

In the long pause that followed their bodies relaxed, and Catherine felt as if she was backing down from a fight.

"Can I ask you something?" she said.

" 'Course you can," Marc said, shifting his body weight to put some space between them.

"Do you want me, Marc? I mean in *that* way. Because we've been seeing each other for a while now and I love talking to you and kissing and I don't even know what I'm asking you really except that do you *really* like me, or do you just kiss me when you haven't got anything to say anymore? Because you feel sorry for me?"

Marc looked dumbstruck. "What?" he asked, sitting up and back on his heels.

"You've never tried to . . ." Catherine was at a loss for words to describe what she barely understood. "Do anything but kiss me."

Marc laughed, flopping back onto the grass. "Oh Christ," he said, his hands over his eyes.

"Don't laugh," she said, punching him lightly in the arm, unable to resist smiling. Suddenly he grabbed her forearm and pulled her on top of him, the expression in his eyes shifting in a second, all trace of humor gone.

"Of course I want you," he said, making Catherine catch her breath. "But I told you. You're different. You're . . . precious. I've never talked to another person in my life the way I've talked to you. You know me, you understand me, and I think I know you. You're pure."

"So does that mean you don't want to . . ." Catherine discovered in that moment that she was becoming very tired of her purity.

"No, it means I want to, I want to a *lot*. But look, Catherine, if we do that—have sex—it will change everything and I don't know, I like this—the way things are. It doesn't feel real, it feels like a dream, another world where it isn't crazy for me to be in love with you."

Catherine lay on top of him, her hair making a curtain for them both as she looked into his eyes.

"You're in love with me?" she asked him.

"I want to be . . . I *am* in love with you," Marc repeated, unable to look at her this time. "But I don't know if that is enough. I'm not the sort of bloke who's going to take you away from this or even stick around . . ."

"I don't care," Catherine said. "I love you too. And I don't care what happens next week or next month. These have been the best days of my life, Marc." She paused, nipping sharply at her lip. "You might as well know I'm a virgin." She saw Marc hide a smile.

"That obvious?" she asked him happily, before looking levelly into his eyes. "But I want more between us. I want us to do more . . . to do everything."

"Are you sure about this?" Marc asked her.

"You said it yourself. We make each other different, better. This is right, I know it is."

Marc brushed her hair back from her face. "It can't be in the park," he told her, his implicit assent making Catherine want to laugh and scream and cry all at once.

"No," she said, blushing only now. He rolled her off of his chest and sat up.

"There's my lodgings, but it's not exactly romantic. You should have somewhere nice, with candles and flowers."

"Marc." Catherine laughed, pulling him to his feet. "Let's go."

Marc picked up her hand and kissed the back of it.

"Come on," he said. And he didn't let her hand go.

The room in the lodging house was small, a single bed against a wall, a sink, a stove, a tiny fridge that burred and hummed in the corner as if it was fighting for its life. The room was neat and clean and it seemed to Catherine that there was hardly anything of Marc there. His fluorescent work jacket hung over the back of the chair. There was a six-pack of beer on the kitchen counter and nothing at all in the fridge.

"Cup of tea?" Marc asked her as she stood in the center of the room.

"Um no, thanks," Catherine said. "Can we just . . ."

"Get on with it?" Marc asked her, laughing. "I'm nervous. I don't know why I'm nervous."

"Don't you be nervous! I'm far more nervous than you," Catherine told him.

"We don't have to go the whole way today, you know," Marc said. "We can just take it slow. One step at a time."

"No," Catherine insisted. "I'm here now. Let's do it."

Marc nodded and took two steps closer to her. Catherine had to refrain from taking the same number of steps backward.

He pulled his T-shirt off over his head and then Catherine's singlet over hers. She felt the touch of air against her skin raise goose bumps across her slender, pale body, the sunlight filtered a bloody orange through the curtains. And then the heat of his hands on her skin, and as he pulled her into an embrace, he was kissing her neck and shoulders. These were not the dreamy, gentle kisses Catherine knew from the park, but new, deeper and commanding kisses. In one movement Marc had undone her bra and slid it off her shoulders, pulling her back onto the bed. She heard a moan deep in his throat and she felt herself respond to him, and at last she knew for certain what it felt like to be desired.

"I love you, Catherine," Marc told her as his hand ran up her thigh. "Always remember that at this moment I love you more than anything in the world."

Catherine snapped back into the present, her wineglass in her hand as she heard a noise on the landing.

"Mummy?" It was Leila.

"Yes, darling?" Catherine called back.

"I went to the toilet on my own!" Leila informed her proudly.

"Good girl, well, get back into bed, then. I'll be up in a minute to kiss you. Don't wake your sister."

"Too late," she heard Eloise call out grumpily.

Catherine set the wineglass down on the table.

Jimmy had told her to remember the last time she was in love, and she had, because despite the huge leap of faith it had taken her to trust her husband with her heart, in the twelve years she had known him she'd never felt the same intensity of emotion for Jimmy that she'd experienced during those few weeks with Marc James. When Marc had walked out of her life, just a few weeks later, she'd felt as if he'd taken with him the part of her that could feel that way again. It frightened Catherine to think that Marc James had been the love of her life. But his was the love that had changed her life—had changed her—forever.

That afternoon in his lodgings had been the most wonderful, most perfect experience of her life.

At last she'd felt that she belonged to someone.

Amazingly she'd felt that he belonged to her.

And then she'd introduced him to Alison.

Six

Alison looked at the clock on the wall. It was almost eleven, the children had long since gone to bed, and Rosie was curled up in a hot little ball at her feet, twitching occasionally as she dreamt about chasing rabbits. Marc was not home.

This was to be expected, she told herself as she took a sip from what was her fourth glass of wine, on the grounds that she deserved a drink after the day she'd had. It was not unusual for Marc to work late, well into the night, without ringing her to tell her what time he would be home. That was what running your own car dealership was like. Sourcing suppliers, keeping on top of the paperwork, taking out big corporate clients in a bid to supply their company fleet. Especially now that he was opening another branch, there would be a lot of work to do to get everything up to a high enough standard. That's what he told Alison, and she accepted it because she knew that Marc would be throwing everything into making this new venture a success. That was just him, or rather that was the way he was now after sixteen years with Alison.

Alison smiled to herself and tried to imagine that dark and brooding young man she had first set eyes on, on that hot summer's day all those years ago, the heat in his eyes blazing almost as intensely as the sun. He had been the most beautiful thing she had ever seen, like an exotic creature that had somehow wandered into their safe white middle-class town, where everything and everyone looked the same. He was a drifter, without aim or purpose, restless and resentful. The young man he was then didn't look anything like a man who would one day work himself like a dog to make his business a success, keep his family secure, and buy himself a life in the very same safe white middle-class town that Alison had once begged him to run away from with her. He didn't look anything like that person she had fallen so hard for at the age of seventeen, the man she'd left everything behind for, including herself.

Once, a lifetime ago, she had dreamt of being a writer. She had talked about it to Catherine often enough, and only Catherine. At school Alison had been the good-time girl, the girl who always sported the shortest skirt she could get away with, or smoke the most lipstick-imprinted cigarettes around the back of the building. Everyone liked her, but nobody took her seriously, except Catherine. When they were about twelve she had confessed to her best friend that she wrote short stories in her diary and that nobody had ever seen them. With her stomach in knots, wild with nerves, she had brought them to school one day and allowed Catherine to read them in secret when they should have been in drama class. Catherine had hugged her and told her the stories were wonderful.

"You could be a writer when you grow up," Catherine had said, wide-eyed with admiration.

"That's what I thought too," Alison had exclaimed happily. "But I wasn't sure if I was any good!"

"You could do it." Catherine had seemed certain. "You could do anything."

Yet the most defining action that Alison had ever taken in her life was to run away with Marc. The moment she had made that decision all of her old dreams had evaporated, and at seventeen she hadn't given a second's thought to their passing. She hadn't really thought about those dreams until now. Until another late night at home on her own without a single thing in her life that felt like hers alone, waiting for the man who was now an entirely different person from the one she had sacrificed everything for.

Alison stopped that train of thought. She could hardly complain that time had changed him; the intervening years and three children had changed her too, even if she worked hard at the gym to try to stem the change as much as possible. Of course Marc was still out at the dealership, getting it ready for the grand opening over the weekend. He would not leave any stone unturned until everything was perfect. Everything else, including his wife, would have to wait until then. Alison knew that because she had created the man he had become, and this, sitting drinking wine alone at eleven o'clock at night, was the price she paid for her creation.

Topping off her wine, Alison looked at the clock again. The house was quiet at last. Dominic had either turned his music off or plugged his headphones in, and the girls had been asleep for hours, Amy drifting into oblivion the second her head touched the pillow, as if her restless dreams would be a welcome escape from the harrowing day her mother had put her through.

Her two daughters' first day at their new school could not have been more different, and Alison was afraid that that was how it was going to be for them for the rest of their lives. Gemma she didn't have to worry about. Gemma was exactly like Alison had been as a child. She breezed through every social situation, supremely confident and happy, utterly unconcerned by the children who did not like her (and there were a few of those because Gemma had a knack for rubbing people the wrong way) and completely besotted by those she chose as her friends.

Amy, on the other hand, could have been a changeling. She was not like her father, driven and single-minded, always chased by nameless demons at his heels, and she was not like her mother. Or perhaps that wasn't entirely true. Because Alison had not been the same woman when she'd conceived Gemma as she was when she'd become pregnant with Amy. During those three years she'd lost a little of her shine, a little of her certainty. Sometimes Alison worried that Amy was a replica of her mother after all, that somehow she had let her youngest daughter down by not being the person she used to be, by not being the kind of woman who had daughters like Gemma.

Gemma had been in the playground when Alison had arrived to pick her girls up, Rosie dancing at her heels and doing her best to chew through her leash. Gemma had raced up full of news for her mother and cuddle for her dog and talk of new best friends who she simply had to have over to tea at the first possible opportunity. They had been about to go round and find Amy when Mrs. Woodruff popped her head out of the reception door and asked Alison to come into her office.

Alison looked down at Rosie.

"I would, but it's the dog, you see. If I tie her up out here she'll howl the place down."

Mrs. Woodruff frowned. "Bring it in, just this once. But for future reference dogs are not permitted on the school grounds."

Amy and Mrs. Pritchard were waiting in Mrs. Woodruff's office. The moment Amy saw Rosie her eyes lit up and she rushed over to the dog, burying her face in its fur, her slender shoulders shaking as she sobbed silently, her small fingers wound tightly in Rosie's coat.

Amy had cried all day. Literally all day, Mrs. Pritchard told her kindly, her sympathetic face crumpled with compassion.

"Why, darling?" Alison asked Amy, gently lifting her face from the dog's coat. "Why did you cry so much?"

"I don't like my new teacher," Amy sobbed woefully. "I want Miss Mill, Miss Mill is *beautiful* and *young*."

"Um, well." Alison looked apologetically at Mrs. Pritchard and was relieved to see a twitch of a smile round the teacher's lips.

Amy's face disappeared into Rosie's fur again.

"Not coming tomorrow," she hiccuped miserably. "Mama, p-please don't make me come again. I'm *worried*."

Alison folded her arms more tightly around Amy and set her mouth in a thin line of determination. She knew she had to be firm and force herself not to give in to her daughter's pleas. Her youngest child had been born fragile and full of fear, equipped with the thinnest of skins, and yet Alison knew that of all of her children Amy was the bravest, because despite her fears, as long as her mother told her everything would be all right, come tomorrow morning she would get up and face the whole terrifying process again.

So now when her tear-stained daughter asked why she had to go to school, even though Alison struggled to find an answer and wanted more than anything to keep her at home and safe by her side, she knew she had to say the right thing. There was no alternative, Amy would have to learn to live her life in this world, as frightening and as harsh as it must seem to her, and all Alison could do for her little girl was to teach her how to cope with it and somehow manage to get through these difficult first few weeks until eventually Amy found the same kind of uneasy peace here that she had found at her old school.

For a second Alison thought of her husband, of his insistence that they move back, and she had to swallow the bitter anger that rose in her throat. They all seemed to be paying the price for his mistakes, even Amy.

"It will take a while for her to adjust," she told Mrs. Woodruff apologetically. "I think there'll be a good few tears till then."

"Of course," Mrs. Pritchard agreed. "It takes a long time to settle into a new life no matter how old you are. We'll get there in the end, won't we Amy?"

"I'll try," Amy said. "It's just that I'm so *worried*."

And then it had been Alison who had to try to stop herself from crying.

At least Alison had been able to get the girls home and know they were safe and in one piece, even if one of them was miserable.

She had made Dominic come out of the gate to meet her before Rock Club because she wanted to go in with him, meet his teacher, and pay for the term. Dominic had flung himself into the car, slapping his body into the seat.

"I've changed my mind," Dominic said, tucking his chin into his neck as a few teenaged girls strutted past. "I don't want to go to Rock Club, it's for losers anyway."

Alison looked at him clutching his guitar by the neck and felt her stomach contract in sympathy. He looked as if he felt pretty much the same way she had ever since they had arrived here: like she was waiting to go home to a place where she could relax and be herself, or rather the self she had spent the last sixteen years inventing.

"Don't be nervous, kiddo," she told him, putting her arm around him. "It will be fine, you're a tough kid. Go and rock the joint."

Dominic's sideways look was one of pure recrimination.

"I'm not nervous," he countered, shrugging her arm off of him. "I just don't want to go in there. It's totally lame, Mum. And anyway, how many other kids do you see whose mums made them wait until they arrived to take them in? They're going to slaughter me and it's all *his* fault."

As if to prove him right, three boys about his age and similarly attired in black combats and printed T-shirts slouched past with that same awkward wheeling gate that all boys of a certain age seemed to have, peering at him through the car window as if he were a piece of dirt.

"Look, I have to come in and pay your teacher. I promise that after today I'll never come near the place again. I'll even walk ten paces behind you now and pretend I don't know you."

She was joking, but Dom exploded out of the car door and took off, taking her at her word.

"Right, well, wait here, girls," she said. "I'll lock you in. Keep an eye on Rosie. Don't let her do any more damage to my leather trim. Don't open the doors to anyone. I won't be long."

"Hurry, Mama," Amy said, her voice quivering, her big brown eyes looking up at the sky as if it might fall on her at any moment.

"Oh come, muffin," Alison heard Gemma say as she grabbed her bag. "Let's play I Spy—I'll let you win."

As she walked back into her old school Alison was unprepared for how the building and its surroundings would make her feel.

It wasn't an especially old building, it had been built in the 1920s, but it was an exact replica of a grand eighteenth-century building complete with palisades, colonnades, and even a chapel. From a distance, set in its own expansive grounds, it looked like a very grand private school, not like the local high school at all.

Close up, though, it was another story. The smell, that slightly musty and acrid combination of disinfectant and damp, was still exactly the same, and as Alison followed Dominic through the impressive paneled double oak doors that marked the main entrance to the school, she was fairly certain that the interior hadn't been redecorated in the intervening seventeen years since she had last set foot in it. The walls were still that insipid grayish green color, with patches of pink plaster showing through where paint had chipped or peeled away. Even the same framed prints lined the corridors, faded and dusty scenes from Shakespeare so grimed with dirt that Alison was sure it had been a long time since anyone had looked at them properly or even noticed they were there.

As she looked around her and breathed in, all at once Alison saw her past reflected, bouncing back at her, almost blinding her like sunlight off a mirror. Once, this place had been the center of her universe. There on the stairs she saw where she had made Cathy wait in vain with her for a whole lunch hour just to catch a glimpse of Jimmy Ashley, the hottest boy in school, who Alison had loved from afar right up until the minute she had met Marc and he had eclipsed everything.

As she walked into the main hall, where her son had already headed, no doubt hoping to disassociate himself from his stalker of a mother, she could see herself onstage, painting the scenery for the school production of *Grease* and imagining herself as Sandy and Jimmy as Danny, while Cathy scoffed at her and told her she had no idea what anybody could see in Jimmy Ashley.

Alison smiled as she remembered the end-of-term dance before the summer she met Marc. Cathy wasn't allowed to go to the dance, or any dances since that time her mother had caught her sneaking off to the Valentine's disco, which left Alison alone to pluck up the courage to talk to Jimmy. Finally, at the end of the evening, after sneaking several slugs of vodka into her orange juice, she had worked up the courage to ask Jimmy to dance with her. Reluctantly he had consented, holding her waist gingerly as they turned in slow circles to a song by the Cars. Alison had not been able to take her eyes off of her feet, certain she would faint clean away if she looked in Jimmy Ashley's eyes. How strange, she thought to herself as she watched Dominic greet a couple of other boys and a girl in a very short skirt with studied nonchalance. She had once considered those three minutes, that dance with Jimmy, as the pinnacle of her life.

Then only a few weeks later she had found out about Cathy's secret boyfriend, and a few weeks after that she had run away with Marc without giving Jimmy Ashley or Cathy a second thought. The course of her life had changed forever.

What surprised Alison the most was that these memories, now so vivid and visceral, hadn't crossed her mind in seventeen years. It was as if on the night she'd decided to run away from home, she'd run away from this part of her life forever, excising it from her heart and her head with the kind of bold decisiveness that only a seventeen-year-old in love can have. She had hoped that the detritus of her youth, the wreck of the life she had abandoned so wholly, all those people and the places would be long gone, rotted into the past.

The school looked as if it had been frozen in aspic. There was even someone over there talking to her son who looked exactly like Jimmy Ashley.

Alison's heart stopped beating for the longest second and she realized. That *was* Jimmy Ashley. When it began to beat again it was racing.

Alison felt a blush extend from her ears downward and pins and needles in the tips of her fingers. She clapped her hand over her mouth to stifle a burst of hysterical laughter. She felt just as she had when he'd put his hand on her waist at the sixth form dance, dizzy and dazzled. It was the shock, Alison told herself, retreating into a shadowy corner to compose herself and regain the sixteen years that seeing him again had swept away.

She simply hadn't expected Jimmy to be there looking almost exactly the same as he did the last time she'd seen him. On the other hand she didn't know where else she expected him to be. He obviously hadn't hit the big time like he'd always said he would, so perhaps teaching guitar back at his old school was the obvious location for this living, breathing relic of her youth.

He didn't look like a relic, though. He looked good, better even than he had at eighteen. His shoulders had filled out and his bare arms were toned and muscled. His skin had cleared up and he looked relaxed, at ease with himself. His hair was still long, but it suited him. It was one of the reasons she had first fallen for him. He had been the only boy in the school brave enough to grow his hair and the only one who could carry it off. Once she had dreamt about tangling her fingers in it.

Biting her lower lip as she hovered in the shadows, Alison was taken aback by how happy she was to see Jimmy again. He still had that hint of a smile on his lips, as if at any second he might start laughing. He still wore jeans so tight that you wondered how he sat down in them without them ripping apart at the seams. Alison had been one of the most popular girls at school, with a new boyfriend every other week from the age of fourteen. Even the older boys asked her out. But not Jimmy, never Jimmy. Not the boy she really wanted. Not her son's new guitar teacher.

Trying to shake off this ridiculous frisson of excitement that had engulfed her the moment she set eyes on him, Alison took a deep breath and determined to pull herself together. Hoping Jimmy wouldn't notice her (and wishing she'd put some makeup on and brushed her hair before leaving the house), she edged over to the table where a register book lay open and leaflets about the club and forthcoming events were on display. She found the amount she owed for Dominic to attend for one term in a leaflet and hurriedly wrote out the check, expecting with a breathless edge that at any moment Jimmy would tap her on the shoulder and say, "Alison Mitchell, how wonderful to see you!"

But before she could even sign the check, a sudden burst of electric rock music crackled in the air, making Alison almost jump out of her skin. Twelve or fifteen kids were standing on the stage, two playing complete drum kits, three or four (including the short-skirted girl) on microphones, and at least seven on guitar, although Alison's limited knowledge told her that included a couple of bassists. Alison didn't recognize what they were playing, and then she realized that was because they weren't playing anything. Jimmy had just got them up on the stage and got them to start making music. The first minute and a half were pretty unbearable, and then suddenly a cohesive tune emerged. Alison saw Jimmy's head go down and his shoulders rock to the rhythm, just like they used to do when he played at the school dance. And then she looked at Dominic and for the first time since they had arrived he was smiling—no, not just smiling, he was grinning from ear to ear with the pure joy of doing something he loved.

She slipped the check into the register book and then walked quickly back to the parking lot, laughing and feeling as light as air, caught up in the moment with the seventeen-year-old girl she once had been. When she got into the car, the thought of seeing Jimmy still living here sobered her.

Coming back to Farmington wasn't going to be nearly as easy as Marc had promised her, because there were ghosts everywhere. Living, breathing ghosts.

Dominic had expressly told Alison that she was not allowed to pick him up from Rock Club, and so even when it had begun to rain, thick gray sheets of water that clattered against the windows in wave after wave, Alison sat tight and waited for him. He was over an hour late when finally his dark and sodden figure emerged out of the storm.

"Where have you been?" Alison asked him as he peeled off his T-shirt and threw it into the laundry basket.

"I got lost," he told her with a shrug.

"Lost? The school's only down the road."

"I know," he told her. "But I wanted to have a look around and some of the kids said there was this crap skate park down by the canal that they go to sometimes. I went to have a look and I got lost."

Alison tried to imagine her son in the canal park, the very same canal park where she had met his father. It seemed like an impossible paradox, as if time had folded back on itself, and not for the first time she got the feeling that her being back here was all wrong. As if somehow Marc was marching her back to the point where they'd met, looking for a way to change a future that was already past.

Alison shivered as she picked up the sodden T-shirt and inhaled deeply. Even in its soaking state it reeked of cigarette smoke.

"Lost with a pack of cigarettes?" she asked him.

"I wasn't smoking, it was the kids I was with," Dominic retorted automatically. "They're all at it at that school. I told you it's a real dump."

"So you were with local kids who know the area but you got lost?" Alison persisted.

"Just leave it out, Mum, all right?" Dominic's voice rose and Alison knew he was reacting to the look on her face, the expression she could see reflected in the glass door of the eye-level microwave oven. In the dark, smoky glass she looked sharp and aged. She looked like the kind of mother who never wanted her teenage son to have any fun, the kind of mother who only wanted to ruin everything for him, the kind of mother who was happy to rule his life but who didn't have the courage to take control of her own. That was who Dominic saw when he looked at her, and at that moment, that alien, hard-faced woman was who Alison was.

"You dragged me to this fucking awful place," Dominic swore at her. "And now I'm just trying to make some mates—is that such a big deal? It's not as if I'm dealing crack, Mother. I couldn't score any in this place if I wanted to."

Alison stared at him for a long moment, waiting, waiting for that woman reflected in the glass to fade away.

"I'm sorry. You're right. I do trust you, Dom," she told him, lowering her tone with some effort. "It's good that you are making friends . . . so tell me all about your first day, then." Alison squeezed all of the tension out of her voice in a bid to make the question sound purely conversational and not like a declaration of war.

"The same old shit," he told her, watching carefully for her reaction to his choice of language. "Just a different fucking place."

"But you made some friends?"

"I said I did, didn't I?" Dominic asked her, lifting a carton of juice from the fridge and taking a swig out of it. Alison considered getting into the "use a glass" argument with him, but then that bitchy mother would be back again for sure, so she let that particular battle go the same way as the "don't swear in the house" debate had gone, which was out the window. Dominic had a lot less respect for her moral qualifications recently, and swilling juice directly from the carton was only one of the ways he chose to show her that. The trouble was Alison felt that her son was largely right about her, so she tried to ignore his challenges, happy to have contact with him at all.

"We can invite your friends over if you like," she told him. "To hang out."

"Ooh, yes, we can have a tea party and jammy dodgers," he teased her. "Tally fucking ho."

He was about to exit the kitchen when he stopped in the door frame for a second and looked back over his shoulder at her.

"How did Muffin get on?" he asked, using the pet name he had coined for Amy when she was born because of her two black button eyes that looked like blueberries in a muffin.

"She found it hard," Alison told him with a sigh. "All she wanted to do was to stay at home with that mutt." She nodded at Rosie, who trotted cheerfully out of the utility room dragging a Wellington boot that was almost twice her size.

"Come here, hound." There was a flicker of a smile on Dominic's face as he bent down and gently retrieved the boot from between Rosie's jaws. "I don't blame Amy, I want to stay at home all day with Rosie too."

Alison smiled, enjoying this brief moment of normality with Dominic. Less than two years ago she and Dominic had always talked like this when he got in from school. He'd been her confidant, her best friend. The struggle with his emergent manhood hadn't gotten to him then, he hadn't discovered his father's imperfections or his mother's weaknesses.

"Did she cry?" Dominic asked, his voice gentle now. He'd been with Alison when Amy was born. Marc had not got there in time because he'd been caught up with something or someone at work.

"She cried a lot," Alison admitted. "And when you didn't come back she was really worried. You know how she is, so make sure you go in and say hi, okay?"

"I don't know why you made us come here," Dominic remarked, turning to face her and leaning against the door frame. "Muffin was pretty happy at home, Gemma was the queen of all her friends. And the stuff I was into wasn't that bad. If you'd told him where to go after that business with the Christmas party and showed some self-respect, then you wouldn't have had to worry about what the neighbors thought and move us all out of the city."

"The neighbors?" Alison laughed harshly. "Is that why you think we left? The month we left London, eight kids your age were stabbed to death in less than two weeks. I didn't want you to be one of those kids, Dom."

Dom shook his head. "That was never going to happen to me. Don't use me as an excuse for this. You're running away from the wrong thing. It's not houses or areas you need to run away from, Mum, it's him. It's Dad that causes all the trouble, not me."

"It wasn't Dad sitting in the back of a stolen car, was it?" Alison asked her son, shamelessly changing the subject. "No fourteen- or fifteen-year-old thinks he's going to walk out of his house and die," Alison said. "None of those boys or girls did. But it happened all the same. I want to protect you because whether you like it or not, I love you."

"Yeah, you reckon," Dominic observed sceptically, his implicit disbelief in her feelings for him hurting Alison more than any insult he could dream up.

"Yes, I do reckon. And anyway it's better for Gemma and Amy, a better place to grow up in, and Amy will settle in eventually. You know how she hates change."

"Sometimes things have to change whether you like them to or not," Dominic replied steadily.

"Yes, they do," Alison said firmly. "Like us moving here. Look, you'll do better out here." And then Alison gave Dominic the list of all the reasons Marc had given her when he had told her he wanted to move here. All of the reasons except for the one that counted, because he wanted to. Because he'd made it almost impossible for them to stay in London and because there was still something that he had to prove to himself here in this town.

Seven

Marc's kiss on her cheek woke her, his face looming over hers as she opened her eyes. She must have fallen asleep in front of the late-night film.

"Hello, beautiful," he said, kissing her lips this time. "Did you know that Rosie has left a little message under the coffee table?"

"Oh, what," Alison said, struggling to orient herself. "That's the perfect end, to a perfect day, that is."

"Don't worry, I'll clean it up." Marc clicked on the table lamp next to where Alison had been sitting, dazzling her temporarily, and dropped a parcel of something heavy into her lap before disappearing into the kitchen to find a cloth. Alison screwed up her eyes to look at it. It looked like a pack of greeting cards.

"I've had a brilliant idea," Marc told her as he cleaned up after a rather sheepish-looking Rosie. "We need to make a splash in this town, right? To get ourselves accepted by the locals. There's so much money to be made here, Al—and not just in the town. The whole area's up to its neck in cash—it's better than Notting Hill any day of the week. No congestion charge, no one picketing the 4x4's on the road. We want to be part of this community. And the best way to do that is to befriend the community, right?"

"Do you mean send them cards or something?" Alison said, her head still muddled by dreams and memories.

"No, I mean by throwing a party here." Marc opened the package, pulling out a card, and handed it to Alison. "Half the invites are already sent. I used the guy from the local business forum and some other contacts I have in the area to get the guest list together. Or at least my guest list. I thought you could invite all the teachers, the head—maybe the PTA committee that I suggested you get involved with. Mothers you meet in the playground, anyone you like. Get yourself a social network so you don't feel so isolated. Don't you see? Instead of waiting for things to take off we can kickstart our new lives by throwing them the best party they've seen in years."

Alison stared at the invitation.

"This date is a week from Saturday," she said numbly. "That's less than two weeks away."

"Yes, it is," Marc said, brushing the hair from her face. "No point in letting the grass grow under our feet, is there?"

"Marc, there is no way we'll be ready to throw a big party in time."

"Well, like I said, half the invites have gone out, so yes we will." Marc grinned at her, that smile that said he'd made up his mind. "Come on, love, you've never let me down yet. And the kids will love it, they can invite all their friends. We'll make a real family event for the young ones too. It might help Amy settle in."

"Amy said she doesn't like people, only dogs, and I know how she feels, except for the dogs bit," Alison mumbled wearily.

"Well, people love you," Marc said, watching her face. "You look beautiful, by the way."

Alison glanced up at him, the muscles in her shoulders tensing as she caught his look.

"I don't . . ." she protested weakly. "I haven't even had a shower . . ."

His hand ran down the side of her face, his forefinger tracing the curve of her neck and breast.

"I remember the first time I saw you," Marc said, unbuttoning her shirt with practiced ease to reveal the lace of her bra. "I wanted you right that minute." He ran his hands over her breasts and then, lowering his head, nipped at the lace of her bra. "The second I saw you all I could think about was what you would look like naked."

"I remember," Alison said. The day they'd first had sex. It was an easy day to remember because it was also the day they'd first met.

It was the last week of the summer holidays. And up until that day everything in Alison's life was going as she had planned and expected, more or less. She had one more year ahead of her at school. One more year to get the boy she really wanted to want her back, one more year to help Cathy escape and then they were off. Free as a pair of birds to study English and art history at Leeds University. She would write her novel and Catherine would study the paintings she loved so much. And Alison knew that once they were there they'd meet a hundred new friends and, best of all, hundreds of new boys, none of whom she'd have a thing to do with because by then she'd have the boyfriend she really wanted.

She'd have Jimmy Ashley. She didn't want him forever, just for a few years, because anyone could see that Jimmy Ashley wasn't the kind of man you married. Her affection and desire for him had been absolutely unshakable up until the very second she'd met Marc.

It happened because she knew that Cathy had a secret, which in itself was unprecedented—Cathy never had anything interesting to hide unless it was some exploit that Alison had arranged for her. That was one of the things that Alison loved about her friend. Yes, she was quirky and different, but at least she had the guts to be absolutely honest herself. Sometimes Alison felt worn-out from the effort she made to be the girl that everyone liked. Catherine might think she was the awkward one, but she had a kind of peace and grace about her that Alison aspired to. Which was why it was even more surprising to realize Cathy was hiding her secret from Alison. And Alison absolutely had to know what it was, because after all, the pair of them had been best friends since they were eight years old, since the day Alison started at her new school.

Cathy had been cowering in the center of the playground surrounded by a ring of girls who were skipping, pointing, and chanting, "Witch, witch, witch!"

"What are you doing?" Alison demanded of them, marching into the center of the circle. The first thing she noticed about the girl standing next to her was that she was very tall, with the skinniest legs Alison had ever seen. Alison took a step in front of her.

"Her mum's a witch, which makes her a witch too," one of the other girls crowed, her soft, young face full of hate.

Alison looked at the girl next to her. "Is your mum a witch?" she asked her conversationally. The girl shook her head.

"Right then, she's not a witch, but I am." Alison marched up to the ringleader until they were nose to nose. "And if you say another word to my friend over there I'll put a curse on you that will make you die the slowest and most horrible and disgusting and painful death you can think of. And if you tell anyone I said that, then I'll curse you anyway. One more word and you're a corpse."

The girls glared at Alison but she remained silent, turning on her heel with a flash of ponytail and saying "Come on" to the tall girl, then marched off, her chin in the air. Gradually the others drifted off too, whispering among themselves about the new girl.

"Got any brothers and sisters?" Alison asked her.

"No." Catherine looked uncertain as she answered.

"Me either, I like you. You're different from all of them," Alison said, holding out her hand, which the other girl took. "I'm Alison, we can be best friends if you like."

"Okay, then," Cathy said. "I'm Catherine."

"Right then, Cathy—want to play hopscotch?"

In the years that followed, that first offer of friendship became a pact, the two unlikely friends confident that the other one was the only person alive who really understood her.

They'd been twelve when Alison got Catherine so drunk on cider that she threw up on her mother's feet as soon as she opened the front door and then lay on the floor laughing. After that Catherine's parents had banned Alison from their daughter's life outside of school. Alison remembered her mother going over to Catherine's house, certain she'd be able to reason with Catherine's mum, blame it on youthful experimentation, high spirits. But she hadn't bargained for Catherine's mother, the coldest and most unbendable human that had ever existed. But best friends were best friends, and a parental ban wasn't about to keep them apart. Alison invented a web of complicated lies that allowed them to go out sometimes to a school disco or a party for a couple of hours, and best of all she'd figured that she could climb out her own bedroom window and into her friend's in less than ten minutes, if she sprinted down the alley behind the houses that separated Catherine's street from hers, without either set of parents knowing.

And the older they got, their friendship, which they still kept a secret from Catherine's parents, fell into an easy pattern. There was Alison and Cathy and Alison and the rest of the world. Alison did her best to be the bridge that Catherine could use to cross over to the normal lives of their peers. Alison threatened anyone who wasn't kind to Cathy and let those who were bask in her approval. But their friendship was always a two-way street. Cathy was her heart and soul, keeping her tethered to the ground when her wilder thoughts and impulses would have had her spinning off into the wild blue yonder. She knew she could tell Cathy what she could never tell her mother. She always thought that Cathy had felt the same, which was why her friend's secret puzzled her. After all, what sort of secret could Cathy have that would require so much guarding?

Alison couldn't imagine it.

Cathy had told her that she wouldn't be around that afternoon. Her mum was making her stay in and study again. But Alison knew it was an excuse, she knew that Catherine's mum would be working in the Christian bookshop and wouldn't know if Cathy was studying at home or not. She couldn't go round and knock for Cathy, so she waited on the iron railing behind the cherry tree just next to the old people's bungalows. It was hot and Alison was bored after ten minutes and thinking about leaving, so it was lucky really that it didn't take much longer for Catherine to emerge.

Alison watched as her friend walked down the road. Something about Cathy had changed—no, that was wrong; everything had.

She was wearing a long white skirt that flowed around her ankles, a skinny ribbed green shirt that set off her rippling copper hair. She had bangles on her wrists and a long beaded necklace that fell between her breasts. Cathy looked beautiful and stylish, sexy even, with a new kind of confidence in the sway of her hips and the way she tossed her waist-length hair over her shoulder.

The way Cathy looked told Alison two things. First, that Catherine's mother was definitely out, otherwise Catherine would never have dared to leave the house in anything other than the clothes her mother bought her. And second, that she was going to meet a male of the species.

Cathy had a boyfriend. Alison marveled at the newfound piece of information and she wondered who it could be. Who at school could possibly have fallen for Cathy Parkin? None of the boys fancied Cathy, not because she wasn't beautiful, it was easy to see that she was, but because she didn't have the yellow hair, the obvious breasts, or the near-naked thighs that boys in their teens appreciated so much. Alison realized it couldn't be a boy from school that Catherine was going to meet. For a split second she thought it might be Jimmy Ashley, but she dismissed it. Even if Jimmy fancied Cathy, which he never would because she was about as far away from being a rock chick as a girl could be, Cathy would never get involved with him. She'd never betray Alison in that way, it just wasn't in her nature.

There were only two ways to find out what was going on. She could either follow Cathy or ask her.

Alison, who was always one to take the fun option, pulled her sunglasses down onto her nose and began trailing her best friend. She giggled as she hopped in and out of bus shelters, cowered behind trees, flattened herself against a shop window. Near to laughing out loud, Alison expected Cathy to turn around at any minute and ask her what she thought she was playing at. And then she realized something: Cathy was in a world of her own, an exclusive little bubble of her own feelings and thoughts that Alison could not even guess at. For the first time in the nine years she had known Cathy, she was on the outside of her head and this boy she was going to meet was on the inside. It took a second or two for Alison to realize, as she slowed to a walk, that what she was feeling now was jealousy.

She had to know at that instant exactly what was going on in Cathy's life.

"Hi, Cathy, where are you going?" she said, falling into step alongside her friend, making her jump.

"I'm . . . oh, hello!" Cathy smiled at her, her cheeks coloring. "I thought you were with Aran. Mum's working so I sneaked out for a walk."

"Liar," Alison said lightly. "Come on, spill, you're on the way to meet a boy, aren't you? You might as well know, if it's Jimmy Ashley, then it's over between you and me for good."

"Jimmy Ashley?" Cathy stopped, wrinkling up her nose. "It's not him!"

"Aha! So it's someone, then!" Alison grabbed hold of Cathy's wrist and swung it back and forth. "Come on, tell me! I'm your best friend, aren't I? I tell *you* everything."

"I was going to tell you," Cathy said anxiously. "It's just I wanted to see what would happen. I didn't think it would last longer than one day. But it has." A slow, shy smile crept over Cathy's face. "We've been seeing each other almost the whole summer."

"Have you?" Alison said. "That's amazing. Can I meet him, then? The love of your life?"

Alison remembered watching Cathy's face as she thought for a moment, unable to believe that she didn't agree immediately, trying not to take it personally but doing exactly that.

"Okay, okay," Cathy said, taking a deep breath and smiling. "You can meet him today. He's amazing, Alison. When you see him you just won't believe that he likes me. I know I don't . . . except . . ."

"Except?" Alison prompted.

"He keeps telling me that he does," Cathy said with a shy smile, her eyes shining so brightly that Alison almost wanted to slap her then and there and tell her to pull herself together.

"It better be one of the New Kids on the Block," Alison remembered saying as they walked across High Street, down through the canal park and over the railway bridge. "I'm only going to forgive you for this if it's one of the New Kids."

Finally they stopped at a square-shaped detached house with a yellow sign hanging outside that read "Rooms to Let."

"He's staying here for now," Cathy said, leading Alison down the overgrown path and through the unkempt garden. A rusted bicycle languished in the seeded grass. "He's on a contract for the railway, it runs out soon. I don't know what will happen then, but he said he might try and get some more work locally, maybe in a garage or on a building site."

"So it's not Donnie Wahlberg, then?" Alison said, wondering just exactly what kind of person Cathy had got herself mixed up with, because if he lived here it wasn't any boy from school.

Cathy pushed the bell and waited, her fingers knotted behind her back.

And as both girls waited, neither of them could have known that this was it: the fulcrum, the moment, the very second when suddenly their fates would tangle and turn forever, and from that point on neither one of them would have the life that was meant for her.

"Hi." Catherine's voice was small when he opened the door. "Um, this is Alison. Remember I told you about her? She wanted to meet you . . . I thought it would be okay, do you mind?"

Marc stopped smiling at Cathy and looked right at Alison and said, "I don't mind."

Alison remembered staring at Marc, open-mouthed.

Yes, in her memory she was definitely open-mouthed, awe-struck as she gawked at him, in his tight black T-shirt and blue jeans, with his skin turned amber by the sun and his dark eyes taking her in under the sweep of his black brows. The first thing she thought, in the first minute of her new life, was that he was the most beautiful living thing that she had ever seen. And the second thing she thought was how on earth did Catherine get him? That couldn't be right.

And then Marc looked into her eyes and she knew that he was seeing her in exactly the same way that the boys at school saw her: her breasts first, then her short skirt and bare golden thighs, her smooth blond hair, and her soft, full mouth. Last of all he noticed her eyes, her pretty blue smiling eyes. And she could tell even as Cathy chatted away, introducing them to each other, that he wanted her. She could feel it in every stroke of his gaze.

"All right." Marc stepped forward and shook her hand lightly, letting his gaze fall from her face to her chest and below.

"So I was thinking maybe the three of us could have a picnic instead of . . . you know . . . what we were planning, down in the park. Under our tree?" Catherine suggested happily.

Alison did her best to stop looking at Marc. "You have a tree?" she teased Cathy gently. "How romantic."

"It's not really our tree, it's just a tree . . . oh, stop it, Ali," Cathy said, blushing and laughing all at once.

Alison watched as Marc dropped his arm around Cathy's pale shoulders and kissed her lightly on the cheek. "We can call it our tree if you like," he said, challenging Alison with a lazy smile.

The tips of Catherine's ears went pink.

"We could go to the supermarket and get a few things," Cathy offered. "Mum won't see us, she's at work, so we should be safe."

"Good idea," Marc said, picking her hand up easily as if it was something he had often done. The easy intimacy between them shocked Alison almost as much as if she had come across them

having sex. Somehow she found it impossible to imagine Cathy
and this creature together. It seemed all wrong that it was Cathy
who was the confident one, the knowing one, and that it was Alison who was feeling awkward, uncomfortable, and out of things.
Alison didn't like it one little bit.

She didn't say a single word as she listened to Cathy chatter on
the way to the supermarket; she couldn't say anything. The feeling
of jealousy and rage and longing that was churning in her kept
her mouth firmly shut. She was afraid, not of what she might say,
but of how her voice would sound when she said something. All
she knew was that this was wrong, it was all wrong. Cathy wasn't
meant to have someone like *him*. Marc wasn't meant to be with a
girl like Cathy.

They must have been seeing each other since the day that
Alison had agreed to go round to Aran Archer's, Alison thought.
Cathy must have met Marc in the park that afternoon when she
had been waiting for Alison. If Alison had shown up that afternoon, there would have been no way that Marc would have looked
at Catherine, no *way*. She would be the one holding hands with
him in the sunshine now, and Catherine would be walking on her
own. And Cathy would have been happy with that, because she
would have understood that that was the right thing, that that was
the way things were.

It must have been about four when Cathy looked at her watch
and scrambled to her feet.

"I've got to go. Mum'll be back in half an hour. Are you walking back, Ali?" Cathy stood, waiting for her friend. Alison guessed
she couldn't wait to hear what she thought of him.

"Um . . . no, I can't. I said I'd drop by Aran's on the way back.
I'll see you later though, okay?" Cathy nodded and smiled. She
looked so happy, as if she felt special for the first time in her life.

"See you at ten," Cathy said. Alison watched as Marc got up

and put his heavy arms over Cathy's fragile shoulders and whispered something in her ear that brought the blood to her cheeks. And then he kissed her, a long, slow, tender kiss.

Alison did not know who she hated the most just then, her friend for stealing away her lover, Marc for not seeing he had met the wrong girl, or herself for what she knew she was about to do.

After Cathy had gone, Marc turned back to Alison and looked at her lying in the sun. He waved a hand halfheartedly.

"See you, then," he said, as if he was going to leave. But he didn't leave.

"Stay and talk to me a bit longer," Alison said, dropping her shoulder back so that her chest pushed forward. She patted a patch of grass next to her.

"Thanks, but I should get some sleep before my shift starts," Marc said, looking at her legs. "You don't want to be too tired working on a railway line, I saw this lad get cut in half in Manchester."

"She was meeting me, you know," Alison said. "The afternoon you two met here."

"Really?" Marc looked over his shoulder at the tunnel under the railway line that led back to his lodgings. "So?"

"Well, who do you think you'd have asked out if I'd turned up that afternoon? Who do you think you would have fancied if you'd met me first?"

Marc looked back at her, his hands on his hips, and he laughed. "Why do you ask?"

"I'm interested, that's all," Alison told him, tipping her head to one side so her hair brushed her bare arm.

"Well, I've never been with anyone like Catherine before," Marc said. "So if I'd met you both at the same time I'd have probably made a move on you. But then I would have missed knowing her. She's a lovely person."

"Lovely?" Alison laughed.

"Well." Marc put his hands in his pockets and looked awkward as he shrugged. "She is."

Alison had never been able to believe the words that had come out of her mouth next. After all, her sexual experience was only slighter greater than Catherine's for all the flirtatious front she put on.

"You can make a move on me now if you like," she offered, her voice sounding shrill and girlish.

Marc stood still and laughed. "I thought you were her best friend. She talks about you all the time."

"I am," Alison said. "But anyone can see you're not right for her. You two don't fit together. You'll just end up hurting her, she deserves better."

"And you don't." Marc sounded skeptical. But he still hadn't walked away.

"I can handle you," Alison said. "And anyway, I know that if you'd met me first you'd be with me now. I know it."

Marc shook his head. "You're very confident," he said, pausing, taking her in, an untranslatable expression crossing his handsome face.

For what seemed like an age neither one of them said anything or moved a muscle, and then suddenly Marc walked decisively over to her and held out a hand.

"Come on, then," he said. "Come back with me."

"What? Now?" Alison said, scrambling to her feet.

"That's what you want, isn't it?" Marc asked her. "To be with me?"

"Yes, yes it is," Alison said.

"If that's what you want, then you have to come now," Marc challenged her, and she wasn't sure if he wanted her to take up the challenge or if he was just trying to frighten her away. "It's now or never, so tell me are you as confident as you think you are?"

Alison remembered feeling as if her heart would pound its way through her rib cage, everything was happening a million miles faster than she had expected, but if this was how it had to be, then she was ready, because he belonged to her and she had to prove that to him. She lifted her chin.

"Let's go, then," she said, with a thousand times more bravado than she felt.

Afterward she lay in the tangle of sheets on his single bed and stared at the ceiling.

"Have you done that with her?" she asked him.

His eyes were shut, his face perfectly still. "I've never done anything like that with her," he said eventually.

Alison found it hard to read the tone of his voice, it was so . . . closed. This moment was not at all like she had expected it to be. She'd expected his arms to be around her, for him to be holding her, kissing her, but he hadn't touched her since he'd pulled out of her. Quite a feat in a single bed. Alison fought the urge to cry, telling herself that this was just the beginning. She still had a way to go but she'd get him in the end. She'd make him understand.

Making herself smile, she sat up and leaned over him so that her breasts brushed his chest. He opened his eyes.

"That was my first time," she told him, careful to erase any trace of vulnerability from her voice.

"I know," he said, watching her face. "I'm sorry if I was a bit . . . rough."

"I liked it," Alison said steadily. "It was passionate."

"You are very sexy," Marc told her, his voice still unyielding. "You've got an amazing body."

"Do you feel bad?" Alison asked him. "About Cathy?"

"I am a bad person," he said. "I told her that the day I met her. I thought I could be better than I am if I was with her, but I can't. This is the way I am."

"You're not a bad person, you just don't fit with her, that's all," Alison said, leaning over him. "If you are with the right person, then you don't even have to change."

Marc didn't move a muscle.

"I don't think anyone can change me," he said eventually, and Alison got the feeling that he'd only spoken half a sentence out loud.

"When you finish with her be kind, okay?" Alison said, sitting up and putting on her bra. A tiny tender and bruised part of her was still wishing for the hearts and romance and flowers that she'd always dreamt would accompany this event, but she knew she had sacrificed any chance of that when she'd agreed to go back to his place with him. Alison told herself all of that would come when she really had him. "Don't break her heart. Don't tell her about us. We'll stay a secret for now, until she's over you."

"What makes you think I'm going to break up with Catherine?" Marc asked her.

Alison looked at him, feeling suddenly out of her depth. "Well, you have to now, don't you?" she asked him. "We've had sex."

"I don't have to do anything," Marc said, turning his face to the window.

Alison felt she should have some right over him now, some extra hold now that she had surrendered to him what Catherine had not. But she had no idea how to play this person, he was nothing like the boys she knew at school, the boys that she could manipulate so easily. Then she realized it was he who had a hold over her. He had her in the palm of his hand.

"Are we going to do this again?" she asked him bluntly, because he seemed to like that about her. Marc turned his face back to her and looked at her, his dark eyes in shadow; one hand reached out and touched her cheek.

"I wish I'd met you first because, you're right. I wouldn't have looked at Catherine, I wouldn't have noticed her at all. I'd have gone straight for you. You're very beautiful, you're . . ." His fingers traced a line down her neck to her shoulder. "You're hard not to touch."

"So?" Alison pressed him, with a little smile. "Are we?"

"Yes," he said simply. "I think we are."

Every time they met after that, each secret hour of afternoon they spent with each other they grew closer and closer, easier and easier together. Alison knew that Marc still saw Cathy whenever she could get away, that they still went walking in the park, or lay in the grass talking about his past, because Cathy would tell her at night, her eyes shining. And somehow Alison could still manage to be happy for her friend because she knew the love that Marc felt for Cathy was entirely different from what he felt for her. He wanted the very bones of her, he wanted to consume her body from the inside out. He couldn't get enough of her body, and every single time they saw each other they went straight to bed.

One evening just as the sun was low in the sky, bathing the room in gold as they lay in his bed, Alison felt that something was different, something had changed between them. And then she realized: he had his arms around her, her head was resting on his chest; the unfamiliar sound she was hearing was the beating of his heart, slow and steady.

It was then she got a sense, the very first inkling that eventually, one day he would love her back.

Now, in the living room of their brand-new house a lifetime later, Alison felt Marc shift his weight on top of her and she wondered where that desire, that unswerving love for him had gone. He kissed her neck just as passionately as he had always done, his fingers as expert as they had always been, knowing how to please her. But although her body responded to him, her heart was still and silent.

What had happened to her love for Marc, which had defined her life for so long? Alison couldn't tell if it would ever come back, she only knew that at that moment she felt nothing.

Not for the first time since she'd found out Marc was bringing her back to Farmington, Alison found herself wondering what had happened to Cathy Parkin.

What she could not have known was that her husband, still wide awake despite his closed eyes and perfectly composed features, was wondering exactly the same thing.

Eight

"This is ridiculous," Catherine said as Kirsty, one palm firmly securing her forehead, plucked her eyebrows.

"Only you would say that," Kirsty said through gritted teeth as she jerked another hair out of Catherine's tender skin. "Only *you* would think that having eyebrows that frame your eyes instead of hanging over them is not a good plan."

"I don't think *anything* about eyebrows, eyebrows are not important to me," Catherine said, beginning to regret agreeing to go out with Kirsty at all.

Kirsty paused for a minute, the tweezers hovering menacingly in front of Catherine's face.

"Tell me you shave your legs," she pleaded.

Catherine looked at her sensible shoes and said nothing.

"Good God, Catherine! What's wrong with you?" Kirsty exclaimed.

"What's right with me, you mean," Catherine retorted. "I don't feel the need to denude myself in order to be attractive to men, and besides, what's the point of shaving my legs? No one ever sees them."

Kirsty attacked Catherine's brow with renewed vigor.

"The point of shaving your legs is the same as always wearing sexy underwear even when you're not on a date. It makes you feel both beautiful and womanly, and then your sexiness exudes from with*in*." Kirsty yanked hard on a particularly stubborn hair, making Catherine yelp. "No wonder you are so . . ." Kirsty struggled to find a suitable adjective and failed. "Look, imagine that you suddenly meet the man of your dreams tonight. There you are in the pub, I'm in the arms of my personal trainer . . ."

"Does your personal trainer have a name?" Catherine asked, hoping in vain to deflect Kirsty's line of questioning. Ever since she'd let herself think about Marc again, it had been hard to stop, and for at least three nights this week he had populated her dreams, dreams in which she was seventeen again, before he'd met Alison, before everything went wrong. She was seventeen and living those few brief weeks when for the first time in her life she had been completely happy. Why she had let him back into her head now, Catherine couldn't comprehend. She was crazy to have listened to Jimmy and his rock psychology, telling her she'd forgotten how to be in love.

The truth was after Marc had gone, after Alison had left the way she did, it had taken Catherine a long time to feel whole again because she'd felt as if her guts had been ripped out. But Alison's abandoning her was a turning point too. It was the beginning of her own life, the life where her head ruled her heart and every other part of her. It was the time when she first got to know Jimmy, when the two of them became friends and then finally more, and he gave her the strength she needed to be able to leave home. It was around that time that Jimmy Ashley had told her he loved her and swore that one day she'd love him back. It was a prediction that she had never been able to fulfill to his satisfaction.

"Of course my trainer has a name," Kirsty replied indignantly, pulling Catherine back into the conversation.

"What is it, then?"

"Sam," Kirsty said firmly. "Or Steve. It's an *S* name and anyway don't try and get me off the subject, you *know* it takes me a long time to remember names. I was calling you Clara for the first six months we knew each other, and it doesn't mean I love him any less. *Anyway*, there I am in his arms—kissing him passionately—and up comes this man. He's tall, dark, handsome and he wants you, sexually. He sweeps you off your feet and into his arms. He takes you to his bed . . ."

"What, in the pub?" Catherine asked.

"Don't be an idiot—unless he's a barman. Anyway, he takes you home and *then* to bed, and as he goes to run his manly hands along your long, lithe limbs, he recoils in horror because he's got carpet burns on his palms."

"If he was the man of my dreams he wouldn't mind," Catherine said stubbornly, remembering with sudden shocking clarity the pressure of Marc's palms on her thighs. For once she welcomed the distracting pain of Kirsty's attack on her eyebrows.

"If he's any man at all, barring a German one, then trust me, he'll mind," Kirsty said. "There are some people that work on the Murphy's Law ethos that if you don't shave your legs and wear your worst pants you are much more likely to hook up. I do not think that way. I think that you have to treat hooking up as if you were in the army in the Special Air Services. Like their motto says, 'Always be prepared.' "

"Isn't that the Boy Scouts?" Catherine asked. "Isn't the SAS 'Who dare wins'?"

"Even better," Kirsty said, making Catherine's eyes water as she removed three or four hairs at once. "And that should be your motto, love. It's much better than your current one."

"Okay." Catherine relented to the inevitable with a sigh. "What's my current one?"

"She who doesn't dare sits about on her arse all day turning herself into a decrepit old woman before the age of thirty-three who is afraid to be happy."

"That's it," Catherine said, folding miserably on the bed, drawing her knees up under chin.

"That's what?" Kirsty asked with some concern, tweezers poised.

"I'm just going to have sex with the first man I meet tonight, whether I like him or not, and then maybe everybody will stop going on at me. Maybe you'll stop telling me I need to have sex to be happy, maybe Jimmy will stop telling me I'm some head case who's trapped in the past just so he can pretend it wasn't his fault our marriage is over and maybe—" Catherine stopped herself. She had been about to say maybe the images of her and Marc that had been crowding her memory would leave her alone. But she'd never told Kirsty about Marc, Alison, and everything that had happened. And she wasn't ready to now.

Contrite, Kirsty sat on the bed next to her and patted her shoulder.

"Don't have sex with the first man you meet tonight," she said gently. "He might be an old man or a fat man, and besides, that's not why I'm taking you out."

"No, I know why you're taking me out, so I can be the gooseberry when you finally catch Sam."

"Or Steve," Kirsty added. "And that's not why either. Well, it is, but it's not the only reason." Kirsty lay on the bed so that she was facing Catherine, looking into her eyes. "You don't see yourself, Catherine, you don't see how stunning you are, with your incredible legs and all that hair and those eyes and those cheekbones. And I just thought if I got you dolled up a bit and we went to the pub, you'd see the way men would look at you. The way they'd *turn their heads* to look at you when you walk past. And no, you don't need to have sex to be happy and you're not some head case who's trapped in the past, whatever the past is. But you are my friend now. And as well as being a mum and an entirely arbitrary wife, you are also a beautiful woman. So don't have sex with any of the men you meet tonight, just come out and stand in a room with your eyebrows plucked, some lipstick on, and smooth legs and see what effect you have. Because when you do I bet you'll feel great, I bet you'll feel free."

"I'd like to feel free," Catherine said thoughtfully. "And actually the thought of having sex with the first or any man I meet makes me want to be sick, so I don't mind leaving that part out after all."

"That's what I thought," Kirsty said, pulling Catherine into a sitting position. "We take baby steps, Catherine, baby steps. Now, where's your razor?"

When Alison got home from the supermarket, her reluctant son in tow, Marc was in the kitchen with the girls. Their heads were bent over the drawings they were creating, felt tips fanned out across the marble counter. As she entered, Rosie skipped around her feet in greeting before sticking her head in the bags that Alison set on the floor.

"This dog is a hooligan," she said, picking the bags up once again and putting them on the countertop. "You can't take your eyes off of her."

Alison looked at her husband leaning over the girls as they colored. The last sixteen years hadn't been as kind to him as they had to Jimmy. Marc had filled out too, but it was a slight paunch and not muscle that had materialized underneath his shirt. And his hair had receded quite considerably, not that either of them ever mentioned it.

Of course the change in his appearance wouldn't matter if she could love him again. If things were right between her and Marc, it wouldn't matter that she had never had the life she'd dreamed of as a girl, never got to university or had a job of her own or really had any part of herself that wasn't wholly dependent on Marc or their children. Take her away from her family and she might as well not exist, she had made such a little mark on the world.

"This is nice!" Amy said happily as she kissed Alison on the cheek. "We're all here in our new big house."

"All right, Muffin." Dom greeted his little sister with the first hint of a smile that Alison had seen since she'd announced to him he was helping her do the food shopping for the weekend. "How was school today?"

"It was okay today," Amy said. "There's this one nice girl I like."

"I had the best time," Gemma told him, glancing up from her coloring. "My teacher is lovely and all the girls like me. Eloise is going to be my best friend, though, because she understands me."

"Oh, does she now?" Marc said, handing Alison a cup of tea. "Eloise must be a very clever girl."

"She is and she's the tallest in our class," Gemma said. "She's the tallest and I'm the prettiest and we're both clever, so we can't fail."

"Except in modesty exams," Dom said, opening the fridge door, looking at the remaining shopping bags at his feet, and closing the door again.

Alison looked at her entire family gathered under one roof, her successful husband who made cups of tea unbidden, her musical son and her two smiling daughters. For a few rare minutes during which nobody was shouting, lying, or crying she could pretend that she had it all. If any other woman was to see her life laid out in a magazine or on a TV show, then chances were she'd feel envious. Three lovely children, a handsome husband who provided for them, a wonderful new home fitted with every luxury. But the one thing Alison didn't have, the one essential ingredient that would enable her to enjoy all of this perfection, was a sense of herself. Somewhere between running away at the age of seventeen and now, she had lost the woman she had always meant to become, and her waning feelings for Marc threw the realization into sharp relief. Despite all the outward trappings of a happy and successful life, Alison was not happy, she was not fulfilled, and worst of all she was not herself.

"How nice, all of us will be in for dinner tonight!" she said brightly, determined to conjure happiness out of so many good things.

"Ah," Marc said, his tone immediately dashing her attempt.

Alison looked at him and realized where the cup of tea had come from. It was a rather low-rent peace offering. "You said you'd be in tonight. It's Friday night, Marc. Remember, you said you'd always be home by four every Friday. That was part of our deal. Family time."

"You sound so surprised," Dominic said sarcastically.

"I know I did and it will be usually," Marc said, ignoring his son's comment, causing the boy to slam out of the room, banging the door behind him. "But it's the lads I've taken on at the showroom. They want to take me out for a drink and I think I need to go. It's a team-building thing, Al. They're young blokes, they need a bit of direction. It'll just be a few drinks at some local pub. I'll be back by ten at the latest."

"Mum, look at this." Gemma held up her drawing. "This is

me and Rosie winning The Crufts Dog Show. This is the big silver trophy. I'm going to teach her to sit and stay this weekend. She's going to be brilliant at it."

"That's beautiful, darling," Alison said, not taking her eyes off of Marc's face.

"But you're not looking!" Gemma protested, thrusting the picture in front of her. For a second Alison took in the bright blue sky, huge smiling sun, and a portrait of Rosie surrounded by deliriously happy smiling stick people. That was how Gemma saw her family. Not like this. Why couldn't she be there, Alison wondered, in the space between the sky and the grass, where the mother and father always held hands?

"Al." Marc offered her a conciliatory smile. "Look, its just a one-time thing, I promise you. And you know I need to network, meet as many people as I can before the party next week, which reminds me, have you sent your invites out?"

Alison noticed his deft change of subject but wearily decided to ignore it, taking a sip of tea instead. She didn't want the kids to witness another fight. They were so rarely all together that even if it was only for a few minutes, she wanted that time to be happy.

"Well, I don't exactly know anyone yet." She thought of Jimmy Ashley. "So I left my invites with this woman named Lois at the school and told her to invite the PTA, and I've asked the girls' teachers and the head. Anyway, how many people are coming to this party, Marc?"

"Couple of hundred, give or take," Marc said, bending over to help Amy color in the remainder of her smiling, benevolent sun.

"And when do you have to confirm final numbers for the caterers?" Alison asked.

"The caterers?" Marc looked up at her sharply.

"You know, the people you found to cater the party at such short notice?"

Marc looked thoughtful, then went back to coloring studiously while Alison began to feel her insides simmer.

"I sort of thought you'd be doing that," he said.

"You thought I'd be making sandwiches for two hundred people?" Alison asked him. "Me?"

"I sort of thought so," Marc said, winking at Gemma, which made her giggle.

"Marc!" Alison exclaimed. "I just can't believe that after everything . . ." She trailed off, unable to detail exactly what "everything" was.

"What I *meant*," Marc added hastily, "is I thought you'd find the caterers. That's the sort of thing you usually do, isn't it?"

"You said all I had to do was send invitations, open my house to the whole of Farmington, and look glamorous. You didn't say anything about catering. And no, I don't usually organize it, usually your PA organizes it, or have you forgotten?"

A brief flash of the Christmas party burned across Alison's eyes and she knew that Marc had seen it too.

They stared at each other for a beat of silence.

"Well, look, darling," Marc said, choosing to brush the bad memory aside like he always did. "How about you find a caterer—there's still over a week to go, after all. Don't worry about the cost—however much it takes."

"It will be 'however much it takes' to find a caterer at this short notice, and if I do end up making two hundred egg mayonnaise sandwiches, there will never be an upper limit on how much it's going to cost you!"

At last Marc got up and came around the table. He put his arms round her waist, and at almost exactly her height, he looked straight into her eyes.

"I messed up," he said frankly. "I forgot something huge and big and I tried to pass the buck on to you. Balloons I remembered, fairy lights and music. I've ordered the champagne, the wine, and the beer. But I forgot food and you remembered it. Which is why I need you, Al. Remember that kid I was when we met? Working nights for the railways? I'd still be doing it now if I hadn't found you. And if you can turn me from that kid into this man, the man who is lucky enough to be your husband, then you can sort out the catering for the party, can't you?"

"Yes, I can," Alison said despite herself. The trouble was he was right. She knew him inside out, just like he knew her. In the end it always came back to this. They'd found each other when they were very young and they had clung to each other from that moment on, riding their choices with the conviction of those who are determined never to be wrong. She'd made her bed a long time ago, and now who was she to complain that it wasn't comfortable anymore?

"You know I love you, don't you?" Marc asked her finally.

Alison made herself look at him. "I do," she conceded, because he did love her, albeit imperfectly.

"Then that's all that matters, right?" he asked her.

Not all that matters, Alison thought. He never asked her if she loved him back.

"Good, well, I'll be back by ten. Make sure you wait up for me, we've still got a lot of rooms to christen."

"You're going now? It's not even six o'clock."

"There's some curry house they want to take me to first, I'd much rather be eating with you, but . . ." Marc shrugged.

"What can he do?" Gemma finished for him with a copycat shrug.

Alison wasn't surprised. It was Marc's favorite phrase, after all.

"Has he looked at me yet?" Kirsty asked Catherine in a whisper as they stood next to the bar in the Three Bells.

It was remarkable really, Catherine thought. Kirsty had stood right next to Steve or Sam at the bar while ordering the drinks, had brushed past him—breasts first—on the way to the ladies' room, and had been laughing and tossing her hair at full capacity ever since in a bid to get his attention, but he hadn't actually looked her way once.

"He might be gay," Catherine ventured. "Or maybe have tunnel vision syndrome and slight deafness in both ears, because that is the only way he would not be able to notice you. You are many things, but subtle isn't one of them."

"He's not gay," Kirsty said firmly. "He used to go out with a pole dancer and anyway, Catherine, I'm ashamed of you conforming to such an obvious stereotype. Just because he's well turned out and takes care of himself doesn't make him gay."

"Okay, then," Catherine said. "Maybe he's just really, *really* interested in what his friend has to say." Steve or Sam was certainly deep in conversation with his friend, a tallish, fair-haired, and pleasant-looking man of about her age, Catherine guessed. This was the friend that Kirsty had deemed it her destiny to distract when she went in for the kill. She studied him covertly. She had no idea how to distract anybody, let alone a man, other than to point at some nameless object over his shoulder and shout, "It's behind you!"

If Kirsty ever did get to talk to her trainer, Catherine was fairly sure that she would mess up the friend-distraction bit. But there was an "if" because what Kirsty hadn't thought of and what Catherine didn't want to point out was that if her personal trainer wasn't gay and didn't have a hearing or vision problem, then the alternative was that he was ignoring her, because he didn't want to have anything to do with her. It didn't seem to be a conclusion that Kirsty was likely to come to on her own, and Catherine didn't want to be the one to bring it up.

"God, you should see that lot over there, a classic midlife crisis in full flow." Kirsty nodded over to the far side of the pub, a corner that Catherine could not see from where she was standing. "That's Joel who used to work in the gym, now he's got a job at the new car dealership in town, so it must be his new boss he's with. Joel told me he's a real entrepreneur, made a lot of money in London and moved out here to make a lot more. Look at him." Kirsty nudged Catherine. "Flirting with girls half his age. I bet his wife wouldn't like that."

"It's none of my business what the man gets up to," Catherine said rather primly.

"Fine," Kirsty sighed. "Anyway, we are supposed to be finding you a man . . ."

"No, we are not!" Catherine was alarmed. "That wasn't on the agenda, I distinctly remember you taking it off the agenda."

"I don't mean to find you one to take home," Kirsty assured her. "I mean find one that's checking you out, so you can see how irresistible you are to men." She scanned the room. "What about him?"

Kirsty nudged her quite hard this time, throwing her a little off balance even in her flat boots.

"What about *who*?" Catherine said.

"Him over there." Kirsty nodded to Catherine's left and when she looked she caught the eye of a fair-haired man, perhaps a little younger than she, who smiled at her fleetingly before dropping his gaze back to his drink.

"He was totally checking you out like a motherfucker," Kirsty exclaimed quite loudly, so that one or two people (but not her trainer) looked over at them.

"Was he?" Catherine said dryly. "I had no idea that one could be checked out in such a way."

"Well, one can, smart arse, and he was. He's been looking at you all night."

"Can we get back to you? What's *your* plan?"

"To be gorgeous, but so far it doesn't seem to be working out too well. Have you got any ideas?"

Catherine thought for a moment. "Well, why don't you go up to him, tap him on the shoulder, and say hi?"

Kirsty shook her head. "Oh, you are so naive, where were you during your teens? Didn't you learn anything from *Beverly Hills 90210*?"

"Why not just talk to him?" Catherine asked with a bemused shrug.

"Because then he'll think I fancy him," Kirsty replied, as if stating the obvious. "I don't want him to know that. I want him to think that I, his beautiful client, am merely flitting by him like a beautiful but unobtainable butterfly that he longs to capture . . . a woman who can only be . . . oh hi, Steve."

Kirsty went bright red as her trainer appeared at her shoulder.

"Kirsty, I *thought* that was you." He smiled at Kirsty. "And it's Sam, by the way."

"I knew it was an *S* name." Kirsty beamed at him. "Can I buy you a drink? I mean water for me because obviously I don't really drink apart from this gin and tonic and honestly it's a lot more tonic than gin, gin-flavored tonic really . . ."

Catherine unconsciously took a step back as Kirsty focused all her attention on Sam. He was nice-looking, Catherine had to concede. He was tallish, with friendly eyes and very nice arms. She could see why Kirsty would be smitten with him even if he was completely bald. Just then Catherine wished very much that Jimmy was there with her in the pub. At least she could always talk to Jimmy; now her prediction had come true and she had become chief gooseberry. Tentatively she glanced in the direction of the fair-haired man across the bar. He smiled at her; she didn't look that way again.

"So that's your friend chatting up my friend, then?" Catherine started as Sam's friend appeared at her side, a little of her drink splashing onto the back of her hand. "Sorry, didn't mean to make you jump. Just thought you might like some company. Looks like your friend's got mine monopolized for the evening. I'm Dave, by the way."

He held out his hand and hesitantly Catherine took it. She hadn't talked to a man she didn't know who wasn't somebody's husband in . . . well, it was certainly months, maybe even years.

"Hello," Catherine said. "I'm Catherine and I'm sure Kirsty won't keep him all evening." She looked over at her friend, who was in full flirt mode. "Actually she might."

"Oh that's *Kirsty*," Dave said with a grin. "No wonder he was trying so hard not to notice her all evening. He digs her big-time."

"Does he dig her big-time?" Catherine said, noticing Dave smile as she repeated his phrase. "That's nice, because she digs him big-time too. Like seriously a lot. I'm probably not meant to tell you that, but she never shuts up about him."

"I won't tell if you don't," Dave said, taking a step closer to her. "So anyway, enough about them, tell me about you."

"Me?" Catherine tried to think of something, anything, but the truth always sounded much worse when spoken out loud than in her head. This time was no exception. "I've got two kids and sort of a husband, who I'm married to but don't live with anymore since he slept with another woman more or less right in front of my eyes, and I work in a local PR company. Oh, and I like growing my own vegetables. That's about it."

"Okay." Dave laughed. "Right, well—just an everyday kind of girl, then."

"That's me," Catherine said with a smile. She quite liked talking to Dave, as it happened.

"So it looks like we've been abandoned, then," Dave said, nodding at Kirsty and Sam, who in the blink of an eye had gone from chatting to deep, deep kissing.

"I expected it," Catherine told him.

"Well, why don't we head off somewhere else, then, somewhere a bit quieter where we can get a drink and talk, what do you think?"

Catherine looked at him. She was fairly sure he was chatting her up. Either that or he just wanted to hang out with a still married yet single mother of two who was two inches taller than him.

"I . . . look, I have to go," she lied. "I've got kids, two under eight—the babysitter goes mad if I'm late."

"But it's only just past ten," Dave said, seemingly unfazed by her children. "Have one more drink with me."

"I'm sorry," Catherine said. "I can't."

And she raced out of the pub and back home as fast as she could until she was safe, back behind her own front door, where she could grow the hair on her legs and cook dinner for her ex, and where she could be safe and shut off and never have to worry about what to say to mildly attractive men in pubs or, worse still, what they might say to her.

Nine

"Mum," Eloise said through a mouthful of toast on Monday morning. "Can I ask Gemma to tea this week, can I, please? She said she's going to train her puppy this weekend, so can I, *please?*"

Catherine looked at her daughter, who had twisted her long hair into her best approximation of a ballerina-style bun and secured it with some frou-frou nonsense that Catherine's mother-in-law had probably inflicted on her during the girls' last visit there. Catherine knew the scrunchie was a silent protest against what her daughter saw as a violation of her human rights: if she was not allowed to have ballet lessons on Monday afternoons, she'd do her best to look like the girls who were.

"Don't talk while you are chewing," Catherine told her. "And anyway, if you are so keen to see her puppy, you should be visiting her house. It's not as if she can bring it here."

Catherine knew something that Eloise didn't, but just for the moment she was refraining from telling her because she liked to be able to eat her breakfast in relative peace.

"Why not? And anyway she's the new girl, like a guest at a party, and I am sort of the host. So I have to ask her first and then she'll ask me back and I'll get to see her puppy, *please,* Mum. You never let us do *anything!*"

Oblique reference to the lack of ballet lessons again reinforced how meager her request was to have one paltry friend back to tea, in the hope that it would elicit a return invitation and the chance to visit a puppy, another treasured wish that Catherine was not able to fulfill for her daughter. Feeling rather inadequate and depressed, Catherine wished she had told Eloise what she had known before this conversation had even started.

The new family was having a housewarming party and Catherine and her daughters were both invited. Lois had rung her yesterday evening just after the girls got back, telling her that all of the PTA and their families had been invited to attend on the following Saturday. Lois told her it was a shameful bid on the part of the mysterious new mother to buy her way onto the PTA committee, despite the fact that new applicants weren't normally considered until September. Still, Lois pointed out it would be an excuse to nose round her house; she'd been dying to look round one of those new houses for months—she'd heard they were terribly vulgar inside. Gold effect taps. Then Lois told Catherine she had already RSVP'd on behalf of the whole committee.

A huge party like that thrown only a couple of weeks after they had arrived meant that Gemma's family must have a lot of money. Catherine was as proud of her daughters as any woman could be, and she loved the ramshackle cut-price charm of her terraced cottage. But it was difficult not to wonder what some of the other parents thought of her when they brought their children to one of the smallest houses in Farmington, with its secondhand sofa and only one loo. What did they really think of the thirty-two-year-old with a philandering long-haired, largely unemployed estranged husband and vegetable patch in the back garden?

Catherine never craved normality in the sense that she wanted *things*. She didn't want things. She would just like sometimes not to feel self-conscious about who she was and the life that she had chosen, or rather the life that had chosen her when she wasn't really paying attention. She supposed when she was a girl she'd had the same expectations as everybody else, that as plain and awkward as she was, one day somebody would love her and then hand in hand they would lead a normal life, get married in their twenties, have children, buy a nice home, and have a steady but modest income. When she married Jimmy she'd hoped for the kind of simple life that seemed to be the right of other people. But their marriage, though often wonderful and occasionally painful, had never been normal.

Farmington normality was a three-car family and a five-bedroom house. Catherine with her part-time job and reliance on tax credits was not anything like the norm. In this money-ugly town she was the oddity. Even so, she couldn't deny Eloise a new friend with a puppy because of her own insecurities.

"Well, actually," she said, bracing herself for the squeals of excitement that were sure to follow her announcement. "You *are* going to be Gemma's guest, because her mum and dad have invited us all, and just about everyone else in Farmington, to a party at her house next Saturday night!"

"A party! A party at Gemma's! Oh, thank you thank you thank you, mum!" Eloise jumped up and planted a buttery kiss on Catherine's cheek before scowling. "We are going, aren't we?"

"Of course we are going," Catherine said.

"Are all of us going? Me too?" Leila asked from the other

end of the table, reserving her excitement until she clarified that point.

Catherine smiled. "Yes, of course."

"And do we get to stay up late?" Leila asked happily.

"A little bit later than usual," Catherine said.

"Thank you, God!" Leila grinned at the ceiling as the girls sprung up from the table and clung on to each other, jumping up and down.

"It's going to be great," Eloise told Leila, her eyes wide. "We'll be able to play with Gemma and Amy as much as we like!"

"Will it be dark, though?" Leila asked.

"Pitch black," Eloise replied.

"Ooooh, goody, goody, goody!" Leila shrieked.

"What's going on?" Jimmy asked as he appeared through the back door. "I've never seen them this keen to go to school on a Monday morning. I'll have to brush up on their antiestablishment training."

"No, silly, we're not being anti-dish-table-is-went, we're all going to a party!" Leila said, flinging herself at her dad's legs, nearly knocking him off balance.

"Are we?" Jimmy asked, steadying himself against the door frame and smiling at Catherine. "Cool, any chance of a quick shower? I'm laying down that demo today and then Mick's going to take some photos to put on the CD cover, and I have to look my best. When's this party?"

"Help yourself to the shower," Catherine told him. "The thing is I don't think you are exactly invited to the party. At least not on my invitation. It's for PTA members and their families."

"But Daddy is our family," Eloise said.

"Yes, he's our *daddy*," Leila added, as if Catherine was being a bit thick. "'Member? Plus mankind is one big family, Mummy."

"I know, darling, but . . ." Catherine looked at Jimmy, who clearly wasn't going to help her out if he could tag along to a party where there would be free booze and free food, two of his favorite things.

"I'm just saying I don't think you were specifically invited, it was an open invitation to the PTA and you are not on the PTA."

"Well, I might as well be, the amount of discount I give that organization for my services. Look, if it's an open invitation, how do you know if I was invited or not? Even the people who are doing the inviting don't know who they've invited in that case."

"It's Gemma's mum and dad," Eloise told him with an air of pride. "She's my new best friend and she's getting a pony."

"And Daddy, we're going to stay up late in the dark!" Leila told him, making a spooky face.

"Are we?" Jimmy grinned down at his daughter as he disengaged her and headed up to the bathroom. "Cool. Give me five minutes and I'll walk you to school."

"Mummy, why does Daddy come here for a shower?" Leila asked as the sound of Jimmy's heavy footsteps sounded on the bathroom floor above their heads.

"Because Daddy doesn't have a shower on the boat," Catherine said absently.

"Daddy practically doesn't even have a *roof* on the boat, it's so leaky," Eloise mumbled.

"Yes." Catherine looked thoughtful. "Daddy really needs somewhere better to live."

"Like here?" Eloise asked hopefully.

"Like a house or a flat with a decent roof," Catherine replied. "And some form of heating."

"Like here, then," Eloise added, and Catherine remembered her agreement with Jimmy.

"Somewhere like here, but either he'll have to sign a record deal or I'll have to win the lottery, because at the moment we can't afford it."

"We could afford it, if he lived here," Eloise said, and Catherine decided it was impossible to argue with her because after all she was right.

"No," Catherine said again as the four of them walked briskly to school, running a good five minutes late.

"But do we really mean no?" Jimmy asked her, striding along beside her. "Think of what an experience it will be for them, how much great music they will hear live."

"No, Jimmy, no, you are not combining your tour of Oxford-shire with your turn to take the girls on holidays. You are not going to drive them around unsecured in the back of a van, make them stay up all night in pubs while you perforate their eardrums, and then put them God knows where while you do . . . whatever you do."

"*Nothing,* I do *nothing* after a gig. I have a pint or two and then go to bed *alone* in whichever B&B we're staying at," Jimmy said, obviously offended.

"Well, even if that's true, you can't do that with a five- and an eight-year-old!" Catherine protested, flinging out her hand in exasperation.

"But the van's just been serviced and I'd put car seats in the front for them to sit on; I'd even throw in a seat belt."

"No," Catherine repeated, throwing him her warrior-queen look. "It's not going to happen."

"But why, Mum?" Eloise asked her. "We could be roadies. Please? It will be fun."

"Daddy said we could be back-up singers," Leila urged her. "Plus the van's just been serviced."

Catherine narrowed her eyes at Jimmy. "I will never forgive you for bringing this up in front of them."

"I'll add that to the list, then," Jimmy said in exasperation.

"That's not fair, Jim, and you know it. I cook for you, wives do not cook for a husband if they still give a damn about . . . well, you know what. Anyway, this isn't about us. It's about our two *little* girls. Sometimes I think you forget that you are their father and not just their friend."

"I know that," Jimmy explained, hurrying to keep up with Catherine's long strides. "That's the one thing I definitely do know . . . look, okay. You're probably right, taking them gigging isn't my best plan. I suppose I thought it would be economical, like killing two birds with one stone. Multitasking. I know you dig that, right?"

"No." Catherine had to raise her voice to be heard over the chorus of pleases that followed Jimmy's suggestion. She suddenly stopped dead, which meant her disparate little family overshot her by a few steps before coming to a juddering halt.

"Jim, please, think about what you are suggesting," she said, looking up into his eyes. Jimmy held her gaze for a moment or two and then dropped his eyes to his boots.

"It's probably not a good idea, after all, girls," he said, his comment greeted by a selection of groans. "Mum's right. When you're a bit older I'm definitely going to take you, but right now you *are* too young. We'll think of something else to do. We could go and visit Nanna Pam?"

Catherine glanced at him before walking on, giving him that look of hers, her specialty, the look that said that he was more of a burden than a partner. It had become a frequent expression of hers during the last year or so they were living together. That constant unspoken disappointment was part of what had driven him to go with Donna Clarke to the ladies' loos.

"Look," Catherine said as she charged along at double-quick pace. "I know you love the girls, I know you do your best for them. But I just wish sometimes that you'd think further ahead than five seconds. You never seem to plan anything."

"I'm more of an instinctive kind of guy," Jimmy said with a half-smile. "Like a ninja."

Catherine's exasperation bloomed into a reluctant smile and Jimmy found to his immense surprise that he had been holding his breath until it appeared.

Neither Gemma nor her younger sister was in the playground when the bell rang, which infuriated Eloise, who was determined to firm up tea arrangements, party or no.

"Where *is* she?" she asked as her classmates filed in around her. "I want you to meet her, Daddy. She's really nice."

"Just chill, babe," Jimmy said. Catherine had left him to wait with Eloise while she took Leila round to her class. "You'll see this Gemma in class, won't you?"

"But I want to go in with her," Eloise said, pawing the ground like an impatient colt. "So everyone will see we're best friends."

Jimmy looked down at his flame-haired girl. "You are everyone's best friend, Ellie. Look, you've got to go in now, otherwise I'll have to sign the late book and your mum will be even more cross with me than she already is."

"Sorry Mummy's angry with you, Dad," Eloise said, hugging Jimmy around his waist.

"She wasn't angry as such, just direct, and that's never a bad thing," Jimmy said, edging both of them toward the school entrance, which was now deserted. "Besides, she was right. It's an irritating habit she has."

"I was thinking on the way to school," Eloise added. "If you got a cold or got sick or something and were *really* poorly and you couldn't stay on the boat anymore because you might *die*, then you'd have to come and stay with us until you got better, wouldn't you?" Eloise looked up at him, her expression serious.

Jimmy took a breath. "But I never get sick," he said. "And I love that old boat, so don't you worry about me, darling. In you go."

Eloise looked disappointed but nevertheless she raced into class, her bright hair flying behind her, calling out over her shoulder, "Gemma's got blond hair and a blue shiny coat and she usually has some sparkly clips in her hair. If you see her with her mum, will you ask her about tea, please?"

"I definitely will," Jimmy called after her, although he had no intention of doing any such thing.

Jimmy glanced around the school yard. All these year-round tanned women with their smart hairdos and high heels just to drop their children off at school did his head in, even more than the groupies that hung around at his gigs. At least he knew what those women wanted with him, and all that was required to deal with them was basic evasive techniques. So making small talk with whatever the name for posh wives was—glamour mamas or something—wasn't on Jimmy's agenda.

"My God, Jimmy Ashley!" Jimmy stopped dead and looked at the blond woman standing in front of him. Good-looking woman, nice shiny hair, a long white raincoat, and high-heeled boots under some faded jeans. She was unquestionably one of them, so how on earth did she know his name? He couldn't see her at one of his gigs.

"Run in, love, you'll just about make it," she said to a blond little girl in a shiny blue coat. "Don't want to sign that book again!"

Another little kid, one about Leila's age, was clutching her arm.

"Right, then," Jimmy said, preparing to leave, but the woman just looked at him expectantly.

"It's great to see you again after all this time," the woman gushed, her face flushing. Jimmy was confused but intrigued.

"Is it?" he said. "I mean it's good to see you too . . ." There was a long gap where the absence of a name flashed like a neon sign.

"Alison," the woman said, her smile fading just a fraction. "You don't remember me, do you?"

While he was fairly certain he had never seen her before in his life, Jimmy thought she looked nice. It seemed wrong to offend her. He smiled at her, interested to see her blush deepen.

"Honestly I don't, but I can't think why. It must have been that serious water skiing accident that I don't remember having last year, because only serious amnesia would be a good enough reason not to remember you."

To his amazement the woman giggled like a sixteen-year-old, and then there was something about her that seemed familiar.

"I'm *Alison*," she told him, as if her name was sure to remind him. "Alison James. When you knew me I was Alison . . ."

"Mrs. James?" The woman looked up as the head teacher leaned out of the reception door. "Any chance of a quick word before you take Amy in? I know you are already running late."

"Of course," Alison said, looking disappointed as she smiled at Jimmy. "Timekeeping is not my strong point." She reached into her bag and handed Jimmy an invitation. "We're having a house-warming party on Saturday, can you come?"

"Oh, you're Gemma's mum," Jimmy said, as if that should be reason enough to know who she was. "I'm already coming with my wife—well, ex-wife, sort of—and my daughters. My Eloise is very keen on your Gemma."

"You're Ellie's dad?" Alison looked surprised. "I'd never pictured you as a dad. I don't know why, maybe because you look the same—you teach my son guitar, he's just started at the school. Dominic?"

"Oh yeah." Jimmy began to relax. "He's a talented kid. When he's not sulking. A lot of them sulk these days. They think if they're not depressed they've got no cred. Only thing is most of them haven't got anything decent to be depressed about."

"Mrs. James?" the head teacher called again, and this time there was a definite edge to her voice.

"Do you know what, Jimmy? It's been really good to see you," Alison said, laying her hand on his arm.

"You too, Alison," Jimmy said, because although he still couldn't place exactly who she was, it was always good to encounter a good-looking woman who was pleased to see him.

"Oh, and if you see a chocolate Labrador tied to a lamppost, howling her head off, tell her I won't be too long, okay?"

"Okay," Jimmy said. "Whatever you say."

Alison flashed him another dazzling smile as she trotted toward the head, her smaller girl lingering a step or two behind her.

Just as she went into the building, Catherine appeared around the corner at full pelt, running right into Jimmy.

"Jimmy! Why are you still here? Please tell me you haven't had to sign Eloise into the late book, have you? I'm only still here because Lois would not stop going on about the school's Easter Festival. You don't fancy dressing up in a bunny costume, do you?"

"I bumped into this woman who thought she knew me," Jimmy began to tell her. "But I don't know how because she's this Gemma's mum, the one whose party we're all going to."

"Oh, was she nice?" Catherine asked, although she clearly didn't want a reply, as she was walking backward toward the gate as she talked. "Anyway, I've got to get to work. I have three minutes to make it down High Street. I'll measure you up for that suit, okay?"

"I'm off to work too," Jimmy called after her as she sprinted off. "Laying down a demo today," he added. "Today's the day. This is the day that's going to change my life."

Alison practically skipped her way to the gym to take up the new membership. She had secured Rosie in the back of her car, parked carefully in the shade with the back window left open a few centimeters so that the puppy wouldn't get overheated. She put a bowl of water next to her and furnished her with a giant chew bone, which she hoped would keep Rosie off the leather trim for at least an hour.

It was foolish, she knew, literally idiotic to feel so happy about bumping into a man who clearly had no idea who she was. So what if he didn't remember that she was the girl who used to lean forward on the edge of the stage in the hopes he'd look right down her top? He'd never noticed that girl anyway. But he'd noticed her now, a grown woman. He'd noticed her and she was fairly sure he'd flirted with her too. It might have been the first time a man had actually flirted with her since the early 1990s.

That, coupled with the tentative smile on Amy's face as Mrs. Woodruff had led her by the hand into class, put her in exactly the right mood for her one-on-one pilates class with her new teacher.

"Hello, there." A woman about her age smiled at her and held out her hand as she walked into the private studio she had booked. "Mrs. James, is it? I'm Kirsty Robinson, I'm going to be teaching you pilates."

"Right," Kirsty said. "From that position step one foot forward and we'll stretch out your hip flexors."

"So?" Alison asked her with some effort as she stretched her left leg behind her. "Are you going to see him again?" Her new teacher had been regaling her with the details of her love life for the last half an hour, something that Alison found most entertaining.

"I think so," Kirsty considered. "We had a nice time in the pub, and he is a great kisser. I let him walk me home and he didn't even *try* to invite himself in for sex, which I was slightly disappointed by even though I would have definitely said no because I hardly ever do sex on the first date with men I like. But he didn't call me over the weekend and today when I saw him he was playing it cool, as if we hadn't spent half an hour with our tongues down each other's throats on Friday night. I still think he likes me, though. And if he doesn't, then I'll just revert to Plan A until I've gotten over him."

"Ignore him and pretend nothing happened," Alison confirmed as she followed Kirsty's movements in the mirror.

"Exactly." Kirsty grinned at her. "Okay, relax into child pose and then roll yourself slowly and carefully up into a standing position, working each vertebra." She and Alison rose in unison in front of the full-length mirror.

"Shake yourself out and you're done," Kirsty told her.

"Thanks, I really enjoyed that," Alison said warmly.

"Me too, it's nice to have a client that's nice and not some stuffy old cow who thinks I'm one of her servants."

"I really hope you get things sorted with Sam and that he asks you out again."

"Well, he will or he won't," Kirsty said with a sigh, catching sight of herself in the mirror and giving herself an admiring glance. "It's not the end of the world if he doesn't. Yes, I'm in love with him. But look at me—I'm gorgeous and still young. I'll love again."

Alison laughed. "And it's better to shop around than buy the first thing you see and find out fifteen years later you don't really want it anymore," she said completely out of the blue. She paused for a moment as she realized what she had just said out loud for the first time.

"You are so right." Kirsty smiled. "You should meet my neighbor. She got married in her twenties to some guy she went to *school* with and of course it didn't work out, and now it's like she's stuck in a time warp. Can't go back, can't go forward. I'm trying to crowbar her out of it, but it's a challenge, let me tell you. So how long have you been married?"

Alison pursed her lips and looked down at her painted toenails.

"Married fourteen years, together nearly sixteen years," she said sheepishly.

"So you bought the first thing you saw in the shop, then?" Kirsty laughed.

"More like shoplifted him out from under my best friend's nose," Alison said. "But you know, when you're seventeen you don't really think."

"Well, it's obviously worked out for you," Kirsty said. "So tell me, what's your secret?"

"I don't know," Alison said with a shrug. "We implement Plan A a lot."

As she picked up her bag, she pulled out her last few remaining invitations. "Listen, we're having a housewarming party and . . ."

"Oh, I already know about that," Kirsty said. "All the sports center staff are coming. Even Sam."

"Well, maybe while you're not ignoring him you'll have a drink with me. I don't know anyone in town yet and the thought of having two hundred strangers in my new house is slightly intimidating."

"I'd love to," Kirsty said. "And I'll introduce you to my neighbor. She's a bit like a young Miss Marple, but once you get to know her she's pretty cool, and then you'll have two friends and I'll know two people to lead astray instead of one."

Alison grinned at her. "I'm perfectly capable of leading myself astray, thank you very much. I'm a world expert at it."

Ten

"Are you sure that you can plug all of those fairy lights into my house and it won't explode?" Alison asked the electrician as he plugged yet another extension into yet another extension on the morning of the party.

He scowled at her. "Yes, I'm completely sure." He hadn't been very amiable since Rosie chewed through one of his extension cords. Fortunately it hadn't been plugged in at the time.

"Okay, well, I'll leave it up to you, then," she said, trying to get back into his good graces so he wouldn't short the fuses just to spite her. "You're the professional. I don't know anything!"

He turned his back on her and resumed plugging more things into more things, which Alison took as a sign of agreement with her self-assessment. She could imagine what he thought of her: a spoiled rich housewife who treated all tradesmen like servants and believed that the working classes were born to serve her. Maybe that *was* what she was like a little bit now, even if her upbringing on the immaculately kept but down-to-earth council estate couldn't have been more different. Her life with Marc had transformed her. Now she was new money and that was the way she sometimes sounded and acted, even if she didn't *truly* feel that way.

It had been a challenging week up to this point, and Alison had had a hard time keeping up the good mood her pilates class had left her in on Monday. The first set of caterers she thought she'd miraculously managed to book for Saturday had let her down, citing some lame excuse like a death in the family and referring her to a friend's brand-new business called Home Hearths.

From that moment Alison had felt that luck was not on her side. She had been well aware that *any* caterer available for booking a scant five days before an event was not exactly going to be top of the range, but by that time she had very little choice but to go with the new company. She'd even booked them blind without any tasting or menu discussion. Alison had told them she wanted canapés for two hundred people and they told her they'd provide the waitstaff. That, as far as Alison was concerned, was as good as it was likely to get.

Marc had not been around for almost the whole week. He'd been at the office until past eleven every night working on getting the new showroom running smoothly. If Alison wasn't asleep by the time he got in, then she was in too bad a mood to make small talk with him, something he always annoyingly wanted to do regardless of the hour, because he'd be high as a kite and wouldn't care that the children and the low-level bone-splintering radioactive stress of her day had drilled her into the ground. But it wasn't just the contrast in their days that infuriated her and nearly drove Alison to murder her husband. No, it was the sheer bloody thoughtless optimism that had infected him ever since they'd decided to come back to Farmington.

She'd never imagined that Marc's determination to change himself would have brought them quite this far. It was as if he was on a quest that would never be satisfied. A three-bedroom house in Kennington would have made Alison happy once. But she had a feeling that no such comforting middle ground was available to her and Marc now. For them the only way was either up, up, and away or a very fast journey back down. It all depended on Marc. Everything had always depended on Marc.

Suddenly Alison remembered everything that still needed to be done, and, furious that she was letting Marc stop her in her tracks again, she found herself saying out loud, "Get a grip, woman—good God, act your age!"

"Forty-seven."

Alison spun around to find Amy standing behind her decked out in her Cinderella outfit, Rosie tugging playfully on the hem.

"Pardon, sweetie?" Alison knelt down to her daughter's level. She loved to see Amy dress up. It was one of her few moments of self-expressiveness and even then she only seemed to be able to manage it if she was pretending to be a Disney princess.

"You said act your age and I said forty-seven. That's your age, isn't it, Mama?"

"Thirty-two, darling," Alison said, unoffended. "But I feel forty-seven a lot of the time, so you're spot-on really."

"You *look* beautiful," Amy told her, wrapping her arms around Alison and whispering in her ear, "Love you, Mama," as if it was their little secret, which Alison sometimes felt it was.

"Love you too, precious," Alison whispered back.

"You're welcome," Amy said, releasing Alison from her embrace. They had been learning manners at her old school and she had been responding arbitrarily to any comment with that phrase ever since. "Dominic said I had to tell you there was some 'old tart' unloading what looks like sandwiches from a beat-up Volvo station wagon out front and that you might want to go and check if it's legal because . . . I forgot the rest."

Alison gave Amy a little hug.

"Thank you for being so helpful, darling, but don't call anyone a tart. It's not a nice word for little girls, okay?"

"You're welcome," Amy replied.

"Run along and try and keep Rosie out of trouble," Alison told Amy, unable to repress a smile as she watched the puppy skid and slide over the polished floor in a bid to keep up with Amy. Her younger daughter had really bonded with the puppy. Perhaps it hadn't been one of Marc's worst ideas after all. But there were still plenty to choose from.

Alison wasn't sure whether to check to see if indeed the caterer had arrived, or to go and strangle her son about his cavalier use of language in front of his sister first. In the end, she made her way to the drive.

"Hello there! Mrs. James?" A surprisingly mature lady in a green raincoat and a red tartan pleated skirt waved at her. "I'm Home Hearth Caterers at your service! It's all gone swimmingly well considering it's our first party. I think you'll be pleased."

Alison looked at Home Hearth Caterers' mud-caked Wellington boots and wondered what "considering it's our first party" meant.

"Mind grabbing a couple of quiches?" Home Hearth Caterers said, piling a couple of platters into Alison's arms. "This way, is it? Don't worry, I'll follow my nose!"

Alison watched helplessly as the old tart tracked mud all across her hallway and she wondered: Where the hell was her husband when she needed someone to blame?

"You can't wear *that*," Kirsty said, looking Catherine up and down.

"I think you'll find I can," Catherine said firmly. "Look, there's only so many times I can take you coming round my house and insulting me. You've made me shave my legs, now leave me alone."

"You do realize that leg shaving is something you have to repeat, don't you?" Kirsty asked her. "Tell me you've done it for tonight, I beg you!"

"Yes, I have," Catherine lied, looking sulkily at the black chiffon shirt with jet beading down the front that she had bought from a charity shop last year, and the straight-legged black trousers with a stay-press pleat ironed down the front that actually reached her ankles. "I *like* my outfit," she said, looking at Kirsty, whose idea it had been to come over three hours before the party to have a girly getting-ready session.

"Three hours?" Catherine had asked her when she suggested it earlier that morning while having breakfast with her and the girls. "Do you mean three actual hours? It doesn't take that long to get ready for *anything*, does it?"

"Yes, it does if you are a proper girl, doesn't it, ladies?" Kirsty had asked Eloise and Leila. "Tell your mum why."

"Well, you have to have a shower, hair wash, hair dry, and hairstyle," Eloise listed, ticking off each item on her fingers.

"*And*," Leila added, "there's choosing what to wear, access-or-eees, see, mummy? That means like earrings and necklaces and nail varnish—ooh, can I wear nail varnish? Nanna Pam gave us some in secret that we are never to tell you about."

"*Also,*" Eloise said, quickly attempting to cover her sister's slip, "there's eye makeup, putting on mascara and lip gloss. Can I wear lip gloss, Mum? Kirsty might lend me some."

"Or we could use the stuff that Nanna Pam gave us . . ."

"Shhhh!" This time Eloise prevented her sister from saying any more by clamping her hand over Leila's mouth. Catherine chose to let the revelations go uncommented on because she had found their secret stash of play cosmetics long ago and thought that everyone, even very small girls, deserved some secrets as long as their mother secretly knew what they were.

"How do they know all this stuff?" Catherine asked Kirsty in amazement. "Are you creeping into their room at night and whispering it in their ears?"

"No, I shout it over the garden fence when you've got them out digging potatoes in the bleak midwinter," Kirsty said, rolling her eyes at the girls and making them giggle. "They know all that stuff because it is ingrained in their DNA. It is the primal urge to make yourself look beautiful. Since the dawn of time, soon after woman invented the wheel and discovered fire, she also realized how much fun it was to paint herself with bright colors." Kirsty clapped a hand on Catherine's shoulder. "You too were born with it once, my friend, but somehow you have lost your feminine way and need to be brought back to the one true path that leads to uncomfortable shoes and exfoliation. Follow the lead of your daughters, follow me, for we have the key to the world of womanhood."

Catherine was unable to resist a smile, particularly when all three of the other females at the table started fluttering their eyelashes at each other, hands arranged under their chins like Botticelli's angels.

It *was* a sort of club, feeling feminine and pretty, and if Kirsty was in it, then maybe she wasn't too old to feel that way too, at least sometimes. Besides, she knew it would make her daughters happy to have a mum that made a bit more of an effort. ("Did you see Isabelle Seaman's mum this morning?" Eloise would often say to her. "She wears high shoes and it's only a Wednesday. Isabelle says that's because she's not letting herself go. That's good, isn't it, Mummy?" And Catherine would give her a talk about looks not being everything and Leila would say something like "Maria von Trapp is pretty and good-hearted and you can be both, look at the Virgin Mary," at which point Catherine would change the subject.) So in short, in a moment of weakness she had agreed to the three-hour preparty preparation party.

It was a decision she regretted the minute she realized that Kirsty had engineered the whole thing firstly so that she could drink the bottle of sparkling wine that Catherine had had in the fridge since Christmas, and secondly so that she could try to get Catherine to wear something that she had brought with her.

"For one thing," Catherine said when Kirsty held up a short black denim skirt that belonged to her, "I am six feet tall. You are five foot two. If I put that on it will barely reach below my butt."

"I *know*," Kirsty said. "That's the advantage of not having one, you'll look great."

"I'll look like a *tart*!" Catherine exclaimed, lowering her voice on the last word lest her daughters stop screaming with excitement for long enough to hear her.

"And looking like a tart is the first in many steps you will need to take to have sex. That's when a man and a woman who like each other very much have a special cuddle and the man puts his . . ."

"You don't need to look like a tart to have sex," Catherine admonished her neighbor. "If I were to ever have sex again, I'd want it to be with someone who respected and cared about me."

"Interesting." Kirsty tipped her head to one side so her sleek brown bob fell at an angle. "You are now not entirely ruling out the possibility of ever having sex again. And okay, you don't *have* to look like a tart to have sex, but it can help. It's sort of the express checkout to shagging, if you like. Ten items of clothing or less get you laid much faster."

"God, you're crass and I'm *not* wearing that skirt." Catherine pushed the bedroom door shut as if to limit the contamination of Kirsty's filthy mind to her own bedroom.

"I knew you'd say that," Kirsty said. "I only brought it to push your boundaries, because what you are actually going to wear is this . . . ta-da!" She pulled out a shopping bag. "I picked up this knee-length pencil skirt for you for a few quid today. Please just try it. I promise you, you'll still have that harbinger-of-doom-at-a-funeral look you like so much, only with your foxy long legs on display."

Catherine said nothing as she looked at the skirt. She hadn't worn a skirt in two years.

"Please try it, for me, Catherine," Kirsty pleaded. "After all, what other friend have you got who is prepared to narrow down her own chances of meeting someone at this party by helping her insanely gorgeous neighbor realize her full potential? That's love. Any other woman would be drawing your eyebrows on, not trying to prune them back."

Kirsty tried her best encouraging you-can-do-it smile on Catherine.

The smile in itself didn't work. What did work was that not only was Kirsty Catherine's only friend who was prepared to try to get her out of her rut and into a short skirt, she was her only real friend period. More than that, Kirsty was the only real female friend she'd had since she was seventeen. Of course there had been lots of friends over the years, girls from work she'd had some laughs with, a couple of women in town who she had known for years. But she'd never been close to anyone apart from Jimmy since Alison had left town. Catherine didn't invest too much in her friendships; if anything she preferred to keep them light and easy, at a comfortable distance. No one told her their secrets and she certainly didn't tell anyone hers. That is, until Kirsty moved in next door. "I'll *try* the skirt," Catherine offered. "But that's all."

The minute she had it on, along with her chiffon shirt, Kirsty called the girls into her bedroom. Having got themselves ready by digging out all the glittery contraband that Nanna Pam smuggled into their lives, and covering more or less every inch of themselves in netting, shiny nylon satin, and glittery bits of lace, the minute they saw Catherine in a simple skirt they oohed and aahhed as if it was she who was dressed up like a psychotic ballerina.

Kirsty, Catherine realized, had pulled a tactical stroke of genius on her. If she took the skirt off now, her girls would be disappointed, and Catherine could not stand disappointing her girls when it was in her power not to.

"I'm wearing it with opaque tights, then," she said, and Kirsty, clearly feeling she had won the war if not the battle, cheered.

"Well, you'll have to, as you lied about shaving your forests . . . I mean legs," Kirsty added.

"And flat shoes," Catherine added, looking at Eloise's clear plastic play heels. That was one secret Nanna Pam item she had not discovered. She'd have to start looking harder.

"Well of *course* flat shoes, we don't want you to tower over all the men, do we?" Kirsty replied glibly. "Actually, put on your long boots, they are like cleavage for the knees, you know—plus it makes you look a bit kinky."

"I'll put them on if you stop saying inappropriate words in front of my children that might get repeated in class," Catherine warned her.

Kirsty nodded in satisfaction at the final effect.

"You are a fox," she said. "You must be the last woman on the planet who doesn't realize what a fox she is."

"Mummy isn't a fox," Leila said, looking perplexed. "She's a human bean, aren't you, Mummy?"

"Well, my darling," Kirsty said, putting an arm around the five-year-old and hugging her. "There is a rumor going round to that effect."

Catherine was brushing out the backcombing that Kirsty had tried out on her hair when the doorbell sounded.

"I'll get it," Kirsty said. "It'll be Jimmy."

"Dad's here, Mum!" Leila said, scrambling into her bedroom and grabbing her by the wrist, dragging her out before she could twist her mass of hair into its customary ponytail. "Come and show him your legs!"

"Leila, I . . ." Catherine felt herself freeze on the stairs. For some bizarre reason, although she had come to terms with half of Farmington seeing her legs from the knees down, the thought of her almost-ex-husband seeing them made her panic.

"Come on, Mummy," Leila said, tugging her down the last few steps. "Look, Daddy—Mummy's got legs!" Leila exclaimed.

Jimmy's charmed chuckle at his daughter's comment faded when he caught sight of Catherine, her head bowed, her hair obscuring half her face. But even though Jimmy knew how much she hated to be looked at, he seemed to spend an inordinately long time, at least five seconds longer than was acceptable, for an almost ex-husband looking at her thin, long legs.

Catherine felt her cheeks grow hot and herself grow cross. This was all Kirsty's fault. She didn't need to know that Jimmy found her effort at dressing up ridiculous. Her life was so much easier when she was in neutral, when he didn't notice her or what she was looking like at all.

"You look . . ." Jimmy struggled to find a compliment.

"What?" Catherine asked him, wincing.

"You scrub up all right, don't you?" Jimmy said with a shrug. "You've pushed the boat out, good for you."

"Oh, how erudite! And they say the art of the compliment is lost," Kirsty observed.

"I'm sorry." Jimmy shrugged. "I mean you look really nice. Or whatever."

"Are you really thirty-three or are you just an extremely old-looking fourteen-year-old?" Kirsty asked Jimmy, hooking her arm through his and leading him out the front door before Catherine had to suffer any more embarrassment under his ham-fisted compliments.

"Right." Catherine looked at her two children, dressed in nylon satin and fake silk and with glitter in their hair.

"I have never seen two such beautiful girls in my life," she told them, her heart glued to every word. "So come on, then, let's go to this party and see what the rest of Gemma's family is like."

"They'll be perfect," Eloise told her, taking the hand Catherine proffered. "They are bound to be perfect, because Gemma is."

Eleven

Bloody hell," Jimmy said as the five of them walked through the wrought-iron electric gate that swung open on their approach.

"Magic gate!" Leila said with a little hop as they walked down the drive that led to the floodlit house.

"Electric gate," Eloise told her, suddenly seeming a little more subdued.

"Nice place," Jimmy said, nodding toward the double-fronted faux Georgian palace.

"Big place," Eloise said quietly. "Much bigger than our house."

"I'd say they paid at least one point two mil," Kirsty added, turning to Catherine. "What do you think?"

"I think that all of those fairy lights are a wanton waste of energy," Catherine said. "Just because you have money to burn doesn't mean that you should."

"And I think I hope there's plenty of booze," Jimmy said, whisking Leila up onto his shoulders and out of the way of a Mercedes SLK as it swept by, leaving a ricochet of gravel in its wake. "I'm going to need it."

The house was already filled with people. Everywhere Catherine looked she saw someone she knew at least by sight. Half the PTA were instantly visible, as well as three or four teachers from the school, including Mrs. Woodruff, and the optician from Boots. It must have been *the* optician, because as soon as he saw Kirsty his eyes lit up and as soon as she saw him she vanished. The massive hallway alone accommodated what had to be fifty or sixty people talking, sipping champagne, and taking sandwiches from a passing teenager with a tray. Catherine looked for someone new who might be one of Gemma's parents, but so far she already knew everyone she saw.

"What do we do now?" Jimmy asked Catherine as the pair of them stood there side by side, one daughter hanging off each of them as they maneuvered their little party toward the relative safety of a sheltering wall.

"We get a drink, I suppose, and mingle," Catherine answered, as if she were suggesting they smear themselves in ketchup and jump into a den full of starving lions. "Make small talk and all that stuff."

"Right," Jimmy said. "Or we could just take the girls to the all-you-can-eat buffet at the place in town, and get drunk on the house white, and forget about it, what do you reckon?"

Catherine looked at Jimmy and felt a sudden rush of warmth toward him. At that exact moment in her life she could think of nothing that she would like to do more than run away with Jimmy and the girls and, yes, maybe even get a little bit tipsy with him over onion relish dip. But before she could accept, Catherine found herself engulfed in squeals and yelps as her daughters were embraced by a blond girl who surely must have been the mythical Gemma.

"Mum, this is her, this is Gemma," Eloise said, tugging dangerously hard on Catherine's chiffon sleeve. "This is my best friend!"

Catherine looked down at the pretty little blond girl standing next to her daughter and suddenly got a vivid flashback. She and Alison standing side by side at Siobhan Murphy's tenth birthday party, admiring the pink Miss Piggy cake. Edward Stone had come up to Catherine and told her that he didn't want to be her boyfriend anymore because she was too ugly. Alison had punched Edward Stone quite hard in the stomach, making him double over in pain and throw up frosted cupcakes on the carpet.

Catherine blinked and suddenly, the moment had passed and she was looking at her own little girl again, standing next to Gemma. For a moment Catherine got the feeling that she wasn't looking back at the past but touching the future. Gemma looked exactly like Alison. Exactly like her but she couldn't be hers . . . because it would just be too . . . Alison wouldn't come *here* after . . .

She stared at the plump little girl with her big blue eyes and smiled at her.

"Hello, Gemma, nice to meet you," she said, hoping she was the only one who noticed the tremble in her voice. "Eloise has talked about you a lot."

"Hello, Mrs. Ashley. Nice to meet you too." Gemma smiled prettily at her. "Eloise has been so kind to me since I started at the school. I feel like I fit right in now."

"That's great, Gemma. By the way, where's your mummy? I'd like to meet her." Catherine glanced quickly around the room, her heart in her throat, afraid of whom she might see, constantly telling herself that there must be a hundred blond little girls in this town who bore a passing resemblance to Alison. This was purely a coincidence. That's what Catherine told herself, yet at exactly the same time she knew with complete certainty what the truth was. Alison was back.

"I think Mummy's in the kitchen being cross about the sandwiches," Gemma told her before saying to Eloise, "and Amy's in the tent being Beauty from *Beauty and the Beast*, dancing to the disco. Want to dance?"

"Yes, yes, yes!" Eloise said. "Can we, Mum? Please?"

Catherine paused. "Okay, then," Catherine agreed reluctantly, because she would rather have kept them close to her just in case she needed to make a quick exit. "But don't go out of the house, okay? Don't talk to anyone you don't know . . . or some people you do know, and when I say it's time to go it's . . ." But the three girls had disappeared.

"There goes the dinner-in-town idea," Jimmy said regretfully. "We definitely can't go without them . . . can we?"

"Jimmy, what's the name of the people whose party this is?" Catherine asked him urgently.

Jimmy looked perplexed. "I don't know, Cat, I never exactly saw the invitation. I met the woman, the mother in the playground. Do you remember? She said her name was . . ." Jimmy trailed off, unaware that Catherine was hanging on every nuance of his silence.

"It's gone," he said, shaking his head and shrugging.

"What did she look like, the mother?" Catherine pressed him.

"What's up, Cat?" Jimmy asked. "I didn't crack on to her if that's what you're worried about, even if she did fancy the arse off me."

Catherine's stomach dropped ten stories.

"Just tell me, what did she look like?"

"Blond, money all over her, you know, the usual. Great teeth, nice smile. Said we used to know each other but I couldn't think how I'd know a chick like that . . ."

"Oh my God," Catherine said, looking around her with wide-eyed horror. "Oh. My. God."

"What?" Jimmy exclaimed.

"It's Alison."

"You're right!" Jimmy clicked his fingers. "Alison, that was her name. How did you . . . ? Oh Christ. It's *that* Alison. The actual Alison."

The two of them stared at each other. Catherine nodded, unable to move.

"How do we feel about that?" he asked her, putting his hand on her arm to steady her.

"I don't know," Catherine told him. "I don't—it shouldn't matter after all these years, should it? So what if she's come back and my daughter is her daughter's new best friend? It's all in the past, water under the bridge, it doesn't matter anymore, right? Right?"

Jimmy didn't say anything for a moment, as he watched Catherine's wide-eyed face drain of any semblance of color.

"We're upset about it, then," he confirmed.

"I don't know how else to feel," Catherine admitted. "I feel sick, Jimmy, why did she have to come back here, that's what I don't get. Why now?"

"Look." Jimmy felt now was his time to be decisive and take control. "I'll get the girls and we'll go, okay? You don't need to deal with this now. You need to go home and think about it. Let it sink in."

"She can't have known I was still here. If she'd known she wouldn't have come back," Catherine said, her voice low and dark. "She wouldn't want to see me."

"Maybe, maybe not—but the point is you don't need to see her

tonight. Wait here. I'll get the girls. We'll go home and talk this
through. Okay?"

Catherine gripped his hand hard in hers.

"Okay," she said. "And thank you. Thank you for not thinking
I'm stupid and irrational and delusional."

"You forget, Cat," Jimmy said, placing the palm of his hand
briefly on her blazing cheek. "I know."

Catherine waited, standing in the hot, crowded room, with all
the good people of Farmington chatting and laughing around her,
and she was glad for once that she had developed the talent of fading into the background.

Even so, her heart was racing, her skin was pulsating with the
blood that was careering around her body. She felt light-headed
and hot, as if she had a fever, as if she'd suddenly been struck down
by the flu.

"It's just a girl you once knew, a girl you fell out with over a
boy," she told herself, braced against any eventuality. "It doesn't
matter. Why should it matter now?" An answering thought slowly
descended, slotting into place with exacting care. Alison hadn't
come back to Farmington alone. She'd come back with two girls
and a teenage son and her husband.

Her husband.

The day after Alison had left Farmington it was as if she had disappeared into a parallel universe. Catherine's parents had banned
any discussion of her, the boy she had run off with, and what
might become of them. Catherine gleaned snippets of rumors,
whispered in hushed tones, but since she had had to leave school
before taking her exams, she had been unable to find out what had
really happened with Alison and Marc. After her mother had discovered the full extent of her involvement with Marc, she decided
that the freedom of school was too dangerous for her daughter and

that was the end of Catherine's education, the end of her hopes of going to university and her dreams of freedom. Catherine could have fought them, she could have left them, but at that point in her life she didn't have the energy. At the age of seventeen she turned her face to the wall and gave up all hope of a normal life.

It took almost a year of working with her mother in the bookshop for her parents to feel that they could trust her again, and it took exactly the same amount of time for Catherine to rebuild her own life in secret. She'd met girls she had used to know from school in the library or the supermarket, and at first all they'd want to know was everything that had happened to her and to Alison, because it seemed as if both Alison and her family had vanished into thin air. But then to Catherine's surprise, when they discovered that she knew less than they did about Alison's fate, they invited her to hang out with them anyway. For the first time in her life Catherine was part of a circle of friends that didn't depend on Alison, and she discovered that if she let them, people liked her. She never once missed the irony that it was only after Alison had gone that she found the courage to climb in and out of her own bedroom window when her parents were both asleep, sneaking off to have a drink in the pub with her newfound friends.

Maybe it was possible that Alison had married Marc, and if she had . . .

Once again Catherine's eyes swept the room, but this time she was looking for something different, and the sight that stopped her heart was the back of a man's head, dark hair cut short into the nape of his neck. That in itself was unremarkable, but the shape of the head and the angle at which it was set on those shoulders was. She was looking at her living, breathing past.

And then, as if he sensed the touch of her gaze on his skin, slowly and uncertainly the man turned around and looked right at her, and recognized her.

In that one second it seemed as if time were standing still and Catherine found it so hard to breathe that for a second she wondered if that thin layer of atmosphere that came between her and the magnitude of space had evaporated, collapsing her lungs and halting the pounding of blood in her ears.

It was Marc. She hadn't seen him for fifteen years and then suddenly there he was. He was smiling at her. He looked happy to see her.

It was Lois's scything voice that brought her back to her senses, shocking her into living again.

"And you must meet our Catherine," Lois said, bringing Marc over to where Catherine was standing, dumbstruck. "She is an absolute treasure, I simply do not know what we would do without her." She looked from Catherine to Marc, and when neither one spoke she filled in the void. "I was telling Marc about the PTA, Catherine?" Silence. "Catherine, are you quite well?"

Catherine tore her eyes away from Marc's face and looked at Lois as if she were the one who was the complete stranger.

"Lois, I'm afraid that Catherine is in shock because of me," Marc said with an easy smile. Catherine was surprised to hear that his voice was different. It was refined now. He had lost his Midlands accent and picked up some *h*'s and *t*'s along the way. "She and I know each other, you see, although we haven't seen each other for a long time. She has probably been struck dumb by how old and fat I've become, and she's got every right to be. She doesn't look a day older than the last time I saw her, only more beautiful."

"Oh? Well, how unusual," Lois said, clearly deflated by Marc's turning his attention from her. "I'll leave you to catch up, then. You can tell me everything later, Catherine."

"I knew it," Marc said a second or two after Lois had left them alone. "I knew I'd find you here."

"At your party?" Catherine asked him banally.

"In Farmington," Marc replied. "I think you're the reason I came back. You might even be the reason for this party. I've been looking for you and I didn't know it until I saw you."

"What?" Catherine asked him. "What are you talking about?"

"Just recently you've been on my mind a lot." Marc took a step closer to her, causing Catherine's heels to graze against the wall's skirting board. He smiled. "I thought about the way I . . . we . . . left and how it must have hurt you back then. Maybe it doesn't matter anymore but I want you to know I didn't plan anything to happen the way it did. I didn't plan period. I didn't plan to get involved with you or Alison, and I didn't know I was leaving with her until the minute she told me I was. I let things happen to me back then, Cathy, and I didn't care about the consequences. But that doesn't mean I don't regret them now." Marc shook his head and laughed. "You know, I didn't expect to have this conversation tonight either, but I'm glad that I am having it. I'm glad I've got the chance to say that I'm sorry. I'm sorry for hurting you, Cathy."

Catherine looked into his dark eyes, at him standing there in the flesh right in front of her, and felt the ground shift a little beneath her feet. A few minutes ago he was a part of her history, a time past that could never be recaptured. Now it seemed as if he had never been gone.

He had no idea, she told herself steadily.

"We are not having this conversation tonight," she told him, making herself smile, shrugging so that her loose hair fell over one shoulder. "When my husband gets back with my daughters we are leaving."

Marc let go of her arm, leaving a residue of heat from a summer fifteen years ago.

"You don't have to go," he said. "It must be a shock, I know, but please don't go. Stay and wait for the shock to wear off. Alison will be here somewhere. I know she'd be so pleased to see you. Catherine, please."

Before Catherine knew it he was embracing her, hugging her thin frame against his. It wasn't the hard, toned body that she had once known that she felt graze against her ribs now, but it was still his body, and at his touch a tiny spark of memory ignited in her belly and made her muscles contract.

She was relieved when he released her, and she glanced over his shoulder looking for Jimmy and the girls. They were nowhere to be seen.

Alison decided that she had spent long enough in the kitchen waiting for her husband to come and tell her what to do about the fact that they had run out of food about half an hour ago. Why she was waiting for him she didn't know, there was nothing they could do about it now anyway. It was just if he was here, if he had come like she had asked him, then she would be able to show him the empty platters that were scattered across the kitchen and say "I told you so." And that would make her feel better. At least they had plenty of champagne. Champagne that Alison had not had nearly enough of. Something she was keen to remedy.

"Right, well," she said to the waitstaff who were hovering about. "Just make sure everyone gets drinks, okay?"

"Can't we have a drink?" one boy asked. "This is a cool party."

Alison looked at him and crossed her arms. If she spent one more minute in her expensive dress in this expensive kitchen with incompetent teenagers, as stone-cold sober as the Italian granite work surfaces, then she would literally implode.

"Just one," she told the boy, "but if I catch any of you getting drunk, there will be trouble, okay?" She watched in relief as the teenagers filed sedately out of the kitchen, trays laden with champagne.

Alison peered into the hallway where many guests were still congregating and searched the crowd for her husband, who was, no doubt, working the room somewhere in the house. She stood on her tiptoes and craned her neck but she couldn't see him out there, and if he wasn't out there then she didn't want to brave the crowd without him, at least not until she'd had at least two more glasses of champagne. Retreating back into the safety of the kitchen, she reapplied her lip gloss and then, taking a bottle out of the fridge, poured herself first one glass and then another. She could feel the bubbles in the wine popping behind her eyes and she decided to go see if Jimmy Ashley had turned up at her party.

She found him in the tent that had been set up in their backyard, trying to persuade his daughters to come off of the dance floor. He wasn't having much luck. The disco lights turned the melee of children green, red, and blue, making them look like multicolored fairies flitting across the floor, but there was something familiar about the tall girl, the one who had to be Gemma's much-loved Ellie. She must take after her father, Alison thought, smiling warmly at Jimmy as he tried to catch his smallest girl and failed.

Tipping the bottle of champagne she had brought with her into her glass and immediately emptying it, Alison thought she might as well be at the sixth-form dance again, trying to pluck up the courage to get Jimmy Ashley to dance with her because that was exactly what she was doing now. Finishing the glass off in one long draft, Alison waited as the room tilted and swayed for a moment before setting itself right, and Alison heard a little sane voice inside her head telling her that this was not the right way to make a good impression as wife and mother and hostess of the party. But unfortunately for the sane little voice, Alison couldn't care less. And besides, it was largely because her husband hadn't introduced her to anyone that she felt fairly safe that most people here wouldn't even know that she was the hostess.

Jimmy hadn't noticed her coming until she was standing right next to him.

"Hi, Jimmy!" she said quite loudly, right in his ear, making him jump. "Come with me and have another drink."

"Alison," Jimmy said, stepping aside so that his daughters could race away from him unhindered.

"Oh, you remembered me!" Alison was thrilled. "Yay! Jimmy remembered me at last!"

"Alison from school," Jimmy said. "That's how I knew you. You hung about at band practice a lot. You were Catherine Parkin's best friend."

"Yes," Alison said, a little more hesitantly this time. "Yes, that was me. I used to know Cathy."

"She got married, Cathy Parkin," Jimmy said. "Her name's Catherine Ashley now."

"Oh," Alison said, her eyes widening, and then, "Oh shit."

"We need to talk," Jimmy told her.

A few minutes later as his eyes adjusted to the light, Jimmy saw Alison perched on what looked like an upturned box with a bottle of champagne in her hand, her bare legs crossed, showing a little upper thigh. She had led him outside to a sort of copse situated in a dip just behind the tent.

As Alison had led him into the darkness, Jimmy had gotten the distinct feeling that he shouldn't be following any woman, never mind this one, into the woods, and that he should really be taking the girls back to Catherine and getting her out of there like he'd promised. He told himself that by talking to Alison he was trying to make things easier for Catherine. Alison had no idea about what had happened to Catherine after she ran way. Catherine had never had the chance to tell her, and now the only people in the world who knew were Catherine's parents, Catherine, and him.

Jimmy was afraid there was a good chance Alison would treat the whole thing as if it were a joke, something they could look back on and laugh over, but Jimmy knew that wasn't the case. He felt he had to warn her. Not for her sake, but for Catherine's.

"Well, talk then," Alison said, retrieving another bottle from one of the boxes next to where she was sitting. She twisted the cork off a bottle, unbalancing herself a little, and realizing she no longer had a glass, she took a swig out of the bottle. "Jimmy Ashley who married Cathy Parkin. That's poetic justice for you, isn't it?" She tipped her head back and laughed like a little girl, which made Jimmy smile despite himself.

She took a long draft from the bottle and then, wiping the back of her hand across her mouth, handed it to Jimmy. "I'm a bit drunk actually. Which is good because when Cathy sees me she's going to kill me."

"Catherine's not like that," Jimmy told her as he took the bottle and a swig. "But you should know it's going to be hard for her. When you went you left her in a real mess. A real mess."

"I know it must have hurt her losing him, Jimmy, but she got over it. Otherwise she wouldn't have married you. You know, I bet she married you to get back at me."

"What?" Jimmy asked her.

"I fancied you at school for years, Jimmy—did you really not notice? God, that is so depressing. I still do fancy you, actually. You're a very sexy man, bringing me out here to talk about your lady wife." Jimmy took a couple of steps back and glanced back at the lights of the house twinkling in the distance. Suddenly he felt very out of his depth.

"But Jimmy," Alison went on. "He might have loved her but

he never would have been any good for her, not in a million years. Trust me, I *know*." Alison's laugh was entirely mirthless. "Funny, really, I got her life and she got mine, all of this is your fault. If you had noticed me throwing myself at you back then, then I would have let her mess herself up with Marc and I would have had you. And we'd be happy."

"I'm sorry," Jimmy said for want of anything else to say. "But the truth is I didn't actually discover women until I was in my twenties. I was too much into my music to get serious with anyone. I never had girlfriends at school, never had anything serious until I met Catherine. I didn't even know I'd gone to school with her for ten years. That's how blind I was. And if I didn't even notice the stunning tall girl with the bright red hair, how would I have noticed you?"

"Mmmmph," Alison said, pouting. "I'll try not to take offense."

"Look," Jimmy said, trying to get back to why he was here in the woods with her. "The fact is that you're here now." He looked up at the house with a million twinkling lights. "And it looks as if you're here to stay—but you're going to have to be . . . sensitive with her, Alison. Allow for what she went through, give her time to adjust. She's never had anyone to talk to about it all, except for me. She still cries about it sometimes. That's how much the whole thing hurt her. It damaged her."

"She still cries about Marc and me running off together?" Alison's laugh was harsh. "Seriously? As her husband, doesn't that piss you off?"

Jimmy looked at her. "She still cries about the abortion. The abortion her parents made her have when she found out that Marc had got her pregnant."

There was a long silence punctuated by a hiccup as Alison stared at Jimmy, the defiant smile on her face faltering and then finally fading.

"You've got that wrong," Alison insisted. "What are you talking about, Jimmy? There *was* no abortion, *she* wasn't the one who he got pregnant," Alison insisted. "I was the one who got pregnant. I know because he never had sex with her, he told me that at the time. He never felt that way about her, they didn't have the passion we had."

Alison swayed a little on her perch as she took another drink.

"Where did you get the story of an abortion from, anyway?" she asked Jimmy defensively. "I had him, I had Marc's baby—my son's in there now, probably secretly drinking and skulking around the waitresses."

Jimmy sighed. How had it fallen on him to break this news to Catherine's archenemy?

"Look, Alison, I don't know what Marc told you back then, I expect he told you a lot of things that weren't true. Men usually lie when they're sleeping with two women at the same time. What I do know for certain is that Catherine was pregnant when you left." Jimmy's hot breath made his words visible, a mist in the chill of the air. "She was pregnant with Marc's baby too, only she didn't get to keep hers. Her parents saw to that."

Jimmy watched as Alison's glassy eyes brightened and filled with tears that glittered in the reflected glory of the decorated house.

"She was having his baby?" Alison asked, her voice a whisper. "She was having his baby too?"

"Yes, she was going to tell him—she wanted to tell you but in the end she decided she couldn't . . ."

"No, you see, that's not right." Alison was determined. "Because it was *me* he wanted, *me* he needed. He played around with her, strung her along, but he didn't do *that* with her. He told me. He told me that *I* was the one he couldn't keep his hands off of. That was what made us special. Jimmy, I'm sorry, but Cathy's made the whole thing up, I don't know why—maybe to get you to feel sorry for her, but anyway, it's a lie."

Jimmy's face darkened as he took a step or two nearer to Alison. "Catherine doesn't lie. Does Marc?"

"No!" Alison stood up abruptly. "He doesn't lie, he doesn't . . . and anyway, don't you see, Jimmy? I can't not have known about that, I *would* have known. We knew everything about each other, Cathy and me."

"Not everything," Jimmy said. "Not this. I'm sorry, Alison, but it happened. Marc got Catherine pregnant, she had an abortion."

Without warning, Alison flung her arms around Jimmy, buried her face in his neck, and wept. At a loss as to how to react, Jimmy stiffly held out his arms at a steady ninety-degree angle as her shoulders shook and he felt her hot breath against his neck.

"This is too much," she said into his neck. "This is one lie too many, and it's not fair because it's the first lie, and if I'd known about the first lie, then maybe I wouldn't have stuck around for the second or the third or the hundredth or the millionth lie." Alison paused and looked up at Jimmy, her face very close to his, and Jimmy couldn't help but notice that despite the drinking and the tears she still looked beautiful. "It must have been hard for Cathy."

"I think that is a bit of an understatement," Jimmy said swiftly, untangling himself from her embrace and stepping away from her. "Like I said before, it damaged her and that's why I'm asking you to back off and take it easy."

"I'm going to kill him!" Alison said, having to steady herself without Jimmy to lean on. "He fucked us both up and now I'm going to kill him."

"Look," Jimmy said, suddenly feeling uneasy. "I suppose it's an obvious question. But Marc? He is here somewhere, isn't he? Sooner or later he'll find Catherine. She's kind of hard to miss."

Alison's head snapped up and before Jimmy realized what was happening she was running past him back toward the house.

"Are you okay?" Marc asked Catherine.

"I'm fine, really. Go and talk to your guests, please. I'm waiting for my husband," Catherine said, but Marc stood stock-still.

"I don't want to leave you like this," he said.

Catherine bit her lip, repressing the obvious retort. She shook her head and conjured an approximation of a smile. "Go, I'll be fine."

Catherine watched him watching her, his dark eyes intense. He'd looked at her in exactly that way on the day they had first met, when he'd kissed her. For one heady petrifying second Catherine got the feeling he might do exactly the same thing now. He took a step closer to her and his hand grazed her shoulder, striking sparks as it passed.

"Liar!" Suddenly Alison was in between them, causing Catherine to stagger backward and into Jimmy, who was following at her heels.

"What?" she asked him.

"Thing is . . ." Jimmy began, but it was then that Alison slapped her husband hard across the face. The whole room stopped and looked.

"Ouch, darling." Marc smiled at his wife. "The caterers weren't that bad."

"Liar!" Alison repeated, and was about to slap him again but this time he caught her wrist.

"Let's take this outside, shall we," he said in a low voice as he gripped her wrist. "Remember our guests?"

"You told me you never had sex with her," Alison accused him. "You were sleeping with both of us the whole time."

"Look, Alison." Marc pulled her closer to him, trying desperately to keep the conversation between themselves. "Please, we'll talk about this later."

"You've lied to me for fifteen years," Alison said, her voice hard and cold. "After everything we've been through and all the promises you made, you've kept on lying. You're still lying now. I used to think it would end one day, but it won't ever end, will it, Marc? It comes as naturally to you as breathing."

She jerked her wrist out of his grasp and looked around at the crowd of guests.

"Ladies and gentlemen, this party is now over due to the unforeseen circumstance of my husband being a disgusting, lying pig. Please collect your coats and make an orderly exit."

Spinning on her heel, she came face-to-face with Catherine.

The two women stared at each other, both aware that not one guest had yet made an attempt to leave.

"Cathy," Alison said quietly, carefully avoiding looking at her husband because she was afraid of how he would react to what she was about to say. "I didn't know. I didn't know about the baby."

"Would it have changed anything?" Catherine asked, and Alison knew she was avoiding looking at Marc too. "If you'd known?"

"It might have," Alison said. "It would have changed something."

Catherine felt the scrutiny of all of those around her and knew that she had to be out of there within the next five seconds.

"I have to go," Catherine said. She looked at Jimmy. "We'll go and find the girls and then leave, okay?"

He nodded.

"Thank you for coming," Alison said to her foolishly. "Will you believe me if I say that it's really good to see you again?"

Catherine nodded, tears standing in her eyes.

"Perhaps I'll see you in the school playground. Perhaps we can talk, sort things out, put things . . . to rest."

Catherine paused, looking at Alison. "Why did you come back?"

"To rescue my family," Alison said. "I don't think it's working out quite as we planned."

Catherine nodded and then, without saying another word, she turned on her heel, slotting her hand into Jimmy's, and walked out of the room as the crowd parted before her.

The cool air soothed her skin as they began their walk back home, Leila asleep on her shoulder and Eloise in Jimmy's arms.

"You handled that amazingly well," Jimmy told her. "I was so proud of you, Cat. You were so serene, and dignified. Even with him, the bastard. You were brilliant."

"I can't believe you told her," Catherine replied. "I can't believe it."

They were silent for the rest of the walk home.

Twelve

Alison lay on her bed, staring at the ceiling. The room lights were out but the thousand or so fairy lights outside of her bedroom window illuminated the room in pulsating glittering bursts of radiance. Rosie lay next to her, a small bundle of warmth, nestling companionably into her side, breaking in one fell swoop Alison's vow that the animal was never to be allowed on beds or the sofa. Alison couldn't bring herself to move the dog; the regular rise and fall of her rib cage was comforting.

Much to her deep irritation the party had not ended when she'd declared that it was over, far from it. That had been a good hour ago and the chatter of Marc's guests still rose in the hallway as if nothing had happened. After Cathy had made her exit, splitting the party crowd like Moses parting the Red Sea, with Jimmy Ashley loyally following in her wake, the room had fallen silent save for the background thrum of the disco in the tent.

Glancing around, Marc had laughed and then he'd put his arm around her and kissed her hard on the cheek.

"May I introduce you all to my wonderful, fiery, impetuous, and amazing wife—Alison James, a woman who certainly knows how to make an entrance."

And somehow Alison had found herself standing at Marc's side, her arm linked through his, smiling graciously while she received a round of applause from the good people of Farmington. Only Marc could have done this, only Marc could have the audacity and magic to turn a martial brawl into a social nicety, into something that was even romantic, while she was still reeling from the news that Jimmy had given her and could have quite happily slapped Marc again.

However, with everyone's eyes on her and the buzz of the champagne having eroded into a head-churning fuzz, not to mention the sight of her two daughters, who had come to find her, Alison realized she didn't have any choice but to go along with the illusion that Marc had created.

She put her arms around his neck and kissed him on the lips.

"Anyone for more champagne?" Marc asked the crowd in general the second the kiss was broken, leaving Alison's side to go and arrange it before anyone could answer.

"I'm tired, Mama," Amy said, putting her arms around Alison's waist and resting her chin on her tummy. "When are all these people going home?"

"Ellie's mummy came and made her and Leila go home. She looked really cross," Gemma said. "I'm not tired, by the way. Can I stay up some more? You could come and dance with us, Mummy. And Daddy and Dominic, we could all dance together."

"I don't think so," Alison said, crouching down so that Amy could hook her arms around Alison's neck, and then hefting her onto her hip. "I think you two girls have had a good run and now it's time for bed, okay?"

" 'Kay," Amy said, resting her head on Alison's shoulder, her thumb in her mouth.

" 'Spose," Gemma sighed. "Although I could dance for at least another hour without getting tired."

And leading her two girls to bed, Alison was finally able to make her escape. With both of them falling asleep as soon as their heads touched the pillow, she briefly peered over the banister to the throng of people below. Marc was the center of attention, talking, throwing his head back with laughter, gesturing like a hypnotist who had the whole room in his thrall. He was rescuing the situation, turning it around, re-creating the facade of their lives from scratch yet again, doing all the things he was so good at, except he hadn't seemed to notice that she was up here on her own and he was down there running all of their lives single-handedly, as if he hadn't lied to her for fifteen years. As if he hadn't been sleeping with them both.

Alison closed her eyes, but the lights still twinkled cheerfully behind her lids, so she pulled the duvet over her head in a bid to blot them out, breathing in the scent of her relationship, her life, that was embedded in the sheets.

Of course he had been sleeping with them both, of course he had. If she'd had any kind of knowledge or experience of men back then other than trying to fend off the wandering hands of the boys from school, she would have realized it was inevitable. She and Cathy were still girls, almost women, but only physically. They were still making the choices and decisions that girls made when it felt as if there would be no consequences and no tomorrow.

And Marc had been a man, a young man, but he'd had to grow up fast, thrown out of the children's home at the age of sixteen and left to fend for himself in a world of brutal and unsympathetic adults. At the age of seventeen Alison had believed that she had sexual power over him. She had the breasts and the legs and the heat that he really wanted. But she was wrong. Cathy had it too, it was just that with Cathy it was much less obvious.

"Have you ever done this with her?" she'd asked him.

"I've never done anything like *that* with her," he'd replied. He hadn't lied, he couldn't have been more blunt. Alison had chosen to believe what she'd wanted to believe.

Alison pressed the heels of her hands against her pounding forehead. Cathy had been pregnant. She had been pregnant with Marc's baby, a baby that would have been conceived only a week or two apart from Dominic, maybe even on the same day as her son. It was possible. Looking back, Alison realized Jimmy was right. Cathy had tried to tell her, after it all came out. After she'd found out that Alison had been sleeping with Marc and everything started to disintegrate around her. Alison remembered she'd felt like she was standing in the eye of a storm, perfectly calm, absolutely determined, while the rest of the world was whipped into chaos around her.

It had been raining; thick rivulets of raindrops blended with her friend's tears as she stood on Alison's doorstep and pleaded with her.

"Please don't do this, Alison," she begged her. "You don't love him, not really. You only want him because I've got him. Please! You don't understand what you're doing to me!"

"It's no good," her seventeen-year-old self replied cruelly. "He loves *me*, Cathy, he wants *me*—not you. You have to realize that. And besides, I need him now. I *really* need him."

"But what about us?" Catherine said, weeping. "You and me? Who will I have if I don't have you? If I lose him I lose you too. I don't know what I'll do, Alison. You don't know what you're doing to me. I need you, I'm . . ."

"Look, I'm pregnant," Alison hissed, taking a few steps forward into the rain and drawing the front door closed behind her so that her parents would not hear. "Nobody knows yet, not even him, but I'm having his *baby,* Cathy. And I *love* him. I love him and he loves me and that's the way we've felt about each other since the minute we met. Tonight I'm going to ask him to leave Farmington with me and he will, I'll make him come with me because I know that he wants me more than anything else in the world. You were never important to him, you have to see that, Cathy—I mean look at you. Can you really picture the two of you together? Now I have to put myself and my baby first and if you can't understand that, then . . ." Alison shrugged.

Catherine didn't say a word. She just stood there in the pouring rain, as if her whole body were melting, her mouth open, speechless as she tried to understand what Alison was telling her. Alison stepped back under the shelter of her porch and waited.

"But you're my best friend," Catherine began. "The only person in the world I could talk to and trust . . ."

"Not anymore," Alison said. "I'm sorry, Catherine. You'll just have to get used to it. Marc belongs to me now."

Alison tried her hardest to get back into the head of the girl she'd been then, and she asked herself what she would have done differently if she had known that her friend was pregnant too. And she couldn't say that she wouldn't still have left Cathy behind. Back then she didn't know any better, she didn't want to know anything except that she was meant to be with Marc and that he belonged to her.

Another uneasy thought was nagging at her as she lay in bed, and that was the memory of her husband standing behind her downstairs at the party when she had told Cathy she didn't know about the baby. It should have been news to Marc too, but he hadn't reacted at all. Not a gasp, not a movement. He was perfectly still. Did that mean that he knew about the baby when he ran away with Alison? It could have been that, or it could just have been Marc maintaining appearances no matter what sledgehammer came swinging out of the past to floor him. It was impossible to know, and Alison decided wearily she didn't want to know. Not yet, at least. She was growing weary of discovering secrets.

There was a knock at the door, rousing Rosie briefly from her slumber before exhaustion overtook her once more and she settled back into sleep. Alison composed herself for Marc, and then she realized he wouldn't knock.

"It's me," Dominic called. He opened the door a crack, the blaze of the hall light momentarily blinding Alison as she peered over the covers. "Are you okay?"

"I'm fine," Alison told him, mustering a smile for him. "I've just got a headache. What's the time?"

Dominic shrugged. Alison glanced at the clock; it was almost midnight.

"What was that all about, Mum?" Dominic asked her. "You shouting at him, and slapping him. You looked really angry. It was wild, well, cool."

Alison frowned; she didn't know how to feel about impressing her son with an act of violence.

"You should have arrived fifteen seconds earlier, he was all over that woman, the tall, scary-looking one. Is she why you slapped him? Has he gone and done it again already?"

Alison, who had been rubbing her eyes, froze for a second. She hated that Dominic knew about Marc. She hated the fact that her son's expectations of his father, of both of his parents, were now so low.

She sat up and turned on the bedside lamp.

"Don't be silly, Dom. Dad hasn't done anything," she told her son as he sat on the edge of the bed, reaching out absently to stroke

Rosie. She reached out and touched his soft, as yet unshaven cheek with the back of her hand. "You know Dad, he's a charmer and a flirt, all touchy-feely. But it doesn't mean anything."

"I call fucking some tart a bit more than being touchy-feely, Mum," Dominic said, his words brutal even if his tone was not. "Look, I'm not a kid anymore. I see things, I hear things. We both know that everyone was talking about him before we left London. And you—they talked about you too. About what kind of woman you must be to put up with him. I know you like to tell everyone including yourself that we moved because I'm such a dead loss and on the verge of becoming a hardened criminal. I don't even care if that's what people think. But we both know that's not the real reason. We left London because you finally found out Dad was fucking that tart at the showroom. But not because of the actual fucking, because you've put up with that in the past and it didn't seem to bother you. No, this time we had to leave because you realized that everybody, all your friends, all his slimy mates knew about it for months and you didn't." Dominic shrugged. "Dad did what he always does and promised that it would never happen again and you did what you always do and believed him. Only this time you couldn't stand living on the same street, going to the same gym and the same school, where everybody knew what he'd done to you, and what a fool you were. So you made us move back here and blamed it on me."

"Dominic," Alison said, still reeling from her son's so nearly accurate portrayal of her life. "You can always talk to me, but please don't use that language. Your father wanted to come here."

"Why?" Dominic asked.

"Because . . ." Alison remembered Marc's reasons, but none of them seemed very plausible anymore. "He said it's a nice place. It's the place where we started and the place where he still has something to prove. And as much as you'd like to deny it, moving here has got plenty to do with you. You of all people shouldn't listen to gossip, Dom. People say things that aren't true . . . maybe that was part of the reason for leaving, but it wasn't all of it. Both your dad and I wanted a fresh start . . ."

"A fresh start?" Dominic looked disgusted with her. "Mum, I don't know what was going on back there with that woman, but this isn't a fresh start, it's an . . . old ending. Are you sure Dad didn't just come here for that? For her?"

Alison stared at her son, the boy who might have been conceived around the same time as Cathy's baby . . . who'd never been born.

"You don't have to worry about any of this . . ." she began, reaching out to pat his hand. Dominic snatched it away.

"Yes I do. Of course I bloody do. Do you think your shit marriage only happens to you two? Do you think the rest of us aren't involved? And it's not just me. Gemma puts on a front but before we moved away she came and asked me to go to her school and beat up this boy who'd been saying things about Dad . . ."

"You didn't, did you?" Alison asked, horrified on both counts.

"Of course I didn't, I'm not a psycho. And do you think Amy would really be so shit scared of everything if it wasn't for the fear of you and Dad busting it all wide open? You think that everyone else looks at us and sees a perfect family, living in a nice house, with a perfect life. But you're wrong. Everyone in London knew the truth about us and before long everyone in this dump will too."

Alison didn't say anything for a moment, she just stared at her hands on the bed covers, flat and immobile.

"You'd be better off without him," Dominic said.

"I . . . you can't say that, Dom," Alison reacted at last. "You don't understand. You don't know what we went through to be together and how hard we've fought for everything. We were only a little bit older than you when we met. No one thought we'd make it, and look at us. Grown-up life isn't pretty, it isn't easy. You do your best, you keep going, you wait for things to even out."

"Me," Dom said matter-of-factly.

"What?" Alison asked.

"What you two had to go through to be together was me. I can do math, Mum, I know he got you pregnant when you were seventeen. You two got together because you had to, because of me, and you've been stuck together ever since even though you don't fit."

"No, no!" Alison said firmly, leaning forward and holding his wrists. "You're a clever boy, Dom, but you've got that bit wrong. I loved your father so much, I wanted him so much. I was mad for him. When I realized I was having you it was a bit of a shock. I was frightened and it was hard to know how to cope. But when your dad and I got together it was because we thought we could make a go of it, not because we had to. Not because of you, even though you would be the best reason in the world. We loved each other."

"But not anymore," Dom stated.

"That's not . . . stop it, Dom, stop saying all of these things just because you are angry with us. This is your father you are talking about and no matter what you say about him, he loves you and you love him."

"I don't," Dom said simply.

"You do," Alison insisted.

"Mum, I don't even know him. I never see him except when he wants to scold me. I never speak to him. He never looks at me. And I think it's because he resents me, because it was me in your belly that got him tied up in this family he's so keen on wrecking."

"Now you're just being silly," Alison said. "You and Dad talk

and spend time together, look at . . . well, what about when . . ."
Alison trailed off. She couldn't remember the two of them talking
in the last month, let alone the last week. "He's very busy at the
moment," she said instead.

Dominic dropped his head so that his dark hair fell over his
face, and Alison wondered if he was crying.

"Leave him, then," he said.

"I can't just—" Alison began.

"Leave him. We'd be all right on our own. I'd help look after
you and the girls and you could be you again."

"I can't just leave him," Alison said with some surprise, because
despite everything, the thought had never once occurred to her
until now.

"You could," Dominic said. "If you wanted to."

"But I don't want to," Alison said automatically. "Look, Dom,
I'm glad we've talked, I really am. Dad and I are going through a
rough patch but it will be over soon. We're not going to split up
because, well, we're just not. We are meant to be together.

"In the morning I'll talk to him about you, about how you're
feeling. We'll sort out some time for you two to spend together—
how about that, huh?"

"Whatever," Dominic said, standing. Alison sensed the connection between them was gone.

"I promise you everything will be fine," Alison told him as he
closed the door on her. He didn't reply.

After Dom had gone Alison lay back on the bed and covered
her eyes with her hands.

Of course it was easy for Dominic to imagine that she could
just walk away from this life, her marriage with Marc. That it was
simply a question of making the choice and completing it. After
all, she'd believed exactly the same thing at his age. She'd made the
choice to be with Marc, to leave behind her home, her parents,

her exams, her future, and it had been a simple choice to make. At the time it hadn't even felt like a choice. It was something she had to do.

Now, though, she was living with the consequences of that decision and at thirty-two it wasn't that easy to simply overturn a lifetime of consequences. You don't just pick up, pack your bags, dump your old life, and take off. It was impossible to imagine living without Marc and all the complications he created. Trying to picture it made Alison's head hurt.

As the noise from downstairs gradually began to ebb and fade away, Alison realized something. She had never thought it would be possible for her to be happy without Marc in her life. The key to happiness, she was sure, lay in finding the way to make their life together work once and for all the way she wanted it, with him at her side, no other women in his bed, and the children happy and secure in their family.

Only now, after the party tonight and Cathy coming back into her life and taking her back to the point when she'd made her reckless choice, could Alison start to glimpse that that resolution might not be possible. Only now did she begin to see that she might never be happy as long as she was married to Marc James.

Thirteen

Jimmy looked out between the still-drawn living room curtains at the cold, misty early morning outside and wondered what exactly had changed last night. The street still looked the same as it always did, except the pavement was gilded in dew and shimmered under the threat of the rising sun. The trees stood like sentinels along both sides of the road, guarding the same row of cars parked nose to tail, in exactly the same order as they always were. Other people were still asleep in their houses—as far as Jimmy knew—living their lives exactly as they had yesterday.

Yet in the space of one night everything had changed for him completely, he just couldn't quite put his finger yet on how. He only knew that for some reason it felt as if this dirty February dawn, so far removed from any promise of spring, was a new start for him. Apart from everything else, this had been the first night he had spent in his home in two years.

His wife had not spoken to him once on the way home from

the party. He'd walked a step or two behind her, weighed down by Eloise, who was actually much heavier than she looked, as Catherine marched on carrying Leila like she was a bag of feathers. Jimmy hadn't attempted any conversation. He couldn't imagine what she was thinking or feeling and he had no idea how to approach her. It wasn't just the reappearance of Alison and Marc that had rattled her, he'd pissed her off too. He'd shared her confidences without seeking her permission, which Jimmy had realized, on reflection, wasn't the best idea he'd ever had.

When they had finally gotten home, Jimmy had followed Catherine up the narrow stairs and helped her get the girls undressed and into their beds. As Jimmy had watched her, murmuring to the half-asleep children, buttoning their pajamas and tucking them in, he'd thought how nice it must be to feel as safe and as warm as his two girls must've felt just then.

After kissing his girls good night he'd walked downstairs and found Catherine standing in the living room, her long arms wrapped around her slender body, her head bowed as she stood in front of the cold grate.

"Will you make a fire?" she asked him before he could say good night. "We never have a real fire anymore. I can never get it to light. And I feel cold, I feel cold in my bones."

"Sure," he said, attempting to mask his surprise at her request.

"I'll make tea," Catherine told him, lifting her head as he walked through the kitchen to the back door. "Or would you prefer something else?"

"Tea, thanks," Jimmy said, pausing by the back door. "Just so I'm clear here, you want me to stick around for a bit, yeah?"

Catherine walked into the kitchen and picked up the kettle.

"Would you?" she asked him. "I'd like it if you'd stay."

And the feeling that Jimmy got in the pit of his stomach, as he headed out into the freezing midnight air to fetch some logs from the shed, frightened him to death.

Once the fire was lit Catherine sat on the rug in front of it, legs curled up under her chin, as she hugged her mug of tea, watching the flames.

Jimmy sat on the armchair, holding his own drink. He wondered about what to say to her. The two of them sat like that for a long time and then finally, Jimmy pulled off first one boot and then the other.

"Look," Jimmy said, because it somehow felt that Catherine was waiting for him to talk. "Okay, she's back. He's back. It's weird, because they were so important to you in the early part of your life, but it doesn't really matter anymore, does it? You came through all of that business, with your parents and the . . . you know. And you made yourself into an amazing woman, a great mother. So yes, they are here and it's weird, but once you've gotten over the weirdness, do you really care?"

Catherine thought for a moment.

"When I saw him my heart just lurched," she said. "It was like I was seventeen again going to meet him in the park. He doesn't look the same, he's older and fatter and he's got less hair, but it was still him. Still that face I've been waiting to see for all of these years."

Jimmy sat up a little in his chair, trying to hide just how much her words wounded him.

"Well, yeah—because it was a shock. But just because you felt that way when you saw him doesn't mean you still have feelings for him . . . does it?"

"I don't know," Catherine said. It was not the answer, Jimmy realized, that he'd been hoping for and he felt his gut clench.

"Right," he said, concentrating on sounding neutral. But he

couldn't help the uneasy churning of his stomach when Catherine talked that way about Marc. He felt sick with jealousy, because he knew Catherine had never felt the way about him that she'd once—and maybe still—felt about Marc.

"Obviously I'm not in love with him, I mean I'm not insane," Catherine said, perhaps reading some expression on Jimmy's face that even he wasn't aware of. "It's just that I saw him and even all these years later I felt like a girl again. I felt drawn to him. I remembered all these powerful feelings and what it was like to love him. What it was like to love like that, so deeply and so much."

"Heavy shit," Jimmy said idiotically to cover the sting her words unwittingly inflicted on him. In all the years they had been married she'd never once talked about her feelings for him that way. He tried hard to regain control of the situation, keep the atmosphere light and easy between them. "But I mean you wouldn't fall for him now, because he's like married, and plus I think we've established that he's a heartless wanker, right?"

Catherine smiled.

"He can't be that bad, he stayed with Alison when she was pregnant, and they are still together, but even so I wouldn't fall for him now, no," she said with less conviction than her words suggested. "I'm just saying that's how I felt when I saw him—all jangled up."

"Good, I mean good for you, not about being jangled up, good about not cracking on to him because I don't think that would help anything . . ." Jimmy stalled. "Just ignore him, I reckon like when you see someone you've slept with who you don't really like anymore, the best thing to do is to ignore them."

"Oh, Jimmy, you are such a kid!" Catherine laughed.

"I'm not a kid, Cat," he replied. "I'm a man, this is what men do. And if you doubt me then wait and see. I bet you Marc, or whatever his name is, ignores you from now on. I bet he acts like he never knew you."

"I hope so," Catherine said, with a wistful tone that belied her words, returning her gaze to the fire.

"And what about her? How do you feel about her?" he asked, referring to Alison.

Catherine set down her teacup and rested her chin on her knees.

"The morning after they'd left, Alison's mum and dad came round to our house. Banging on the door at seven in the morning. Her mum had gone to take Alison some tea in bed and found her daughter had gone, leaving only a note. 'Mum, I've run away with the man I love, we have to be together. Love Alison.'

"Alison's mum was clutching it when she came round, they all thought I would know where she'd gone. My mum dragged me downstairs to see them but I could see she was pleased that Alison's parents were going through this. It was proof, proof of what kind of daughter they had. My mum was enjoying it.

"I told them I didn't know where they had gone. I could see that Mum was itching to slap me across the face. She told me now was not the time to be protecting my friend.

"I said I'm not protecting her, I hate her.

"That shut them all up.

" 'What do you mean you hate her?' Alison's mum asked me.

"So I told them: because she stole my boyfriend from me. She took the one good, happy thing I had in my life and she ran away with him. I don't know where. Mum hit me then, she couldn't stop herself even though it shocked Alison's parents. I didn't cry, I didn't even flinch. I told them his name and where he worked, where he had been staying. And I waited for Alison's parents to leave because I knew that the moment they did, my mum would really wallop me.

"I would have just taken it normally, wouldn't have said a word. But now there was the baby. I was worried about the baby, so I begged her not to hit me. I told her I was pregnant.

"She stopped in midstrike, her fist raised. I closed my eyes because I expected her to really lay into me, but she didn't. She just stood there, staring at me, then she walked away. It was this thing that Mum used to do if she was really angry with me, she wouldn't punish me then and there. She'd go all quiet and walk away. Just to let me know that she was thinking about how to really hurt me. Just to let me know that when the punishment came it would be especially bad.

"What I should have done then was what Alison did. I should have climbed out of my bedroom window and never come back. I was seventeen, nearly a grown woman. If I'd had guts I would have gone out of that window. But I didn't. I just lay on the bed waiting for my mother. I was scared. I had no idea where to go or how to look after myself on my own and pregnant. And the one person I could have trusted, the one person who I could have relied on had gone. Not Marc, but Alison.

"It was dark by the time Mum opened the door again.

"You do nothing but bring shame and disgrace on this family," she said, her voice as cold as ice. "Fortunately now that I've uncovered your lie nobody else needs to know. We'll sort this out between ourselves. Get rid of it and get back to normal life."

" 'Can I keep it?' I asked her. I remember my voice sounded like a child's in the darkness. 'I want to keep it.'

" 'Don't be ridiculous,' she said, and that was it. The decision was made. I should have fought it, fought for myself and the baby. But I didn't. I let everything happen around me and all I could think about was how much I hated Alison.

"I felt like she'd run away with my life, almost as if she'd run away with my baby. She had everything. She had Marc, her baby, she had her freedom. I didn't even have the guts to fight them, Jim. I didn't even have the guts to protect my baby. I didn't know how to. I lay there in the dark and I hated Alison, I hated her with every single cell in my body.

"In the clinic with my parents sitting on either side of me like prison guards I gave the doctor my consent to abort. I hated Alison, because it was her fault that I was there alone with no one to stand up for me. And when the baby was gone, and when I felt so empty and used up and lost, I hated her more than anything.

"It was like an energy, like a power source. It was hating her that finally got me away from home. It was hating Alison that night I slapped my mother back, the night I told her about you. I hated Alison when I walked out of the house and told them I was never coming back. Even on the day Eloise was born, even at the moment they put my baby in my arms and I was so full of joy and love I hated Alison . . .

"And then I saw her tonight out of the blue after all these years and I . . ." Catherine trailed off, gazing into the fire.

"What?" Jimmy said.

"I missed her," Catherine said, perplexed. "I looked at her and the first thing I wanted to say was, 'Oh, hello, it's you. I've missed you.' "

"And then the hate came back?" Jimmy asked her.

"No." Catherine frowned. "Just sadness, a lot of sadness. And some bitterness and anger, but not hate. I don't hate her."

"What does that mean?" Jimmy asked, leaning forward in his seat.

"I don't know," Catherine said. "All I know is that she's here now and I don't think they are going anywhere. How I cope with it, I don't know. I don't know anything, Jimmy. I'm a mess. You'd think that in all of these years I'd have grown up, gotten stronger. I'm a mother now, and a wife . . . I've been a wife. I've had a life

since they left. A whole huge massive, wonderful, painful important life. But I'm still that silly little girl, I'm still that mess that
couldn't do a thing to stop her parents from aborting her baby."

Jimmy had gotten up out of the chair and down onto the rug,
kneeling next to his wife, before he realized what he was doing.
The moment he put an arm around Catherine he felt certain she
would bat it away. But she didn't; instead he felt her body relax
and mold into his.

"You are the strongest person I know," he told her. "Coura-
geous, brave, fierce, loyal. You grew up with a woman who beat
you, who hated you, and yet look at you. You are a wonderful
mother to our two girls. To be able to be the parent you are after
having grown up like that makes you incredible. What happened
when you were seventeen wasn't your fault, Catherine, you can't
go back in the past and change the person you used to be. It's the
person you used to be that's made you who you are now. You were
a child, with evil fuckers for parents and no one in the world to
turn to. I just wish . . . I just wish . . ."

"What?" Catherine tipped her face to look up at him.

"I wish I'd found you earlier," Jimmy told her, dropping his
gaze from hers. "Before Marc did, before Alison left, before your
mum could do what she did to you. I would have protected you.
I'd have battered that old bag."

Catherine smiled, her head dropping onto Jimmy's shoulder
causing him to hold his breath, in case the slightest movement
from him would make her move.

"I can't imagine you battering anyone," she said.

"Only because I've never had to batter anyone yet," Jimmy
told her. "But I will if the need arises. I'm like a tightly coiled
spring. Ready for action at any minute."

Catherine moved and sat up away from him, brushing her hair
behind her ear.

"Jimmy, I've known you a long time now, you've never once been tightly coiled in your life."

"How long is it?" Jimmy asked, even though he knew exactly. "Not counting all those years we were at school together. It must be almost twelve years. I remember the first time I saw you. The first time I really noticed you, that is. You were at that party the band was playing, some bird's twenty-first. We were on a break and I was at the bar getting a drink. You were standing at one end of it looking a bit lost, dressed all in black like you'd come to a funeral. I remember thinking to myself, that chick is *tall*." Catherine laughed and rolled her eyes. "You were looking like you'd rather be anywhere else but there and then the girl whose party it was—what was her name? Denise something—came over and hugged you and she said something to you that made you laugh. And you lit up, Cat, sort of from the inside out, like a lantern. I wanted to get to know you then. You didn't make it easy."

"Because the whole of the town was queuing up to go out with you, I couldn't think why you'd want me," Catherine said.

"I wanted to be the one to make you laugh," Jimmy said. "I wanted to be the one who lit you up every day. I blew that. I blew it big-time."

He'd blown it because he'd cheated on Catherine exactly like Marc had, Jimmy thought bitterly to himself. He'd behaved no better than the other man. In fact, his act of betrayal was far worse than Marc's because Marc had never loved Catherine the way he did. He'd hurt her because he loved her, and what kind of coward does that?

"No, you didn't blow it," Catherine said. "I mean you did, but it wasn't just you. It was me too . . ." She sat up, pushing her fingers through her hair, shaking it from her shoulders as if she were trying to wake herself up from a dream. "Look, Jimmy, let's not rake all this over now. Not now when we're friends at last, okay?

Let's just agree that we both did things wrong. That we're better suited to being friends than husband and wife. Now that Alison and Marc are here, well, I don't know what's going to happen, but I know I'm going to need you to be my friend. And I don't want us to run the risk of falling out again."

"That's not what I was trying to do," Jimmy said awkwardly. "All I was trying to do was to . . . I don't know. Make you see that you have changed, you're not the same person you were at seventeen. You might feel like it tonight, but it's temporary, I swear."

"Will you stay here tonight?" Catherine asked. Jimmy felt his chest tighten. "The sofa's quite comfy."

"Yeah? I mean yeah, 'course. If you like."

"I would," Catherine said. "Do you want some more tea?"

"On second thought, have you got any whiskey?" Jimmy asked, and they got up and found the bottle that had been in the cupboard for two years, since Catherine won it in a raffle at the school fair.

Catherine had had perhaps two or three sips before she had fallen asleep upright on the sofa. Gently, Jimmy had taken the glass from her hand and then with infinite care had lifted her legs up onto the sofa and eased her shoulders down, placing a cushion beneath her head and drawing the crocheted throw over her. That had been about four hours ago and she still lay there now, her hair trailing over her face, one hand clenched around the corner of the cushion as if it were the last straw.

Jimmy had tried to sleep in the chair, but sleep had not come. Every time he'd closed his eyes, fireworks went off behind his lids, his brain hummed and his body ached. At some point during the night or early morning something had changed inside him, because whenever he looked over at Catherine sleeping on the sofa, he felt as if his whole body had been cleaved in half by the sight of her.

And then as the sun rose in the sky and burned the mist away, the realization that had been nudging at his thoughts all night suddenly dawned. Nothing had changed, nothing was different. For the last twelve years he had always felt like this, and only recently had he managed to convince himself that he didn't. But now when she needed him, that pretense had fallen away like a sandcastle disintegrating under the incoming tide.

Jimmy still loved Catherine. It felt as if he always had.

He bit his lip and rested his head against the back of the chair. As he closed his eyes, he felt a tear trickle down his cheek.

The fact that he loved his wife was not in question.

Whether or not he'd have the guts to try to do anything about it, he couldn't say.

Fourteen

Alison opened her eyes and waited for the second or two it took for her to remember her life. She had been dreaming about being a child again. Not about any event in particular, but just about her and Cathy when they were around Gemma's age, running along the canal towpath in the sunlight, the heat of the sun on their shoulders as Alison chased after Cathy, whose hair was made amber by the sunshine. That was all; nothing else had happened in the dream except that Alison had felt light inside, she had felt free.

Now that her eyes were open and she had reabsorbed her daily life back into her bones, she felt the weight of reality sinking into her skin. She truly had seen Cathy last night, she hadn't dreamt that.

It was Rosie and not Marc who was in bed next to her. She rolled onto her side and looked at his side of the bed. The pillow was plumped and smooth, the duvet unruffled. He had not come to bed at all. Briefly Alison wondered if he had followed Cathy home and was with her right now, and an ember of jealousy flickered in her throat, but she swallowed it down.

Pushing herself up onto her elbows, Alison made herself get out of bed, the dog springing off the bed after her, skipping around her ankles, keen to be let out. Alison opened the bedroom door, hearing Rosie yap once as she scampered headlong down the stairs.

She found that her legs felt heavy, her arms ached, and she felt as if her brain was somehow insulated by one or two layers from reality. Everything seemed just a little bit farther away than it normally did.

It couldn't be a hangover, she told herself. Yes, she'd drunk a good deal of champagne very quickly, but champagne usually didn't affect her poorly. If she was hungover from anything it was her life and its culmination the previous night. The choices she had made that had somehow brought her life to this point had finally caught up with her. There was nowhere left to hide anymore.

In the bathroom Alison dunked her face in a basin full of cold water and then rubbed some more on her neck and between her breasts with a sponge, feeling the cold water trickle down over her belly. Roughly rubbing herself dry, she took a deep breath and looked in the mirror. Her reflection looked tired, her skin thin and frail. The trouble was, Alison thought, that all those years when she hadn't seen Cathy, it had been easy not to think about her or about the kind of person that Alison had been. She hadn't had to face up to that selfish, spoiled little brat, the thoughtless girl who had wrecked half a dozen lives just to get what she wanted.

But now Alison had seen Cathy face-to-face, and she had to acknowledge the truth.

This person, the woman looking back out of the mirror at her, was the very same girl who had abandoned Cathy to her parents.

Of course, Alison hadn't known that Cathy was pregnant. But in the cold light of day, as she looked at her reflection in the mirror, she knew that even if Cathy had told her, she would have left anyway. She would have done anything to be with the man she loved.

Tired of looking at her tired self, Alison went to check on her children.

Dominic was sprawled facedown diagonally across his bed, one arm flung over his guitar, his iPod still plugged into his ears. He looked fifteen again and nothing like the enraged and passionate young man who had visited her in her bedroom last night. Alison tiptoed carefully across the detritus of his teenage life and carefully pulled the earbud from his left ear. When she realized she couldn't reach the left one she carefully located the iPod and switched it off.

Dominic mumbled something, brushing one hand outward in a spasm, as if he were attempting to swat a fly, before settling back into sleep, and then he didn't look fifteen anymore but five, his face relaxing into that little boy who had once been her guide and beacon. Alison looked at those dark lashes and that soft mouth that used to tremble whenever he was sad, frightened, or furious, and, unable to resist, she bent and kissed him lightly on the head.

He wanted her to leave Marc, to strike out on her own. But he was young, and angry and full of fire. For the first time last night Alison had tried to think of a life without her husband and found she couldn't imagine what it might be like. Perhaps she had created Marc, but he had made her too, he'd made her a mother and a wife, a woman who lived for her family or at least who told herself she did. But did she?

Alison dragged Dominic's duvet cover over both boy and guitar and crept back out of the room to check on her daughters.

Gemma was arranged as neatly as always, the back of one hand resting demurely against her cheek, the other tucked neatly under the cover, like a true sleeping princess.

Amy, on the other hand, looked as if she had wrestled a crocodile in her sleep, which wasn't past the realm of possibility, Alison thought as she looked at her, one leg hanging out of bed, soft vulnerable toes touching the floor. Her quilt was flung to one end of the bed, her head was twisted awkwardly to one side, and her pillow was on the floor.

Alison crept over to the bed and, kneeling tenderly, lifted Amy's leg back onto the mattress and covered her with the duvet.

Perhaps Dominic was right, perhaps she had been so busy creating and re-creating this perfect family life for her children that she hadn't noticed how the stress and tension between her and Marc was affecting her children. Gemma was so easy, that's how Alison always described her middle child. She assumed that Gemma's confidence was due to happiness but perhaps it was like armor, concealing her anxieties. Maybe her eight-year-old little girl was trying to protect herself. And Amy's fears weren't nameless or imaginary, not if she sensed that the fairy-tale castle her parents had built for her to live in might crumble away to nothing. If that was true, then no wonder she only ever relaxed when the whole family was in one room.

Alison sat on the pink wicker chair opposite Amy's bed and put her face in her hands.

Her life had come full circle back here in her hometown. It was ironic that she had had to walk back into her past to finally face her future. The trick was going to be trying to work out exactly how to face it, how to face Cathy and Jimmy and especially her husband. How to make sense of the accidental life she had forced herself into, and of the accidental wife she had become.

The house smelled of stale alcohol and egg- and-watercress sandwiches, some of which were trodden into the stair carpet or ground into the hall tiles. Abandoned glasses were everywhere, filled with various liquids to varying degrees, giving Alison the almost irresistible urge to pick up her son's drumsticks and play with them.

Marc was not in the kitchen or any of the downstairs rooms. From the looks of things he hadn't even slept on the sofa.

Alison walked gingerly over broken chips to the French windows.

The sun was almost up, burning the mist off the lawn, spiralling up into the air like magician's smoke. Marc was in the garden, huddled up in his wool coat, sitting on the white wrought iron garden furniture he had bought at a job lot from the show home in the development. He had his back to the house and was looking at the hills that swelled and rolled across the valley, lush green and gold in the early morning, the horizon garlanded with trees. Above the mist, the sky looked bright blue and clear. Alison thought that this might be the first sunny day of the year.

The grass was wet and cold under her bare feet, slick with dew, but she didn't go back into the house to find shoes or slippers, sensing that if she turned back she'd lose this moment.

As she approached Marc, he looked up and smiled at her.

"Good morning, beautiful," he said. "You really should have something on your feet. It's a bit nippy out here. Thought I'd take the morning air and survey my kingdom and have a think." He nodded at Rosie, who was enthusiastically digging in the flower bed. "The dog did her business in the garden for once. That's got to be something to celebrate."

Alison sat down on one of the wrought iron chairs, drawing her feet up onto its seat and tucking her knees beneath her chin. She felt the cold of the dew seep through her nightdress.

They smiled at each other for a moment, like two old cohorts who were finally realizing the game was up.

"Well, I certainly didn't picture this when we came back,"

Marc said eventually. "I just didn't think Cathy Parkin would still be here. That was a surprise, wasn't it?"

"Didn't you?" Alison asked. He looked at her; his nose and cheeks were red from the chill and his eyes looked puffy and sore. Briefly Alison wondered if Marc had been crying, but in all the years she had been with him she'd never seen him shed a tear.

"I didn't plan it," Marc said. "I swear to you."

"I'm sorry I slapped you," Alison said, hugging her arms around her knees.

"I deserved it," Marc said.

"Maybe fifteen years ago you did. I mean of course you were sleeping with her," Alison said. "I don't know why I hadn't worked that out years ago. I don't even think that was why I slapped you. Or the fact that you'd gotten her pregnant too. It was seeing her there in front of me. I realized I'd missed her and I blamed you. So I slapped you. And I shouldn't have. It must have been very embarrassing."

"I carried it off, though," Marc said. "And anyway I understand, because I felt the same way."

"Embarrassed?" Alison said, tucking the hem of her nightgown under her toes.

"No, when I saw her, I missed her. Missed the way she used to make me feel back then . . . missed who I was when I was with her."

They sat in silence and Alison tried to work out if the burning she felt in her chest was caused by hurt or relief. Because although Marc's comments were painful, at least he was being honest with her.

"What would you have done?" Alison asked him. "If you'd known she was pregnant too? Would you have stood by her as well? That would have given the town something to talk about. 'Man Fathers Two Children Born Within a Week of Each Other.' "

Marc's laugh surprised Alison. "I knew she was pregnant," he explained. "I think I knew long before she did. I was waiting for her to tell me that we couldn't go to bed because her period had come. I waited for three weeks, four weeks, five weeks and the subject never came up. I knew we couldn't carry on forever then. I knew there would be a moment when she had to tell me and I wanted to leave before it arrived. "

"You knew she was pregnant and you still chose me?" Alison said. Once she would have left it at that, let herself believe that that one action fifteen years ago stood as a testament to how much she had meant to Marc, but not today. Because for once in his life he was being honest and she needed to know the truth. "Why?"

Marc didn't answer for a moment as he looked out toward the horizon. Then taking a breath, he began to talk.

"You told Catherine about us, I knew you would sooner or later," he said. "I'd been expecting it since that first afternoon. It must have been a school day because Catherine turned up at the rooming house in her uniform. I'll never forget it, seeing her there in her blue-checked kilt and school sweater.

"She was crying. She asked me if it was true that I'd been sleeping with you and I said that it was. And she asked me if that meant me and her were over. I was shocked, upset for her even if I didn't show it. She should have told me it was over, not asked me. She should have been stronger than she was. But she wasn't strong, I knew that when I got involved with her. I warned her. So I told her that it was; it was over.

"I braced myself, waiting for her to tell me she was pregnant, but she didn't. She must have known by then that she was but she didn't mention it. She just turned on her heel and walked away." Marc looked up at the clear sky. "It was pouring rain."

"She was coming to see me," Alison said, more to herself than to Marc. "She tried to tell me about the baby. But I wouldn't let her."

"I went to the pub that night, my first night off in ages. I wanted to get drunk, really out of it, I didn't want to think about anything. The work in Farmington was coming to an end, I heard there was some work coming up near Croyden. Not that far away, but that night it seemed like a welcome refuge. And then suddenly you appeared. I don't know how you found me . . ."

"I looked in every single pub."

"You walked in and all the blokes looked at you, your hair all wet, your top soaked through. All that eyeliner you used to wear running down your cheeks. I saw you and my heart sank. I thought, here we go again. Ding, ding, round two. But I was ready to take whatever you wanted to dish out, I thought I deserved it."

"I asked you to go outside with me," Alison remembered. "Told you I needed to talk to you. I had no idea what I was going to do if you didn't come, but you did come."

"We stood outside in the rain," Marc went on. "I had both my hands in my pockets and I was staring at my work boots, I couldn't look at you. Because you were the one thing I hadn't been able to resist, like a bloody greedy kid in a sweet shop. You were the one thing that made me mess up again."

"I said, I'm running away from home. I've done it already. I'm going anyway, whatever. But I want you to come with me. Will you come with me? And I felt like screaming because I was so frightened," Alison recalled.

"I just kept on staring at my boots, I heard you talking but words weren't going in. And then you said, 'I want to be with you more than anything, I have to be with you and you have to be with me because I know that we are meant to be together. Come with me and I'll be your family. I'll stand by you, I'll help you. I'll look after you.' That's what you said. 'I'll look after you.'

"You said you'd look after me," Marc repeated. "I knew that there was no way a seventeen-year-old girl would be able to look after *me*, but nobody had ever said that to me before. Not anyone. I didn't realize how much I wanted to hear it."

"And is that why?" Alison prompted him. "Is that why you came with me?"

Marc shook his head, taking a deep breath.

"It was one reason, but there was another one. A stronger one." He looked Alison in the eye. "I was obsessed with Cathy, Alison. Back then at that very moment, standing outside of the pub in the rain, when you asked me to run away with you like I was some kid in a play and not a twenty-year-old railway worker. Catherine had got to me, got inside of me. I was consumed by her, but I couldn't be a better person for her. I couldn't make myself be good enough to deserve her. Even feeling as deeply and as passionately as I did about her I still went to bed with you, and I kept on going to bed with you because I couldn't stop.

"For most of my life I'd had nothing, so when I got the chance to have everything I took it." Marc paused. "I tried to imagine what it would be like to do the right thing, to stay with Cathy and try to look after her baby. But I couldn't. All I knew was that Catherine was having my baby and that I couldn't, *wouldn't* be there for her or her kid. I was frightened, I wanted to get away. Then suddenly there you were standing in the rain, shivering, asking me to run away with you, telling me you'd take care of me. And that meant a lot to me. I didn't love you, but I knew you loved me, I needed to be loved by someone I wasn't frightened of loving back. So I took my hands out of my pockets and put my arms around you and held you until you stopped shivering and I said, 'Okay, then.' I said 'Okay, come on, let's go.' "

He let out a deep sigh.

"The thing is I didn't run away with you, Al. I ran away from her."

Alison put her chin on her knees and rubbed her toes.

"So when I told you about my baby, why didn't you leave me then?" she asked. "Why weren't you scared then?"

Marc stood up and shrugged his coat off; underneath it he was still wearing the shirt and trousers he'd worn to the party. He draped the coat around Alison's shoulders and she gathered the edges close around her.

"You had the most balls of anyone I'd ever seen," Marc told her. "Putting up with that shitty flea-ridden room when I knew you wanted to go home about a million times a day. You stuck it out, you didn't cave. The longer you did that the more I respected you. The more I believed you meant what you said. And then you told me. You said, 'Well, I'm having a baby, so there. You know about it now. I'm keeping it, it's up to you what you do—stay or go, I don't care.'"

"I was scared shitless," Alison said. "I wanted my mum, I wanted Cathy."

"I know," Marc told her. "I looked at you—seventeen, runaway from home with some bloke you hardly knew and not a clue about how to look after yourself, let alone my baby in your belly, and I knew I couldn't leave you. You needed me, and I liked you needing me. I started to need you, looking after you made me get things done. Made me look for regular work and a decent place to live. I don't know, but I could do it for you. You made it easy."

"But you say you love me now," Alison said. "You are always saying that you love me. Is that a lie too?"

"Dominic was born and we got the flat, I got the job in the garage. Your dad came round a few times and threatened to kill me; those first couple of years seemed like a blur and I didn't have time to think about Catherine, I didn't have time to think about what had happened to her and the baby. Before I knew it Dominic was four and I'd got the promotion at the garage, remember?"

Alison smiled. "Yes, they said they'd put you on sales because all the ladies loved you."

"And we'd taken that flat. The two-bedroom on Seven Sisters Road. I came home from work and you were sitting on the living room floor with Dominic, playing with Legos or something. You had the window open, and it was a sunny evening, it sort of lit up the back of your hair like a halo. I looked at you and my son sitting on the floor and I felt as if I'd been kicked in the chest by a mule. I realized I loved you both more than anything. I don't know when it happened exactly, but it was then that I realized. I loved you. I love you. I still do."

Alison looked out at the hills. A horse in a field on the hillside opposite was galloping through the wet grass, mane and tail flying, tossing its head in sheer abandon. Alison shut her eyes and tried with all her might to will herself onto that hillside with that horse. But when she opened them again Marc was still sitting on the white painted wrought iron garden furniture, watching her.

"Everything's changed now that we've moved back here," she said. "Now that we've found Cathy again. Things can't go on as they are."

"Yes they can," Marc insisted. "Yes they can. I know it's weird seeing Cathy again, I know we put her through a lot. But we can come through it, Al, like we always do. We've had our problems, and coming back here has stirred up old memories and opened up old wounds, but maybe that is a good thing. Because maybe now we can clean them and let them heal for good. And I love you, I love you so much, Alison."

Alison looked at him, shielding her eyes against the advancing sun so that she could see his face clearly. He was watching her intently, waiting for her to smile and acquiesce like she always did.

"The trouble is, Marc," she said after a long pause, "I'm not sure that I love you anymore."

Fifteen

Are you sure you don't mind?" Catherine asked Jimmy again as he stood at the door with the girls.

"Of course I don't mind," Jimmy said. "Why would I mind taking my own daughters to school? I've done it loads of times before."

"I just feel so . . ." Catherine looked at her two girls kicking at pebbles in the front garden, Leila with her coat hanging off her shoulders as always and Eloise pointing her toes like a dancer. "I can't see her today. Or anyone. I'm not ready. I'll probably never be ready, actually, so while you're out I'll be checking property prices in the Outer Hebrides."

"That seems like a long way to go to visit," Jimmy said.

"Well, obviously you'd have to come too," Catherine said, lifting Jimmy's heart for a fraction of a second. "You could buy the house next door."

"Right, well," he said. "I've got this thing up in London later."

"What thing?" Catherine asked. "Don't tell me you've been discovered at last?"

"No, well, not exactly. Maybe some session work coming up, I'm going to a sort of informal audition. Pays well, so if I can land it I could maybe get a deposit together on a flat, couple of months' rent to get me sorted."

"That would be fantastic, Jimmy." Catherine's face lit up.

"Yeah, I'd probably have to stay up in London for a few weeks . . . you know how these musicians are. Sometimes it's a twenty-four-hour job . . ."

"Well, if that's what it takes to get you off that boat," Catherine said without hesitation. "And it's not as if we're that far away. There'll be weekends."

"Maybe," Jimmy said slowly. "It's not really a nine-to-five sort of gig. But anyway, I haven't got it yet, let's wait and see. Might not have to worry about it after all."

"Good luck," she said, kissing him briefly on the lips. "Oh, and . . ."

Jimmy waited.

"If she's there, if you see her, just . . . don't tell her anything we talked about, okay? I don't know what's going to happen between us, I'm just not ready to face up to it yet."

"Okay," Jimmy said. "Probably won't see her, probably wouldn't say anything to her even if I did see her."

"She used to have the major hots for you, you know," Catherine said. "In all the years we've been married I've never told you that. Didn't want to. But she was mental about you, to basic stalker levels."

"Well," Jimmy said lightly. "She's only human, right?"

Catherine looked at the girls who were peering rather nosily into Kirsty's front-room window.

"She probably *still* fancies you," she added, lowering her voice.

"Cat." Jimmy looked offended, as he thought about Alison's arms around his neck at the party. "She's a married woman."

"Yes," Catherine said. "And you're a married man, but that's never stopped you before." Catherine's smile faltered when she saw the stricken look on Jimmy's face. "I'm sorry, I was only joking," she said. "What you get up to is your business, I was trying to lighten the mood, you know, after the whole depressing, soul-searching, mortifying weekend of doom. I didn't mean to make you feel bad."

"I know," Jimmy told her. "But it was only once. I only did it once."

The two looked at each other for a moment, but just as Catherine was about to speak, she heard the girls burst into excited laughter as Kirsty slammed her front door shut and climbed over the low brick wall, still wearing her pajamas.

"Bloody men," she said, staring hard at Jimmy. "Bloody bastard men. And by the way where did you go to at that party?"

"Come in," Catherine said, waving at her daughters as they set off for school with their father. "Tell me all about it."

"Not up to scratch, then?" Catherine asked Kirsty, who was wearing red-checked flannel pajamas and pink fluffy slippers, items that Catherine presumed she had donned in utmost secrecy. "Not the love of your life after all?"

Kirsty wandered into the front room and sat heavily on the sofa.

"No, everything went *great*. He was funny, charming, and gorgeous and so was I. At the party we were chatting away, getting on like a house on fire one minute and then the next we were in the downstairs loo going at it like a pair of freight trains. I thought this is it: this is the end of my life as a single philandering hussy and the beginning of my life with the *love* of my life, with Steve."

"Sam, and doing it with a man you hardly know in a loo was your perfect scenario for true love?"

"It wasn't where we did it, it was how. It was so sexy, Cat, and slow and sensuous. And the sink was pretty sturdy too, so that was a bonus. Anyway, we made ourselves presentable and came out but I couldn't find you anywhere. So I let Sam walk me home. And I let him come in and I let him stay for the whole weekend. It was wonderful. The whole weekend, just the two of us in bed. Getting up to make bacon sandwiches, or uncork a bottle of wine, but mainly just us in bed doing it and laughing and talking and sometimes sleeping. It was *lovely.*"

"So?" Catherine pressed her, sitting down beside her on the sofa. "If it was all so wonderful, why are you so down—wait, was the 'doing it' bit not up to scratch? Was he funny, charming, and handsome but a narcissistic and selfish lover? After all that buildup did you have to endure a weekend of anticlimactic sex?"

Kirsty sat up and straightened her shoulders. "No, my dear, the sex was perfect. It was multiclimactic. He was attentive, generous, and very well hung. God, can that man fuck."

"Right—so why are you here looking all cross and fed up?" Catherine was perplexed. "Did he snore or talk in his sleep? Has he unwittingly revealed he has a thing for ladies' underwear?"

"None of those would necessarily be a deal breaker," Kirsty said on a heavy sigh. "I'm here because he's gone. I woke up, and it was so nice, Catherine, to be all achy and sore in all the right places, the sort of feeling you only ever have after a great night of sex, and I thought I was about ready for some more, so I rolled over to wake him up and . . . he was gone." She shrugged, dropping her chin onto her chest.

"To the loo?" Catherine asked optimistically.

"Nope, gone out of the house. Left. Not a good-bye, not a note, not a thing. After that whole lovely long weekend he just got up before dawn and went home. I don't even have his number."

"Well, he probably knows he'll see you at the gym later," Catherine said.

"Yes, he probably does," Kirsty said miserably. "But after a whole weekend of sex and talking and laughing and kissing, Catherine, you don't just get up and leave without saying good-bye. It's not done. It isn't sex etiquette. It's not sexiquette."

Kirsty sniffed loudly. "I really thought he liked me."

"Are you going to cry?" Catherine asked nervously.

"No," Kirsty said, promptly bursting into tears.

"I'll make tea," Catherine said.

"I'm fine, really," Kirsty said some time and several tissues later. "I mean yes, he was handsome and funny and great at sex—but he wasn't really my type, not really."

"I didn't think he was," Catherine said with a wry smile. "I always thought you were more into the ugly, dull, and impotent men myself."

"Catherine, this is no time to be teasing me. I know you're rusty at this best friend thing but this part is where you give me a pep talk and say something to make me feel better, okay?"

"Okay," Catherine said. She had never considered herself to be Kirsty's best friend, but now that Kirsty had mentioned it, the idea made her feel quite pleased. The old best friend had stalked back into town all high and mighty and married to her first love, but it was okay because Catherine had a new best friend. One she was fairly sure would not run off with her husband. She thought for a moment.

"There are plenty more fish in the sea," she said.

"That is a bollocks pep talk," Kirsty said, sniffing. "You're so right, you know. I never thought I'd say it but you, Catherine Ashley, are absolutely right about everything. I take it all back. Men are shit and you and me, we're old, we're past thirty. Boys in gas stations calls us *madam*, men don't look at us when we walk by anymore. Our bosoms—or at least those of us who have bosoms—are collapsing. The wrinkle creams don't work. The hair dye doesn't cover all the gray. We've had it. All we can do is what you're doing, give up on love and sex and hope and life because it's horrible out there, Catherine. It's horrible being single and old."

"And you think *I'm* bad at pep talks," Catherine said mildly. "Look, you are nothing like me. First of all, you are not old, and second of all, men love you, Kirsty. You're pretty and funny and fit and hardly have any wrinkles and have really nice shiny hair that always goes into a style. You go out there and grab life and look for happiness instead of just waiting for it to somehow find you tucked away in a terraced two-bedroom house. And probably Sam was just being an idiot, a stupid idiot who doesn't know the rules of—what did you call it—sexiquette and thinks he'll see you later at the gym to get your number off you and arrange a date. He's a personal trainer, Kirsty. He probably had to go for a fifty-mile run before breakfast or something."

Kirsty smiled at Catherine. "Now that was a pep talk," she said. "But still, how will I know if he really loves me? How will I know?"

"When you see him today go up to him and say hi there, great weekend—let's hook up again, how about tonight? And if he says yes, then he likes you, and if he says no, then he might be busy tonight, so suggest another date and if he still says no, then he probably doesn't like you."

Kirsty stared at her. "That seems an awfully *literal* way of finding out."

"Well, what else can you do? Employ a psychic?"

"Oh, you are so naive," Kirsty said. She rubbed her eyes with the heels of her hands, completing the panda look. "Never mind all this asking business—what I'll do is implement Universal Plan A."

"What's Plan A?" Catherine asked.

"Catherine, where have you *been* all of your life?" Kirsty exclaimed. "Universal Plan A is to act as if nothing has happened. You meet boy, you like boy, you and boy have sex, boy disappears into the night, but you still have an appointment with boy to work on your buttocks on Monday morning at eleven fifteen. You attend the aforementioned appointment. You act as if none of the above has happened. Either the mystery of it will do boy's head in and he'll be forced to ask me if I'm still into him, or he'll be so grateful I don't want to pursue it anymore that he'll act as if nothing happened and we'll be able to put it behind us forever. And then I'll know. I'll know if he really loves me."

Kirsty looked resolute. "That's a much better way of sorting things out. Never mind asking him straight questions and expecting straight answers. That would blow all his circuits for sure!"

"I'm not sure." Catherine sounded unconvinced by Universal Plan A. "Would it not be better perhaps to try and talk to him about last night, clear the air at least? Find out what happened so you don't drive yourself mad thinking about it?"

Kirsty looked at her friend, an expression of pure pity on her face.

"Oh my dear," she said. "For one so old you have so very much to learn. Rarely in the history of humanity has a woman actually talking to a man about anything ever got her anywhere. You have to manipulate them, Catherine. It's the only language they understand. But don't worry, I actually feel better now that I've talked to you. So tell me. Where did you go to at the party and why aren't you getting ready for work now? If you tell me that you went home and had sex with your husband, you owe me five hundred pounds because I bet you months ago that that would eventually happen."

"No, you didn't!" Catherine exclaimed.

"I did, I just haven't told you yet."

"Well, anyway, I didn't have sex with Jimmy. Of course I didn't. We are well past all that now. No, what happened was far more weird and strange and . . . I don't know what I'm going to do about it, Kirsty. I have no idea how to handle it . . ."

"So tell me, then!" Kirsty shouted. "I've got hours to kill before I have to go to the gym to ignore Sam."

Catherine looked at Kirsty's empty mug. "I'd better make another cup of tea first," she said.

"Da-ad," Eloise said, stretching out the word as she swung Jimmy's hand.

"Yes, love," Jimmy said. He was watching Leila, who had run a few feet ahead and was midperformance in her latest staging of "Leila: The Musical" as she danced and sang her way along High Street.

"Litter bin! Litter bin!" she sang as she stopped to do star jumps in front of a rubbish bin. "People put litter in you and that is goooooooooood! Yeah!"

One thing Jimmy could say about his younger daughter was that she was never afraid to express herself in public. He wasn't sure if that was a good or a bad thing.

"Well . . . is Mum okay? I know you stayed up all night after the party talking and you've stayed in the house all weekend and now she's having a day off work. What does it mean, Dad? Does it mean you're moving back home for good?"

Jimmy was very careful not to let the question break the rhythm of his stride.

"No, love," he said. "No, I'm not moving back in. Mum just needed a friend around this weekend to talk to and I'm her friend now."

"Kirsty next door is her *friend*," Eloise said. "You're her husband and she wanted you around all weekend so that might mean she wants you to move back in, mightn't it, Dad? It might mean that it's nearly time?" Eloise hopped a little, tugging on Jimmy's hand.

"Ellie," Jimmy began purposefully. "I don't think I am going to be moving back home at all, in fact I might get this job soon that means—"

"But you would, wouldn't you?" Eloise interrupted him. "If Mummy said you could move back home for good, you would, right?"

Jimmy sighed inwardly; he'd promised Catherine never to lie when it came to questions like this one, that he'd never gloss over the truth or give the girls false hope. Yet how could he, a grown man—a parent—confide in his eight-year-old daughter everything that he was still struggling to come to terms with? Of course he'd move back in if Catherine asked him to, he'd move back in like a shot. But she wasn't going to and the nearest he was ever going to get to her now was being her friend, her children's father, and soon enough even those roles would lead to his being nothing more than a peripheral character in her life as she blossomed and grew and found her own way in life, which she was bound to do. Jimmy knew that Catherine was really only at the beginning of herself, even if she didn't realize it yet. But how could he explain all of that to Eloise, who just wanted to hear that her daddy would come home if he could?

"I don't know," Jimmy tried to explain uncomfortably. "I live on the boat now . . ."

"Yes, I know, but if Mummy says you can come home, you will, won't you?" Eloise persisted.

"No, I mean I would but . . ." Jimmy got the distinct feeling he'd said something that he shouldn't.

"But what?" Eloise asked him. "You do want to come home, don't you, Daddy? You do miss us, you've just said so. So but what?"

"But Mummy doesn't want me to move back home," Jimmy blurted out before he really knew it. He grabbed Leila's hand as they came to the pedestrian crossing and for a few awkward moments Leila performed her self-taught version of Irish dancing over the black and white stripes while Eloise was silent, holding on to his hand tightly. Once on the other side, Jimmy released Leila again and watched her gallop off through the school gate and into the playground, where she immediately commenced skipping around in a circle, an activity that soon attracted four other participants. Those were the days, Jimmy thought, the days when all you had to do to feel good was skip in a circle.

He looked down at Eloise, whose face was filled with thunderclouds. She was so like her mother, it made his breath catch in his chest.

"Look, it's not really Mummy's fault," he attempted to explain, resorting guiltily to trotting out the standard speech. "These things happen. Sometimes grown-ups who still care about each other just can't live together and it doesn't mean they don't love their children . . ."

"I hate her," Eloise said quietly as they followed Leila into the playground.

"Now listen." Jimmy stopped and put his hand on his daughter's shoulders, bending to look into her green eyes. "You don't hate your mummy, you love your mummy."

"But you've said you are sorry and you want to come back, and me and Leila want you to come back. And anyway in assembly Mrs. Pritchard said that when someone's done something bad you should try to forgive them."

"That *is* what Jesus would do," Leila counseled as she skipped by.

"Right." Jimmy paused; it was hard to argue with the son of God. "Well, I expect he would, but the thing is when you're grown-up it's not always as simple as saying sorry and forgiving people and stuff . . . like that."

"Why isn't it?" Eloise asked, pinning him to the spot with her mother's eyes.

Jimmy couldn't answer her for a moment.

"Because when you're grown up and you do something wrong, more people are affected. More people get hurt and it's very complicated."

"But what about me and her?" Eloise asked baldly, nodding at her sister. "We're people, we got hurt—why doesn't what we think matter? We think you should come home."

As Jimmy looked at his daughters he felt the crushing weight of failure on his shoulders. He'd let them down.

"Sometimes," he said finally, heavily, "even though grown-ups love their children very much, they just can't live together anymore . . ."

He watched his daughter as her eyes darkened like a stormy sea.

"You shouldn't have got married and had kids if you couldn't keep loving each other properly. It's not fair!"

The bell rang and Eloise snatched her school bag from Jimmy's hand and ran into her classroom, along with most of the rest of her class.

"That didn't go quite the way I planned," Jimmy said, watching her go, feeling her words stinging like slaps on his skin. She was right, of course, according to all the songs ever written, many of them by him. It was impossible to make somebody love you just because you wanted them to. And yet with Catherine he had truly believed that he would be able to make it happen, because he loved her so much. You couldn't love a woman as much as he loved her and not inspire something similar in her, you just couldn't. At least that was what he had always believed, and it was hard to let go of that kind of faith even when the facts had discounted it long ago.

Life had been very simple before Jimmy Ashley got to know Catherine Parkin. There had been the band, music, the band, his friends, the band, a few girls here and there, and the band. Jimmy hadn't needed or wanted anything else. At the time he'd put his single-mindedness down to his ambition, but just recently he'd wondered if it wasn't more to do with his dad dying when he was seventeen. Knowing that his dad wasn't at home meant he didn't want to be there either.

So when his mum had told him she was moving away to Ayles-bury just as Jimmy was approaching his nineteenth birthday, it was with some relief that he told her he was going to be staying in Farmington, sharing a place with the rest of the band. Jimmy liked the feeling of being rootless, he liked the freedom it brought him, the idea that at any moment he could pack a bag and be gone, not that he ever did. But it didn't matter that he hadn't done that, what mattered was that he could. He had been ready, poised for life.

And then he met Catherine, no, not exactly met her, because she'd always been around on the periphery of his life, the skinny ginger-haired girl who hung out with the blond bombshell. But it was when he was twenty-one and Catherine was twenty that he first truly saw her. And once he started looking at her he couldn't stop. She wasn't good-looking in the traditional sense, the sense in which he and Billy had always defined an attractive woman, by her hair, breasts, and general availability for sex. Catherine had plenty of hair, that was true, but her body was long and thin with skin that seemed almost translucent. Jimmy remembered that Catherine reminded him of his mum's best bone china. If you held a piece of it up to the light, you could see your fingers through it.

He had known that something had happened with Catherine and her blond friend with the short skirts a few years before he first noticed her properly. He knew that she had dropped out of her A levels and never made it to university and that she still lived at home and worked in the Christian bookshop. But until he saw her smiling at that twenty-first birthday party he hadn't wanted to know any more than that.

It had started with a conversation, his love for Catherine, a conversation that had begun with Catherine glancing over her shoulder as Jimmy approached her, unable to understand why he wanted to talk to her. There had been many conversations after that. Jimmy became a regular visitor to the Christian bookshop on the days that Catherine worked there and her mother did not. Eventually he managed to persuade her to come to a gig, made her promise that she would try to come so he could show her what he did best. He was proud of his music, but more than that he'd hoped that when she saw him up onstage she'd fancy him—it seemed to work on a lot of girls that way.

Jimmy remembered scanning the crowd at the gig until he caught sight of her, a good head taller than most people there, and then he'd played all night to her, never taking his eyes off of her.

"What is it with you and that skinny chick?" Billy asked him after he tried and failed to get Catherine to stay and have a drink with him after the gig.

"I like her, that's all," Jimmy said, disappointed that he'd played his very best and she still hadn't let him buy her a drink, let alone fallen into bed with him.

"Don't go falling in love, mate," Billy warned him. "We can't conquer the world with our music if one of us is in love."

"Not me," Jimmy told his friend. "Never me."

But it was already too late. Before he'd ever kissed her he'd loved her.

Actually, getting to kiss her had been a lengthy process that had taken almost four months. It was hard to see her because her mother watched her like a hawk, but Catherine had developed a number of ways of getting time to herself, an act of rebellion that had made Jimmy love her all the more, especially when she used that precious stolen time to be with him. Mostly they would go for a drink, the two of them sitting in a quiet corner of a pub and talking about everything and anything. Jimmy found it became his mission to make her laugh, his heart quickening every time she smiled. A couple of times he'd taken her to the movies, to see films he couldn't care less about, just so he'd be able to sit next to her in the dark and steal glances of her profile lit by the big screen. Funny, he remembered thinking, how he yearned to have the courage to simply pick up her hand and hold it. Once, though, she had a whole day to herself. When Jimmy asked her if she would like to hang out with him she refused, telling him she was going to London to visit art galleries. Without thinking, Jimmy found himself volunteering to go with her.

Eventually he found himself standing by her side opposite a painting of some red-haired chick in a lake.

"She looks like you a bit," Jimmy said as Catherine stared very hard at the painting.

"She's Ophelia," Catherine said. "Driven mad by love. I'm not like her at all. I'm never going to be like her."

Then one spring evening Jimmy walked her home after a gig she had stayed at long enough to have one drink. As always they stopped at the bottom of her road.

"I can walk you to your door if you like," Jimmy offered. "I'm also available for coffee and the full range of hot drinks."

Catherine laughed at his joke, standing underneath a cherry tree in full blossom, the scent of it mingling with his memories. The sound of her laughter made him happy.

"You can't walk me home," Catherine told him. "My mum doesn't know I went out to a gig in a pub with a man. She thinks I went to a book group. And she can't know about you, because if she did it would spoil everything. I'm not supposed to listen to rock music."

"What?" Jimmy exclaimed. "Am I in *Footloose*? You're twenty, you can do what you like."

"I do do what I like," Catherine replied defiantly. "Which is why I have to keep secrets from her . . . she's very hard to live with."

"Then leave home," Jimmy told her.

"It's harder than you think," Catherine said, and suddenly she looked hopeless. "I don't know how to."

On impulse and after weeks of being too afraid to touch her, Jimmy put his arms around Catherine and held her close to him. He'd waited for a long time in the moonlight, the night silent and still, until her rigid body, which had stiffened instantly when he'd touched her, relaxed and softened. He remembered the feeling of her bones against his.

"I like you, Catherine," he said, holding her, her chin resting on his shoulder.

"I'd worked that out," Catherine replied. "I don't get it, why *you* would like *me* of all people, but I know that you do."

"Do you like me at all?" Jimmy asked her nervously, because in the four months they had spent together he had no idea what she felt about him other than that she tolerated him with a certain degree of fondness.

"I like you . . ." Catherine began. "I don't know about anything else, Jimmy. I don't know if I can do anything else. I'm not sure I know how to love someone. I don't want to be like Ophelia."

Jimmy pulled back from the embrace just as a warm breeze disturbed the branches of the cherry tree, causing its blossom to waft lightly into her hair, glowing silver in the moonlight.

"Listen," he said softly. "I don't know what's happened to you to make you feel like you can't love someone, but you can. You of all people could love better than any of those half-asleep idiots in their houses who think they've got it all. You just need to believe that you can be free to grow, and go to gigs and invite blokes in for coffee whenever you like, especially if they are me because I am so in love with you, but anyway you can do it. You just need someone to show you how."

"What did you say?" Catherine asked him.

Puzzled, Jimmy started ticking off the major points in his speech on his fingers.

"I said you can find love, grow . . . er . . . go to gigs and um, oh yeah, invite guys in—"

"You said you were in love with me," Catherine interrupted him, and Jimmy realized she was angry. "You shouldn't go around telling girls that you love them just because you want to sleep with them." She pushed herself out of his arms. "I'm not that naive, Jimmy."

"Huh?" Jimmy was confused. "Did I say that? I never meant to say it out loud, at least not yet, I haven't spent four months getting you to let me spend time with you to freak you out now. But you might as well know I do love you, which is pretty weird considering all we've ever done together is talk and hang out. But I do love you and I'm not even trying to get you into bed, talking about extreme weirdness. I just want to be near you. Obviously I'd like to have sex with you too but not until you're ready. I can wait for as long as it takes, and for the record I actually mean that. I love you, Cat."

Catherine was silent for a long time before she said anything.

"Cat?" she asked him.

"Yeah, sorry," Jimmy said, shrugging. "It's your eyes, cat's eyes. I won't call you that again."

"I like it," she said. "It's new. And I like you, Jimmy. A lot, but maybe not like you want me to, and I don't know why because you are a great guy."

Jimmy picked up one of her hands. "Plus way sexy too," he added.

"Yes." Catherine smiled slowly. "I suppose so."

"Never thought I'd be trying to get a girl to like me," Jimmy said. "Normally it's the other way around."

"Perhaps it's the thrill of the chase you can't give up," Catherine suggested. "Maybe once you've got me you won't want me anymore. I'm not very experienced at sex, for example."

Jimmy had to take a minute to think about that.

"Are you implying that I may have a chance of 'getting you,' as you put it?" he asked her.

Catherine took a step closer to him.

"What if I don't fall in love with you?" she said.

"I'm Jimmy Ashley," he told her. "Of course you're going to fall in love with me."

And then as the cherry blossoms drifted down, he kissed Catherine for the very first time, completely certain that he was right.

Only now, with the benefit of hindsight, could he finally accept that he had been wrong. Because no matter how much Catherine cared for him, desired him, protected him, and relied on him, she had never once looked him in the eyes and told him she loved him.

Which meant that Eloise and the pantheon of rock was right. He never should have believed that he could make the impossible happen.

Jimmy pulled himself back into the present as his younger daughter hopped over to him.

"Was Ellie mean to you, because never mind, because she's mean to me all the time and she doesn't mean it really."

"Right," Jimmy said. "Come on, love, I'll take you round to your classroom."

"Mind if we join you?"

Jimmy turned around to find Alison at his side, her hair brushed and smooth, just the right amount of makeup on. She was wearing a pristine white wool coat and caramel-colored boots. It seemed as if the night of the party hadn't affected her at all. When he looked at her he was conscious of his fifteen-year-old leather jacket creaking at every movement.

"So that was some party," he said, not knowing exactly what he should say to this woman, the other woman. Yes, she had betrayed his wife, but if she hadn't betrayed Cat there was a good chance he would never have gotten together with Cat, which despite everything was something he couldn't regret.

"Yeah, I'm sorry about that, weird or what?" Alison said, making Jimmy smile, because she sounded about fifteen instead of thirty-two.

"Weird is one way of saying it," Jimmy said. "Definite proof of a small world."

"Is she okay?" Alison asked. "Not too totally freaked?"

"She is totally too freaked," Jimmy said, unable not to smile again. "Her head is completely done in."

"Heavy, man," Alison replied, and the pair of them chuckled. Once again Jimmy wondered if he should be trying harder not to like her as they reached the younger girls' classroom door. Catherine hadn't explicitly said don't like her, but Jimmy felt it was probably more honorable not to.

"Come on, then," Leila said, offering her hand to Amy, who

was half hidden behind her mother. "You can come in with me if you like and sit next to me at snack time; hopefully we won't have raisins today because I can't eat them because they look like dead flies with their arms and wings pulled off, don't they?"

Hesitantly Amy took Leila's hand and with one last glance at her mother followed Leila into school.

"That's the first time since she's started that she's gone in without a fuss," Alison said, suddenly reaching out to hold Jimmy's forearm. He looked at her smooth hand with the perfectly manicured nails on the arm of his leather jacket and noticed she was not wearing her wedding ring.

"It would be so great if Amy and Leila would become friends."

"Would it?" Jimmy asked her. "Or would it be seriously complicated and difficult?"

Alison looked at her watch as if she had somewhere particular to be.

"Can you come for a coffee with me?" she asked.

Jimmy looked at his watch, as if he had somewhere particular to be, and for once he did. He had a train to catch to town, but not for another half hour. "I don't know . . ." he began.

"Why, don't want to fraternize with the enemy?" Alison asked. She laughed but there was no humor in it. "Please, Jimmy, I think we have a lot in common in all of this, you and I."

"But I'm on Cat's side," Jimmy said.

"Oh God, Jimmy, we're not at school!" Alison exclaimed, which for a second made Jimmy feel exactly like he was.

She smiled at him, tucked her arm through his, and dragged him in the direction of the coffee shop, tossing her blond hair over her shoulder.

Jimmy put up no resistance as he went with her, telling himself he wasn't fraternizing with the enemy, he was going under-cover.

"So you like, slapped your husband," Jimmy said conversation-ally once Alison had ensconced them on the sofa at the back of the coffee shop. The location was a little too clandestine to make Jimmy feel entirely comfortable. "How did that go down?"

"He dealt with it," Alison said, loading her skinny latte with sugar. "Just like he deals with everything. He's a master at it. It's funny, really, because the man I met, the man Cathy met back then, isn't there now. I don't know where he is. I don't even know when he disappeared. But when I . . . we fell in love with him he was tough and dangerous but sort of vulnerable and gentle too. Every teen girl's, no every woman's idea of heaven. Then he changed, and he changed because of me. Suddenly he was respon-sible for me and our baby. Being with me made him into the kind of man who could support a family, build a business—become successful. But not everything about him changed. He kept the bad bits. The bits that sleep around with other women right under my nose."

Jimmy thought about the ladies' loo in the Goat Pub.

"Well, nobody's perfect," he said. Alison looked up at him over the rim of her coffee cup with her tranquil blue eyes.

"Did you cheat on Cathy?" she asked. "Is that why you two aren't living together anymore?"

Jimmy shrugged and nodded. The whole town knew about him and Cat, so there was no point in trying to cover it up. "It was only once, though."

He waited for Alison to pass judgment but she didn't, she just watched him through the steam from her drink and finally said, "Have you noticed that all of us have been unfaithful to Cathy in some way? We've all betrayed her."

"Yeah, but me and Cat don't have anything to do with you and him and her," Jimmy said, shifting in his seat and glancing at his watch again. "We're not part of that."

"I think you are," Alison said. "I think the mistakes we all made back then affected your chances of having a successful marriage with Cathy. I think I've stolen her life and she got mine by mistake."

"What?" Jimmy leaned forward in his seat. "Alison, *what* are you talking about?"

"I don't love Marc anymore," Alison said, finding that saying it was oddly liberating. "I'm thinking of leaving him, which is a freaky and terrifying thought, but if I can get myself together and find the guts I need to be on my own for the first time ever in my life, maybe it might be the right thing to do. What really worries me is that I was always so sure that it was right for us to be together. I loved him so much that I couldn't see how my life could ever be any other way. I wanted him, I was jealous of Cathy having him right from the moment I set eyes on him. I was obsessed with him, to the point that nothing else mattered but finding a way to be with him. Not my mum and dad, not Cathy, even the risk I was taking having unprotected sex with him, I'd do anything just to have those few minutes of his attention . . ."

"Okay," Jimmy said, tapping the table. "Slightly too much info there."

"Well, Cathy did it too," Alison said, looking slightly hurt.

Jimmy was silent. He didn't want to think about that.

"Anyway," Alison went on. "What's been driving me mad ever since I saw Cathy again and you is this—now that I don't love him anymore, what have I got? I gave my future to him, gave up my dreams of university, a career for him. I conducted the last fifteen years of my life, had his children, put up with his affairs for nothing. If I still loved him it would almost be bearable, but I don't. And if I don't love him then what's left? An uneducated woman in her thirties with three children and no prospects."

Jimmy looked over his shoulder as if he was hopeful of making a quick exit through the unisex toilets.

"Look," he said after a while. "I'm not really qualified for all this chick stuff, about feelings and love. I don't really know why you're talking to me about it."

"But this is important to you too," Alison said.

"Er, how exactly?" Jimmy said.

"I stole Marc from Cathy, like a jealous child snatching a toy. He said he wouldn't have stayed with her, but he never really got the chance to find out. Maybe if he had, things would have been different, right? Maybe he would have been different. If he'd stayed with her he might have changed for her, but in the right ways. By dropping all the bad bits and keeping all the good. He might have been a whole man for her. She might have been able to keep her baby."

"And what about your baby?" Jimmy asked. "What would have happened to Dominic?"

Alison thought of her son, who she had delivered half asleep to the school gate earlier that morning, his tousled hair pulled over his eyes in a bid to try to hide the eyeliner he had applied that morning. She thought about him, his bravery and determination, and her heart ached. She'd like to think she would have kept him whatever had happened, but she remembered the terror that had engulfed her the second she realized what was happening to her body. And the absolute total determination she'd had to have Marc by her side while she had his baby no matter what. She couldn't be sure that if Marc hadn't yielded to her persuasions and her demands, then she wouldn't have done the same thing Cathy and a hundred other lonely and frightened seventeen-year-olds had done. All that mattered, she told herself, was that Dominic was here now and she loved him.

"Dominic exists and I love him," Alison said. "He's a fact."

"Good," Jimmy started, tapping his fingers restlessly on the arm of the leather sofa. "I'm glad you feel that way about him. But there's no way Marc and Cat were meant to be together. It would never have worked, he couldn't love her the way that . . . that she needs to be loved."

"Maybe you're right." Alison looked at him thoughtfully, leaning a little closer to him. "But I don't think Marc feels the same way."

"What?" Jimmy leaned backward as far as the sofa's plump cushions would allow him. "You think *what?*"

"I know my husband," Alison said urgently. "I know that sooner or later his curiosity is going to take him back to Cathy. He is going to want to see how he feels around her, if he can recapture anything that he's lost. He's going to want to know how he makes her feel. And I'm going to let that happen. If he wants to try and get back anything of what he once had with her, then I won't stand in his way because I want that too, I want her back too."

"Look, if you want to be Cat's friend again then that's cool. I actually think she might go for it," Jimmy said. "But there is no way, there is no way at all that I'm letting that creep back into my wife's life again to mess with her all over again. No way."

"But she's not your wife anymore, is she?" Alison said. "I mean for all practical purposes you are single. If you wanted to you could . . ." Alison caught herself on the verge of saying something highly inappropriate to Jimmy Ashley. "You could come to bed with me," she had been about to say, but instead she bit her tongue, her heart pounding with the thought of what she had nearly said.

"Could what?" Jimmy said.

"Could be with anyone you wanted," Alison said, dropping her gaze and studying the contents of her cup. "Like I said, you're not really Catherine's husband anymore."

"She's . . . look, I know that, but I still care about her." Stung from the slap of reality that Alison had just dealt him, Jimmy stood up quickly. "I've got to go," he said, and he walked away.

As Jimmy's train rolled into the station he hesitated. Maybe he shouldn't get on the train after all, maybe he should go straight back round to the house and see how Cat was. Alison might be right. Marc might be heading there right now. Jimmy had no idea what would happen. But given that he'd only just worked out that he had never stopped loving her, he wasn't quite ready for her to move on yet. The train squealed to a halt alongside the platform and a handful of people got out, walking past Jimmy as he stared at the carriage.

Sixteen

Alison looked at herself in the wall of mirrors in the private exercise room as she waited for Kirsty. Her cheeks were pink, her eyes were hot and glittering, and she hadn't done a stroke of exercise yet.

Since she had told Marc she didn't love him anymore she felt as if she was going a little bit more mad as each minute passed, especially in that second when she had almost asked Jimmy to go to bed with her. The thought of saying those words out loud shocked and exhilarated her almost as much as saying them. It was as if, after fifteen years of keeping herself on track, suddenly she'd derailed and was careering out of control downhill. Alison had no idea what was happening with her and Marc, because since they'd talked on the lawn in the morning mist they hadn't spoken at all. She had barely even seen him. He'd spent the rest of the weekend at the dealership and when he came home he went to sleep in one of the guest bedrooms. Alison felt as if she should feel more about what was happening, but it was hard to accept that this was reality. It was hard to accept that things wouldn't eventually go back to the way they had always been, even though this time she knew this was really the end. She should be crying, she supposed. She should be screaming and tearing her eyes out, but just at that moment there was nothing there, a void. A vacuum of emotion waiting to be filled with a sudden indrawn breath.

The door swung open and Kirsty walked in. Alison smiled at her. Kirsty didn't smile back.

"You might as well know, I'm Catherine's best friend," she said, crossing her arms under her chest. "I had no idea who you were when I started teaching you. But if it's a question of sides, then I'm on hers and don't try and make it any different. Got it?"

Alison looked at her. "God. It's exhausting always being the villain," she said, and sat down on the floor and wept.

"Well," Kirsty said, handing her a tissue she had retrieved from her handbag. "I didn't expect you to cry. That's kind of thrown me a bit."

"All this is happening to me too, you know," Alison sobbed into the tissue. "I don't want you to take sides, I don't want there to be sides. It's just that I'm breaking up with my husband and I've just come face-to-face with my best friend again after fifteen years and it's very confusing. I'm not evil, you know. I'm not some crazy scheming witch, I'm just trying to sort out this whole mess and put things right again."

"I didn't know you and him were breaking up," Kirsty said. "Catherine doesn't know that."

"No, well, I didn't know it until I saw Cathy. Until I realized there was an alternative to being miserable married to him. I don't love him anymore and when I saw how he looked at her . . . I don't know if the way he loves me will ever be enough. And now my only friend is a fifteen-year-old boy who wears eyeliner and periodically despises me."

"Catherine doesn't hate you," Kirsty said after a while. "She's extremely freaked out that you are back. But when we talked about it, about how she felt when she saw you, 'hate' was not a word that cropped up."

"I miss her," Alison said, drying her tears. "Especially now. I feel like I've been in suspended animation for fifteen years playing at being a grown-up, but really I haven't matured by one second. Today I almost asked Jimmy Ashley to have sex with me."

"You did *what?*" Kirsty exclaimed. "You nearly asked Catherine's husband to have sex with you? Thank God you didn't say it out loud to him because I don't think that is necessarily the best way to get back into Catherine's good books, given that the last time she saw you you were running off with the love of her life."

"They've split up, haven't they?" Alison challenged her weakly.

"Technically yes, but in my book splitting up means burning photos and never speaking to each other again, it doesn't include sharing meals, taking long country walks, and always living in each other's pocket, which is pretty much what they do. There's something unfinished there and if you hope to be Catherine's friend, I suggest you stay well out of it, at least until they've worked out how to finish it."

"Don't worry," Alison sniffed. "I wouldn't ever say it out loud. He doesn't look at me that way anyway. In fact I can't remember the last time anyone ever looked at me that way, apart from Marc." Alison sighed and sniffed again. "Look at me, I'm crying because you were a bit mean to me, but I can't cry over my marriage disintegrating. I'm a mess. I'm a big fat useless pointless mess. I've got two little girls who don't know their lives are about to fall apart, a son who holds me in contempt for about ninety-five percent of the time, and a husband who . . . who I don't love anymore."

"Right, well I didn't know any of that, either," Kirsty said. "You are in a pickle, aren't you?"

"That's one way of looking at it," Alison said, stifling a sob.

"I tell you what," Kirsty said. "How about we sack the pilates and go for a cup of coffee instead. Maybe between you and me we can work something out." ·

"I don't know," Alison said with a watery smile. "The last time I went for a coffee I was on the verge of making random offers of sex to men who patently aren't interested in me."

"Oh, honey," Kirsty told Alison as she pulled her up onto her feet. "Welcome to my world."

Catherine lay on the sofa and stretched her toes. It was the afternoon and she had been lying on the sofa since she got back from work at just after ten that morning.

For the first time ever in her three years of employment at the Stratham and Shah Agency Catherine had been sent home from work.

She'd gone in as usual, her hair drawn back in a bun, a black sweater over black trousers, aware that her skin looked even more pale and stark than usual and that there were lilac shadows under her eyes. Catherine had been tempted not to go to work at all, but she refused to let herself give in so readily to the impulse to crawl into bed, pull the covers over her head, and stay there. She was not going to let anyone see that what had happened on Saturday night had affected her, and besides, she was hopeful that very few people had noticed her part in the drama. She was sure that the other guests would've all been looking at Alison, beautiful, glittering, golden Alison, as she slapped her husband across the face, eclipsing Catherine in her shadow as nothing more than a minor player in the drama.

"There you are!" Emma, the receptionist, beamed at Catherine as she walked in the door. Catherine started. She never usually got more than a disinterested "Morning" from Emma.

"Am I late?" Catherine asked, checking her watch. It had been a struggle to get Kirsty to stop talking about Sam and out of the house so that she could leave for work, but according to her watch she'd made it in on time.

"Tell me all," Emma said wide-eyed, leaning across the reception counter so that the glass beads she wore around her neck clattered on the wooden surface. "What have you got to do with Marc James? Is it all true?"

Catherine blinked at Emma, and pressing her lips together, she put her head down and walked into the open-plan office. People stopped talking as she entered the large, busy room. Unspoken words hovered in midsentence above her head, eyes dropped, and swivel chairs rotated away from close conversations.

"Morning, Catherine!" Her boss, Sunita, must have been looking for her because she came out of her office the second Catherine arrived. "Can you come in when you're ready, please, I need to firm up some event dates with you."

"Will do," Catherine said, conscious of everyone not looking at her. She sat down at her desk, flanked on two sides by dividing panels, and switched on her PC. She sat there staring at the screen as it leapt to life. Everyone was talking about her.

"Did you enjoy the party, Cathy?" Francesca, a twentysomething bright young thing who had come to the office straight from university, appeared over the top of one of the dividers.

"It was fine," Catherine said, looking intently in her desk drawer for some unknown object.

"So did you used to know the Jameses, then?" Francesca pursued.

"A long, long time ago," Catherine said.

"And he got you both *pregnant*?" Francesca questioned.

Catherine stood up abruptly, suddenly towering over diminutive Francesca.

"I don't think that's any of your business," Catherine said stiffly, feeling her fury and embarrassment searing her skin.

Francesca looked around at some of the other women in the office who were trying not to catch her eye, their hands covering their mouths.

"It's just that it all came out right in front of *everyone* and I thought you might like to set the story straight . . ."

Catherine picked up her diary, walked around the partition, and stared down at Francesca, who wilted like a flower beneath her gaze.

"No thank you," she said before turning on her heel and setting off for Sunita's office. She heard gasps and giggles as she closed the door behind her.

"They love gossip," Sunita said as Catherine sat down.

"It's not gossip," Catherine said. "It's nothing."

Sunita gazed at her for a moment. "You look tired, Catherine," she said. "Perhaps you should take the rest of the day off, let it all blow over."

"I can't." Catherine shook her head. "If I do, then they will think they've won."

"Who will?" Sunita laughed. "Silly Francesca or nosy Emma? No one cares about them. Everyone here respects you and loves you, Catherine. We worry about you and we care for you. It's almost impossible to ignore what happened on Saturday night, but I'm certain that most people here don't want to pry or make things any harder for you. In a day or two everything will be back to normal. It's just come as a bit of a surprise to us all to find out that . . ." Sunita trailed off.

"What?" Catherine said.

"Well, that you've had another life. One before the woman you are now. You always seem so serene and calm." Sunita laughed. "It was a shock to discover you had a secret life."

"I don't have a secret life," Catherine said, surprising both herself and Sunita with the anger in her voice.

"Go home," Sunita said. "Don't worry about what anyone thinks. Go home and rest and come back tomorrow. By that time Francesca will have a new boyfriend and Emma will have new nail polish, and everything will be as it always was and no one will give you a second thought."

Catherine looked down at her hands, folded in her lap. She didn't know why Sunita's choice of words stung her quite so much.

As soon as she had gotten through the front door Catherine had flopped down onto the sofa and she hadn't moved since, trying to make sense of everything that was happening.

Seeing Marc and Alison again had taken her by surprise, but somehow the way she felt about seeing them again surprised her more than the actual event. It was almost as if on some level she had always been expecting this moment, knowing that one day it would come. Now that they were back she felt curiously complete, as if a missing part of her life had been returned to her. Knowing where they were and what they were doing released the pressure of the past that had been building inside her, like a dam that had burst, and she could feel it flowing free out of her fingers and toes.

As she'd looked into the face of her old friend she'd felt happy and sad simultaneously, but the bitterness and anger she'd expected were not there at all. Alison looked almost exactly the same, except that in the brief moment Catherine had talked to her she hadn't seen Alison's fearlessness, that passion for life that had propelled Catherine through most of her teens, connecting her to the world outside of her parents' house. Seeing Alison as she was now, the real woman and not some imagined paragon leading a perfect stolen life, Catherine found herself wondering what had changed her friend so much over the years. She found herself wondering how Alison was.

Being confronted with Marc was altogether different. Jimmy had asked her how seeing Marc again had made her feel, and she hadn't exactly lied but had edited the truth, because she couldn't tell anyone, especially not Jimmy, how it made her feel to look into his eyes again.

Stretching her arms out over her head, Catherine sat up and looked at the clock; it was almost two. She had to get up and go get the girls soon.

The knock at the front door made her jump, sitting forward on the sofa. She looked at the door and for a few long seconds considered the possibility of not opening it because she knew who was standing on the other side of it.

She knew that she was wearing her work clothes, which were crumpled now, that her hair was messed up from lying on the sofa, and that the traces of makeup she'd put on that morning would have run around her eyes. And she knew the very last person in the whole world she wanted to see was on the other side of that door. But Catherine didn't seem to have any control over her own limbs; just as she was thinking about sneaking out of the back door and taking refuge in Kirsty's shed, her body had gotten up and opened the door.

And there he was. There was Marc.

And with the cooling insulation of her husband gone, she could feel how he burned with heat, as if he had somehow captured all the sunshine from that distant summer in his eyes.

"Morning," Marc said. "I looked you up in the phone book. I was going to phone but the address was there and I just got this feeling I should call round, see for myself how you were after the party. Maybe talk a bit about . . . everything."

He paused. "So how are you?" he asked.

Catherine felt her rebellious body stepping aside to allow him in even though her head was shouting at her to slam the door in his face. "Fine. Just tired."

She held her breath as Marc walked into her tiny living room. She suddenly saw her home through new eyes, through his eyes. The tiny room, the shabby sofa, the grubby carpet, and breakfast things still piled on the dining table. She wondered if it would have been possible for their lives to take more divergent paths than they had.

Marc turned and looked at her where she was still standing by the front door. He was wearing a camel coat over a suit and he held a pair of black leather gloves in his hand. She could still feel the heat of him even from three or four feet away.

"Drink?" she asked him, unable to think of anything else to say.

"Coffee?" Marc suggested.

Five minutes later, she sat down at the table and took a sip of coffee. While she was making the coffee she'd been trying to adjust to this new reality. Marc James, *the* Marc James, the man who had stalked her dreams for so long, was sitting at her table in her house. He'd even helped clear away the breakfast dishes. It was as if by allowing herself to think about him again, to dream about him, she had conjured him up out of thin air, like letting a genie loose from its lamp.

"This is all a bit odd, isn't it?" Marc said finally.

"Yes," Catherine agreed. "I sort of can't believe that you are here."

"Do you hate me?" Marc asked, glancing briefly sideways at her.

"I don't think I ever hated you," Catherine said. "But even if I did, all of that business was a long time ago. I got married, had children, moved on."

Catherine wasn't sure if she was lying or not, but it seemed like a sensible thing to say. It was a way to put distance between herself and him, even across this three-foot-wide table.

He looked at her, his sudden smile causing her to grip the sides of her chair beneath the table.

"You haven't changed," he said.

"I have," Catherine replied. "And so have you."

Marc laughed once and nodded. "I think about the kid I was back then, and wonder if I am the same person. I mean I can't understand how I turned from him into me. It doesn't seem possible."

"Alison made it possible, I suppose," Catherine said carefully. "It looks as if you two were meant to be together after all."

"I didn't want to let her down," Marc said. "But I have. I never learned to resist that urge to spoil things that were good for me. You were good for me, you made me feel human. I couldn't wait to ruin that."

Catherine didn't say anything for a long time.

"We were all young," she said. "How many twenty-year-old men would turn down the chance to have two teenage girls on the go? I was naive and so were you. I was passive. Alison fought for you, she won you. She deserved you."

"Some would say she got what she deserved," Marc said. "You do realize I only left with her because I didn't love her. It seemed easier to be with a girl I didn't love than to be with one I did."

Catherine looked out the back window down her long, thin garden where the grass was overgrown and the vegetable patch was covered in polyethylene sheeting to protect the seedlings from the frost.

She had absolutely no idea where the next few seconds and minutes would take her, and knowing that made her feel dizzy, as if she were balancing on a knife's edge.

"Why are you here, Marc?" Catherine asked him. "Not why are you back in Farmington, although I could ask you that too. I mean why are you here now, sitting at my table drinking instant coffee?"

"For the same reason I'm back in Farmington," Marc said, sitting very still. "To find you." Catherine heard the sound of her own indrawn breath, and she knew that Marc must have heard it too.

"I don't suppose I expected to actually find you standing in my hallway at a party. I honestly thought you'd be long gone. But I wanted to find the *memory* of you. I wanted to get close to that person I was for those weeks I was with you. I've never been like him since then, Catherine. That person was the best I've ever been. Almost since the day Alison and I left I keep letting people down. I keep hurting them even when I don't want to. It just seems to happen around me. I thought in this place I might find you and I might find the man I was when I was with you. I thought that you, the memory of you at least, might heal me and make me whole." Marc smiled and looked at his hands. "And then there you were, the living, breathing you, standing right in front of me in the hallway, and now I don't know what to do."

"There is nothing to do, is there?" Catherine said.

"Isn't there?" he said, looking up at her. "Look, on Sunday morning Alison told me she didn't love me anymore. It's been like a set of scales. Over the years the more I loved her the more I hurt her and the less she loved me. I love her, Catherine, but I've used up all the love she had for me."

"And now you want me to make things better?" Catherine asked him, frowning.

"No, I just want you," Marc said. "I want you."

Catherine made herself look at him and they held each other's gaze for what felt like an age. He just walked back into her life after fifteen years and told her that he wanted her back even though he was still in love with his wife, who was leaving him. She should be furious. She should be incandescent with rage, but all she could feel was the pull in her guts when he told her he wanted her.

She needed to put distance between herself and him right now.

"I have to pick up my daughters," Catherine said, scuffing the chair on the carpet as she stood up.

Marc stood up too.

"Are you happy?" he asked her, reaching out and catching her hand. His fingers felt hot on hers.

"Yes, thank you," Catherine said, unable to muster the energy required to withdraw her hand from his.

Marc drew her hand closer to him, and her treacherous body followed it.

"Wouldn't you like to know," he said, his voice diminishing to a whisper, "if our kiss would still feel the same?"

He drew her body flush into his and brought his lips to within a whisper of hers.

"I . . ." Catherine had no idea what she was about to say, and just as her lips formed a nameless word the back door opened.

She sprung away from Marc as if he had just given her an electric shock.

Jimmy stood in the kitchen doorway and looked from Catherine to Marc. Catherine discovered that she could not look at her husband.

"I came back," Jimmy said flatly.

Marc turned and smiled at Jimmy, holding out his hand. "We

meet again!" he said pleasantly. At last Catherine made herself look up at Jimmy. His jaw was set, his hazel eyes clouded and dark.

"What are you doing here?" he asked Marc, advancing two or three steps toward him. "What do you think you're doing?"

Catherine rubbed her hands over her face, trying to wake herself from the stupor she'd been lulled into. As Marc dropped his hand back to his side, she saw the muscles in his jaw tighten.

"He just popped in to say hello, to catch up," she said, as guilty as Marc was of acting as if nothing had happened but desperate to defuse the tension in the room. "Anyway, why aren't you in London?"

Jimmy did not take his eyes off Marc, the fury he felt illustrated quite clearly in the tense way his shoulders were pulled back. "I got to Euston and I changed my mind. I came by to tell you I'd pick the girls up if you like. Now that I'm here I think we should pick our children up together."

Catherine could not hide her surprise at the violence in Jimmy's voice. Was he concerned about her welfare or had he decided to get territorial about two years too late?

Marc hadn't budged, if anything he'd squared up to her taller, leaner husband.

"I don't suppose it's any of your business who Catherine spends her time with," he said.

Before Catherine knew it Jimmy lunged at Marc, pushing him abruptly against the wall.

"You leave her alone, do you understand me?" Jimmy said to Marc, his pointed finger millimeters from the tip of Marc's nose. "She didn't have anyone the first time you got to her, but now she has me and I won't let you hurt her again. I don't want you anywhere near her."

"Jimmy!" Catherine was astonished, pulling him away from Marc. "Jimmy, just leave it, I know what I'm doing!"

"Do you?" Jimmy looked sharply at her as Marc straightened his tie.

Catherine shook her head at him, silently admonishing him. "Well," she said, looking at Marc. "You'd better go."

"Okay." Marc was careful to appear completely unflustered, and Catherine could sense it was designed to enrage Jimmy all the more. "It was so good to see you again, Catherine. I'll look forward to picking up where we left off."

"Me too," she replied automatically, providing him with enough ammunition for a triumphant smile as he headed out the front door.

As Catherine watched him leave, suddenly all of the air rushed back into the room and she could breathe again. She sat down on the dining chair with a thud.

"What was going on?" Jimmy demanded.

"How can you ask me that? What was going on with you, you idiot!"

"You were about to kiss him!" Jimmy shouted, catching his voice as it rose and struggling to contain it. "You were going to *kiss* him, Cat!"

"Jimmy, back off," Catherine told him. "It was nothing . . . nothing happened."

Jimmy looked at her as if he had never met her before in his life.

"So suddenly everything he did to you is forgotten?" Jimmy asked her. "And you, you just felt like giving it away?"

"Jimmy!" Catherine gasped. "I didn't plan it, I don't know if I wanted it. Maybe it would have been one way to finish things . . . or start something."

She had no idea why she was being so antagonistic. It was just that Marc had left and she felt furious, and Jimmy was the only one here to turn on.

"He's a married man!" Jimmy blurted out.

"Yes, I know that, Jimmy, but it's funny I thought you'd be the last one to judge what a married man should or should not do."

"He messed you up, Cat. For years and years he blighted you, blighted our marriage, even the birth of our children. He made it almost impossible for me to keep loving you and impossible for you to love me. *Him*, that . . . shit of a man did that. And you let him breeze back in here and what? You were about to climb back into bed with him?"

"Why do I have to tell you *anything*?" Catherine shouted at him, her fury giving her strength. "And who says Marc was the reason I didn't love you? Maybe I just couldn't love *you*. And anyway, none of this has got anything to do with you."

The instant the words were out of her mouth Catherine regretted them, but they were out there now and she knew they had hit Jimmy hard.

"This has got everything to do with me," Jimmy told her darkly, his anger making him tremble. "I'm the one who sat up all night listening to you talk about how confused you were. I'm the father of your kids, I'm the man who . . . the man who really cares about what happens to you despite what you may think about me. I'm the one who is always here for you." Jimmy stood firm. "Whether you like it or not this has got everything to do with me. So you tell me right now—were you going to kiss him back?"

Catherine flung her hands in the air as she slammed past Jimmy and marched to the front door.

"Leave me alone, Jimmy. Go back to London and make some money for a change."

"Were you going to *kiss* him?" Jimmy demanded once more.

"Why do you care?" Catherine asked. Then she turned and looked at him. "Really, what difference does it make to you?"

"I need to know, Catherine." His voice caught, making Catherine pause and take a breath.

"I'm fine," Catherine replied. "Nothing happened and everything's fine."

"Would you have kissed him?" Jimmy said, frustration and fury saturating every word.

Catherine took her hand off the door latch.

"Yes." She threw the word at him with full force. "Yes, I think I would have kissed him. I wanted to kiss him."

Jimmy seemed to deflate in front of Catherine's eyes, the tension draining out of his muscles. "Right. You would have kissed him."

"Look." Catherine paused. "I get that you are worried about me and I appreciate that, but I don't need you to march in here and start laying down the law. I've got to handle this my way and you should have stayed in London. This mess shouldn't stop you from getting on with your life."

"But you are my life," Jimmy said almost to himself. He looked up and caught Catherine's expression. "I mean you and the girls. Like it or not, you are a big part of my life. Whether we are together or not I have to make sure you are okay. You'd do the same for me, right?"

Catherine thought for a moment and then, dropping her bag, she walked across the small room, put her arms around him, and held him. His heart was still racing.

"Of course I'd do the same for you," she said. "I needed you over the weekend and you were there for me, but now—I've got to sort this out my own way, Jimmy. I've got to work out how to handle this. I've never really been on my own, never really had to stand on my own two feet. I always had Alison or my mother telling me what to do and then there was you, rescuing me, taking me away from my parents. But I can't let you rescue me this time—it's not your place to even try anymore. I have to sort this out for myself, you understand that, right?"

"I understand that," Jimmy said, briefly hugging her back before stepping away from her.

"Coming to get the girls, then?" Catherine asked.

Jimmy shook his head mutely.

"I need some air," he said. "Unpack my rucksack, that sort of stuff."

"See you later, then?" Catherine offered.

"Maybe," Jimmy said. "I don't know."

"Okay." Catherine shut the front door behind her, leaving Jimmy standing alone in what had once been his living room.

He knew he couldn't rescue Catherine this time. He'd understood that long before he'd seen her on the brink of kissing the man who had once ripped her life to shreds.

Seventeen

D o you ever think," Kirsty asked Catherine later that night as they sat in her back garden sipping tea, "that there is anything out there? You know, like a higher force or something? A God sort of thing?"

Catherine looked up at the dark and crisp February night sky. The evening was chilly but the sky was perfectly clear; the stars glittered with a particular brightness and a kind of intensity that made Catherine catch her breath, thinking that just a tiny bubble of atmosphere was keeping her here on the earth instead of wheeling out there lost in the magnitude of space. Only a couple of miles away from where she was sitting now, a huge sucking, gaping, gulping universe waited to swallow her up, and after the events of the last few days, there was a little part of her that couldn't quite extinguish the desire to find a pin big enough to burst the bubble so she could go sailing out among the stars.

"No," she said to Kirsty, her voice perfectly level despite the set of coincidences and consequences that had suddenly beset her, making her feel exactly like a rather panicky chess piece on some cosmic board. "Not really."

"I do," Kirsty said. "I think there has to be. Because otherwise why are we here?"

"Because this planet happened to be the right distance from the sun to allow the production of water and facilitate life. Probably a billion- or even a trillion-in-one occurrence. Our existence is completely random," Catherine told her, because that was what she wanted to believe. It was easier to accept the tangled and chaotic mess her life had snowballed into if it was an accident. If some sentient being had thrust all this upon her, then she was not only confused, she was extremely pissed off.

"Now *that's* madness, of course that is madness—you don't get all of this . . . you and me, your children and love and heartbreak and happiness and music and *orgasms* from a freak random occurrence. You just don't. There's something else out there."

Catherine sipped her tea, tasting the sweetness of the sugar on the back of her tongue.

"There probably are aliens," Catherine conceded. "Given the vastness of the universe it would be insane to think that we lived on the only planet capable of sustaining life in some form. Probably on some planet far away from here male aliens are messing up the lives of female aliens with a wanton disregard for manners or decency."

"You say you didn't actually kiss him," Kirsty said thoughtfully. Catherine had filled her in on Marc's unscheduled visit that afternoon about five minutes after she had climbed over the back fence for a cup of tea, and unusually Kirsty had not said a word about it until now. For the first time in their friendship, Catherine realized uneasily, she was waiting to find out what Kirsty was thinking.

"No, I didn't actually kiss him," she said. "But if Jimmy hadn't turned up when he did, I think I would have kissed him. And what then? What would have happened then?"

"Well, based on my experience, probably foreplay followed by sex, possibly on the living room floor," Kirsty remarked flatly, before adding a touch wistfully, "Do you know one of the saddest things about being over thirty is that you never get to just kiss anymore. A kiss is always followed by sex these days. Kiss, sex, kiss, sex, kiss, sex. What ever happened to just making out?"

"But what if I had slept with him?" Catherine went on. "What would it have proved? Would it have changed anything except to make a really complicated situation worse? What was I trying to do—steal him back, get revenge? Why would I kiss him?"

"Because you wanted to get your rocks off?" Kirsty suggested, tipping her head to one side. "Not quite as emotionally delving as your reasons why, but the most likely one. It's like you're a bottle of milk of magnesia . . ."

"A *what*?" Catherine scowled at her friend.

"And you've been sitting on the shelf in the back of the bathroom cabinet since 1994, well past your sell-by date, just going a bit stagnant and moldy, and then *suddenly* along comes this great big fuck-off complicated situation and it shakes you right up. Kick-starts your natural womanly urges. You got turned on by seeing Marc again, he is quite hot in a sort of paunchy, suited way, so I don't totally blame you. You experienced a physical reaction, not some deep psychological one. Seriously, Catherine—think about it, it's not rocket science. This whole situation is actually extremely interesting, beats *Desperate Housewives* any day of the week . . ."

"Oh, I'm so glad that you find my messed-up life interesting," Catherine said. "At last I'm the interesting one!"

"I wouldn't go quite that far," Kirsty said with a little smile. She took a sip of her tea. "What is interesting, though, is that you, 'Catherine the Nun,' as I like to call you sometimes . . ."

"I've never heard you call me that," Catherine said.

"Not to your face, obviously. Anyway, *you*, the world's most cautious, uptight, and sexually stunted woman, nearly threw caution and your pants to the wind over this particular man. You weren't thinking about consequences and implications. You weren't thinking at all. Your lady parts were doing all the thinking, and that's interesting because that is not you. Or maybe it is you, but a you you never knew you were until now."

Catherine set down her tea and looked utterly appalled.

"Promise me something," she said.

"Anything," Kirsty offered.

"Never give up pilates to become a psychiatrist. The suicide rates would soar."

"God, you're ungrateful," Kirsty said mildly, gazing up at the sky, her feet up on the bench seat, her knees tucked beneath her chin. "I believe in fate, I believe things happen for a reason. Like a sort of cosmic symphony, maybe it's the stars or God or . . . aliens. The two people who were a big part of making you into who you are today are back here for a reason. You can't just go along pretending that nothing's changed and go around all day going 'La-de-da-de-da I nearly snogged the face off my married ex after about five minutes but everything is still normal and fine'! You can't. You have to face up to it all. Face up to fancying him and wanting to shag him, if that's what it takes."

"But if anything happened between me and Marc it would be a terrible, terrible mistake," Catherine moaned, leaning forward and dropping her forehead to her knees, so that the tips of her hair grazed the patio stones.

"Yes, I *know*," Kirsty said with some emphasis. "You are talking to the queen of terrible, terrible mistakes here. But you have to crack a few eggs to make an omelette, right? Whole and grown-up people are made up of all the terrible, terrible mistakes they've made and learned from. If you are too afraid to take chances, if you're too cautious, then you're bound to get stuck in one great big fat boring-as-a-motherfucking-bastard rut."

Catherine turned her head sideways and one eye glinted in the reflected light from the kitchen window as she peered at Kirsty.

"I must be going mad because you are starting to sound quite sane," she said, straightening her back and even sitting up. "Even slightly wise."

"I have hidden depths," Kirsty told her. "That's why I'm so popular with men. Look, I've got an idea," Kirsty said. "The girls are off with Jimmy this weekend, right?"

"Yes," Catherine said. "He's taking them to his mother's on the boat."

"Come over to my house, we'll have girly night in. I'll cook, we'll drink a load of wine, we'll have a proper girls' night in and it will be lovely, you can stay over."

"Are you sure?" Catherine asked her. "I mean I know you hate cooking and cleaning your house so that it's fit for visitors."

"For you, my love, I'll get in takeaway and push things under the sofa."

"It's a lovely idea, but we could always do it here if you like," Catherine offered.

"No." Kirsty was quite firm. "You'd only be looking at your table and thinking about Marc bending you backward over it all the time, no, my place it is. I've decided."

"That's the trouble, the thought of Marc and me in the living room. That's what I can't get out of my head." Catherine looked at Kirsty. "Maybe I should just have sex with him, behind Alison's back, behind Jimmy's back, no matter what the consequences are."

Kirsty sighed and crossed her arms.

"Ordinarily I'd agree, but I think that if you do it you might spontaneously combust from the shock. You need to be careful, just follow your instincts for a bit. Find out why you felt the way you did around Marc, explore the way you're reacting to him and his wife being back in your life. Perhaps," she added carefully, "you should see Alison too, see how that goes."

"I can't," Catherine said. "I think I would have, but then I almost got off with her husband. Funny, I can stand her stealing him away from me much better than I can stand the reverse, it seems. And anyway, while I'm off following my instincts and exploring my feelings, what about Jimmy?" Catherine paused, feeling some nameless form of anxiety well in her chest when she thought of the expression on Jimmy's face when he'd seen her and Marc together. Since that moment, whenever she thought about her husband, she felt jangled and disconnected and she couldn't quite work out why, except that it was something more than the embarrassment and discomfort she had felt at being found in such an unorthodox situation.

"You should have seen him. He was so angry when he came back."

"Why do you care?" Kirsty asked her flatly. "He has all the half-wit women in the county after him and you still make him Sunday dinner. You nearly snog the only other man you've slept with in your entire life and he goes nuclear. What a hypocrite. Ignore it, Catherine, he's just getting all male and territorial when he had no business to be and he should know better. Don't feel bad about him, you're not together anymore, remember?"

Catherine nodded. "I know, but he's such a big part of my life and the girls and I don't want to fall out with him."

"You don't fall out with him over his girlfriends, do you?" Kirsty reminded her. "Why should you fall out with him over what you do?"

Catherine didn't give an answer because she couldn't think of one.

"If I ask you a full and frank question, will you give me a full and frank answer?" Kirsty said, leaning a little closer and peering at Catherine in the darkness.

"I suppose," Catherine replied cautiously.

Kirsty smirked. "That's not exactly the affirmative I was hoping for, but nevertheless it will have to do." She sat up straight. "Are you, Catherine Elizabeth Ashley, still in love with your sham of an ex-husband, Jimmy Ashley?"

"No!" Catherine said immediately. "No, don't be stupid! Of course I am not still in love with him. If I was still in love with him, would I have been tempted to kiss Marc? No, I wouldn't. It was hard for me to get everything under control after he did what he did, but I have done that. And we've got a relationship now that I care about. But I don't love him. Of course I don't love him."

"Well, then," Kirsty said. "All I'm saying is that at some point you will have to make a choice, between what you want for you and being Jimmy's friend. And if when it comes to it you put Jimmy's friendship first, then maybe you'll want to rethink your answer."

"What does this mean?" Catherine asked the sky, standing up suddenly. "If I still have one type of feelings for Jimmy and another altogether for Marc—what does that mean?"

The two women were silent for a moment, as if both of them hoped for a reply, but the night was silent, except for the distant sound of traffic.

"I don't know what to do," Catherine groaned. "I don't know how to be, or how to feel about anything!"

Kirsty stood up and put an arm around her friend.

"This is actually all good," she said.

"How is this good?" Catherine said, her voice small.

"Because you are awake and *feeling*, Catherine," Kirsty told her. "Your heart is racing, your blood is pumping, you're scared and confused, and you have no idea what is going to happen to you. You're alive, my friend, you're alive!"

Catherine paused and looked up at the star-spangled sky.

"I'm not sure I like it," she said.

Eighteen

Four o'clock on Friday afternoon: this was family time, the afternoon when Marc was supposed to come home early and they were all supposed to eat dinner together.

Gemma and Amy were sitting at the table already in anticipation of the roast chicken Mummy was cooking, even though it was a good half hour away from being ready. Rosie was sitting at Amy's feet, staring fixedly at the chocolate cheesecake that Alison was defrosting, proof positive in Alison's opinion that telekinesis could not be possible, because if it were, that dog would have moved the cheesecake from the counter and into her mouth by the power of her mind alone.

The men of the household were nowhere to be seen and Alison wasn't surprised. Dominic made it his business to be late for everything, and if Marc arrived at all before the entire family had gone to bed, Alison would be stunned. In a way she was relieved that he wouldn't turn up, just as she had been relieved that he'd been avoiding her all week, because she'd had no idea that he'd react to her revelation in the way that he had. And so far she had no idea how to deal with it. She had barely seen her husband since they talked after the party. For some reason she had expected for things to go on as usual after she told him that she didn't love him. That he'd simply accept the information and their lives would go on without anything else really changing. But then, of course, that would be how *she* would have reacted if he'd told her the same thing, or at least that was how she always reacted when he told her about an affair.

Alison would scream and cry, she'd throw things and swear, but by the next morning she'd be up in the kitchen making coffee, getting the kids breakfast, carrying on as before. Over the years she had become an expert at absorbing the pain and carrying it within her, accepting it as her lot, unable to find the courage or direction to fight against it.

Marc hadn't screamed or shouted or gotten angry with her; instead he'd vanished. Perhaps the reality of seeing her, knowing how she felt about him, was too hard for him to bear. There was a part of Alison that was glad about that. Finally she had found a way to hurt him back. But another, greater part of her was afraid. She simply didn't know what to do next.

This has to be it, she thought to herself as she watched her daughters sitting at the table, laughing together. This has to be the rock bottom that people are so fond of talking about. Surely things had to take an upward turn from here. Alison hoped Saturday night would change everything in one way or another. After Saturday she'd know what to do. Because tomorrow night she and Cathy were meeting at Kirsty's for dinner. The very fact that Cathy had agreed to go gave Alison hope that something good would come out of their move to Farmington, because now more than ever she longed to see her friend again. To hug her and laugh with her and ask her, "What should I do?"

"Mummy, it's nearly quarter past four, where is everyone?" Gemma asked primly. "Where is Daddy?"

"Well, the thing is, Daddy . . ." Alison was just about to conjure up some explanation when she heard the front door close.

"Here's Dom anyway," she said brightly, winking at the girls and calling out, "Count yourself lucky that you've showed up more or less on time, young man. Ten more minutes and your dinner would have been in the . . . dog. Oh, hello darling."

Alison masked her surprise with a smile for Marc as he walked into the kitchen and kissed her lightly on the cheek. He'd shaved that morning, and his skin was cool, soft, and smooth against the heat of hers.

They held each other's gaze for a moment but Marc did not return her smile.

"Daddy!" Amy exclaimed, running to hug him around his legs, accompanied by an equally delighted puppy. "I had the best day today, Daddy. We saw an actual play at the school, actual real people came and did a play and it wasn't on the TV or anything, and I sat next to Leila Ashley, who is my new friend. She let me eat her carrots at snack, which her mummy grew in the *ground*."

"Did she, darling?" Marc said, ruffling her hair and sitting her on his knee as the two of them joined Gemma at the table. "Well, it's great that you two are friends with the Ashley sisters. It's sort of like history repeating itself, right, Al?"

"I suppose so," Alison said uneasily, as she peered into the oven where the chicken was roasting. After testing one leg, she took it out of the oven and covered it with foil. Rosie now fixed her unwavering attention on the chicken, making hopeful little whining noises in her throat as she stared at it.

Marc had come to eat dinner at "family time" to make a point, and it was clear what it was.

"What do you mean, Daddy?" Gemma asked Marc as he shifted Amy off of his knee and unbuttoned his shirt collar. "How can the past repeat its self. Is it like Dr. Who?"

"Not like Dr. Who. You know, don't you," Marc said to his daughters, "that once, a long time ago, when Mummy was a little girl she used to live in Farmington?"

"Yes," the girls chorused at once.

"Well, Mummy used to be best friends with Leila and Eloise's mummy, didn't you, darling?"

Her back to her family, Alison felt her shoulders tense as she strained her supermarket-bought carrots, tipping the water into the pan to make gravy. There was an edge to Marc's voice that unnerved her. Perhaps this was it, after a week of lying in wait, now she'd finally find out how he'd deal with the end of her love for him.

"Yes," she said over her shoulder. "A long time ago now, though. Practically a lifetime."

"Does Eloise's mummy know that you are you?" Gemma asked her excitedly. "I bet she'll be so pleased to see you, Mummy! Then all of us can all be friends and we can all go round to teas and things. Won't it be great, Mummy?"

"Well," Alison said. "Maybe, we'll see."

"Pleeeaasssse," Gemma pleaded, which was her stock response to the phrase "We'll see."

"The thing is that Mummy and Eloise and Leila's mummy fell out and they've never made up since."

"Why, Mama?" Leila said. "Didn't you make up?"

"And why did you fall out?" Gemma asked. "Was it over sharing?"

"Sort of," Marc said before Alison could answer. "Your mummy and Eloise's mummy fell out over me." He grinned and waggled his eyebrows, making the girls giggle.

"Don't be silly, Daddy," Amy said. "Mama didn't even know you when she was little."

"Well, Mummy wasn't quite as little as you when she fell out with Eloise's mum," Marc explained. Alison shot him a glance across the kitchen as she stirred the gravy, but he ignored her.

"I'm not little, actually," Gemma interjected primly.

"Or me, I'm not little either," Amy added. "Much."

"Well, Mummy was only a little bit older than Dom is now when she met me and fell madly in love with me, and who can blame her?"

"Because you are handsome," Amy said. "Like the prince in Cinderella."

"Only fatter," Gemma added. "And sometimes you can see the skin on the back of your head through your hair."

"Well, anyway," Marc said. "The trouble was that Eloise's mummy had met me first. And she was already in love with me."

"Ooooooh," Gemma said, wide-eyed. "What happened?"

"I chose your mummy, of course," Marc said. "I gave up everything to choose your mummy and Dom, and you two girls, and I worked very, very hard to make you all as happy and as secure as I could."

"Was Eloise's mummy sad?" Gemma asked, frowning slightly.

"I think she was sad," Marc said. "And a bit cross."

"And are they still not friends even now?" Gemma asked him. "That's a long time not to be friends. I wasn't friends with Emily Shawcross once for two weeks at our old school. That was the longest time I've ever not been friends with someone." She looked concerned as a thought suddenly occurred to her.

"Mummy, this doesn't mean I won't be able to be friends with Ellie, does it?"

"No, of course not." Alison looked crossly at Marc, but he only winked at her. Dominic was not here, the food was getting cold, and Marc was doing his level best to rattle her, for what purpose she could not imagine except to try to exert some power over her. Well, she had some news she knew would shut him up.

"Everything will be fine because I'm going to see Eloise's mum, and hopefully after we've had a good talk about things, we'll make up."

"When?" Marc sat up in his chair. "When are you seeing her?"

"Tomorrow," Alison said. "Amazingly, the one friend I've made since we moved here is her next-door neighbor. She's invited us both to dinner. You don't mind babysitting, do you?"

"And Catherine's fine about that?" Marc asked, his brow furrowed.

"Yes, clearly she is, otherwise Kirsty would have told me by now," Alison replied, smiling at the girls. "So by Sunday morning everything will be straightened out. It will be nice, actually, after all of these years." She looked at Marc. "After all, I knew her before I knew your dad. I miss her."

"You can make up, Mama," Amy suggested.

"And things will go back to how they were before you knew me," Marc said, his face closed.

"I doubt that very much," Alison said, keeping her voice light as she watched him.

"Where's Dom?" Amy said, looking anxiously at the cloud-heavy sky.

"I'm here," Dom said, sauntering in through the back door, causing Rosie to briefly greet him before returning her attention to the chicken. The smell of stale cigarette smoke drifted in with him, along with a girl who was thin as a blade. A curtain of black hair revealed only one kohl-blackened eye and an ear that had been pierced several times. She seemed to be holding Dominic's hand, although Alison couldn't tell conclusively because her sleeve was pulled well past the tips of her fingers, as were his.

"This is Ciara," Dom announced. "I've brought her home for dinner, like you said, Mum."

Alison pressed her lips together, balancing her irritation with a need to get through this dinner unscathed. Yes, she had told Dominic to bring his friends home, but she had foolishly hoped that he might give her some notice. At least a guest would defuse some of the tension, she hoped. Marc was always at his most charming in front of strangers

"Hello, Ciara," Alison said, still coming to terms with the sight of her son possibly holding hands with a girl. "How lovely that Dom's brought you home. Have you told your parents? Would you like me to ring them?"

"I've told them, thanks, Mrs. James," Ciara said, producing a mobile from her pocket and waving it with one fingerless gloved hand. "Thanks very much for having me."

"My pleasure." Alison smiled warmly at the girl, who sounded much nicer than she looked. "Gemma, set another place at the table, please."

"So, Ciara," Marc smiled at the young girl as she sat down next to Dom. "Do you go to Rock Club too?"

"Yes," Ciara said, tossing her hair back and revealing quite a pretty face. "I do vocals mainly, but I'm learning to play the bass too because Mr. Ashley says that versatility is key in the industry. You've got to have a USP."

"Everybody needs a USP," Marc agreed. "Dom loves his guitar, don't you, Dom? Sometimes he actually sleeps with it."

Ciara looked at the table and smiled, raising one finely plucked eyebrow.

"I don't sleep with it," Dominic said, glowering at his father. "Sometimes I fall asleep playing it, because I'm always playing it. It's the only fucking thing to do in this shithole of a town."

Ciara breathed in sharply, this time her eyes wide with awe.

"Dominic." Alison slammed a pan down, making Rosie start, and stared at her son.

Dominic returned her gaze.

"You never, ever use those words in front of your sisters," she said, her voice low, noting how Marc was doing nothing. How Marc always did nothing about his son until a situation reached crisis point. "I treat you like an adult when you behave like one. So don't show off just because you've got a friend here. Don't make me embarrass you."

"Which words were bad words, Mummy?" Amy asked as Alison set two plates of food in front of Gemma and Amy.

"Never you mind," Alison said. "I'm sure Ciara doesn't use that kind of language, do you, Ciara?"

"I don't, actually," Ciara said. "I think the use of swearwords demeans and cheapens a person, it makes us look weak and ineffectual."

Marc laughed out loud, making the girls giggle too.

Dominic sat perfectly still in his chair, his hands on the table, tapping his chipped black nails on the surface.

"So are you two an item, then?" Marc asked Ciara as Alison gave them both a plate of food. Dominic chewed the inside of his cheek furiously.

"We've hooked up a few times," Ciara said quite calmly.

"Young love is so sweet," Marc said, causing Alison to shoot him a warning glance that he deflected with a shrug. "Well, it is at your age. It's nice, uncomplicated."

"We're not in love, right?" Dom said, looking at Ciara, who merely shrugged in agreement. "Look, Mum, I thought I'd bring a friend home for dinner. I thought you'd like that. I didn't think she'd get the third degree. From *him*." He jabbed a nod in the direction of his father.

"I don't mind, actually," Ciara told him. "I'm quite good with parents."

"I mind! It's none of his business," Dom said. He got up and went to the fridge. "Do you want a drink?" he asked Ciara.

"Please," she said. When Dom sat back down he set two bottles of beer in front of him and the girl.

"Cool," Ciara said, picking hers up and taking a swig straight out of the bottle.

"I don't think so." Alison reached over and picked up the bottles. "Look, Ciara, I'm sorry, but we don't let Dom drink alcohol at home. I know he's probably trying to impress you, but I'm not sending you home to your mother with beer on your breath. I don't condone underage drinking."

"That's okay, Mrs. James," Ciara said politely. "Although actually once you're fifteen you can legally drink in the home, if your parents allow it. My parents let me have a glass of wine with Sunday lunch because they feel that if I'm familiar with alcohol I'm less likely to go overboard and binge on it when I'm unsupervised."

"Really," Alison said, sitting back down with a jug of orange juice. "Well, if you'd like to give me your mother's number, I'll ring her and ask her if she minds your having a glass of wine with your meal."

"That's okay Mrs. James," Ciara said. "Juice is fine by me."

Except for the three girls, who fought the tension bravely with chatter, they were silent at the table. Gemma asked Ciara about all of her earrings, and Amy quizzed her on her makeup. Alison was surprisingly grateful for the girl, who fielded her daughters' questions with good grace and didn't seem to mind that the boy who had invited her over was silent and sullen. Perhaps that was what she liked about him. Perhaps to her he seemed mysterious and misunderstood.

She was so deep in thought trying to imagine how her son must appear to teenage girls that she was completely unprepared for what happened next.

"This is a fucking joke," Dominic said under his breath.

It took Alison a second's delay to register what he had said.

"Dom," she warned him. "One more word and you'll go to your room and Ciara will have to go home."

"Oh, come on, Mum," Dominic said, shoving his untouched plate away from him. "Admit it. We're sitting round the table on so-called family night and it means nothing, there's no family here. It's a fucking joke and you know it. This isn't a family, it's a sham."

"Dom! Stop it, stop it! Mummy, make him stop," Amy said, covering her ears, her face crumpling.

"Go to your room, now," Alison told him, her voice shaking.

"No!" Dominic stood up abruptly, leaning across the table so that his hot breath and spittle collided with her face. "I will not go to my fucking room. Admit it, admit that all of this is bollocks and that this whole family is just one big fucking mess that's falling to pieces. I won't move until you tell me that he"—he stabbed a finger at his father—"is a useless, lying, cheating waste of space and we'd all be better off without him!"

"Get out of here!" Suddenly Marc sprung up from the table and hauled Dominic away from it by the collar of his shirt, slamming him back hard against the kitchen wall.

Dominic just laughed in his father's face. "Yeah, that's it, hit me. Show your true colors, Marc, show us what you really are. Just a thug who can't keep his dick in his trousers, that's the real you, isn't it, Dad? Might as well knock your kids around too!"

Before Alison could move she saw Marc grab Dominic with his left hand and draw back his right fist.

"Daddy don't!" Gemma screamed over her sister, who was

wailing uncontrollably. "Don't hit him, don't hit him," Gemma sobbed.

Marc paused, and Alison saw that his arm was trembling.

He released Dominic, taking a step back, staring at the boy as if he had no idea who he was. Shrugging his ripped shirt back onto his shoulders, Dominic pulled himself off the wall and, looking Marc right in eye, spat in his face. Picking up one of the opened beer bottles Alison had left on the counter, he slammed out the back door.

Able to move at last, Alison gathered Amy up onto her lap and put her arms around Gemma. She felt something pawing her foot and realized that Rosie was cowering under the table.

"Never mind, never mind," she whispered to them. "Silly old Dom and Daddy. They didn't mean it . . . never mind . . ."

Ciara looked regretfully at the plate of food that was still steaming in front of her.

"I'll go after him, Mrs. James," she said, standing up. "He's been wound up all week, really angry about something, but he wouldn't say what. I didn't know he was going to do that or I would have tried to stop him." Ciara paused, not quite sure how to exit. "Don't worry, I'll make sure he's okay. And thanks very much for dinner."

She edged quite calmly past Marc, who was still standing facing the wall, his fists clenched.

"I'm going out," Marc said once the girl had gone.

"Marc," Alison said as evenly as she could. "Don't go, wait, please. We need to talk about this."

"Do we?" Marc said. "It's quite clear who you talk to in this family and it isn't me. You didn't have to do that, Alison. You didn't have to turn my own son against me."

"Me turn him against you?" Alison snapped. "You *lie* to him, you *ignore* him, you threaten him, and you think *I* turned him against you? I didn't have to say a word to him. You did that all by yourself."

Marc turned to Alison, who was still shielding her daughters, and she saw the fury in his face. The two of them stared at each other across the tops of their childrens' heads, the unspoken anger crackling in the air.

"I'm going out," Marc repeated, and he left, picking up his wallet and keys on the way.

Alison sat with her two crying girls and she rocked them, all three of them going back and forth until all she could hear was the ticking of the kitchen clock.

When both her husband and her son had come in tonight they had both planned to hurt her. They'd both wanted, for very different reasons, to show her what she was doing to their family.

Marc wanted things back the way they once were and Dom wanted everything to change. Strange, then, given how different they wanted things to be, that they'd both gone about it in exactly the same way.

It had taken Alison a long time to get the girls to sleep, and only when she allowed Amy to climb into bed with Gemma and Rosie did they eventually drift off, after insisting that Alison sit by them until they were asleep.

It was Amy, who had done most of the crying, and her puppy who had surrendered to sleep first. Fighting sleep willfully, Gemma had looked at her mum from the bed.

"Will you and Daddy split up, Mummy?" she asked Alison.

Alison closed her eyes, feeling as if she were crumbling and collapsing from the inside out.

"No," she said because she wanted her eight-year-old to be able to go to sleep without being afraid. "It was just a silly row, that's all, between Daddy and Dom."

"But Daddy and you don't like each other as much as you used to," Gemma said. "You pretend to, but I can tell. You're all . . .far apart."

"Things are just a bit funny at the moment because we've moved to a new house, and we're both a bit tired and grumpy, that's all. You'll see, when things calm down everything will be fine." Alison fought to maintain the soft, calm timbre of her voice.

"Do you promise, Mummy?" Gemma asked. Alison bent over and kissed Gemma on her smooth round cheek.

"I promise you," she said.

And as she walked out of the room, she didn't care what she had to do or give up to keep that promise, she just knew she had to make it true. So what if other people risked failure to be happy? Perhaps happiness wasn't as important as the world kept on insisting that it was. Perhaps it didn't matter if she didn't love Marc the way she used to. Maybe if she stuck with him the feeling would come back. Dominic thought he knew what was best for her but he was just a boy, he had no idea what it really meant to be married, committed to a relationship come what may. Marc had behaved badly in the past, and almost unforgivably tonight, but like he'd said he cared about her, he loved her the very most that he could, and perhaps she'd just have to learn to live with that.

As Alison walked down the stairs in the dark, she told herself again and again that she could make it work. Maybe after tomorrow she and Cathy would be friends again and perhaps in time good friends. If she had Cathy to lean on, she thought she could manage it, she thought she could do anything for her daughters. Anything that would prevent Gemma from knowing that her mother was a liar.

At just past eleven Alison was trying to work out exactly who it was she was waiting up for.

She'd called Dominic several times, but of course his phone wasn't switched on.

At one point she almost phoned Marc, to tell him that Dom was wrong and he was right, that the family was worth staying together for no matter how difficult it would be. But her thumb hovered over the call button and eventually she set the phone down. She had to see his face when she told him that, she had to see the way he looked so she could be sure she was doing the right thing.

She sprung awake when she heard the front door open and close; sitting up, she saw Dominic appear from the hallway.

"Is he here?" he asked her.

"He stormed out too," Alison said. "The two of you are so alike."

"Don't say that," Dom said, but his voice was drained of all aggression.

Alison held a hand out to him and reluctantly he came and sat down next to her.

"Why did you do that?" Alison asked him. "Why do that to your sisters? They were so upset."

"They're going to be upset sooner or later," Dom said. "Divorce is hard on the kids, but if you're up front with them they'll take it better."

"No," Alison said. "No, they won't . . ."

"Honestly, Mum, I'm sorry," Dom said as if he hadn't heard her. "I just lost it tonight. I didn't mean to do it, I didn't even plan it. I just couldn't stand him being at the table with us. Acting as if he cared, acting as if this family meant anything to him. And you're wrong, Gemma and Amy will be able to handle you and Dad breaking up. In fact, probably once it's out in the open they'll be fine, because they'll know where they stand and they won't be worrying so much."

"They already know where they stand," Alison said, bracing herself.

"You talked to them?" Dominic asked.

"Yes." Alison paused and picked up her son's hand. "Dom, I told them that everything was going to be all right between me and your dad. I told them we weren't going to split up. They won't have to deal with anything . . . I'm going to fix things."

"Mum . . ." Dominic shook his head. "Mum, wait, listen . . ."

"No, Dom, I've decided. I'm not leaving your dad. I know things aren't perfect, but, well, your dad and I talked. I've made my feelings really clear, and it's shocked him. It's hurt him and I don't think he really understood before what was at stake, what he risked losing. I think that if I . . . if *we* make an effort now, then we can really make it. I think this time your dad really listened to and understood how I felt. I think he'll change, Dom. I think he'll do his best to keep us all together. It's what he wants and it's what the girls want and so it's what I want too. And I need you to support me. Who knows, perhaps once things have calmed down you'll start to get on better with Dad. "

"You've talked and he's changed," Dominic said, shaking his head as if he hadn't heard half of what Alison said. "When did you talk? Tonight, after I'd gone? Tell me, Mum, when did you talk?"

"Last Sunday after the party," Alison said. "He's been really good since then, I think he's tried to be considerate, until tonight, that is."

"Last Sunday," Dom said. "That's funny because on Monday I saw him with another woman."

"What?" Alison was stunned into silence. "What do you mean? How—you were supposed to be in school."

"We had a free period and it was almost the end of school, so I went down to the canal with some of the other kids," Dominic said.

"You saw your dad in the park with another woman?" Alison laughed, the image was so absurd, it was as if Dominic had somehow glimpsed into the past.

"No, I was walking on the road down the bridge and I saw him at the door of a house. I was going to sneak by because I didn't want him to see me, but then the door opened, and it was that woman. The woman who was at the party, Mum. Tall, with red hair. She let him in and closed the door."

"He was at Cathy's . . ." Alison whispered almost to herself. "I knew he'd go there. I knew he would . . ."

"That's not all," Dom said. Alison looked up at him. "He was in there for a while, so I thought I'd hang around, you know, see if he came out, ask him what he was doing. But he was in there for so long I crept up and looked through the window. They were holding each other. It was pretty obvious what was going to happen next. I didn't want to see that so I legged it. I didn't know how to tell you, Mum. I hoped I wouldn't have to tell you, but—"

"I really thought I'd know if he'd been with Cathy," Alison said bleakly. "I really thought I would."

"I'm sorry," Dom said. "But I'm not lying."

"I know," Alison told him. "I know."

She felt something flare in her chest, a reignited spark of that old passion, the fury and jealousy that had driven her to take Marc from Cathy fifteen years ago. That's what had been between her and Marc at the beginning. And after any love they might have managed to conjure up between them had finally vanished for good, that was all that remained, fury and jealousy.

"So when you thought he was hurt and worried and upset he was already trying to get off with someone else," Dominic said triumphantly. "Don't you see that's why we can't go on like this? You have to end it."

Alison was silent.

"I'm going to bed, before he gets in," Dom said. "Maybe now you can see why I got so angry tonight."

Alison nodded, "I see."

Once her son had gone up she found that she was crying. But not only because Marc had betrayed her again. Because her friend had. And for the first time in sixteen years Alison knew what that felt like.

Nineteen

Catherine lay in bed and listened to her empty house. If it had been her weekend to have the girls they would be downstairs by now, bashing about in the kitchen making themselves cereal, slopping milk onto the floor, and sloshing juice into cups. And then they'd eat, sitting on the carpet in front of the TV because it was the only day of the week their mother would let them get away with it.

But this weekend they were away with Jimmy and the house was quiet—no, it was more than quiet, it was hollow. It echoed with their absence.

Catherine stretched her fingers above her head and her toes toward the bottom of the bed, sat up, and paused not for the first time to reflect on how her absent family had been thrown off balance by everything that had happened. The return of Marc and Alison hadn't thrown just her into turmoil, but the feelings and thoughts of those around her too, including her children, and she couldn't stand that.

It frightened Catherine to death when she thought about the sane and steady life that she had worked so hard to sure up over the last couple of years being threatened, and she knew she had to do whatever she could to try to protect the makeshift harmony that she had created for her daughters. But, just as she was resolved to do just that at any cost, there'd appear a stealth image of Marc and the remembrance of the heat of his touch; her heart would beat a little faster and she'd feel the blood pumping in her veins, and for a few terrifying seconds she'd feel the impulse to throw everything away just to feel like that again, damn the consequences. She had felt like that once before and it hadn't ended well.

Catherine got out of bed and pulled the curtain back; it was cold outside, a sharp blue sky promising chilly sunshine. She crossed the heat of her cheeks against the cool glass for a moment until the thought of what might have happened next if Marc had kissed her faded to a bearable level.

It was all very well for Kirsty to tell her to rejoice in being fully alive, but when you weren't used to it, it wasn't that easy. It was like waking up one hundred years into the future; everything seemed louder, faster and a whole lot more frightening—a world full of terrifying possibilities.

Despite what had happened on Monday, Jimmy had still been around for most of the week. He had still picked up the girls and taken them to school every other day, and on Tuesday he'd walked with Catherine to work because he knew she was dreading it even if she didn't say so. He'd had dinner with them on Wednesday night and on Thursday had come round to replace the rotting floorboard in the bathroom, a job he'd been promising to do for at least three months. He'd been there physically, but he'd seemed emotionally absent.

On Friday afternoon, he came round to pick up the girls' luggage before he collected them from school to take them straight off to his mother's. He stood there in silence holding up the rucksack while Catherine folded in changes of clothes for the girls and then carefully stowed favorite toys, books, blankets, and pillows.

They hadn't talked again about what Jimmy had seen on Monday, but Catherine felt that she should be talking about something, because it just wasn't like the two of them to be silent and polite, so she asked him another question.

"Are you sorry you missed the audition for session work?" she said. "I feel so bad that you missed it because of me. Maybe if you called them now it wouldn't be too late." Jimmy shook his head, bending to scoop one of Leila's soft toys from the floor where Catherine had dropped it. He picked it up and squeezed it tenderly before dropping it into the bag.

"No," he said. "I was of two minds about it anyway, and besides, I'm needed here right now."

By his usual standards he was being singularly uncommunicative, and although Catherine could understand that walking in on her and Marc had made him angry, territorial even, unusually macho, she couldn't work out why he'd seemed so sad. Catherine hated to see him sad.

"I just don't like to think about you missing out because of me," she said. "Because of my stupid mess. I can manage without you, if you want to go."

"I know," Jimmy said with a shrug, staring at the toes of his cowboy boots. "Session work is for losers anyway. I've got the band to think about. Right now the band needs me, we're at a crucial writing stage. Plus we've got that wedding at the Holiday Inn week after next."

"Jimmy?" Catherine said uncertainly, afraid that his sadness was a symptom of regret. "Do you ever wish you'd never met me, that we'd never gotten together and you'd never become a dad so young? Because then you wouldn't feel obliged to hang around me now and make sure I don't make a total idiot of myself?"

Jimmy looked at her for a long time.

"I felt like that once, on one night for about half an hour, and that was enough to end our marriage." He shrugged and, as Catherine put in the last toy, bent to strap up the rucksack. "But I've never felt that way for one moment before or since. Why do you ask? Is it because you think if you didn't have me or the children in your life *you'd* be free now? Free to run off with arse-face?"

Catherine knew her laugh at the insult was probably ill advised, but it escaped before she could repress it. Jimmy glowered at her.

"I'm sorry," she said, composing herself. "It's just—look, I know you think I'm an idiot and possibly some kind of slut for getting as close to him as I did after knowing him again for about five seconds, but you know me, Jim. You know that in the last twelve years you're the only person I've . . . I'm not the kind of woman who jumps into bed with people for the sake of it. I got swept away in the moment, in the past. I know what's at stake and besides, I've never stolen another woman's husband yet and I'm not going to start now. Please don't be angry with me, please don't be so . . . disappointed in me. For one thing I can't take it, I need you to like me because what you think of me matters to me more than what anyone else thinks, and for another Kirsty says you are being a right royal hypocrite and that I should punch you for being so up your own arse."

This time Jimmy's mouth twitched a little, but only a little.

"Maybe it's just hitting me now," he said. "Maybe that's why I'm so . . . down."

"What is hitting you? Marc and Alison turning up?"

"No, us breaking up. The end of our marriage." Jimmy sighed and looked at the ceiling. "Look, I've got a reputation, girls hang around me a lot of the time. I can't blame them, I am Jimmy

Ashley, after all. But for what it's worth, I want you to know that I haven't been with anyone else in twelve years either. Apart from Donna Clarke in the ladies' loos of the Goat Pub. At first I let you think I did what I did because I was angry at you for not forgiving me and I wanted to hurt you even more. And then I did it because I thought I actually might meet someone new, and sometimes, recently just because it seems easier to pretend that I'm something I'm not. That version of me is a lot easier to live with, the version that doesn't give a bollock about what he's messed up." Jimmy shrugged. "Look, I know you have every right to see other men and move on, even arse-face if you really want to. I know that, but when I saw you with him then it hit me. We're over. We're really over, and sooner or later everything will change forever because we can't go on like this and live our lives."

Catherine was silent for a moment, listening to the radiators rumbling against the cold and the whoosh of the traffic splattering through the puddles outside of the window, and to her astonishment, as Jimmy's words sunk in, she found she had to fight the well of tears in her eyes and blink them away.

"You'd better get the children," she said, dipping her head to use her own hair as a curtain as she composed herself. "Got all their stuff?"

Jimmy picked up the big and battered old rucksack, the same one he'd had when he left home at the age of nineteen.

"Right here," he said, mustering a smile. "Although why they need this much stuff for a weekend at my mother's I don't know."

"Especially when she'll send them home with a whole new wardrobe of pink anyway," Catherine said, grateful for his smile. "Never could get her head round redheads and hot pink."

The pair stood up and eyed each other cautiously.

"Have a good weekend," Jimmy said, hugging her briefly. "And take care of yourself."

"I will," Catherine promised him. "And you make sure you keep the girls warm and dry. I want them on that rust bucket for the least amount of time possible. Give my love to your mother."

"Seriously?" Jimmy said wryly. "She won't send you any back, you know."

"Well, give her my regards, then," Catherine told him with a smile. "I can be magnanimous."

And then on impulse she threw her arms around him and hugged him until his arms encircled her waist and he was holding her.

"No matter what has to change, you'll always mean the world to me," she told him.

Jimmy peered out from the hatch of his boat on Saturday morning and looked up at the rain; it was slicing down in thick sheets, colliding with the tin roof with a violent clatter.

He looked back at the girls, who were wrapped as one in his duvet, sitting on the bed and cowering from the leaky roof.

"We'll try calling her again in a minute," Jimmy said. His mother had been out when they arrived in Aylesbury on Friday evening. After mooring the boat they had waited for a break in the weather until it became apparent that no break was going to come, and Leila said she thought they'd be drier outside anyway. With no umbrellas, they had run the two hundred yards or so from the towpath to his mother's house and Jimmy had knocked on the door, but no one answered.

After a few moments he'd knocked again, and again, and then he had gone round the back and peered through the French windows. The living room was silent and dark. Sensing his daughters' expectancy, Jimmy knelt down and peered through the letter box; the hallway light was on. But that could mean anything. His mother had always lived by the conviction that burglars would never rob a house with a hallway light on, on the off chance that the entire family plus a guard dog might be convening on the landing.

Shepherding the girls under the meager protection of the porch, he phoned both her home (although Leila pointed out that if she was in to answer it, they wouldn't have been standing outside in the rain) and mobile number several times. Then Eloise noticed a milk bottle with a note sticking out of the top of it.

It was written in his mother's loose handwriting; the ink was faded and had bled into the paper where the rain had reached it. It read, "No milk for two weeks, please."

Jimmy stared at the note and got an uneasy feeling in the pit of his stomach. Mum never missed her chance to see the girls, and in the winter Jimmy always brought them here when it was his weekend. He didn't like them spending the night on his boat. Especially not in this weather. He hated them having to see past the romance and fun of how he lived to the damp, cold reality.

Jimmy recalled the last conversation he'd had with his mum when he'd phoned to give her the dates they'd be visiting in February.

"Now, that third weekend I won't be back from Spain till Saturday morning, okay? So bring them on Saturday at about eleven. It'll be lovely to see their little faces and I'll bring them back some presents."

"Okay," Jimmy had said, or something like that.

"Did you get that?" his mum had persisted. "Bring them Saturday morning? Write it down, James. You know what you're like."

He had forgotten that his mum wasn't going to be back until Saturday morning. He had known, but then he'd caught Marc and Catherine together and suddenly there wasn't space for anything else in his head except for the two of them, together. He'd been so busy trying to picture Catherine with that man that he'd forgotten. He'd let his girls down.

Jimmy looked at his girls huddled on the porch and did his best to hide his frustration from them. At a loss over what to do, he took the girls to McDonald's, where they sat over three happy meals until the early evening crowd thinned out and the late evening groups of angry-looking boys and bored-looking girls began to fill it up. At that point even Jimmy, who was noted for being hip with the kids, thought the girls probably didn't need to hear language quite so Anglo-Saxon. By the time they got back to the boat it was almost ten, and he could see his girls were cold and damp and miserable, even though they were trying their best to look like they were having a good time, especially Eloise, who was determined to prove that nothing her father did could ever be wrong.

Jimmy had made them a hot chocolate and they'd huddled together around the stove singing Meat Loaf songs until finally sleep overtook first Leila and then Eloise. Jimmy had still been kicking himself when he'd drifted off.

The rain hadn't stopped all night. It was just after six when a hint of gray daylight struggled to appear through the sodden gloom and Jimmy woke up. He'd been phoning his mother's mobile on and off ever since, but true to form he knew she wouldn't turn it on until she got back into the house.

"Try again," Eloise whined miserably, nodding at Jimmy's phone. "It must be past eleven now and I want to be warm, Daddy."

"We've had a lovely time," Leila said consolingly. "It's just we can't feel our noses now. It's a bit like when Jesus spent forty days and nights in the desert. Only cold." She sank her chin into the collar of her coat, which she had worn all night, adding, "I love you, Daddy," just before the lower half of her face disappeared completely.

Jimmy bit the inside of his mouth and pressed the redial on his phone.

As his mother answered, he knew at least one thing for certain: he was *never* going to hear the end of this.

"Look at my girls," Pam said as she put another plate of toast in front of the children, who were bathed and changed into the brand-new and largely pink outfits that she had bought them in duty-free. "Pretty as a picture."

Pam was always buying her granddaughters things, pretty things, nice things. The things their mother didn't seem to give two hoots about.

"I've missed you," she said, hugging first one and then the other, and then adjusting the bow in Leila's hair.

"We missed you too, Nanna Pam," Leila said, with feeling. "Especially when we were freezing like ice cubes and penguins."

"Hmph . . ." Pam caught her son's look and bit her tongue. "Well, if your daddy didn't love that leaky old boat so much."

"I'm like a pirate, girls," Jimmy said, mustering himself, now that he had his own plate of toast, not to mention some dry old clothes that his mum still kept in his wardrobe. "I sail the high seas looking for adventure."

"You sail the canal, you mean," Leila said.

"And you don't even sail it cos you haven't got a sail," Eloise added.

Jimmy sipped his tea and said nothing. Sometimes he felt like he was the best father in the history of fathers. Like last night, yes, he'd gotten his daughters cold and wet because of his own stupidity, but when he and the girls had been singing "Bat Out of Hell" and he realized they knew all the words, at that moment he was officially the coolest father in the world. But then the real world came crashing in and he'd realized that a comprehensive knowledge of the Meat Loaf catalog was not what an eight- and five-year-old really needed from their father. They didn't know exactly how much he'd messed up their little lives. And even worse, Eloise was now blaming the whole sorry mess on Catherine.

This wasn't what he had planned when he'd met Catherine twelve years ago. He'd planned to marry her, yes, about twelve minutes after he'd met her. And after half an hour he'd wanted to have children with her, that was right. But not like this. He'd never seen his future panning out like this.

"Well, it's chucking it down out there," Leila said, making everyone laugh. "What are we going to do, Nanna? Not another puzzle of kittens, please—I'm bored of puzzles of kittens."

"How about shopping?" Pam suggested, which always got a roar of approval from the consumerism-starved girls. Their mother wouldn't like it, which was principally why Pam did.

"Ooh, yes, can I get some nail varnish?" Leila asked, her hand clasped to her face in excitement. "I really need some."

"I'd like some new hair ribbons, please, Nanna," Eloise added. "Some of those floaty sparkly ones with the stars and hearts on that the girls who go to ballet class wear."

"Okay, well, you go and wash your hands and brush your hair and we'll set off in a few minutes, okay?" Pam smiled as the girls scrambled up the stairs, climbing over each other in a race to the summit.

"Why don't they go to ballet class?" she asked Jimmy. "Doesn't she approve of ballet?"

"It's expensive, and money's tight," Jimmy said.

Pam spent several silent moments clearly trying to hold back the words that threatened. She failed.

"All night in that . . . that . . . *boat*," she huffed at Jimmy, keeping her voice low so that only he would hear her disapproval. "That's no way for two girls their age to live."

"It was one night," Jimmy sighed.

"It's no way for a man of *your* age to live," Pam added, her voice tight with frustration. "It's a wonder you're not dead of pneumonia."

"It's temporary," Jimmy said. "I sent off a new demo to record and publishing companies last week. It's the best material I've ever written. It'll get picked up, you'll see."

Pam sniffed dismissively. "Two years ago that boat was temporary. It's been two years since you and Catherine separated and you're still stuck living on that leaky old boat, still in the same situation as you were the day you left her. Why don't you divorce her, James? At least then you can split your assets. It's not right. Half that house is yours."

Jimmy looked at his mum and took a painful breath.

"All of that house is Leila's and Eloise's, it's their *home*. It's about the one steady thing they've got. Even if we did get the divorce I wouldn't have them move out, they need stability, Mum. It's not their fault that me and Catherine didn't work out."

"No, well, if you'd listened to me and never married her in the first place . . ."

"Then there would be no Leila or Ellie—is that what you want?" Jimmy asked her. If he had a pound for every time he and Pam had had this identical conversation, then he'd be living in one of those penthouses in the new block they were building across the canal from his boat. But his mum never tired of having it. She never tired of being right.

"You need to get a flat of your own," she told him. "Start afresh, face up to reality. Honestly, James, you've lived your life in limbo since you were seventeen years old. When are you going to grow up? Get a *proper* job, a teaching qualification like we've talked about. They'll take anyone these days. I'd help you. You could live here while you went back to college."

"No, that is not who I am," Jimmy said, gesturing down at himself. "*This* is who I am. I'm a musician, a songwriter—a *guitarist*. *This* is my life. I'm not going to get a qualification or a 'proper job' as you call it. I *love* what I do, Mum, I'm going to keep on doing it until I get my break or I die, whichever comes first, and if either one of those things happens while I'm living on a rotting old boat, then so be it. But what I'm not going to do is give up. You don't give up your passion."

Pam sat back in her chair so that one chin tucked into another.

"Is that why you've never divorced her?" she asked.

"I cheated on *her*, I left *her*," Jimmy said painfully. "I was the one who broke the marriage up, I did it. The reason we haven't got the divorce settled is because of the girls. The girls aren't ready to deal with it yet."

"Are you sure it's the girls who aren't ready?" Pam said, sighing heavily. "I don't know what your father would have said."

Jimmy looked sideways at his mother. "He'd support me," he said quietly. "Because he always told me to follow my dream and not let myself get trapped in a life that didn't belong to me like he . . ." Jimmy trailed off. His dad had died of bowel cancer when Jimmy was seventeen, something that neither he nor his mother had ever quite recovered from. "Dad always told me to give it my best shot, never give up. Don't be a quitter, son, that's what he said."

"Well, he should have said quit while you're ahead, James. Look, if everyone who ever wanted to be a pop star made it, then you wouldn't be able to walk out your front door without bumping into them. Wanting something to happen is not enough to make it happen. You can chase your dreams when you're thirteen or twenty-three, but you're *thirty*-three now. It's time you grew up." Pam leaned forward so the girls wouldn't hear her. "James, you've got two smashing girls. Wouldn't you like to give them what they want, a few ribbons and some nail varnish—a couple of ballet lessons? It's not that much to ask."

"I . . ." Jimmy had been about to launch into his usual defense when suddenly all his strength left him and he reached out across the table to grip his mother's hand. Pam looked up, startled.

"What is it, son?" she asked him.

"I still love her, Mum," he said. "I love her and I'm going to lose her. After everything I did, two years after we split up and I've only just realized it. I thought I could go on pretending that everything was fine between us, but I can't. I'm going to lose her and there's nothing I can do about it now."

Pam watched him for a moment, her lipstick-bright lips pressed into a thin line, and then she covered his wrist with her free hand.

"There are more out there for you, James, a whole world of nice decent women who'll treat you the way you deserve to be treated. Who'll appreciate you like she never has. Look at that lovely Sally Mitchell from my bingo game. She's a lovely girl, steady, does a lovely roast. I could invite her for lunch tomorrow."

"No, Mum," Jim said sadly. "It doesn't matter how nice Sally Mitchell is, or how many other women there are out there who'd be good for me. It's Catherine I love, it's her I want. It will always be her I want."

"You know I don't think she is good enough for you," Pam said, catching hold of Jimmy's hand when he tried to withdraw from her. "But I must say I'm surprised at you, James Ashley."

"What? Why?" Jimmy said.

"You're the boy who spent his entire adult life chasing after one dream and never giving up. You had good A levels. You could have gone to university, could have a good job now doing something in an office with a pension plan. But no, not my Jimmy. My

Jimmy never said 'It's no good I'm never going to make it I think I'll chuck it all in and become an accountant.' You never give up, Jimmy, you never do. And yet here you are telling me you're giving her up without even the ghost of a fight. Now, after all these years of devoting yourself to her and your children, you're rolling over and playing dead while she does as she pleases. That's not my Jimmy."

"What are you saying?" Jimmy asked warily.

"She's the mother of your children, and I suppose a good one judging by how those angels have turned out, despite the clothes she puts them in. And you say you've only just realized now, but I don't think that's true, James. I think the light went out of you when you walked out on her and I've been waiting for it to come back on but it hasn't, so . . . so just think—what would your father say? What did he say when he was encouraging you to learn the guitar?"

Jimmy looked puzzled for a moment and then his face cleared.

"He'd say give it your best shot, never give up, don't be a quitter. If he was here now he'd tell me I've got to fight for her, go back to Farmington and tell her how I feel, tell her how she feels and why we were meant to be together. Why we were never meant to be apart. To tell her she can't make any choices about what to do next until she knows that I still love her and that I always have. That's what he'd tell me." Jimmy sat up a little straighter and squared his shoulders.

"That's what he'd say, wouldn't he, Mum? He'd tell me to give it one more shot to make sure that I knew, absolutely knew that I had done my best."

Pam nodded, pursing her lips. "He talked a lot of rubbish, your father," she said, but she squeezed his hand as she said it.

Twenty

O h my God, look at the face on you," Kirsty said when she opened the door to Alison. She quickly glanced over Alison's shoulder and then dragged her indoors, slamming the door behind her.

"What was that all about?" Alison asked her, smoothing herself down as she slipped off her coat.

"What was what all about?" Kirsty looked perplexed, as if she always greeted her visitors by hurling them into the living room. She looked Alison up and down, admiring her straight, knee-length claret cord skirt, worn with soft light brown leather-heeled boots and topped off with a tightly fitting cream cashmere sweater. "Is that your standard reunion-with-an-estranged-friend outfit? I'm just asking because it doesn't seem to provide the option for a catfight. You'd never get the blood out of that sweater."

"Ha, ha," Alison said mirthlessly. "Don't wind me up, Kirsty. I don't care how much this sweater costs, the way I'm feeling . . ." Alison clenched her fists and actually growled.

"What's up?" Kirsty asked, hurriedly pouring Alison a large glass of white wine.

"When we moved here, back when I still thought we could salvage *something* from the wreckage of our marriage, Marc agreed that Friday afternoons would be family time. The one day of the week when we could guarantee that we would all sit down together and eat dinner as a family. I knew it wouldn't ever happen and it hasn't. Yesterday Dominic turned up and went ballistic, just wound Marc up until he blew his top and they both walked out. The girls were there, they got so upset, Gemma asked me if Marc and I were going to divorce." Alison looked unhappily at Kirsty. "I couldn't bear to see her any more upset, so I said no, and I meant it. I thought, I don't care about anything except making my children happy. You see those old couples, don't you, couples who've been married for about a hundred years and you think, there is no way they have loved each other for all that time, at some point they must have hated each other's guts. But then they come to a point where they can just rub along. And for the girls' sakes, for all our sakes I thought I could do that too, believe it or not."

"Okay," Kirsty said slowly, looking at the door. "Far be it from me to judge your insane reasoning, but what's changed and made you so cross?"

"I found out Marc went round to see Cathy. I knew he would. I knew he wouldn't be able to resist it. But I'd hoped that he had, because if he had, there might still have been a chance for us. After everything he's done to me I was still hoping for one last chance! I'm so stupid!"

"Oh *that*." Kristy rolled her eyes. "That was nothing, it wasn't even a kiss. It was barely a bit of hand holding, it was all very repressed, all very *Brief Encounter*. Besides, Jimmy walked in at the last minute and broke it up."

"You knew?" Alison exclaimed, finishing her drink and pouring herself another one from the bottle that Kirsty had left on the mantelpiece. "And you didn't tell me?"

Kirsty pursed her lips, looking at her watch as she folded her arms.

"Listen, she'll be here in a minute, so let's get this straight. First of all I'm doing you a favor here that you begged me to do even though I've only known you five minutes. And secondly, no, I didn't tell you, but neither have I told her that you wanted to have sex with her husband. So can it with the condemnations, lady, I am not part of your Jacobean tragedy."

"Oh," Alison said, her crossness stalling and stuttering until it came to a standstill. "Well, okay, then."

"And if Catherine's not kissing Marc is enough to make you doubt your genius master plan to remain locked forever in a sham marriage, then maybe she actually did you a favor."

"Oh, I don't know," Alison said a little sheepishly. "I heard that a lot of women are perfectly happy in sham marriages. They have the money, the status, sex with their personal trainers on tap."

"Don't talk to me about sex with personal trainers," Kirsty said crossly. "Now look, let's get this evening back on track and concentrate on what it's really about. Getting you and Catherine talking again."

"Okay," Alison said, glancing at the door nervously.

"Good, well I'm nothing if not a good hostess. So help me microwave these curries."

"I must admit," Alison said as she vigorously stabbed the film of one of the dishes. "I was surprised that she agreed to meet me quite so easily. What on earth did you say to her to get her to agree just like that?"

"Nothing," Kirsty said, studiously reading the back of a package of microwaveable rice as if it held the secret to eternal life.

"Nothing?" Alison stopped stabbing, her fork hovering in midair.

"Well, obviously she doesn't know you're going to be here!" Kirsty exclaimed impatiently. "She would have never come, then! No, this way is best, like ripping a bandage off a wound quickly. She'll get here, she'll be shocked and angry, possibly violent. And then we'll all have a glass of wine and laugh about it." Kirsty bit her lip. "Hopefully."

Alison put down the fork. "I'm going home," she said blankly, heading for the front door. Kirsty stood in her way.

"No, you're not. You're the wound I've got to rip the bandage off of." There was a sharp rap at the front door. "And besides, here she is now. Don't worry, this is Catherine. As far as I know she's never hit anyone. Not since she decked that tart who slept with her husband."

"Hi!" Catherine chimed as Kirsty opened the front door. She handed Kirsty a bottle of sparkling rosé wine. "Do I ever need a drink. I hate it when the girls aren't around, even if Eloise hates me. All I've done all day is pace around and think about—"

Catherine tried to step past Kirsty and into the living room, but Kirsty blocked her way. Catherine laughed and then frowned.

"What's going on?" she asked Kirsty sternly. "Don't tell me you've gone and ditched me for Sam, have you? Have you got him in there naked on the rug?"

Kirsty stood on her tiptoes as Catherine peered over her head.

"Now look," Kirsty said. "Don't get cross or don't say anything . . . *loud*. Try to remember that I'm your friend and I love you, and believe it or not I listen to you. And so the only reason I've told this tiny little white lie is because I honestly thought that this was a really good idea, the perfect opportunity to banish all the demons and start afresh."

"What have you done?" Catherine asked her, snatching back the bottle of wine on impulse.

Taking a breath, Kirsty stood aside and let Catherine in.

Alison was standing by the fireplace, clutching a glass of wine as if it were a life jacket.

"Hi, Cathy," she said. "Fancy meeting you here."

"I'm going home," Catherine said, turning on her heel, but Kirsty stood with her back against the closed front door.

"Normally it's men I have to prevent from leaving," she joked for Alison's benefit before lowering her voice. "No, you're not leaving. Remember what you said to me? Remember that you said that when you saw her you didn't hate her like you thought you would, that you even missed her a bit. Remember?"

"I know, but I'm not ready for this, and you know I'm not ready and that's why you didn't tell me."

"I know you. I know you'd never be ready. Just like you'll never be ready to divorce Jimmy unless someone makes you. Well, now you have to be ready. Just give her a chance, see how it goes. Wouldn't it be nice to just clear this whole thing up once and for all and forget about it?"

"Look, I'll leave," Alison said, cutting into their whispered conversation.

"Oh for goodness' sake, will everybody stop trying to leave before I start to take offense!" Kirsty stared hard at Catherine, who returned it with a look that said "I'll get you later for this."

"No," Catherine said, backing away from the door and turning to face Alison. "No, don't go. We're here now and Kirsty's microwave curries are famous for miles around."

"Good," Kirsty said efficiently. "Well, dinner will be ready in approximately forty-five seconds, so let me take that bottle and your coat and why don't you two sit down and talk amongst yourselves."

She waited for a moment as Catherine and Alison watched each other warily, then went into the kitchen.

"I didn't know," Alison said. "That you didn't know. I wouldn't have come if I'd realized she'd set us up. I thought you were happy to come. I was really pleased."

"That's Kirsty for you," Catherine said. "Full of idiotic plans."

"It's weird seeing you after all this time," Alison said tentatively. "You look great. I can see why my husband tried to kiss you." Catherine's mouth dropped open and she looked over her shoulder toward the kitchen. "No, no, Kirsty didn't tell me and neither did he. I just found out. I'm not going to get upset about it now. I just thought that as we're here on a new page, we might as well get everything out in the open."

"I'm sorry," Catherine said, with a shrug that hinted she wasn't that sorry.

Alison raised her eyebrows.

"Well, don't be too sorry. The last time I saw your husband I was on the verge of asking him to go to bed with me." She tilted her head, adding a touch sharply, "I didn't . . . that time."

"As if I'd care what you did," Catherine said, surprised by the tension she felt in her chest. "It's got nothing to do with me."

Alison watched her for a second. "If you say so," she replied, unconvinced, adding with a smile, "Do you remember all those years I used to follow him around? He's still a fox."

"I know," Catherine replied defensively, suddenly thinking of Jimmy and the way he'd looked at her when he'd found her with Marc. The intensity in his eyes had caught her off guard. No other man had ever looked at her the way he had. "But we're split up, so . . ."

She trailed off, furious that Alison had managed to unnerve

her so with her half-baked revelation. This was not how it should be going. Catherine glowered at her erstwhile friend.

"So how's it going in here?" Kirsty asked brightly as she came in with plates of steaming and largely orange food, adding proudly, "I chopped that coriander."

"Awkwardly," Catherine said, shooting her friend a look that Kirsty studiously ignored.

"Well, drink some more and that will sort *that* out," Kirsty said, opening another bottle of wine. "Now come on, dinner is served and I haven't slaved over this for, well, minutes just for it to spoil."

There was silence as Kirsty refilled Catherine's wineglass for the third time, watching her neighbor push a bit of irradiated chicken round her plate with a distinct lack of enthusiasm.

As soon as she topped off Alison's glass, Alison emptied it almost immediately.

"It seems to be taking a lot of wine to loosen you two up," Kirsty observed, looking at the empty bottle. "At this rate I'll have to go to the liquor store."

Neither one of her guests replied.

"Okay," Kirsty said. "The way I look at it we can do one of two things here. Either we could treat this as a sort of therapy session. You two could air all of your grievances, talk about the sense of loss, the betrayal. You know, purge yourselves of all the bitterness and recriminations, hurl insults and accusations, make each other cry, and blah, blah, blah, *or* . . ."

"Or what?" Catherine asked.

"Go home?" Alison added hopefully, her eyes meeting Catherine's briefly, as for the first time in fifteen years they had something in common.

"I've told you. Not an option," Kirsty said quite sternly before erupting into a smile once again. "*Or* we can make my house Switzerland. We can pretend we don't know anything about stealing husbands, abandoning friends, inappropriate passes, and all of that sordid business you married types get up to, and just hang out and try to have a laugh. Tonight you are on neutral territory and from now on we shall not talk about anything to do with either of you. Here we shall talk woman to woman, friend to friend, and only of the truly important issues in today's world."

"Which are?" Catherine asked her.

"Me and how I can get Sam to like me, of course!" Kirsty replied. "You two men stealers must have a few tips on *that*. So drink up, we've got a lot of planning to do, and I always find the drunker I am the better my plans get."

Kirsty put her palms on the table and looked around her.

"Speaking of which, where did I put that bottle of tequila?"

"I'm not sure this is a good plan," Catherine said, screwing up her eyes as she sucked a wedge of lemon and then downed another shot of tequila.

"Don't be crazy, it's a genius plan," Alison countered. "How could it possibly go wrong?"

Catherine wagged an unsteady finger at Alison. "You would say that, you're the girl who thought it would be a good idea to smuggle vodka into school in Coke bottles."

"I don't know why you're complaining, I took the fall for that one," Alison said, turning to Kirsty. "Three days' suspension I got, when she was just as drunk as me, except when I'm drunk I get all loud and hilarious and when she's drunk she gets all quiet and sullen so no one could tell she was drunk."

"I didn't even know the vodka was in the Coke . . ." Catherine complained.

Kirsty topped off their shot glasses.

"Okay, let's recap the plan. We go round to Sam's flat and then what . . ."

"That's as far as the plan got," Alison said, downing her shot.

"That's why it's a terrible plan," Catherine said, her eyes watering as she downed her shot. "Going round to a man's flat at past . . . one in the morning to spy on him qualifies as stalking, not wooing. "

"She's right," Kirsty said. "I can't just turn up there and peer in through his windows to look at him. That would be wrong. Also he lives on the second floor, so it would be dangerous too. When we're there I'll tell him I love him and then . . . then he'll know."

"Perfect," Alison said.

"You are insane," Catherine said, leaning forward on her elbows so that her nose was mere millimeters from Kirsty's.

"I told you," Alison said, tipping her chair back at a dangerous angle. "Sullen and morose, every time. She's not a happy drunk."

"I am not sullen," Catherine protested, swinging her head in Alison's direction. "I'm a very funny drunk. And anyway it's better than being a slutty drunk . . ."

"*Anyway*," Kirsty said, slapping her palm down on the table. "Catherine, you should be pleased. You're always telling me I shouldn't try to play games with him, that the whole ignoring him thing wouldn't work. Well, *now* I'm listening to you. *Now* I'm going to talk to him. Woman to woman. Man to man. Man to woman to . . .whatever. I'm following your advice so actually this is *your* plan that you're dissing."

Catherine shook her head and began to stand up. "The pair of you are mentals and I'm not coming," she said, swaying forward and using the table to steady herself. "I want no part of this madness!"

"Which is his flat?" Catherine hissed at the two other women crouched in the somewhat thorny bushes outside the Longsdale House Apartment building.

"It's either that one," Kirsty said, pointing rather vaguely at three or four windows at once, "or that one. Or that one."

"The lights are on in that one," Alison said, pointing at one set of illuminated windows. "Let's try that one."

"Hang on!" Catherine held her palms up in the universal stop sign. "What if that is not his flat?"

"Then we'll try another one, obviously," Alison said.

"That's not a good idea." Catherine frowned at her. "I don't know why, I can't remember just at the moment. But it'll come back to me."

"Yeah, yeah, yeah," Alison said, making a *w* with her fingers. "What*ever*."

Kirsty had gotten up while they were squabbling and was kicking about on the ground; then she bent down rather unsteadily and picked up half a brick she found lurking in the bushes.

"And what are you going to do with that?" Alison asked her. "Brain him?"

"No, I'm going to chuck it at his window, you know—like they do in the films," Kirsty replied, limbering up.

"That will go right through his window, you moron," Catherine said. "If it even is his window. Come on. Let's find some stones, pebbles. If you're going to throw stones at a random window, you might as well do it properly."

"Creep," Alison said under her breath as she joined in the search on her hands and knees to look for pebbles.

"Tart," Catherine replied as she clawed through the dirt.

"Ladder," Kirsty added.

"What?" Catherine and Alison both said at once.

"Ladder, I could really do with a ladder," Kirsty explained.

After a few minutes they had gotten together a handful of small stones for Kirsty to throw at the window that might or might not belong to Sam.

"Right, I'm ready," Kirsty said, taking a deep breath. "This is it, girls. Showtime."

She chucked the meager handful with all her might and they peppered the soil about a foot and a half in front of her.

"Oh. That didn't go so well," Kirsty said, looking confusedly at the ground. The three women stood in silence for a moment, puzzled by the anticlimax.

"I know!" Alison shouted before she remembered that this was a stealth operation. "Sing him a song."

"Oooh, good idea," Catherine said before immediately checking her enthusiasm for the plan. "Better than chucking bricks is what I mean. This whole thing is *mainly* a bad idea, but that particular part of it was a bit less bad than the rest."

"What shall I sing him?" Kirsty asked them.

"Well, what's your song? What number sums up the precious moments that you've spent together?" Alison asked.

Kirsty thought for a moment. "Well, his mobile phone did go off once during sex. Apart from that we haven't got a song, unless you count the combat training megamix workout at the gym. We used to take that class together."

"Well . . . how does it go?" Alison encouraged her.

"Sort of da, da, da *da da*, da da *da da, da! Da! Da!*"

Catherine and Alison joined in with gusto if not exactly any skill, and leaning haphazardly against one another, the three of them sang at the tops of their voices.

Once they'd run out of breath they paused, looking up at the lit window, waiting for a response. None came.

" 'S not working," Kirsty said, her shoulders dropping.

"Double bastard glazing," Alison said. "Keeps out singing, which in my opinion is an unforeseen drawback. No wonder romance is dead in the modern world."

"We need to drink more," Catherine suggested. "If we drank

more we'd have a better plan. I think I'm sobering up. For some reason I seem to have a terrible headache."

"Wait!" Kirsty grabbed both of them and froze to the spot like a meerkat in the desert. The lights in the communal stairwell were coming on one floor at a time. Someone was coming down the stairs.

"Hide!" Catherine hissed, tackling the others into the bush just outside the door.

"I've broken a nail because of you!" Alison groaned miserably, wiping her muddy hand on her sweater. "Bitch."

"I wonder who's going out at this time of night," Catherine said somberly as they waited for the front door to open. "Must be a drug addict. Only a drug addict would be out now."

"Right, wait until whoever it is opens the door and then rush the door," Alison said.

"Okay," Kirsty said. "Why?"

"Because then we'll be inside, of course," Alison said. "I bet the doors inside aren't double-glazed."

The three held their breaths as the last sets of lights switched on.

"Now!" Kirsty yelled, making one poor unsuspecting man jump out of his skin, gripping onto the door for dear life.

"Please don't hurt me, just take my wallet, plea—Kirsty, what the fuck are you doing here and why are you all covered in mud?" Sam eyed Catherine and Alison warily.

"Are you all in some kind of coven?"

"Oh, do you live here?" Kirsty asked him. "What a coincidence. We were just out on the town having a carefree, devil-may-care girls' night out, like happy single women do, when Alison here lost her car keys and so we were looking for them."

"Here?" Sam smiled at her. "She lost her car keys here? What were you doing with your car here and . . . well, anyway,

I'm not being funny but I don't think any of you should be driving."

"I know," Alison said, tottering over to Sam, putting her arm around his neck, and fluttering her lashes. "Which is why it's your civic duty to make us all coffee."

Sam laughed. "I haven't got any milk," he said. "I was just off to the twenty-four-hour gas station to get milk. I couldn't sleep."

"That's okay," Alison said in a husky voice. "We like it strong and dark."

"And bitter," Kirsty added.

"And slutty," Catherine piped up.

Sam rubbed his hand over the top of his head.

"I must be crazy, but you'd better come in before you get arrested."

"Oh God, I love you," Kirsty gushed before catching herself and saying, "I mean thanks ever so. Most kind of you."

"Plus you have a very nice arse," Catherine said as she walked in. It took her the three flights of stairs to believe what had just come out of her mouth.

"Coffee was a bad idea," Alison said to Catherine, peering down at her ruined sweater. "Because now I'm starting to realize I'm in some strange man's flat covered in mud with a jackhammer going off in my head."

Catherine leaned her head against the cool pane of the window she was looking out and sipped her coffee.

"I don't think I've stayed up this late since . . . since Jimmy played this gig at the Marquee in London. It was supposed to be his big break, supporting some American band. We all got excited and stayed out all night, watched the sun come up in Regents Park. Nothing came of it, of course, but I think that was the last time I stayed out this late, before Eloise was born." She paused and pinched her temple. "My eyes hurt. Is it possible for eyeballs to explode?"

She shifted her attention to the kitchen, where Kirsty was helping Sam with the instant coffee.

"Do you think they're talking in there or having sex?" she asked Alison blurrily. "Based on the coffee I'd say having sex."

But to Catherine's surprise Kirsty walked out of the kitchen fully dressed and sat on the couch, nursing a mug of steaming coffee.

"I'm sorry about all this," she said to Sam as he sat down precisely one cushion apart from her. "We drank tequila and then they said we should come over and do stupid stuff." She pointed at Catherine and Alison. "They made me do it."

"We did," Alison said, winking at Catherine. "We're evil."

"It's the coven, you see," Catherine said. "It demands a sacrifice."

"We all just wanted to see you, all of us together," Kirsty attempted to explain. "To, you know, see how you are. How's Sam? we wondered, and the next thing we knew we were here. That's tequila for you, because you know I'd . . . we'd never do anything so stalkery without the demon tequila."

"You didn't have to do mud wrestling to get my attention." Sam smiled. "If you wanted to see me you should have rung the bell. I was up anyway. Like I said, I couldn't sleep."

"*We* didn't know if you wanted to see *us*," Kirsty said with heavy emphasis on the plural. "*We* thought you might be with some other slut."

"Of course I wanted to see you," Sam said, looking puzzled. "You're the reason I can't sleep. I thought that you . . . all . . . didn't want to see me. You haven't spoken to me since we spent the weekend together. I thought that you weren't interested anymore and that you'd had your fun and moved on. It's been getting me down, actually, because I can't stop thinking about you, by which I mean just you and not those two other scary women you brought with you, no offense."

"Ahhh," Catherine and Alison chorused, catching each other's eye and giggling.

"What—pardon?" Kirsty said, rubbing her ear vigorously just in case she'd misheard.

"I like you Kirsty, a lot," Sam told her.

"But you left without saying good-bye or anything," Kirsty said. "You just went. I thought that was your way of telling me it was a one-off."

"I had a run scheduled with a client," Sam explained. "Six a.m. every Monday before he goes to work in the city. He's training for the London marathon. I left you a note on the pillow next to you."

"Oh," Kirsty said. "I'm a very restless sleeper."

"You didn't see it on the floor?" Sam asked her.

"There're a lot of things on my floor," Kirsty said. "Sort of hard to pick one thing out from another if you don't know what to look for."

"Oh, so he's not a heartless philandering sex pest after all," Alison cut in happily. "Shame."

"So," Sam said. "What do you want to do now?"

"Go to bed with you, please," Kirsty replied instantly.

"And after that?" Sam smiled.

"I don't know, maybe breakfast and then more bed . . . ?"

"No, I mean, do you want to go out with me? Be my . . . actual girlfriend?"

"Oh." Kirsty looked thoughtful. "Okay, then. Can we go to bed *now*?"

"A-hem," Catherine coughed loudly. "And what about us?"

"You know the way home, don't you?" Kirsty said, unable to take her eyes off of Sam.

"Actually, no," Alison said. "This block of flats wasn't even here last time I lived in Farmington. I have no idea where I am."

Kirsty looked pleadingly at Catherine.

Catherine sighed.

"You can come back with me, I suppose," she said. "It will be morning soon anyway."

Kirsty got up and hugged both of the women.

"You see, this evening has gone exactly as I planned. It's gone perfectly. I so totally knew what I was doing. I never had a single doubt."

"Of course you didn't," Catherine said to Kirsty in a low voice, as Alison made her way out of the flat and gingerly began the descent down the stairs. "Just one more thing."

"What's that?" Kirsty asked her.

"I'll deal with you later," Catherine promised her.

"Like I care," Kirsty said, and she slammed the door shut in her face.

Twenty-one

Catherine handed Alison a cup of tea, conscious of her old ex-friend looking around her tiny living room.

"Bit different from your place," she said.

"Yes," Alison admitted, taking the tea carefully as if she expected that at any second Catherine might throw it in her face. "But if anything, it's nicer—more homey. Marc picked out our house. Sometimes it feels like a bit of a mausoleum. Sort of a fitting setting, really, for the death of our marriage."

"Homey is one way to describe it," Catherine said, glossing over Alison's reference to her marriage. "Pokey and tatty is another."

The pair sipped their tea in silence for a few minutes, sitting at the small square oak table, each one trying to work out how to talk to the other, or even if she had anything to say.

"This is not at all how I imagined meeting you again would be," Alison said suddenly, setting her mug down firmly and looking at Catherine.

Catherine sat back in her chair and took a steadying breath. The moment to really talk had finally come. "Me neither," she said. "I could never have imagined on our first proper meeting after sixteen years we'd be high on tequila and trying to break into some strange man's flat. But that's Kirsty for you. She's got the brain of an eighteen-year-old inside the body of a thirty-year-old woman, although she would also insist she had the body of an eighteen-year-old if you asked her."

"But haven't we all?" Alison asked her. "I think I have, especially now things are coming to an end with Marc. Especially in Farmington. I feel like I've been playacting at being grown-up for the last fifteen years and now that I am actually a proper grown woman I don't want to play anymore."

Catherine looked at her. "No," she said simply, half shaking her head. "I don't feel like that. I feel more comfortable in my own skin now than I ever did when I was a teenager. It's taken me a long time to get here, but now I'm here. I'm . . . strong."

The two of them watched each other for a moment. It was Alison who dropped her gaze first.

"I thought that when we, *if* we saw each other again there would be a lot more shouting and tears. And a lot more bitterness and recrimination," Alison said.

"I don't really shout," Catherine said. "I hardly ever cry, but I do still have some bitterness and recrimination. I do still feel . . . *angry*, Alison. I thought I didn't, but then we spent tonight together and it was fun and I liked being with you." She shrugged and glanced out the window where the sunrise was bleeding into the sky. "So now I'm angry, don't ask me why."

"I was only seventeen," Alison said quietly, offering a tentative excuse.

"So was I," Catherine pointed out. "I look back now at what I was doing, getting involved with some older strange man I met in a park, when I'd never even kissed a boy, never mind had sex with one. Letting him take me home, and take me to bed. I think about that and I can't believe that was me, that I did something so idiotic and dangerous. It makes me terrified for my daughters." Catherine shook her head in disbelief. "Marc told me on that first day that he would be no good for me but I didn't care. It was almost as if I *wanted* to be hurt by him, I *wanted* to have my heart broken because then I'd feel something that would be mine and only mine. It was like living in a dream. But I always knew he would have hurt me anyway, all the signs were there if I'd known where or how to look for them. We never once talked about contraception. He told me that if he was careful we wouldn't need it. He never spoke about a future beyond the summer holidays, about what would happen to our great love affair once his contract was finished and he had to move on. And he knew I was pregnant, Alison. The night he ran away with you he knew and he didn't look back once, didn't call, didn't write, didn't try to check on what happened to me and his child. Not once.

"I got involved with a bad guy just as my mother said. And I think that that's why I'm not angry at Marc. Because he never tried to hide who or what he was from me. He never put on an act, or made promises he couldn't keep. Even when he said he loved me I knew instinctively that it was a temporary emotion, one that might even vanish the second I left his sight, and I wasn't too far wrong, was I? I was stupid enough and naive enough to hope that with me he could be better than he was. But that was my fault, not his. So rightly or wrongly, I'm not angry with him."

Catherine paused, and Alison watched the muscles in her jaw tighten and her face tense. "But *you* . . . since we were six years old you'd spent almost every day telling me to trust you, to follow your lead, that I could rely on you because you were my best friend, my family, my hero. And then in one second?" Catherine snapped her fingers, making Alison start. "All of that went up in smoke and you sacrificed our friendship, you sacrificed me to get what you wanted and I don't care if you were only seventeen and that we were both foolish girls caught up in a moment. What I *care* about is that after everything you left me. You left me all alone, too weak to be able to stand up for myself, because I'd never had to before. You always did it for me. I didn't know how to cope without you. I wasn't strong enough to stand up to my parents about the abortion. And if you'd have been there with me I would have been. So at the end of the day it's not that you slept with Marc behind my back. It's that you chose him over me. That's why I'm angry at you—and at me—and I know that it's not fair, but it's how I feel, even now after all of this time."

Gradually the morning sunlight seeped into the room, illuminating the condensation on the window and creeping across the carpet, briefly turning it into a field of shimmering gold. Catherine stretched out her palms facedown on the table and let the sun warm them.

"For a while," Alison began hesitantly, "for years, actually, I was so convinced that I'd done the right thing, for me *and* for you. I honestly believed that I'd rescued you from Marc and him from his life and had won myself the only man I could ever love in the process." Alison glanced tentatively at Catherine's face, trying to read her expression. But her features were locked. So she took a breath and went on.

"It was horrible being away from home for those few weeks, truly awful. We stayed in hostel after hostel because we couldn't afford anything better, places that stank, were crawling with vermin, and where you couldn't leave anything lying around because the second you turned your back it would be gone. Every night I'd cry, but when Marc was asleep, because I didn't want him to know. I wanted to come back home so badly, have a bath, sleep in a clean bed, have my mum cook for me. Those first couple of weeks were hard, but even though I wanted to go home and I missed Mum, I never once considered actually going because I was so convinced that I'd done the right thing. I thought I loved him.

"But it was more than that. I was jealous of you, Catherine, and angry that a plain quiet mouse like you had gotten to him, when it should have been me. I didn't want you to have him so I took him, without realizing what I was getting myself into. And then when I found out I was pregnant and I realized it was real life and not some little girl's game, I was terrified. I knew I couldn't let him go. I knew I had to say anything, do anything to make him come with me. I knew he felt lonely, that he missed having a proper family. I knew that not because he told me, but because you had. Because you were the one who really knew him. So I used that to make him choose me. I told him I'd be his family, I'd look after him. But what I really meant was that I needed him to look after me. I didn't tell him about the baby until after he left with me. I tricked him into going with me and I manipulated him into staying. Or at least I thought I did. Looking back now, I don't think he would have stayed with me if it hadn't suited him, no matter what I said."

"Eventually Marc got some casual work in a car dealership, washing the cars, cleaning up, and they let him watch them work so he could learn a few things. Once we got the cash together we rented this little studio apartment in Camden. This one room, with a shitty little electric hob that didn't get hot and a fridge that didn't get cold. After about a month at the dealership Marc told me that they agreed to apprentice him and help him go back to college. He was so pleased with himself, so proud. And I looked at him and I thought he feels like that because of me, because he's doing all of that for me, and I think that's when the jealousy and fear began to drain away and I realized that if I could hang on to him now, even though I'd won him so unfairly, then I would be able to love him and he would be able to love me. After about six weeks, Dad found us. He'd been looking all that time, apparently. Poor Dad, every day and all night walking the street trying to spot me. One of the hostels we'd stayed in gave him our address.

"He and Marc had a fight—a proper fistfight. You should have seen me, Cathy, I was on Marc's back trying to drag him off of my dad, begging him not to hurt him. But when I finally got in between them I told Dad to go home alone. It was the hardest thing I've ever done because I missed him and Mum so much and I'd have given anything for a hug from him. But I couldn't go home because by then I loved Marc and I was crazy about him, I just couldn't get enough of him, I was always thirsty and hungry for him, always starving for his attention. And he never left my side during those first couple of months, except when he was working. He never once suggested that I go back home or get off his back but he *was* distant, just a little bit removed from us. He was thinking of you, I expect, but I didn't know that then, or want to know it.

"He worked, and worked and worked until finally he and I and our lives began to knit together. We felt close, *I* felt close to *him*. The years after Dominic was born were the happiest years with him. When we didn't have much but we had enough and he was proud of himself, felt good about himself because he was improving our lives day by day, taking care of his son and then after a few years his daughter too. If he was seeing other women back then, I didn't know about it. Or I didn't want to know about it. I was so happy."

Alison paused. "I didn't think about you much then, I blocked you out of my memory, cut you out of my life. And if you did ever cross my mind, I'd tell myself I'd done what was best and I'd look around at our flat, at Dom and Gemma and at how happy Marc and I were, and I'd tell myself there's the proof, there is the proof that I was right to do what I did.

"It was while I was pregnant with Amy that I found out about the first woman, the first one I was aware of, anyway." Alison took a breath and rubbed her hands over her face. Catherine noticed that her fingers were trembling as she rested them back on the table.

"It was a nurse, from Gemma's nursery. I couldn't believe it when I found out because Marc never picked Gemma up from nursery except for this one time when I'd been so tired with the pregnancy that I'd begged him to leave work early and do it for me. And then a few days after that I began to notice that this girl, Lou her name was, who'd always been so polite and friendly, began acting all off with me, and while once she would happily chat about Gemma with me, she would barely speak a word to me now. I didn't know what I'd done to upset her. She was only a young girl about nineteen but you know, when you're pregnant you become sensitive about everything. I was really worried about it. I even mentioned it to Marc and he told me it was hormones playing up again. We even laughed about it.

"Then one day after dropping Gemma off I asked Lou if everything was all right. I told her I was sorry if I'd offended her in some way. She burst into tears and told me she'd been seeing Marc, and that she hated herself because she knew he had two kids and another on the way but she couldn't help it, she loved him . . ." Alison trailed off into silence and Catherine waited impassively for her to go on. Perhaps almost a minute passed before Catherine prompted her.

"What happened?" she asked.

"I took Gemma out of nursery. I hadn't wanted her to go in the first place. It was Marc's idea. He thought I'd need a break from both the kids during my pregnancy. And I waited until Marc came home that night and I said to him very politely that if he didn't stop seeing Lou at the nursery I would be leaving with both of his children. He wasn't shocked or horrified that I'd discovered him, just . . . regretful. He apologized, said it wouldn't happen again, and that was that. At first I screamed and shouted and there were tears, things broken. I threatened to leave him but I didn't mean it and he knew that. Looking back, I can't believe how calm I was after the first outburst. All I wanted was for the whole incident to be over and for me to not have to think about it again, to go on as before and pretend it never happened. I think I was more upset about Lou being uncomfortable with me than about her sleeping with Marc. I think that I had been expecting him to stray sooner or later. I'd prepared myself to accept it without even realizing. All I could think was that I had a baby on the way. I was in my twenties with three kids and I'd never had a job. I couldn't think of a job I could do. Being on my own just wasn't an option."

"But that wasn't the last time?" Catherine asked her.

"No." Alison shrugged. "There were four more that I know of after that. The last time was at Christmas. One of his salesman's wives came up to me at the Christmas party and said, 'Look, Alison, I don't want to do this to you, but it's not right. Everyone knows what he's doing except you. He's with her right now.' And she told me he was with his personal assistant in the office." Alison's laugh was mirthless. "The thing was his PA was my next-door neighbor, a woman of about my age. *I'd* got her the job with him because she wanted something part-time now that her children were at school. We used to go to pilates together on Thursday mornings. And the salesman's wife was right, this time Marc had been extra careful that *I* shouldn't find out. But everybody else knew. All the mums at school, the families on our street, the people at the dealership, even Dominic. It was as if my whole life was colluding to keep Marc's secret from me. For the first time in a long time I hadn't seen it coming and that's why I think it hit me, hit us so hard. The love and passion I had for him had begun ebbing away long before that night. But I think I used up the last little bit I had right then." Alison turned her face to the window, her features fading in the glare of the sun. She closed her eyes briefly and then turned back to Catherine. "I look at him now and really try to feel something, but I don't, not a thing. And the funny thing is, the really hilarious thing is, that one minute he's crying his eyes out over me telling him I don't love him and the very next . . . he's come round to pick up where he left off with you."

"It's hard when someone has cheated on you," Catherine said, her expression still implacable. "I know that. I sympathize. But if I'm honest there's a bit of me right now that's saying, 'Serves you right.' It's not a bit of me I like very much but it's there. And there's no point in me pretending not to feel how I do. Otherwise we'd never get anywhere."

"Fair enough," Alison said, pausing for a second. "It was just after Christmas that I started wondering if I'd made a terrible mistake. I started to think that instead of fixing things, I'd run off with your life and you'd accidentally ended up with mine. I began to think that that was why Marc and I never really fitted properly, not even when we were happy. When Marc moved us back here and I found out that you were married to Jimmy Ashley, *my* Jimmy Ashley, it seemed even more possible. I let myself think that the reason you and Jimmy weren't together was for the same reason that Marc and I couldn't be happy. Because we had each other's lives."

"Really," Catherine said without emotion.

"I know, it sounds deluded and I was, a bit. I was looking for meaning and symbols where there weren't any. The truth is when I left with Marc I was too young to know what I was doing to me, to my parents, and most of all to you. I thought I was in love, and I was if being in love means being jealous and obsessed and competitive." Impulsively she picked up Catherine's sun-warmed hand, holding on to it when Catherine tried to pull it away.

"Please, listen," Alison pleaded. She felt Catherine's hand relax in hers.

"I did the wrong thing. I should never have slept with him behind your back or run away with him. But I realize now, it wasn't your life I stole. It was mine. It was the ten more years I could have had with you of messing around like we did last night, having fun, being free, being young. I should have grown up with you. Instead I tried to grow up alone, overnight, and I failed.

"I'm sorry, Catherine, I'm sorry for everything I did, and if I thought there was any way that you and I could be even just polite to each other in the playground, I'd feel so much better. I'd feel so much stronger. Even if that's all that we can manage—what do you think?"

Catherine paused, pursing her lips.

"I don't know, Alison," she said, slowly withdrawing her hand from Alison's. "You sitting here in front of me and my knowing where you are again makes me feel, I don't know, sort of completed, but at the same time I can't just accept that our being friends again should be that easy. It doesn't seem right."

Alison sighed. "Do you remember that time when we were about nine that we fell out and the whole of our class fell out along with us? I mean you were either on Cathy's side or you were on Alison's, you got all the nerds and I got all the cool kids, remember?"

Catherine nodded. "I remember," she said. "It was horrible. I used to dread going to school. I can't even remember why we fell out."

"Heather Hargreves invited you to her party and not me. I got jealous and uppity and I took it out on you because Heather Hargreves was too scary, that's why we fell out," Alison said. "I could be a little cow even then."

Catherine shrugged. "How is this relevant?"

"I remember it so clearly, Cathy," Alison said. "I remember how awfully sad I felt every single day and how empty. I was so angry with myself for falling out with you but I couldn't admit that I'd behaved stupidly. I couldn't bring myself to apologize. I'd see you in the playground hanging around with those other girls and all I wanted to do was to come over and say hi. I knew that all I had to do was to say hi and that we'd be friends again, just like that."

"It took you long enough," Catherine commented.

"I was waiting for you to do it first," Alison said. "But you were stronger than me. You stuck it out because you knew I was in the wrong. It seemed to go on forever."

"It was probably about a week, if that," Catherine said.

"Do you remember how we made up?" Alison asked.

Catherine nodded, the ghost of a smile on her lips.

"We were in gym getting changed. I sat down next to you on the bench and I said, 'Hi, Cathy, I'm sorry.' And you said 'That's okay' and that was it. In an instant we were best friends again. It was back to you and me against the world, and I can still remember to this second the enormous relief that I felt in that moment. It was as easy as saying hi, that's all it took to make everything all right again. And I think I've been living with that sense of loss and panic all these years, waiting to see you and say hi and tell you that I'm sorry." Alison paused as she studied Catherine's profile. "What I'm trying to say is that if you want to get to know me again it doesn't have to be hard or painful. You can just decide to do it."

Catherine was silent for a long time and then she turned to Alison, the morning sun igniting her hair.

"I'm going to have to insist that you don't try to sleep with my ex-husband," she said. "I know I don't have a right to insist it. But if you did, that would be it between us because I . . . I just wouldn't like it."

"Don't worry," Alison said. "I won't."

Catherine nodded once. "One day, when you and I know each other properly and when I . . . *if* I feel like I can trust you again, I'll tell you about the abortion. I have to tell you about it, Alison, about everything that happened with my parents after you left and how I got the courage up to leave home and why it's taken me years to be able to feel good about myself again. I'll have to tell you about it even though it will be painful and difficult. And I'll blame you for some of what happened, which I know isn't fair because you were only a seventeen-year-old girl and you weren't responsible for me, but I will anyway and I think you'll need to accept that."

"Okay," Alison said steadily. "I'll be ready."

"I've missed you," Catherine said, and suddenly tears sprang to her eyes. "I've missed you a lot."

"Me too!" Alison said, and then briefly, clumsily the two women reached across the table and hugged each other very hard.

And then both of them laughed, the tension in the room deflating in an instant like a popped balloon, sucking out fifteen years of time with it.

"Your face, when Kirsty picked up that brick," Alison said with a giggle.

"And your singing," Catherine retorted. "Thank God those windows were double-glazed, otherwise we'd have been arrested for noise pollution." They chuckled again.

"Well, I'd better go, Marc will want to go into the dealership, I expect," Alison said. "It's going to wind him up something rotten that I was out with you all night. It will make him competitive, you know; he'll want you to like him more than me."

Catherine raised her brows and rubbed the back of her aching neck.

"Well, if you're going to promise not to sleep with my husband, I think I can manage to return the favor."

"No, don't," Alison said, making Catherine's head snap up in surprise.

"Pardon?" she asked.

"I'm not saying sleep with him if you don't want to. But as much as I hope I could do something with our marriage, I know now that I can't. All I can do is try to find the best way to end it for all of us, the children especially. When Marc brought us back here, part of the reason was to try and find that ideal version of himself that he's never quite been able to pin down since the summer he met you. Maybe that man exists, maybe he doesn't. But I'd like him to find out if he does and I think maybe he needs you to help him with that. So if you want to, I won't mind."

"Right," Catherine said, looking disbelievingly at Alison.

"So I'd like to have your girls over for tea," Alison said. "Maybe next Wednesday?"

"They'd love that," Catherine said slowly, suddenly feeling that her life had taken a decidedly surreal turn.

Twenty-two

"This has got to be the first properly sunny morning we've had in months," Jimmy said as he steered the boat back down the canal toward Farmington. "You can even feel the warmth on your face. Maybe spring's on its way at last, hey, girls?"

"Maybe," said Leila, who was sitting at his feet, happily chalking a masterpiece depiction of Jesus and a lot of angels in heaven, having tea with God, on the painted floor of the boat. Eloise sat opposite him on the little bench at the helm of the boat, her arms crossed, her face turned away from him, looking at the canal bank as it slowly drifted by.

"Did you have a good weekend, Ellie?" he asked her. "I mean after the bit where we all nearly froze to death."

" 'Course I did," Eloise said, smiling at him. "I liked going to the multiplex with you and Nanna Pam and Leila. I love this . . ." She put her hand on her new sparkling hot pink and silver scarf that Jimmy's mother had bought her, which clashed violently with her hair. "And even the cold and rainy night on the boat was fun, because we were with you. I just wish I didn't have to go home, that's all. I'd rather spend a hundred cold and rainy nights on the boat than go home to *her.*"

"I wouldn't, so don't try and make me," Leila scoffed as she continued to draw.

Jimmy sighed. Eloise had been making digs about her mother all weekend, just the odd word here and there, and of course his mother had loved it, but it had upset both him and Leila, who at one point had punched Eloise hard in the arm, causing a full-blown fight to break out.

"Look, you can't be angry at your mum, Ellie," Jimmy said. "Your mum didn't make us break up."

"She did," Ellie said. "*I* remember it. She got really, really cross and threw you and all your stuff onto the street. And me and her were crying and crying but she still did it, even though she could see that we were crying because of what she was doing. She made you go and she won't let you come back again even though you are sorry and she said you only ever had one chance and you blew it."

Jimmy thought for a moment, realizing that if his daughter was right about that, then he was in an even bigger mess than he'd first thought.

"She threw me out because I'd done something really, *really* bad," Jimmy said. "Mummy's never told you what I did because she doesn't want you to hate *me,* but if I hadn't done the really, *really* bad thing—then who knows? We might all still be together now."

"What did you do?" Leila asked, looking up from her drawing. "Stealing? Lying? Worshipping a false idol? Did you covet thy neighbor's wife?"

Jimmy swallowed; when he started this talk he hadn't planned far enough ahead to know quite how to answer that question.

"Do you know what covet means?" he asked both the girls.

"No," Leila said.

"Not sure," Eloise mumbled.

"Well, that's what I did, I coveted my neighbor's wife."

Leila screwed up her face in an expression of disgust. "Mrs. Beesley? But she's got a beard, Daddy!"

"No, not my actual neighbor's wife," Jimmy corrected her hastily, desperately wondering if he was doing the right thing by talking to them like this, or if this conversation was destined to come back to haunt him. "Not *anybody's* wife, actually, she wasn't married. But I did covet another lady, a lady that wasn't as beautiful or as wonderful or as important to me as your mummy is, but I did it anyway because I was stupid and confused. And your mum found out I was coveting her and she got really, *really* upset. So she told me to covet off."

"Huh?" Eloise said.

"Nothing," Jimmy answered. "Anyway, the point is that I don't blame her at all. I deserved it."

"You liked another lady apart from Mummy?" Leila asked him, frowning deeply. "That's wrong, Daddy, because you are married."

"I know and the funny thing is that I didn't even really like the other lady," Jimmy said. "I certainly didn't love her the way I love, loved your mum. But I coveted her and I was stupid, which you'll find as you grow up most boys are."

"I know that already," Eloise said, rolling her eyes.

"Me too," Leila said. "And stinky."

"Okay, well, that's good, I think," Jimmy replied. "But the point is that the breakup was my fault. I risked everything I had for the chance to feel free and young and footloose again," Jimmy said. "But the funny thing is that ever since I've actually been free and footloose, all I've felt is lonely and sad and as if something is missing in my life. And the thing that's missing is the thing I had to begin with. All of you."

"But you've still got us!" Leila said. "Even if you did covert that lady, which is a bad sin. But we forgive you because we love you."

"I don't forgive you," Eloise said. "I hate both of you now."

"Grown-ups are often a bit rubbish," Jimmy said. He paused and grinned at his daughter. "Do you really hate me, Ellie?"

"No," Ellie said sulkily.

"And do you really hate Mummy? Especially now that you know the truth?"

"Well, she could let you come back now that you're sorry, couldn't she?" Eloise asked. "If she wanted to."

"She could," Jimmy said, feeling his chest tighten with hope. "But if she doesn't want me to, then we still can't be cross with her, okay? Not ever. She loves you two. She'd do anything for you. The pair of you are her sunshine."

Jimmy looked up at the faultless blue sky. "You make her feel like spring is on its way even when it's a rainy and cold day. So don't be hard on her anymore, okay? I know you don't want to be."

"I have felt bad about it, actually," Eloise said. "Poor Mummy. It wasn't like me at all to be so mean to her."

"That's what I said," Leila said, chalking with enthusiasm. "Turn the other cheek."

The house was quiet when Jimmy let himself and the girls in through the back door. Dust spiraled in the still air of the living room where the sunlight streamed in through the windows. Jimmy looked around; there were two cold cups of tea on the table. Two cups, someone had been round. Probably Kirsty, he reasoned, but still he stared hard at the cups for a moment as if he might be able to determine some masculine aura around one of them. Realizing what he was doing, Jimmy blinked and shook his head briefly; this was not him. He had never been, as Lennon put it, a jealous guy. And now was not the time to start.

"Cat!" he called out. "Cat? Babe? We're back!"

"Mum!" Eloise and Leila shouted at once. "Mummy! Mum! We're here!"

They heard a creak of a floorboard upstairs as somebody got out of bed and Jimmy composed himself, methodically shutting down every single image of Catherine's long, white limbs entangled in Marc's hairy, dark ones that appeared to him on each heartbeat as he heard the sound of footsteps on the stairs. He fully expected his wife to appear with her hair tousled, wrapped in a sheet and sleepy from a sex marathon.

He'd never been so glad to see her looking so terrible.

"Hello," Catherine yawned, appearing in her pajamas. She mustered a weary smile. "Hello, girls," she said, holding her arms out. The girls ran to her and hugged her hard.

"Oh, what a lovely hug," Catherine said, sitting down with a thump on the carpet and then toppling onto her back, a daughter in either arm. Jimmy smiled at the three of them giggling helplessly on the carpet.

"You look terrible, Mummy," Leila said, peering at Catherine through the ropes of hair that lay across her face.

"Thank you, darling," Catherine said. "I feel pretty awful. How was Nanna Pam?"

"She was great," Leila said. "We went to the multiplex and McDonald's, and Nanna Pam bought us loads of lovely things, and best of all at Nanna's house it was warm so our noses and toes didn't turn blue like—"

"Sounds lovely," Catherine said, smiling up at Jimmy. "I haven't had much sleep so I'm a bit—"

"Good night?" Jimmy asked hesitantly.

"Weird night." Catherine chuckled. "Kirsty set me up on a blind date with . . . Alison."

"Gemma's mummy, Alison James?" Eloise asked her. "Are you friends too now, Mummy?"

"I think so," Catherine said.

"Really?" Jimmy said as he crouched down on the carpet. "What was that like?" he asked, wishing very much he could lean over and kiss that smile.

"Tense, bitchy, and in the end sort of good," Catherine said. "And I *think*, I actually think we might be able to coexist at the very least. Maybe even be friends again. I don't know if it's because I'm tired or if it's because of Alison, but I feel lighter suddenly. Like I could float away." She hugged the two girls to her. "But we didn't get in until six this morning so . . ." The sentence evolved into a self-explanatory yawn.

"Is that why you are in your pajamas, Mummy?" Eloise asked her, leaning up on one elbow to peer at her mother's face. "Were you in bed at four o'clock in the afternoon?"

" 'Fraid so," Catherine said, closing her eyes.

"Well, I think that's cool," Jimmy said. "Living it up, having a good time, remembering you're still young and beautiful . . . it's all good, so why not?"

Catherine screwed up her shut eyes. "Because it hurts," she moaned.

"Well, if you like," Jimmy suggested hesitantly, "if you're okay to watch the girls for a bit, I'll pop back to the boat, sort a few bits and bobs out, and then I can come back and cook dinner, if you want. I mean I don't have to. But as you're feeling rough, I could. If you like, but not if you don't, but—"

"Would you?" Catherine asked, opening one eye. "*Could* you?"

" 'Course I can, I don't just live on ready meals and pot noodles when I'm on my own, you know," Jimmy told her happily. "I can do a roast. Stick a chicken in an oven, how hard can it be?"

"Then thank you, Jimmy," Catherine said, opening both eyes to smile at him, feeling a sudden rush of warmth and gratitude toward him. "You're my hero."

Jimmy looked at her lying there, flanked on either side by their daughters, and he knew that if he sat on that carpet for one more second the sight would bring him to tears.

"Right, then," he said, jumping up in one agile move. "I'll be back in an hour."

Catherine flopped her head left to look at one daughter and then right to look at the other.

"You are going to have tea with Gemma and Amy next Wednesday," she told them, wincing as they cheered at the news. Leila kissed her on one cheek, and then after a second of hesitation Eloise kissed her on the other.

"Mummy," Eloise said, propping herself up on one elbow.

"Yes, darling," Catherine said, smiling at her.

"I haven't been kind to you very much, about you and Daddy. I thought that it was your fault, but Daddy explained it to me, about how he made you sad and angry even though he loved you and that really grown-ups are stupid a lot of the time, especially him so don't blame you for it. So I'm sorry. I love you."

"I love you too," Catherine said, feeling tears spring to her eyes that somehow made the day seem all the more bright and clear. "You feel very sad, don't you, about me and Daddy." She looked at Leila. "You both do."

Both girls nodded, but did not speak.

"It is sad, and I am so sorry," Catherine told them, looking at each of them in turn. "And I am so sorry that it happened to you. When I married your daddy and we had you we never, *ever* planned that this would happen; we thought we would always be together, all of us. But sometimes life has a way of sweeping you off course when you are not looking and turning things upside down. So I'm sorry, I'm so sorry you have to feel sad because of me and Daddy getting swept off course. But you know, we both love you so much and we will always look after you. We will always be a family."

She hugged the girls close to her and kissed each one on the forehead.

"I expect God is proud of you, Mum," Leila said into her hair. "Because you are trying very hard, and God loves a trier, Mrs. Woodruff says."

"Glad to hear it," Catherine said.

Twenty-three

Alison took a deep breath before slotting her key into the lock and opening the front door. She had no idea how Marc was going to react to her being out all night and most of Sunday. She knew since she had missed breakfast and lunch and was only just making it home in time for tea that he was bound to have noticed, but her phone had run out of charge at some point in the night and had been spared any demanding or angry messages he might have left her. So, deciding that ignorance was bliss, Alison took a long time to get back home, because she didn't want to face Marc. Besides, she knew what would happen the moment she saw him. He'd want to know all about her night with Catherine and she didn't want to tell him. The time she'd spent with her old friend had gone better than she could have imagined and this morning she felt for the first time in a long time as if some unnamed disjointed part of her life had clicked back into place. After she had left Catherine's, as tired and as nauseous as she was feeling, she did for the first time what she had either neglected to do or had been unable to do since she had arrived back in Farmington. She went for a walk in her heeled tan boots and visited all of their old places.

At last Alison felt as if she had been handed a passport to her past.

Her first port of call was the tree in Butts meadow where they both used to climb and hide out for hours in its canopy, telling each other stories and jokes, reading comics and later magazines. Alison was delighted to see that the tree was still there, its branches bare now and braced for spring. She stood at the foot of its trunk and looked up into its tightly laced branches. It was there as a nine-year-old that Alison had persuaded Catherine to wind the hands on her watch back one hour so they could have some more time to finish their game. The following Monday at school Catherine had shown Alison the bruises on her legs she had suffered for the extra hour. Then Alison walked through the near silent town to the coffee shop, Annie's Kitchen it used to be called. Alison pressed her nose against the window and peered through the glass, trying to imagine it as it used to be; now it was a PC repair shop.

It was in Annie's Kitchen that she and Catherine had both tasted their first cappuccino when they were twelve, and where Alison had made them come back every single day until they got a taste for its bittersweetness and could tell the other girls with all honesty that they were bunking off from PE to go for a coffee. Thanks to Alison, Annie's Kitchen had become the hot spot for schoolchildren for several years.

Taking a step back, Alison looked at her wan and transparent reflection in the glass and wondered how long the café had lasted in Farmington after she left, how long it had taken for change to overcome it so that all that remained of that hot and crowded landscape of her childhood existed only in her memory. It was then, with her head pounding and her mouth parched, that she retraced her steps to her son's school on the hill, the school that had once been hers and Cathy's.

She felt the heels on her boots sink into the churned mud and grass as she crossed the playing field to find the copse at the back of the school, backing onto a paddock of horses. This had once been, and still was, judging by the butts that littered the muddy floor, the smokers' den. It was here Cathy would sit, and smile and listen while Alison and the other girls smoked like troupers but did not inhale.

Once when they had been alone Alison tried to explain to Cathy that all you had to do to fit in and look cool was to hold the smoke in your mouth and then blow it out again, tapping the ash off the end of your cigarette as often as possible so that it would burn down quicker. Eventually she had managed to get Cathy to try it, but Cathy had accidentally inhaled and thrown up all over her feet just as the other girls arrived.

Now Alison sat down on the same low branch of a tree in the copse that she always used to—and that somewhere under all the moss and mold still bore both her and Cathy's names, carved rather inexpertly with a knife nicked from the canteen—and looked out across the field that glittered fiercely as the sun strove to evaporate the morning dew.

Even on that night when she had left Farmington with Marc, she'd always told herself that she was Cathy's savior, her crusader, and her hero. Was the true sum of their friendship that she was always getting Cathy in trouble for being late, encouraged her to skip school, even tried to get her hooked on smoking? Not to mention breaking her heart. Alison had always thought that she was the strong one, the one that Cathy needed, but now she realized that was no longer true; it had never been true.

The girl she had been fifteen years ago, Alison, the hip kid, the sexy girl, the one who was in with the in crowd and fighting off the boys, had always needed Catherine to keep her anchored to the ground. And it was the moment, the very second that she had chosen to let go of her friend that her life had begun, ever so slowly at first, to spin out of control. But with each revolution had come a fractional increase in speed, like the earth spinning on its axis at over a thousand miles per hour, so fast that you don't even notice it. So fast that Alison didn't notice it until finally her world had spun off of its axis and she was floating free, flaying around in free fall without a clue how to land safely.

Cathy had always been the strong one, she'd always been the brave one, and if Alison was honest, she'd always been the beautiful one too. All Alison had even managed to do was to burn a little brighter than Cathy for a short while, to burn so angrily that she put her friend in the shade. Now, though, Alison's light was almost extinguished.

And here she was now, in this town that Marc had brought her back to. Here with her children and one hundred promises she could not keep.

As Alison sat there, the sun beginning to warm the sky, she understood that now she had to be strong, she had to stand on her two feet alone for the first time in her life. Because now there was only her, and no one else to blame if she got it all wrong.

At eight o'clock Alison headed back to the gym, where she showered and changed into the workout gear she kept in her locker there, and rang home to speak to her daughters from a pay phone. But the home phone was engaged, probably knocked off the hook at one of its many extensions, and it went straight to voice mail.

"Hi guys, I stayed at Cathy's last night, sorry I didn't call but it was late by the time I decided to stay over. I'll be home in a little while. See you then!" Alison hung up the phone knowing that the message would languish undiscovered until someone picked up the phone to make a call, which on a Sunday might not be for hours.

Alison left the gym and was on her way home when she saw a train rumbling into the station. And the impulse to be anywhere except at home with Marc overtook her and she caught the next train to London, where she walked and shopped and ate a quiet lunch until she knew she could not put off returning home any longer.

It was just after four when she finally arrived home, hesitating with her key in the lock. But before Alison could turn the key, Marc opened the door, his clothes crumpled and his face heavy with dark stubble.

"Where have you been?" he demanded, his body barring her entrance to the house.

"Don't start," she said, ducking under his arm and heading for the stairs. "I've been out, Marc, I stayed out with Kirsty and Cathy last night and today I just needed some time to myself." She leaned over and made a fuss of Rosie, who had come skidding round the corner to greet her. "And I'm sorry if you actually had to spend some time with your children instead of breezing in and out of their lives in five minutes flat, but frankly you are such a hypocrite. I left a message on the answering machine, at least. How many times have you never bothered coming home without ringing?"

Alison was racing up the stairs when Marc's words stopped her in her tracks.

"Dominic went out last night and he hasn't come home since," Marc shouted. "I called you, I left you message after message. Where were you?"

Alison turned on her heel and looked at him.

"My phone went flat. What do you mean he hasn't come home? Is he with friends?" she asked him urgently.

"You went out," Marc began. "I was cooking the girls their tea when he came in, he'd obviously been drinking and he reeked of smoke. He said a few things, swore in front of the girls. So I said a few things and . . . it got out of hand."

"Got out of hand?" Alison asked him, her voice tense. "Marc? Did you hit him?"

"Did I . . . ?" Marc looked stricken. "No, Alison, I did not hit our son. At least I didn't mean to . . . he just makes me so furious, but I'd *never* hit him. I said a few things I shouldn't have, but he . . . he makes me so mad. I don't understand him, I don't know him anymore."

Alison stared at Marc for one fraught second as she attempted to decipher what he was saying to her.

"Marc," she said, keeping her voice steady and calm. "Did you hit him?"

"I didn't mean to." Marc shook his head, as if the details were irrelevant. "He stormed off and I haven't seen him since. I tried his mobile, it's off. I've tried you a hundred times, where *were* you?"

"Oh my God, was he hurt, was he bleeding? . . . Marc?" Alison said, feeling the panic and fury surge in her chest. "Marc, what have you done?"

"No, no—I wouldn't . . ." Marc trailed off. "He was angry, his pride was hurt more than anything. Like I said, he stormed off and I haven't seen him since."

She turned and walked slowly down the stairs, each descending step drawing her nearer to the fear she was beginning to feel for Dominic.

"I tried to find him," Marc said, taking a step back as Alison approached him. "But I don't know any of his friends. I don't know where he goes, I don't know anything about him. I put the girls in the car last night and again this morning and we drove around the school and a few other places but we couldn't see him. I don't know where he is, I didn't know what to do without you. I didn't know what to tell the girls. I told them you were at a sleep-over. Amy cried for you."

"We need to find him," Alison said, focusing on finding Dominic. "We'll both go, I'll take the girls with me and you go in your car. But if you see him . . . just phone me. Let me talk to him first. Don't frighten him, Marc."

"Frighten him? Alison it was nothing more than a slap, it wasn't as hard as when you slapped me at the party," Marc said, offering a smile.

Alison took a step closer to him, keeping her voice very low. "Our son, our child has been out alone all night because of you. You do understand that this is your fault, don't you, Marc?"

Marc took a breath, unable to meet her eyes. "I know that," he said. "I didn't mean for it to happen."

"But it did," Alison said, biting back the obvious retort, determined to focus on her son. "And now we have to find him."

"Mama!" Amy shrieked, crashing down the stairs, closely followed by her sister, hitting Alison's legs with full force and buckling them so that she had to sit down on the bottom stair. "Where *were* you, Mama? Dom's gone away and we don't know where he is or where you were. Were you with him?"

"No." Alison forced a smile for Amy as she put her arms around her daughter. "I was having a sleepover with a friend, with Leila and Eloise's mum, remember? I didn't know Dom was gone until just now."

"Daddy didn't know where to find him," Gemma told her. "We thought of everywhere we could look but he isn't anywhere."

"Mama?" Amy's voice was low, her eyes huge as she wound her arms around Alison's neck. "Is Dominic dead, like the teenagers on the news? Is he shot?"

"Of course not, of course he isn't. He'll be fine, I promise you," Alison said, hoping her daughter didn't hear the hollow echo in her words. She had a feeling, a cold, hard feeling in the pit of her stomach that frightened her.

She felt the weight of Marc's stare on her and looked up at him; his whole body was clenched with anxiety.

"I'll head out now," he said.

"Okay." Alison remembered something. "Ciara told us her surname, I'll look in the book. I'll try all the numbers under that name. If I can find her, maybe she can tell me some people he might be with. But if he's not with her . . ."

"What?" Marc asked her.

Carefully Alison kissed first Amy and then Gemma on the cheek.

"Why don't you girls go and get some snacks to eat while we're out looking for Dom, I'm ever so hungry," she asked them brightly.

"I can do that easily," Gemma said.

"I'll help," Amy said, and the two girls and one dog trotted off to the kitchen, reassured for the time being.

"What if he's run away, Marc?" Alison asked. "Gone back up to London? We might never find him then, not if he's gone back up there . . ."

Marc took her in his arms and held her for a moment.

"Come on, you were right the first time, he'll be fine," he said. "He'll be holed up somewhere hoping like hell that he's causing all of the fuss and grief that he is. He'll turn up."

"Okay," Alison said, feeling suddenly imprisoned in his embrace.

"You know that you and I are a good team," Marc said, holding her a little tighter for a second. Alison disengaged herself from his grasp.

"Just find him, Marc," she said. "Once upon a time you and he used to be such good friends. Don't throw that away too."

Twenty-four

Jimmy was determined to be prepared for what he was planning to say to Catherine as he climbed back on board his boat. This time he was going to get it right.

The best things that had ever happened to him, apart from his daughters, had been the one thing he'd put all of his forethought and planning strategies into. And that was getting Catherine to marry him. It had taken him ten months to get her to agree, ten months to persuade her that one day she would love him as much as he loved her. Every single day he'd offer her another little bit of carefully gleaned proof that he was the man for her, until she dropped the last of her defenses and let him love her the way he knew he could—forever. For ten months she'd resisted him, and then one morning as he'd been proposing to her between kissing each one of her toes, she'd said yes.

Or more precisely, "Yes, yes okay! Yes! Just stop it, *please*!"

"Yes what?" Jimmy had said, sitting up at the end of the bed, his heart in his mouth.

"Yes, I will marry you, you idiot," Catherine had said.

"Why?" Jimmy had asked, crawling along the bed and stretching out next to her.

"Because you won't shut up about it," Catherine had retorted, pulling the sheet over her breasts. "And I'm tired of lying to my mother about where I am."

"Your mother doesn't know you have a lover?" Jimmy had asked her playfully, enjoying the illicit implications of the word.

"No, she doesn't," Catherine had told him, her smile dimming. "I need to get out, I need to be myself, and when I'm with you that's who I am. You let me be completely me and you still seem to like me, so yes, I will marry you, Jimmy. You're the best thing in my life."

"That's the most romantic thing you've ever said to me," Jimmy had said, grinning from ear to ear.

Laughing with pure happiness, Jimmy had pulled her into his arms and kissed as much of her as he could before she squirmed away, rolling herself up in the sheet.

"I love you so much too," he'd told her, intent on revealing those lovely breasts again.

"I know." She'd laughed as he pulled her close to him. "And knowing that makes me the happiest I've ever been."

Ten years ago, months of careful planning and persistence had got him his wife in the end. And that was exactly what he needed to do now to get her back. Because when Jimmy thought of himself and Catherine back then, laughing and happy, entangled in that sheet, he knew he loved her just as much now as he ever did. No, he loved her more, because after everything they'd been through she still had the strength and generosity not to hate his guts for it. She was the most amazing person he was ever likely to know, and even if she was never able to love him back in the same way he loved her, he still had to try to make her see that he was still the man for her. He had to be able to know that at least he had tried.

So now he was going to think through how he was going to tell Catherine he still loved her and persuade her to give him a second chance from about a million different angles. He was going to be prepared for any eventuality. Every single one of them. He was going into this like a barrister: sharp-witted, determined to win, and impossible to distract . . .

"Afternoon, Jim," one of his neighbors, Leo, called as he hopped off his boat with his Jack Russell terrier yapping at his heels. "Lovely day for a walk."

Leo paused and watched as his dog terrorized the ducks, sending them splashing and quaking into the water, shaking their feathers in distress. And then the dog spotted a swan, hissing a warning with wings spread, advancing toward him. Sensibly the dog retreated, heading instead for the undergrowth on the other side of the towpath.

"Yep," Jimmy called back, hoping Leo wouldn't want to draw him into a conversation. He was a nice old man, but he liked to talk, mostly about his dog. Fergus.

"He's all bark, no bite, that one." Leo smiled indulgently as Fergus broke out into insistent barking in the hedgerow. "He'll have found something down there. Water rat probably, but he wouldn't hurt it," Leo said. "He acts all high and mighty, but when push comes to shove he's a big softy. Or should I say a little softy."

Leo chuckled, but Jimmy frowned as he looked at the bush that Fergus had disappeared into; something was driving the small dog to bark frenetically, so much so that the leaves of the bush trembled. Something white caught his eye. Fergus was tugging on it, growling between barks. Was that a . . . ? It was the sole of a running shoe. And it was attached to a leg.

Jumping down from his boat, Jimmy crouched down and crawled into the bush.

Fergus had found a boy lying on his side, his hood pulled up over his face, arms crossed over his chest, his legs drawn up against his body. Now that Jimmy had arrived, Fergus dropped the toe of the boy's shoe and was barking in his face, but the boy didn't move a muscle. There was a sharp acrid smell and Jimmy noticed that the boy had been sick, probably shortly before he passed out. In the grass next to him lay an empty bottle of whiskey.

"Christ," Jimmy said, scooping the boy up in his arms and lifting him out of the undergrowth and onto the pathway.

"Fergus has found a kid!" he yelled to Leo. "He's cold, looks like he's been here all night."

"Is he all right?" Leo asked him, bending to pick Fergus up. The dog continued his tirade, a high-pitched insistent yap that made Jimmy have to shout to be heard over him.

"I don't know." Jimmy pulled the hood back from the boy's still-white face, devoid of color except for his bluish lips.

"Oh God, it's Dominic," he whispered to himself.

"What did you say?" Leo asked him, bundling Fergus back into his boat and shutting the door on him. "Drug addict, is it?"

"No, I know this boy," Jimmy said as he watched Dominic's chest. "He's not breathing. Call an ambulance, Leo." Jimmy rested his head on the boy's chest and tried to block out everything around him as he listened; after an impossibly long moment he heard a heartbeat. "Tell them there's a slow heartbeat—but he's not breathing. Tell them to be quick."

"I haven't got a phone," Leo said, looking bewildered and frightened.

Jimmy threw his mobile at Leo's feet, where it landed in the dirt. "Here, use mine, call them now. Do it now, Leo!"

He turned back to Dominic and took a breath, sensing that each precious second that passed was irretrievable.

"Right." Jimmy closed his eyes. Last summer the school had sent him on a first aid course. All teachers had to know CPR. It was school policy. He knew what to do, he knew CPR, he just had to focus and think, and eventually it would come back to him. He took a breath and thought of Alison sitting in the café, talking about her son. He saw his own daughters lying there. Imagining in an instant their faces white and still. He couldn't afford to get this wrong.

"Recovery position first," Jimmy spoke aloud as he carefully tilted Dom's head back to keep his airway open. He was dimly aware of Leo in the background trying to explain where they were. He peered inside Dom's mouth: it was blocked with vomit, which must have been why he'd stopped breathing. He'd been choking. Jimmy cleared it away with his fingers, wiping them clean on the grass, hoping that suddenly Dom would take a deep breath, cough, and splutter into life. But the boy remained still.

"Rescue breathing, create a seal," Jimmy whispered to himself. He pinched Dominic's nose with one hand and held his mouth open with the other. He took a deep breath and blew it into Dominic's mouth, watching the boy's chest rise with each of the breaths he gave him. That meant he was doing it right; if the chest rose, that meant the air was going into the lungs.

What next? Jimmy thought as he continued to breathe, counting to ten. Wait and watch. You were supposed to give them ten breaths and then wait to see if they would start breathing on their own. He sat back on his heels and watched Dominic intently, holding his own breath, willing the boy's chest to rise. Dominic was perfectly still. But there was no time to panic, no time to think or worry about what the next minute or even the next second would bring. All Jimmy knew was that he had to keep him breathing, he had to keep oxygen going to his brain and hope that would be enough.

Circulation, he remembered, the *C* of the ABC during the set of ten breaths.

"Compressions. I haven't done compressions." Jimmy waited, watching Dominic again; his rib cage remained immobile. Hesitantly he placed the heels of his hands over Dominic's breastbone; was this the right thing to do?

"They're coming," Leo told him. "They said they'd be ten minutes. What are you doing?"

"Compressions . . . no, wait." Jimmy looked at his hands on Dominic's chest and then snatched them away. "No, no—his heart is beating, compressions could make it worse. I just need to keep breathing for him. Ten breaths and see if he starts on his own. Then ten more breaths. That's right. That's right. I just need to keep on breathing for him. Go and stand by the bridge, Leo, keep an eye out for them. You'll need to show them where we are."

"You're doing well, son," Leo said as he headed off, but Jimmy didn't hear him.

It seemed like an age before the ambulance crew arrived. They had to park a few hundred yards away and run the rest of the way. By the time the first paramedic sat down beside Jimmy and took over resuscitation, Jimmy's knees had gone numb, his legs had cramped, and he felt heady from the deep breathing. But he didn't notice any of those things. In those ten minutes his whole world had become about counting ten breaths, watching the rise and fall of Dom's chest, and hoping. But not once did Dominic breathe on his own.

"Can I have a word, sir," the second paramedic asked him as her colleague worked on Dom.

"His heart is beating," Jimmy told her. "I've been breathing for him, but he hasn't done it on his own yet."

"Do you know how long he'd stopped breathing for?" she asked him.

Jimmy shook his head. "I don't know. We found him in the bushes, me and Leo. He was white and cold, and he'd been drinking." Jimmy nodded toward the empty bottle. "He'd been sick, I don't know when . . . I teach him guitar. Maybe he came to see me to talk to me, but I wasn't here last night. I'd gone up the canal to see my mum. Maybe he was waiting for me and I wasn't here . . ."

"You've done all you can," the paramedic told him.

"Let's bag him and move him, this is about as stable as he's going to get here," her partner told her, and Jimmy watched as they expertly inserted a tube into the boy's throat.

"We've got to take him in now," the paramedic told Jimmy. "You say you teach him, can you give us his parents' names and phone numbers?"

"Yes," Jimmy said. "I can, I . . . I have a folder on the boat . . ." Jimmy stopped midsentence, staring at the place where Dominic had been.

"Great, can you grab that and come to the hospital with him until we track down his parents?" the woman said.

"Of course." Jimmy didn't hesitate. The boy needed him.

Jimmy stood looking at the clock in the hospital waiting room. It seemed as if hours had passed since they'd arrived in the emergency room and he'd stood, watching as Dominic was rushed through swinging doors. He had been instructed to wait outside. He'd been staring at the clock. Hours seemed to pass but the hands on the clock barely moved. If Jimmy stared at the second hand for long enough it even seemed to go backward. If he could stop time, turn it back. If only he'd found Dom earlier, got to him before he stopped breathing. If he had been on the boat when Dom came looking for him. Had the boy been looking for him? They'd played together three times now, had a laugh, talked about chord structure. The last time Jimmy had seen him Dom had waited for everyone else to go and then hesitantly asked him to listen while he played through a song he'd been writing. The boy's voice had trembled, caught somewhere between a child's voice and a man's voice, but it had been a good song. He'd told Dominic it was a good song. Dominic had smiled. Would that exchange have been enough for him to come and find Jimmy? Or had he been looking for a place off the beaten track where he could drink himself to death?

"Mr. Ashley?" A young doctor approached him.

"That's me," Jimmy said, holding his breath. "Is he okay?"

"I'm Dr. Malik. We've had to ventilate Dominic, but we're hopeful that that is a temporary measure. It looks like severe alcohol poisoning and respiratory failure caused by vomiting. Your actions probably saved his life." She produced Jimmy's folder of student contact details. "I've contacted his father. He's on his way in."

Jimmy took the folder and nodded.

"You say he's going to be fine?" he asked her.

The doctor didn't reply right away. "We're hopeful. You can go home now, if you like."

Jimmy thought of Catherine sitting at home, waiting for him with his daughters, and his heart and body ached to be near her. But he knew he couldn't go.

"I'll wait until his parents get here," he said.

Catherine winced at the loud banging on the door that roused her from where she had been dozing on the sofa, her girls watching TV slumped on either side of her.

"If that's your dad, forgetting his key . . ." she grumbled happily, aware of how much she was looking forward to seeing Jimmy, to watching him as he cooked dinner, teasing him about his culinary skills, the two of them laughing together again. She pulled herself up and went to the front door.

"Why didn't you go round the back . . ." Catherine stopped in midsentence. Alison, Gemma, and Amy were standing on the doorstep.

"Alison?" Catherine was confused. "Didn't we say next Wednesday?"

"Can you have the girls to play?" Alison's voice was light and she was smiling, but Catherine could see something else in her eyes. "It's just that silly old Dom has had an accident and he's been taken to the hospital . . ." Her voice wavered on the last word, and she took a deep breath. "Jimmy's with him, Marc's on his way and I didn't think I should take these two . . ."

"Jimmy?" Catherine asked her, her heart suddenly pounding in her chest. "Is Jimmy hurt, what happened?"

"Jimmy's fine. He found Dom. Marc said he gave him mouth-to-mouth or something . . ."

"Mouth-to-mouth?" Catherine looked down at the two girls.

"In you go, you two. Eloise and Leila will be over the moon to see you!"

The children were silent as their mother kissed them on the tops of their heads.

"In you go, I'll be back soon," Alison said.

"Is it bad?" Catherine asked her once the girls had gone in. Tears stood in Alison's eyes. "I don't know, he was drinking and he stopped breathing and I don't know what else. I have to go. Say if it's too much to ask. I didn't know who else to go to."

"Its fine," Catherine said. She reached out and touched Alison's arm. "Just let me know what happens. Now go."

The first thing Jimmy knew was the skull-splitting, searing pain that shot through his head. The second thing was finding himself on the floor outside the emergency room. Then he realized Marc James had punched him.

"What did you do to my son?" Marc demanded, standing over Jimmy, his fists clenched.

"Nothing." Jimmy clambered up, tasting blood on his tongue, fighting to control the surge of adrenaline that made him want to hit Marc back very hard. "I found him. He'd probably been out there all night. There was an empty bottle of whiskey next to him. I don't know what happened. I know you're worried and scared. That's the only reason I'm not hitting you back. But seriously, if you want to do something useful you should be in there finding out how your son is and not out here throwing punches at the man who tried to help him."

Gingerly Jimmy touched his jaw; it was sore, but it had been a glancing blow that had taken him by surprise, rather than a knockout punch.

Marc shook his head, his lips tight. "I can't," he said.

"What do you mean you can't?" Jimmy exclaimed.

"This is my fault," Marc told him. "I made this happen. We argued, he ran out of the house and didn't come back. If I could talk to him, if I could be a father to him . . . this is all my fault."

"Yes," Jimmy said. "Yes, it is all your fault. But you still have to go in there. You still have to talk to the doctors and find out what's happening. You don't get to run away. You're his father."

"What if he's not okay?" Marc said, looking into the room.

"You still have to go in," Jimmy told him. "If you are any kind of father—if you are any kind of man, you still have to go in. You don't have a choice."

"He's never tried to understand me," Marc said, and Jimmy guessed he was talking about his son. "He made up his mind about me, and the conclusion he's come to is that I'm a terrible person. I know what he thinks of me. So I try and stay out of his way. I try not to let his windups get to me. If I let him get under my skin I lose it with him. I don't mean to, because I love the boy. And I know I don't have any right to get angry with him, but I do. And now this happened because he doesn't try to see how difficult things are for me. There is nothing I can do."

"Bollocks," Jimmy said simply.

"What did you say?" Marc asked, looking confused.

"Listen, you're not talking to a chick now," Jimmy told him. "Don't try all your touchy-feely-nobody-understands-me crap out on *me*. We're both men. We know the score. You've been busy with work and quite possibly a woman other than your wife and maybe even mine. You're caught up in your own midlife crisis, wondering how you ended up with a lovely wife and three great kids—something that I find hard to believe too, as it happens. You're so involved with you and what everything means to you that you don't have time for your son. Your little girls are cute and adoring so you give them your attention whenever you're around, but he"—Jimmy hooked his thumb toward the entrance of the emergency room—"he can see right through, and he's angry and prickly and difficult to handle, and on your long list of priorities that mainly reads 'me, me, me' you've put him at the bottom because that's the kind of fucked-up selfish prick you are."

"Don't talk to me like that," Marc threatened, advancing a step toward Jimmy.

"Next time you raise a fist to me I'll knock you out," Jimmy replied, squaring his shoulders. "For Christ's sake, think about what you're doing here. The question is, Marc, do you want to do the right thing? Or do you want to run away from the mess you've made yet again? Do you want to fuck up some more lives and then just disappear? I'm a father and I know that no matter what happened I could never walk away from my children for even one second. If you don't go in there now, then you might as well leave for good because you won't ever be able to come back."

Marc stared at him with those dark eyes, cold and hard.

"Is this about me and your ex-wife?" he asked Jimmy.

"There is no you and my wife, and she's still my wife. We're still married. And anyway listen to yourself, man, you're here because your son, your fifteen-year-old son is seriously ill in the hospital and you want to talk about me and Catherine?" Jimmy shook his head. "What kind of man are you?"

Marc dropped his shoulders, staring hard at the floor before looking back up at Jimmy.

"I don't know anymore," he said, looking as if he had been defeated by his own anger. "He used to think I was a god, that I was the greatest. And I loved that, you know. I'd never had a dad myself, but I thought this is what it's all about. Father and son. I never had that. I *need* to get this right somehow, but I keep getting it wrong and now . . . now he's in there and I don't know what's going to happen."

"You have to be there for him," Jimmy said. "He's a good kid, your son. He's funny and smart. He's got real musical talent. He loves his mum and his sisters. You can't be that faultless, perfect man for him anymore but you can still be his dad, if you try. You're the parent. It's up to you to make the first move. If you spend all your time waiting for him to forgive you, you'll never work things out. But if you ask him to forgive you, then he will because he loves you. And if you do, then you have to be certain that you will never let him down again, because you can only ever ask someone to forgive you once and mean it."

"What's happening?" Alison arrived suddenly, breathless, her face pink. "I couldn't find anywhere to park and then I didn't have any change and . . . why are you out here? How is he? Is he okay?"

"I've just arrived," Marc told her. "I was just about to go in."

"You haven't seen him yet?" Alison asked. "You've known for nearly half an hour."

"I had the same problems as you—parking, change," Marc said, his effortless lies running off his shoulders like water. He avoided looking at Jimmy.

Alison looked at Jimmy, her face pinched and tight with fear. "Thank you for being there for him," she said.

"I just did what anybody would have," Jimmy said.

"No, not anybody," Alison replied, pointedly looking at her husband. "Are you coming in?"

"I'm coming," Marc said.

Jimmy stood for a moment watching as Dominic's parents disappeared down a corridor. Marc had always figured so large in his life, even before he'd met him. He was this mythical man, the man Catherine had loved, the memory he had never been able to compete with. And when he'd arrived in the flesh, with all his money and confidence, Jimmy had been even more frightened by Marc. But not anymore.

As Jimmy began to make his way back home to his wife and kids, he knew. He knew that whatever happened next, he was ten times the man Marc James would ever be.

Twenty-five

It took Catherine and Jimmy quite a while to settle the four girls down to sleep. Alison had phoned about an hour after Jimmy got back and told them that Dominic had finally begun breathing on his own.

"It was frightening at first, I didn't know what was happening," Alison explained, her voice trembling. "We were sitting there with him and suddenly he started spluttering and choking on the tube. The doctors came and took it out and he's been breathing on his own ever since. He's still weak and he's not really conscious yet. The doctor . . ." Her voice broke and she paused for a moment, then continued. "The doctor said its likely he's damaged his liver permanently. But he's young and strong. They think he'll make a good recovery. They said that Jimmy saved his life."

"Really?" Catherine glanced over at Jimmy sitting on the sofa, playing Beatles numbers for the girls to sing along to, a half-smile on his face as he and the girls rewrote the lyrics. She recalled the few microseconds when she had believed that Jimmy had been hurt too and how frightened she'd been. He'd saved a boy's life today and yet here he was playing "Lucy in the Sky with Diamonds" as if nothing out of the ordinary had happened.

"If Jimmy hadn't found Dominic when he did, then . . ." Catherine heard the break in Alison's voice and tore her eyes away from her husband.

"He's going to be okay," she reassured Alison. "Just focus on that and not what could have been."

"Are you sure you're okay about keeping the girls tonight?" Alison asked.

"Of course," Catherine reassured her. "We'll cobble together some uniforms for tomorrow and take them to school. They'll be fine here."

"If I hadn't spent last night with you," Alison said, "then this wouldn't have happened, but I did and . . . you've been very kind to me."

"Anyone would have helped you out," Catherine said.

"I know," Alison told her, "but I am so glad that it's you."

When Jimmy came down from reading the girls their final story he found Catherine lying on her back on the sofa, a cushion over her face.

"I'm sorry you ended up having to cook after all," he told her, a smile in his voice. "Not to mention get lumbered with houseguests."

"I don't mind," Catherine said, her voice a little muffled by the cushion. After a moment or two she sat up and looked at Jimmy through her tousled hair. "You were pretty amazing today."

"No need to sound so surprised." Jimmy smiled ruefully.

"I'm not surprised, I'm just . . . I'm proud of you," Catherine said, smiling at him.

The pair looked at each other for a moment, Jimmy standing at the foot of the stairs, Catherine perched on the edge of the sofa. Suddenly it seemed like neither one of them knew what to do or say next.

If was Catherine who broke the tension, slumping back onto the sofa. "What a weekend. You must be exhausted, I know I am. I feel too tired to go to bed," she half groaned, half-giggled.

"I could take you up if you like," Jimmy offered. "Like I did the night we moved in, do you remember?"

Catherine laughed, pushing her hair back from her face.

"Yes, I remember, I bumped my head about four times and you put your back out for a week! I don't think it's quite come to that yet." Wearily she pushed herself into a sitting position, rubbing the palms of her hands over her face.

Jimmy looked at her, feeling his blood pounding in his veins. Earlier today he had been determined to tell her how he felt about her, how he loved her so much that he ached deep in his bones when he wasn't with her.

"I could stay over if you like, help you with the girls in the morning," he offered.

Catherine shook her head. "Thank you, but you should go, you must be worn-out after everything. You should go and get a proper night's sleep."

"What, on that boat, are you joking?" Jimmy said. "Actually . . . I feel a bit . . . well, everything that happened today made me feel a bit . . ."

"Shaky?" Catherine offered. Jimmy watched in dismay as she held her hand out to him, offering him her gesture of friendship. He took her hand and looked at it, her strong, pale fingers in his. The sight of them brought a lump to his throat and for a moment he was afraid to say anything else.

"I'm sorry," Catherine said gently. "I should have realized, after everything that's happened, you don't want to be alone. Of course you can stay over, we can sit up and drink a bottle of wine and you can talk about it. I think there's a bottle in the fridge, I'll get it."

"I would like to talk," Jimmy said quietly, his eyes still fixed on Catherine's hand.

"Great, will you pull me up?" Catherine held out her other hand to him, and Jimmy pulled her onto her feet a little more robustly than he planned so that she collided with his chest, and for a second they were nose to nose. Jimmy caught his breath as she stood so close to him.

"I love you," he said seemingly out of the blue, dropping the three words into the millimeters of air between them without warning. Catherine stared at him for a second, her green eyes clear as glass, and then she smiled.

"Me too, you idiot," she said, and she wrapped her arms around him and hugged him tightly. For a moment, for about two seconds as his arms enclosed her waist and he felt her warmth crushed against his rib cage, Jimmy marveled that it could be that easy, that to turn his life around completely was as simple as telling her he loved her. And then he felt Catherine tense in his arms and putting the palms of her hands on his chest. She pushed him away from her a few inches so she could look at his face again.

"God, Jimmy, your heart is pounding," she said, her smile faltering as her hand rested on his chest.

"Because I love you," he said quietly. "Like I said, I love you. And standing this close to the woman you love does tend to make a man's heart pound a little."

"You've been through a lot today . . ." Catherine said.

"I know, but that doesn't change the fact that I love you. I don't want to spend another moment apart from you.

"You're fond of me," Catherine insisted, fear suddenly lighting her eyes. "You care for me, the same way that I care for you. We're *close*."

"Yes, yes, we are close and I am fond of you and we are good friends," Jimmy replied.

"Well, there you go, then," Catherine said, conscious suddenly of the length of his thigh pressed against hers.

"But that's not what I'm trying to tell you. What I am telling you is that I fully, madly, passionately *love* you," Jimmy said, his voice dropping almost to a whisper. "And I need you, every single atom of my body needs you."

"Jimmy." Catherine couldn't look into his eyes anymore. "Think about what you are saying," she whispered urgently. "You've had a shock, you're feeling muddled and confused."

"I've tried so hard not to love you, Catherine," Jimmy told her. "I wanted to forget I loved you because it seemed so bloody pointless. But love is love and there it is. I can't do anything to stop it. It was the night Marc and Alison came back and you were so upset and confused that I understood. I realized I'd do anything to stop you hurting, because I still love you. I love you, Cat." He took a deep breath. "And I wanted to ask you if . . ."

Catherine took three steps backward and sat down heavily on the sofa.

"Jimmy, don't," she said, shaking her head. "Don't say it. I can't hear this right now, I can't say what you want me to say. I'm tired."

"I know," Jimmy said, impulsively kneeling at her feet. "I know you're tired and I know I probably shouldn't say any of this now, but I have to because I can't go on hanging around you all day every day without you knowing how I feel. You don't have to say anything, decide *anything*. Just listen."

Catherine dropped her head into her hands, but she did not say no. Jimmy watched her for a second, her hair flowing over her fingers like water. This was it, he told himself. This was his moment.

"When I had sex in the loo with Donna Clarke at the Goat I made a mistake," Jimmy said, watching Catherine's fingers tighten in her hair. "Not just because I had sex with her, although that was a massive, *massive* mistake. I made the mistake because I thought I didn't want our marriage anymore. I thought I was worn-out with loving you. I thought I wanted to be young and free and single and alive again. Billy had drunk himself to death and I didn't want to go the same way as him, I didn't want to have the hopelessness he had at the end. That sense of losing something he'd never even had.

"I thought about the gigs the band got, the weddings and parties, and I thought about the tutoring I did and how you and I managed just about from hand to mouth, week to week and month to month, and I thought this isn't it, this isn't *my* life. It can't be because sooner or later I'm going to end up dead like Billy or Dad and I won't have lived *my* life. Touring Japan and bedding groupies, that was the life I was supposed to have. I was angry with Billy for giving up the way he did, I was angry at myself for failing, and I blamed you for not bloody delivering something you never once promised. For not loving me. And I've never told you how sorry I am about that. So now I'm telling you. I'm sorry, Cat, because while I was with you I had the best life I could have ever hoped for, I had everything that a bum of a musician like me didn't deserve and everything Billy deserved but couldn't have. But I couldn't see it. So I'm asking you to forgive me for what I did, for what I threw away, and to say that you'll give me another chance, because I promise you I won't let you down ever again and I know there isn't another man alive who can love you as much as I do."

Slowly Catherine lifted her head, raking her hair off of her face with her fingers. She looked white, all traces of color drained from her cheeks, her expression taut.

"I . . . I don't know what you want me to do," she said, her voice expressionless. "I don't know why you are saying all of this to me now, *now*, Jimmy, when things are finally at peace between us. Is it because of Marc? Is it because suddenly he's back on the scene and you've decided to get protective of me? Jimmy, this is typical you, you think you love me but you don't, not really. You care about me, you're worried about what I might do, and you love your children and you'd like them to be happy. You're thirty-three and the band isn't taking off, maybe it never will. You're feeling low, and maybe all of those things muddled up inside you make you think that you love me, but you don't. This is just a phase. It will pass."

"It won't pass," Jimmy said urgently. "Christ, Catherine, can't you see how much I want you, how much I need you, if I could only touch you . . ."

"Jimmy, stop it," Catherine pleaded with him urgently. "Don't say all this, don't make things difficult between us again. You and me being together that way is in the past. Finally, *finally* I can deal with that. I can accept it. We've made peace for us and for the children. I don't want to rake it up again, Jimmy. I don't want to . . ."

"But don't you see, you don't *have* to accept it," Jimmy said, grabbing her hands in his. "You don't have to. Because I love you and I think that finally you could love me if only you'd let yourself. We can be together again. After all, we're still married. I could move back in tomorrow and it would be as if the last two years had never happened."

Sharply Catherine pulled her hands out of his.

"The last two years happened, Jimmy," she said, an edge of anger flashing on the blade of her voice. "Donna Clarke in the ladies' loos *happened*. Me trying to get used to the idea that the man who *begged* me from one month to the next for almost a whole year to marry him, who *promised* me that he loved me and he would never let me down and kept on promising until I believed him, just ripped all of those promises and that marriage to shreds and in a matter of minutes *happened*." Catherine stopped catching the rise in her voice and closed her eyes for a second as she steadied herself. "You say you still love me, but I don't think you do. And even if you did, even if you were as stupid and as arrogant to think that after everything you've put me and your children through you can just waltz back in here and pick up where you left off, well, then I don't love you. I got over you, Jimmy. It *happened*."

Jimmy didn't move, he didn't breathe, he felt caught in that moment, afraid to break it because the very next second and every second that would ever follow it seemed pointless to him if she didn't feel the same way.

"We get on okay, don't we?" Catherine asked him, leveling her voice. "I like you being around. The girls need you around. So please let's just both go to bed and forget we ever had this conversation. I think you should go back to the boat and tomorrow we will carry on as if nothing happened. Please, Jimmy."

"I can't do that," Jimmy said, standing slowly. "I can't because I've said it now, it's out there and I can't hide it or lie about it anymore. I can't go back to the way things were before tonight." He paused, looking around him as if he didn't recognize where he was anymore. "Look, I knew you might not feel the same, I knew that maybe I got it wrong, but for a few seconds when I was holding you just then it felt so right, so perfect, Cat. And I thought . . . I thought I could sense you felt the same way."

"But you didn't sense that," Catherine said doggedly. "I don't feel that way about you."

"Right." Jimmy stood up straight and squared his shoulders. "I think I'll catch the late train to town. See my mates about that session work, after all. You've got the situation covered here. And besides, I could really do with the money, and you never know what it might lead to."

"Jimmy, don't." Catherine stood up. "Don't go because of this. Please."

"You're not being fair to me, Cat," Jimmy said, his voice tense. "You don't want me, but you want me to stay. And I can't live like that anymore. I can't hang around and be your friend and your babysitter, because I need more. So I have to go for a bit. Tell the girls I'll call them and I'll see them soon, but right now I have to go."

"Please, Jimmy, don't go like this . . ." Catherine began.

"Don't!" Jimmy raised his voice, making Catherine start a little. "Don't ask me to stay if you don't feel the same," Jimmy said. "It's not fair. You must see that."

Catherine reached out a hesitant hand and touched his face. "Take care up there," she said.

"You know me," Jimmy said, with a twist of a smile. "It's London that had better take care."

He leaned forward and kissed her just barely on the cheek.

"I'll see you," he said.

"See you," Catherine said, standing perfectly still in the middle of the room.

Jimmy closed the front door softly behind him so as not to wake the girls, and he headed for the boat. He would have just about enough time to pick up his guitar and catch the late train into town.

After that he had no idea what he was going to do.

Twenty-six

Alison sat down opposite Marc at the table and waited for him to say something.

The hospital had discharged Dominic earlier that afternoon. Alison was frightened, afraid it was too soon. How could they be sending him home hardly more than twenty-four hours after he'd been found not breathing in a ditch? But Dr. Malik insisted that Dominic was well enough. She had told them the results of Dominic's test, explaining gravely that her son was exceptionally lucky to be alive, not to mention surviving without any kind of brain damage and escaping with relatively little damage to his liver. They had made an outpatient appointment for him, and while he was still in the hospital he had seen a counselor.

Alison didn't know what had been said between her son and the sensible-looking middle-aged man who referred to himself as Mike. She and Marc had been asked to wait outside while the two of them talked. Since coming round Dominic had barely said three words to either of them, let alone looked either her or Marc in the eye.

It had been down to Alison to do the talking for all three of them, filling the room with senseless, pointless chatter, as if her words could cement the three of them together against their will.

She couldn't imagine what Dominic would say to Mike, but after forty-five minutes the sensible-looking man emerged and told Alison and Marc that he was confident that Dominic had not been trying to kill himself, that he was a normal adolescent boy who had let things get out of hand. In need of some care and attention, but he wasn't at risk of suicide.

"Does he know?" Alison asked the man urgently. "Does he understand that he could have died?"

"He does," Mike told her. "It's frightened him, so go easy on him. Take things slowly. He says he doesn't want to talk to me again, but if I were you I'd encourage him to talk to a professional counselor. Give it a few days until things have settled down a bit."

When they got back from the hospital Alison followed Dominic up to his room, running a bath for him while he sat on the bed, enduring a comprehensive wash from Rosie with a kind of boyish pleasure that made Alison's heart contract.

"It will be time to go and fetch the girls soon," she said. "I bet they'll be glad to see you. They were so worried."

"I know," Dominic said. Alison sat next to him. As she put her arm around him she felt as if her robust and vivid son had become fragile and thin overnight.

"I'm sorry I wasn't here for you, Dom," she said.

"I know," he replied.

"Look, Dom, what Dad did was wrong, but . . ."

"Mum, I just want to get in the bath and then get some sleep," Dom told her. "Can we talk about this later?"

"Okay." Alison looked at the tub of steaming water through the bathroom door anxiously.

"I could sit in here and chat to you while you're in the bath if you like," she offered.

Dominic raised one sardonic eyebrow, a familiar gesture of affectionate disdain that lifted Alison's heart more than she thought possible.

"Yeah, because it's every teenage boy's dream to have his mummy chat to him at bath time," he teased her gently. He put his hand over hers. "Look, I'm not going to drown myself, I promise. I never wanted to die. I was angry and I wanted to get drunk. I went to find Mr. Ashley because I figured that he really gets me, you know? And thought he probably hated Dad as much as I did. But he wasn't there. So I sat down under a bush and I drank and I waited. I fucked up. But I don't want to die, Mum, even if it does seem tempting with this hangover."

He rallied a smile for her and Alison had done her best to return it.

"You are so precious to me," she told him.

"Yeah, yeah, whatever," Dom said with an embarrassed smile. "Now go, before my bath gets cold."

At the door Alison paused and then asked her son the question she had been dreading. "Dom, what about your father?"

"What about him?" Dom asked. He closed the bathroom door behind him.

As she watched Marc, he remained immobile, his eyes fixed on the tabletop, his hand gripping a bottle of beer he had opened soon after they had arrived back from the hospital.

"Do you want another beer?" Alison asked him, hoping to break his silence.

Marc looked up at her. "No," he said. "I'm fine, really."

"I'll go and pick the girls up from school soon, they'll be so relieved to see Dom home. He gave us all quite a scare."

Marc did not reply and Alison closed her eyes momentarily, tried to calm herself and failed.

"You can't do this," she said finally, the tone of her voice causing Marc to look up and meet her eyes.

"What do you mean?" he asked her.

"You can't make this all about you," she said.

"It is all about me," Marc told her, suddenly animated. "I hit my own son, Alison. I drove him out into the night where he was so angry and hurt that he almost drank himself to death. It *is* about me. I did this to him. I did this to us." He paused, a frown slotted between his brows. "Perhaps I'm like my father. Do you think my father was a violent man? The type of man to hit women and children and sleep around? If I'd known him, if he'd raised me, I'd be able to understand why I am like I am. But I don't have a single memory of him. I don't even think I ever set eyes on him. So I can't blame him, can I? But I want to blame someone."

"Blame yourself," Alison said bleakly.

Marc looked into her eyes. "I do."

Alison paused, struggling to frame the words she knew she had to say into a sentence.

"Listen, Marc, if there was ever a chance for us, even the smallest chance that somehow we'd make it through and stay together, then that was lost when you hit Dominic." Marc flinched at Alison's graphic explanation of what he had done. "You're not a violent man, God knows you're not even an angry man. You're not even really a bad man. But you are weak and careless. You are a careless man, careless with the people you are supposed to love and more careless still with those who love you. You've destroyed my love for you and—for now, at least—you've done the same to Dom too. I don't want to see that happen to Gemma and Amy. I thought that if we stayed together that would be the best for them, but I was wrong. I can't be married to you anymore. For your sake, for my sake, and for our children."

"I'll change," Marc began.

"You won't," Alison told him. "Not while you're married to me. You'll always be the same. We make each other the same."

"No, you're wrong. This has been a wake-up call," Marc protested. "I know you hate me now, I can see it in your eyes. And I know Dom feels the same, but if you let me I can change that. I can make things better. Don't I always fix things, Al? I always make them better."

"Not this time." Alison's voice was tight. "Not that way."

"But Al . . ."

"No, *stop* it," Alison shouted. "Stop it! *Stop* it! Accept that you've done this. That you can't change it. The only way you are going to be able to have any kind of relationship with your children now is outside of this home and outside of this marriage. There are no more second, third, fourth chances, Marc. It's over."

Marc stared at her for a second and she braced herself for a barrage of reasons and explanations as to why she was wrong. But he shook his head, his shoulder slumped, and she watched the fight drain out of him, leaving only a shell of a defeated man behind.

"I know," Marc said simply on a sigh, all resistance gone. "I know. I'll move out. I'll find a place to stay tomorrow. Somewhere local. I'll talk to my lawyer. You should find one too. We'll make it as easy as possible for everyone. I'll give you whatever you want, the house, the car, maintenance—I don't want you to suffer because of me."

As Marc spoke, Alison felt ice-cold panic grip her heart and squeeze it, and a sense of dizzying unreality, as if she were watching this next turn her life was taking on a movie screen.

"No . . . I mean yes, I need your help. I don't think we should move the children again, not just yet. And you should support the children. But both of us have something to prove here, Marc. Me too, I need to be able to do something for myself. I need to *be* myself. I don't want you to support me. I'll find my own way." Alison felt a surge of confidence as she said the words and she knew Marc had seen it too. "This time I'll look after myself."

And that was it. This was the moment she had seen coming for months, possibly years, and yet had never quite believed would arrive. Marc was really going. After all this time he was going to leave her to stand alone in the world, and even if this had been the very thing she knew had to happen, hearing him say it shocked and terrified her and all at once she felt so terribly, terribly sad. A dream that had been born on a summer's afternoon fifteen years ago had finally ended and yet outside the kitchen window the world still seemed to go on as if nothing had happened.

"I'd better go and collect the girls," she said, picking up her bag and car keys.

She hesitated by the back door.

"You'll be here when I get back?" she asked him.

Marc nodded. "We need to talk to Gemma and Amy."

Alison nodded but just as she opened the door Marc spoke again.

"Al?" he called.

"Yes?" She did not look at him.

"I always loved you. I never lied about that."

"I know," she said, and closed the door behind her.

Twenty-seven

Do you think you can sprain your vagina?" Kirsty asked Catherine and Alison when they met for lunch on Monday. "Do you think it's possible that too much sex in too many positions can actually make you pull an internal muscle, let's call it the love muscle, because I'm telling you I've had so much incredible sex this weekend I think I might actually have sprained my vagina. I might have made medical history, because you know what, it is actually true. Sex is better when you're in love with someone, isn't it?"

Catherine ignored her tuna salad sandwich and Alison sipped her coffee.

"God, I thought the whole point of you two making up was that the world would be a happier, lighter place, cease-fire would be called across international war zones, mammals on the verge of extinction would start mating again, the ozone layer would repair itself overnight. If I'd known you were both going to be so miserable, I wouldn't have bothered getting you back together again, let alone asking you to meet for lunch. What is the point of me being blissfully happy and in love if I can't share it?"

Catherine looked at her. "I think that being blissfully happy and in love *is* sort of the point."

Kirsty raised a brow.

"If you say so," she said. She looked from Alison to Catherine.

"Okay, I give in, go on, tell me what the problems are and make it snappy because I want to talk about me and Sam and the sex we're having again before I have to go back to work, although if I'm lucky I probably could have sex in the storage closet with Sam if I got back before my two o'clock, so . . ."

"Jimmy told me he loved me, that he wanted to get back with me, and then he went to London," Catherine blurted out.

"That's incredible," Alison said.

"According to Jimmy, he's always been in love with me," Catherine said bleakly. "Never stopped for a second. And then he was all passionate and sexy and I'm really, really pissed off with him."

"Interesting," Kirsty said on a yawn, wincing as both women looked daggers at her. "Well, the fact that he's in love with you and wants to get back together with you is old news. I could have told you *that* months ago. The part where he gets on a train and goes to London is a bit confusing. How does he think that's going to help?"

"He doesn't," Catherine said. When Kirsty looked perplexed she went on. "Of course I'm not going to get back with him, am I?"

"Aren't you?" Kirsty asked her.

"Of course I'm not!" Catherine exclaimed. "I told him that I didn't love him. I told him that we weren't going to get back together. And he looked really sad and said he was going to London to find work."

"And let me guess, now you're feeling really sad?" Kirsty asked her.

"What if I am? I don't want things to be bad between us, do I?" Catherine snapped at her. "He's the father of my children . . ."

"The love of your life . . ." Kirsty mumbled.

"He's not," Catherine protested. "I told him. It took me long enough to get over him. But I did. Our relationship is finished and that's that."

"Okay," Kirsty said, more than a little skeptically. "If you say so. What about you, Alison? Why are you in such a mope? I mean I know your son had a near-death experience that was really bad, but he's over the worst now, right? Yet you still look like you're going to a funeral."

"I am in a way," Alison said. "My marriage is in the coffin. Marc is moving out of the house at the end of the week. We're appointing solicitors. We're doing it, we're getting a divorce."

"I'm sorry," Catherine said, reaching over the table and touching her arm briefly. "I suppose everything that happened with Dom brought it to a head?"

"Among other things," Alison said, biting down on her lip hard. "What's so stupid is that I keep crying. But it's me that wanted it. It's me that doesn't love him anymore and it's him that's a selfish, unfaithful pig, so why am I *crying*?"

"Because it's the end of a part of your life," Catherine told her. "A part of your life that when you started it you believed would always be wonderful, and would always be happy. And when you have to face up to the fact that that isn't going to happen anymore it's sad, it makes you want to cry."

"Bloody hell," Kirsty said. "You two are really bringing me down here." She turned to Alison. "Look, you're doing the right thing. You've just got to tough it out now because things will sort themselves out. You might even end up being best friends like Catherine and Jimmy, although that degree of closeness can lead to confusion for some ex-spouses, particularly the less intelligent ones like Jimmy."

"He is not less intelligent," Catherine said indignantly. "He's one of the cleverest, most brilliant and sensitive men I know, the ignorant pig."

"Is he?" Kirsty said mildly. "You should marry him, then, oh no, wait, you already have."

"He saved Dominic's life," Alison said.

"That was impressive," Kirsty conceded.

"It was incredible," Alison said, looking at Catherine. "He was incredible."

Catherine stared at her tuna salad sandwich, "He is such a bastard."

"Sorry?" Kirsty asked, confused.

"Jimmy. Jimmy is such a bastard," Catherine said furiously. "I was happy with him, I trusted him—it nearly killed me to let myself do that after . . . well, after you know what. But I did it. And then he had sex with Donna Clarke in the ladies' loos at the Goat. Now he's saying that he still loves me, that he still wants me, and he's going around rescuing teenage boys and he's doing it all too late. Two years too late. And that makes him a selfish fucking bastard. And I hate him. I hate him because I can't love him now. It's too late."

"Have you ever thought," Alison said, laying each word down ever so carefully, "that the reason you feel so angry toward him is because you do still have feelings for him?"

"No," Catherine said firmly.

"Okay, then," Alison said, catching Kirsty's eye.

"Come on, ladies, snap out of it," Kirsty said, banging her fists on the table, so hard it made the two old ladies at the next table send her disapproving glances.

"Let's summarize. You," she said, pointing at Catherine. "The man you say you don't love has just cleared off to London for a few days. What's the big deal? There is no big deal, that's what." Kirsty shifted her attention to Alison. "And as for you, your no-good cheating husband who you don't love anyway has finally packed his bags, leaving you in the nice house with every chance of a great big fat divorce settlement. We should be celebrating! I know, let's go out tonight. Let's go to the Goat, I hear there's a great new band playing and there's every chance of catching some action if you play your cards right."

Catherine and Alison looked at each other across the table.

"I suppose I've got free babysitting until the end of the week," Alison said. "I should probably make the most of it."

"And I'm sure Mrs. Beesley would babysit if I asked her," Catherine said, a little less certainly.

"Great," Kirsty said. "Let's tear this town up. Monday night in Farmington, rock on! Two bitter single chicks and their blissfully happy friend—how can we fail to have a great time?" Kirsty flashed her best smile at the outraged old ladies. "Now, can we get back to talking about me and my vagina?"

"Mummy, what are you doing?" Eloise asked Catherine as she hovered in front of the mirror that hung over the fireplace, her nose about an inch from its surface.

"Applying eyeliner," Catherine told her. "The trouble is, I don't know how people do it, because as soon as I get this sharpened pencil anywhere near my eyes I want to screw them up, so I can't see what I'm doing. I don't understand eyeliner. It's not natural. Why would anyone ever want to wear it?"

"You are trying to wear it," Eloise observed, tilting her head to one side as she watched her mother jabbing at her eye. "Trying quite hard, and you never normally wear eyeliner, especially not green eyeliner."

Catherine put the pencil down on the mantelpiece and looked at Eloise.

"On the way back to work from lunch today I bought a magazine. I thought spring is here, it's a new start, a fresh beginning, I'll give myself a spring cleaning . . ."

"Are you dirty, Mummy?" Leila asked as she stomped down the stairs in a pair of Nanna Pam's special clear plastic high heels that set off her Dalmatian pajamas particularly well.

"No, not that sort of clean," Catherine said, looking rather perplexed at the magazine article she had opened, balancing precariously on top of the TV so that she could refer to it while attempting eyeliner in the mirror. "Give Your Makeup a Spring Cleaning and Put a Spring in Your Step!" it yelled at her, the headline feeling more like a set of orders than a suggestion.

Catherine never normally bought magazines, especially not women's magazines, because she supposed, perhaps a little loftily, that on some level she didn't consider herself to be that kind of woman, concerned with earthly things such as shoes and makeup and . . . hairdos. But in the last couple of weeks her life had changed completely. Old wounds had closed and healed over, final breaks between herself and the past had been made at last, and she felt as if she should be a new woman. Somehow her tentative renewal of her friendship with Alison had helped her see her life from a new perspective, as though through a fresh pair of eyes. She hadn't realized until she had told Jimmy point-blank that she was over what had happened between then, that it didn't hurt her at all anymore. And seeing Alison again now, as an adult, a mother with her own problems engulfing her made Catherine realize she couldn't blame either the woman she now knew or the seventeen-year-old Alison had once been for what had happened to her back then.

She couldn't even blame Marc because all that had happened to her was the same set of wrong turns and bad choices that had beset almost every seventeen-year-old girl since the dawn of time, mistakes that had to be made and owned up to in order to become a whole person, a grown-up woman. Just recently everyone had been telling her how strong she was, but it was only now that Catherine believed it. She would always mourn the loss of the baby that she never knew, always regret that she couldn't have been close to her parents, but whereas once she thought those two things defined her, now she realized that although they were a part of her, they did not represent her whole. At the age of thirty-two, Catherine was finally ready to become herself.

The only trouble was she wasn't entirely sure how to go about it.

And when she walked past WHSmith and saw the headline on a magazine that shouted out "Ten Steps to a New You!" she picked it up and bought it, because it seemed a good place to start, and after a quick scan of the article so did buying some eyeliner.

"When I say a cleaning, darling," she told Leila, who had found her Dalmatian ears headband behind a cushion on the sofa and had shoved it unthinkingly on her head at a rather rakish angle, "I mean more like . . . well, a makeover."

"A makeover?" Eloise perked up. "I can make you over, Mummy, I know all about makeovers. I've got makeover Barbie plus Nanna Pam makes us over all the time."

"Yes," Leila said. "From Orphan Annie to little princesses," she said as if she was remembering a direct quote, which she no doubt was. "Nanna Pam said we could always look beautiful if only you put in some effort. Is that what you want to do to your-self, Mummy, put in some effort?"

"Like Isabelle Seaman's mum?" Eloise asked her. "She always puts in effort and she's . . ." Eloise trailed off thoughtfully.

"You could have colored streaks in your hair," Leila said, her eyes widening in awe. "And glittery eye shadow, Mummy. I've got some of that!" Leila was poised to race upstairs and retrieve it.

"No, no, not that kind of makeover either," Catherine said hastily as she envisioned her youngest child tearing her room apart in a bid to locate all of her secret cosmetics stash. "Apart from perhaps a bit of eyeliner. More than changing how I look, I mean, it's just trying to be a bit different, maybe doing things I wouldn't normally do, being a bit more adventurous and impul-sive."

"What's impulsive?" Leila asked her begrudgingly, clearly dis-appointed that she was not going to get to apply the glittery eye shadow.

"Doing things without thinking," Catherine said.

"Like buying eyeliner?" Leila asked dubiously.

"Well, yes," Catherine said, looking at the offending pencil and putting it back in her capacious and barely filled makeup bag.

"But why?" Leila asked. Catherine blinked at her.

"Because, you know, it's spring, new plants, new . . . lambs everywhere, new me."

"I like the old you," Leila said. "I like the you that's you, Mummy, only I don't mind if we give up eating so many veg-etables and maybe eat more cake. Is cake impulsive? Anyway, Jesus loves you if you wear eyeliner or not . . ." Leila thought for a moment. "He might actually prefer if you didn't wear it, though, especially if it's green."

"What I'm trying to explain to you," Catherine started again, well aware that it was more herself she was trying to enlighten

than her persistently curious five-year-old, "is that I'm not changing into a different person, I'm more sort of becoming more like
me than I am already. Sort of Mummy, but more so."

"Mummy but more vegetables so?" Leila asked.

"No, I just mean that from now on I might wear eyeliner
sometimes and perhaps the odd skirt . . ."

"That is an odd skirt," Leila said, looking at Catherine's
knees.

"And go out for drinks on a Monday night," Eloise said, speaking for the first time in a while.

Catherine turned to her.

"Yes, you don't mind me going out, do you?"

"Isabelle Seaman's mum started putting on eyeliner, and wearing skirts and going out for drinks . . ." Eloise said with a tone of
foreboding that made Leila widen her eyes. "And now she's got a
boyfriend with a beard. Is that what you are doing, Mummy, looking for a boyfriend?"

"Mummy!" Leila looked scandalized and Catherine wondered
how her back-handed attempts to apply eyeliner had come to
this.

"No, I am not looking for a boyfriend. I am trying out eyeliner. It's not the same thing, Eloise, at all. I mean look at Kirsty,
she always looks nice and . . . bad example. The thing is a person
can decide to change how they look for other reasons than to get a
boyfriend, so you don't have to worry about that at all, ever, okay?
I promise."

"Mummy," Eloise said in a slightly chiding tone, "you shouldn't
promise that. One day you might want to have a boyfriend, just
like Isabelle Seaman's mummy, and Daddy might want to have a
proper girlfriend that he likes."

Catherine tried to imagine herself with some unknown,
unnamed, absurdly titled "boy" friend and for some reason all

she could picture was a beard. Was that really what this was about, buying a magazine and some eyeliner? Were these her first tentative steps to trying to meet someone again? She tried to imagine herself out there, like Kirsty had been for so many months, getting involved with opticians, among others, dating and dancing and flirting and chatting all because of the faint possibility that it might deliver her into the arms of a man who could make her happy. But she found it impossible to imagine. To even comprehend spending time with a man who wasn't Jimmy—apart from that near kiss with Marc, which she was determined not to think about at all—and thinking about Jimmy with a proper girlfriend made her feel cross. She put the image out of her head and decided that she wasn't ready for eyeliner of any shade.

"Perhaps you're right," Catherine said. "I think I'll stay in tonight after all."

"Hooray!" Leila yelled.

Eloise put her hand on Catherine's shoulder and looked at her with that unnerving green-eyed stare. "I'm ever so proud of you, Mummy," she said.

Catherine smiled and put an arm around Eloise.

"Are you, darling, I'm glad." She considered leaving it at that, but the temptation to fish was just too great. "Why?"

"Because even when grown-up things are happening to you, you remember to love us," Eloise said. "And because you know when not to wear green eyeliner."

"Not coming?" Kirsty groaned, leaning against the door. "But it's *arranged*. Alison is coming and this is important, it's phase two of my plan to reunite you two. We've gotten over the hard bit, we've had an intermediate coffee. Now you need to get drunk together again and reaffirm your fledgling bond."

"You see, I don't think inebriation is necessary to get to know a person," Catherine said. "Unlike you, I haven't based all of my relationships on the consumption of alcohol."

"Ouch," Kirsty said. "And anyway, it's not true. Not with Sam; when we went round there the other night he was stone-cold sober."

"Yes, *he* was," Catherine replied, raising a brow. "Look, it's been a big weekend, a massive one, seeing Alison again, drinking tequila, things finally coming to a head with Jimmy. I need time to readjust and get used to the life I have now. At the moment it doesn't seem real."

"But you and Jimmy were over two years ago," Kirsty said. "How much readjusting do you need?"

"Yes, but back then we were over because he cheated on me and I was devastated, and now we're over because I told him we are and now he's devastated, which makes me feel . . ."

"Devastated too?" Kirsty chanced.

"Sad," Catherine said, nodding.

"Well, you are sad," Kirsty said. "I won't argue with that. Come on, come down to the Goat and celebrate your freedom."

Catherine pursed her lips. "Another time, but maybe not at the Goat."

"But you just said you're over the Goat, come on," Kirsty encouraged her. "It's been two years, what could be more symbolic of your moving on?"

"Eyeliner," Catherine said. "And I'm not ready for that either."

"What in God's name are you talking about?" Kirsty asked, peering at her. "Did you eat the worm in the tequila bottle? Because you don't seem like someone who's just found her best friend and ditched her deadweight husband at all."

"Just go out and have a nice time with Alison and cheer her

up," Catherine said. "I just want to stay at home tonight and re-adjust. That's what I want. I'm doing what I want."

"God, you're selfish," Kirsty said. "I was hoping to sneak off with Sam after half an hour or so, now I'll have to keep an eye on her all night."

"Ah, well," Catherine said with a cheery smile as she closed the door on Kirsty. "That's what friends are for!"

Twenty-eight

So Marc was okay with you going out on the town after you finally split?" Kirsty asked Alison as she led her into the music bar at the Goat; it was a small space and packed to the rafters with the Monday night crowd who always turned up for the live music. "He didn't expect you to observe a period of mourning like Catherine seems to think she has to?"

"He wasn't there," Alison said, having to speak up as the band struck up. "He didn't come back from the office before I left. I thought about phoning him but then I thought what if he's flat hunting or talking to a solicitor or knocking off his secretary. And somehow it doesn't seem right for me to ask him to come home so that I can go out. I couldn't leave Dominic in charge after his recent escapades. I think he needs someone to be in charge of him. So I asked the neighbor instead. She lent me her au pair, German girl. Very no-nonsense."

"How generous," Kirsty said loudly, as she waved a ten-pound note at the barman and grinned at him. "I hope one day I'll be rich enough to lend other human beings to people."

"You know what I mean," Alison said. "Anyway, I don't think I'm going to be rich enough to be borrowing them from people for very long. A three-bedroom house and some kind of job is what my future holds." She smiled and took a gin and tonic from Kirsty. They made their way through the crowd to the back of the room, where they could get a good view of the whole room.

"So tell me," Alison said, leaning close to Kirsty so that she could hear her. "I haven't been on the dating scene in fifteen years. What do you do these days?" Kirsty laughed.

"I see you don't have to go through a period of readjustment, like some people." She grinned.

"The last fifteen years of my life have been about readjusting," Alison said. "And probably the next fifteen will be too, but now I want to have some fun."

"Well, first you scan the room, look for someone you fancy," Kirsty instructed her, "and then you catch his eye, make sure he knows you are checking him out, and then you go over there and flirt."

"You make it sound like falling off a log," Alison said skeptically.

"It's usually a lot easier if you are so drunk that if you were standing on a log you would fall off it," Kirsty replied. "To be fair, a lot of people think that when a girl gets to a certain age she should start to be a little more reserved and a little less naked. But I say fuck 'em. Now, see anything you like?"

Alison trawled the busy room until through a gap in the crowd she glimpsed the back of a man's head, long hair pulled back into a ponytail, a battered leather jacket on the back of his chair. He looked exactly like Jimmy Ashley from behind. He was the only person in the room who wasn't facing the small stage.

"Okay," she said, target identified. "What next?"

"Make eye contact," Kirsty said, looking in the opposite direction for her boyfriend.

"He's got his back to me," Alison said. Kirsty looked at her.

"You've decided you fancy someone from the back of his head?" she asked. "You're not fussy, are you?"

"I'm only practicing," Alison said.

"Okay, well go over to where he is standing and make eye contact," Kirsty ordered her.

"You mean just go over and stand in front of him and stare at him until he looks at me?" Alison asked her. "He'll think I'm nuts."

"You asked me how to meet men, not how to become a secret agent," Kirsty said. "Go on."

Alison looked at the back of the man's head. This seemed like a very odd place to come for a quiet drink.

"What if he's a serial killer?" she said.

"Perfect, then he won't be too needy," Kirsty said, her face lighting up as Sam walked in the door. "Now, off you go. I'm not buying you another drink until you report back. Think of it as rehabilitation."

Alison watched the look on Kirsty's face as her boyfriend crossed the room and kissed her. She wondered if she would ever feel that way about someone again, or if anyone would ever feel that way about her. Well, every journey started with a single step, even if in this case it was in all likelihood a very ill-advised one. Alison took a breath and began to make her way through the crowd toward the back of the man's head.

"If I get all this way and he turns out to be a woman . . ." she thought to herself as she approached him, getting past the thickest part of the crowd and emerging in the near-empty seating area that was strewn with jackets and coats and where only one person was sitting. Not quite sure how to position herself in order to make eye contact with him (or change her mind and hurriedly make her exit), Alison walked over to the jukebox. She took a deep breath and turned around, hoping that the man looked a little bit like Jimmy Ashley.

Which was why she had mixed feelings when she found out he actually was Jimmy Ashley.

"You're not supposed to be here," Alison said just as the band took a break and the room filled with cheering and applause. Jimmy did not look up from his beer.

Taking another steadying breath, Alison went and sat opposite him. After a second or two he looked up.

"Oh, hi," he said miserably. "Great band, right? Really good, really . . . young."

"Why are you here?" Alison asked him. "Catherine said you'd gone to London."

"I did, got there last night, there was no session work, but a mate tipped me off about something else and I went to an audition this morning." Jimmy sighed. "I got the job."

"Jimmy, that's fantastic," Alison said, reaching out impulsively and covering his hand with her own.

"It's with this Gothic rock band my mate knows," Jimmy said desolately. "Their guitarist accidentally cut off his thumb during a fake satanic ritual; they picked it up and managed to sew it back on but he'll be out for weeks and they've got a tour coming up. The stuff they play is pretty basic, so I picked it up quick. They said with some black eyeliner and hair dye I'd be perfect. Oh yeah, and I've got to straighten my hair too, because apparently the minions of hell don't have a natural curl."

"Wow, that is exciting," Alison said, struggling to keep up her enthusiasm when his misery was like a huge gaping chasm that sucked all the joy from the room. "What are they called?"

"Skull Incursion," Jimmy said dolefully. "Shit name."

"I've heard of them!" Alison said excitedly. "Dom likes them . . . they're *awful*."

"I know," Jimmy said. "But it's not forever. Just while they're touring and this guy's thumb graft takes. But it's good money and eight weeks' work while they're on tour."

"On tour," Alison said. "With a band, that's cool, right?"

"In Croatia," Jimmy added. "Skull Incursion are big in Croatia."

"Oh," Alison said, desperately wishing she had ordered another drink before she came over here. "I hear it's lovely out there in the spring."

"It probably is, but Skull Incursion doesn't play in direct sunlight, it contravenes vampire health-and-safety-in-the-workplace regulations. Anyway, the flight leaves at five o'clock in the morning."

"Tomorrow?" Alison looked at her watch. "Then why are you here?"

"I came to say good-bye to Cat and the girls," Jimmy said. "Couldn't just go without saying good-bye to them."

Alison looked at her watch.

"Okay, so then why are you in the pub?"

"I thought I'd revisit the scene of my downfall first," Jimmy said. "The place where I fucked up so badly that one day I'd be taking a nocturnal tour with a bunch of faux vampires. I had a couple of pints and now . . . now I don't think I can see her. She'll just be all beautiful and amazing and not in love with me, and when I tell her I'm going away for eight weeks she'll be really supportive and pleased for me and I don't want her to be. I want her to fling her arms around me and say, Don't go, Jim, don't go because I love you and I can't live without you no matter how much you get paid for dyeing your hair black and wearing a pair of fangs."

Alison couldn't help but smile at him. He was even sexy when he was being all miserable over another woman.

"Jimmy, just go and see her," she told him. "If you don't you'll regret it."

"There's hours yet. Buy me a drink first," Jimmy said, looking at her directly for the first time, which made Alison sit back a little in her chair.

"Okay, then," she said slowly as Jimmy watched her. "I will. Back in a minute."

"Two Jack Daniel's and Coke, please," Alison shouted across the bar as the band began their second set. Kirsty appeared at her side and clapped her on the back.

"I must say I didn't think you'd actually go through with it," she said admiringly in Alison's ear as she picked up a drink. "Thanks for this, I don't normally drink whiskey, but . . ."

"Ah, that's not for you," Alison said. "It's for the man I picked up who is not a man but Jimmy Ashley. He's here in Farmington incognito and he needs someone to talk to before he goes round to see Cathy."

Kirsty narrowed her eyes.

"Are you going to offer him sex again?" she asked her.

"No, I am not," Alison stated firmly. "Even if I do really fancy him and I'm fairly sure he'd go for it because he's depressed and confused and a bit drunk. But I do have some standards and taking advantage of a vulnerable man is not one of them. Besides, I ruled him out when Cathy and I called a truce. I'm not going to make that mistake again."

"Hmm," Kirsty said, scrutinizing Alison for a moment. "Well, if it wasn't for the fact that my gorgeous and incredibly well-hung boyfriend wants to take me home, I'd come with you, but as it is, I'd much rather be snogging him than listening to Jimmy go on about how rubbish he is. Will you be okay if we shoot off?"

Alison looked over at where Jimmy was sitting.

"Yes," she said firmly.

"Are you sure?" Kirsty asked her. "You could come with us now, we'll walk you home."

"No, you go," Alison said. "I can handle him. I can do this for Catherine. After all, I'm a grown-up now."

Catherine looked at the TV screen and sipped her wine. Sometimes she wished that Jimmy had a mobile phone like the rest of the planet. Then at least she could call him and find out how he was doing. Ask him if he'd found a place to stay, got anyone to give him some food, that sort of thing.

Then she kicked herself hard.

He was a grown man, he could cope in the world on his own without her worrying about him. In fact, the very last thing he'd want would be her worrying about him. The trouble was over the last nine years she'd gotten into the habit of caring about him. It would be a hard habit to get out of. It unsettled her that he hadn't phoned to say good night to the girls, something he always did when he was away. It was probably nothing to worry about, either he was working in some studio and couldn't get out in time to find a pay phone or . . . well, there was always the possibility that he was dead in an alleyway somewhere, because there were very few things that would keep him from saying good night to his daughters, and death was one of them. Catherine was determined not to worry about that, however. She was determined not to think about Jimmy, period. The only trouble was the more she thought about ways to not think about him the more she thought about him. Turning her brain off was much harder than she'd thought it should be.

Eloise had been right, even if she hadn't known it. Going out today, buying eyeliner and magazines of all things, Catherine supposed she was trying to transform herself into the kind of woman that might attract a very tall man who likes redheads. She had been trying to find her feet again and part of that balancing act was feeling good about herself, feeling sexy and even sexual. For two years she'd shut that part of herself away as she concentrated on healing herself and keeping her children happy. It had gotten almost to the point where she didn't think she cared anymore if she never had sex again. Then Marc walked back into her life and nearly kissed her and that part of her hadn't slowly roused so much as rudely awoken. Eyeliner was Catherine's body's way of saying she was ready for a man in her life again.

She and Jimmy had taken a long time to get to know each other's bodies, they had taken it very slowly, inch by inch over several weeks before they finally went to bed, and then, even though it was still awkward and embarrassing, it didn't matter because they were already so close, and so bonded. With him Catherine hadn't felt self-conscious about her long, white body and boyish figure. With him she'd felt womanly, she'd felt beautiful. It had hurt her so badly when she discovered that she was not enough for Jimmy. It had hurt her even though she had no right to feel that way. How long could she have realistically expected him to go on running on empty in their marriage? Why had she felt it was okay for her to allow him to live that way? The anguish of finding him with another woman had ripped her to shreds, even if she knew that she had been just as responsible as Jimmy for driving him into Donna Clarke's arms. Jimmy had done what he wanted with Donna Clarke, but Catherine had made him want it.

She felt relief now that the pain of that discovery had ebbed away to nothing at last. That finally after two years she could look him in the eye and smile and be close to him again, because that sense of completeness she had known when she was with him had been hard to live without . . . Catherine metaphorically kicked herself hard again, only harder this time.

These warm feelings and thoughts she was having about Jimmy weren't real. They were a confused muddle of simply caring for him as a friend and the fear of being without him, of having to stand on her own two feet like she claimed she wanted but was really terrified of doing. They were feelings that she had to get over, feelings that were simply a reaction to truly being without him for the first time, like when you take off a warm coat and you feel the chill of winter. She had to keep reminding herself that these feelings weren't real, that they were just illusions that would fade soon enough, because it would be so wrong not to let someone go just because you felt half naked without them. And she had to let Jimmy go now, because despite everything she had said to him before he left for London, Catherine knew their marriage had failed because she couldn't love him enough. To bring him back to her side now with more false hope and half-baked promises would be too cruel, it was so much less than he deserved.

Catherine kicked herself really hard again and then gave herself a metaphorical slap for good measure. The reason she was thinking about Jimmy so much wasn't because she loved him, it was because she didn't love him. Her brain knew that, but her heart hadn't quite been able to believe it yet.

Just then there was a knock at the front door. Catherine looked at her watch. It was late. Past ten. It had to be Jimmy. He was the only one who would show up at this hour and he hadn't called because he was on his way back from London. He probably hadn't come to the back door because after the way they parted he felt that formal was the way to go.

It was only when Catherine reached the front door that she realized she'd run to answer it. But that was okay, it was okay to be pleased to see him as long as she didn't give him any kind of false hope, because that simply wouldn't be fair. She took a breath and composed her smile before she opened the door.

But it wasn't Jimmy at the door.

"Marc," Catherine said. "What are you doing here?"

"I wasn't in the neighborhood," Marc said, holding up a bottle of wine. "So I thought I'd make quite a long detour and drop by."

"I'm supposed to be out," Catherine said. "With your wife."

"Really?" Marc said, his smile faltering fractionally. "She didn't tell me. She's avoiding me at the moment, we're avoiding each other. It's awkward—the end of a relationship—when one of you hasn't exactly left yet and neither of you especially hates the other. It's like sharing a house with someone you don't know very well. She's trying to be kind to me even though I don't deserve it. We haven't told the girls yet. We were supposed to do it today but they were so happy this morning, getting ready for school. It just goes to show you what our marriage had come to. Their parents are barely speaking and they don't notice the difference."

"They notice," Catherine assured him. "They always notice."

She looked at Marc standing on the doorstep in his coat, clutching the bottle of wine. Asking him in had implications. But Catherine didn't have a choice. She had to ask him in.

She had to know.

"It's like a film," Jimmy said, downing his third Jack Daniel's and Coke since Alison had sat down with him. "A bad film. Boy meets girl, boy loses girl, boy ends up in Croatia. Where's the happy ending? My film's going to be a flop at the box office, story of my life, really."

"There's always a happy ending," Alison tried to reassure him. "It just might not be the one you expected."

Jimmy looked up at her again, making her tummy do a backward flip. She wished he would stop doing that. One minute he'd be all maudlin and pathetic, still cute but quite easy to cope with, and then she'd say or do something and he'd get this look in his eye, like she imagined a particularly disillusioned wolf might have when it's sizing up a nice lamb because steak is off the menu. And when he looked at her that way, she got the distinct impression that this evening could go a whole different way if only she would let it.

"Maybe you're right," he said, leaning forward a little bit, looking at her as if he was preparing for a bite. "Maybe I'm not in love with her at all and what I need is for someone to show me."

"Actually, I think you are in love with her," Alison squeaked nervously as Jimmy focused his attention fully on her, placing one hand on her knee. "I think you're crazy about her."

"I like *you*," Jimmy said, patting her knee. "You've got pretty hair and a very nice cleavage in that top." For one or two simultaneously mortifying and electrifying moments, Alison endured Jimmy's staring at her breasts.

"Got a lot of buttons, that top," he added. "I like a challenge."

"What I think you need," Alison said, "is a nice cup of coffee and some focus. You have to go and see her, Jimmy, you have to tell her you're leaving the country. Give her a chance to ask you to stay."

"I don't know why she fell out with you, because you are lovely," Jimmy said. "Apart from the whole sleeping with her boyfriend and then running off to abandon her with her psycho parents thing, but then everyone makes mistakes. Even her, even Catherine. I bet you that right now she's somewhere making a mistake, a really big terrible mistake. Yeah, and then who's she going to come running to, huh? Huh? Not me, because I'll be in Croatia. Oh God I love her."

"Right," Alison said. "Well, if this is the attitude you're going to take, then maybe Croatia is a good idea."

"How do you work that out?" Jimmy asked, looking bemused. "Are you drunk?"

"No, well yes, a bit," Alison admitted. "But what I mean is you've given up at the first hurdle. You told her you love her and she's told you she doesn't love you and now you're all drunk and on the next flight to Croatia. That doesn't strike me as really loving someone; I think if you really loved her you'd stay and fight for her."

"She doesn't want me to fight for her," Jimmy said, frowning deeply. "I'm doing what she wants because I love her. The funny thing is all my life I thought that this, touring with a band, and playing a gig every night to thousands of people, was my ultimate dream. And it's not anymore—yeah, I want to play, and write and be in a band and earn a bit more cash. But I want to do it here, in my hometown with my girls, so I can kiss them all good night every night, all three of them. Why does God do that, why does he move the goalposts just when you've finally scored? Well, I'll show him, I've just signed up with the other side."

"Right, I've had enough of this," Alison said. "If you're not going to go and see her, then stop whining and just go to Croatia. It helps a lot not seeing the person you have unreciprocated feelings for, and if you manage to stay away from them for long enough the feelings wear off quite a lot. Sometimes even totally. It's when they keep popping up at inopportune moments it gets a bit tricky . . ." Alison trailed off and looked into Jimmy's hazel eyes. "And there would be no chance of Catherine popping up in Croatia, would there, so if you haven't got the guts to go and see her, then shut up and get on the train."

"Can't," Jimmy said. "Can't go without saying good-bye because first of all she is the mother of my children, second of all she is my best friend, and third of all I bloody love her, I do."

"Go and see her, Jimmy," Alison said.

"Or," Jimmy said. "I could just take my mind off things with someone else. Someone sexy and friendly and smiley with a nice buttony top . . ."

"I think," Alison said carefully, "I might just nip to the ladies. Look, wait here, when I come back I'll get you a coffee and you can pop round to Catherine's before she goes to bed."

"You're very sensible," Jimmy said as Alison stood up. "You never used to be so sensible when you were Catherine's friend in your tight tops and little skirts."

"I thought you said you never noticed me," Alison said.

"I only said that because I was afraid you were going to make a pass at me. I would have had to have been blind to have never noticed you," Jimmy said, leaning rather far back in his chair so that it rocked dangerously.

Alison couldn't help but beam, and then Jimmy crashed backward in his chair.

"Get up," Alison ordered him as she helped him up, glad that the din of the music had covered the commotion. "When I get back I'll bring you a coffee."

Once she got into the relative safety of the ladies' loos, Alison splashed some cool water on her heated cheeks and looked at her damp face framed in the mirror.

Jimmy Ashley had noticed her when she was seventeen, he had admired her in her tight tops and little skirts. And who knew, perhaps . . . perhaps if she had never found out about Catherine's secret boyfriend, perhaps while Cathy was busy with Marc, Jimmy Ashley would have finally noticed how much she fancied him and put down his guitar long enough to ask her out. Alison closed her eyes and tried to imagine what it would have been like to be Jimmy Ashley's girlfriend back then, holding hands with him in the corridors, sitting with him at lunch, kissing him like crazy in the smokers' den at the back of the playing fields. Would he have stayed with her for a couple of weeks or months, or maybe, just maybe, if she hadn't left town and he hadn't fallen for Catherine, maybe he would have always stayed in love with her. Maybe if she'd never known Marc they'd still be together now . . . except they weren't together now and she had met Marc and Jimmy Ashley was in love with Cathy.

Alison shook her head and patted her cheeks; if only he wasn't so hot. Even when he was drunk and miserable he was gorgeous. Even when he was clearly sizing her up only because he was desperately in love with Cathy and wanted someone to take his mind off that, to stop him from taking any positive action, he made her knees tremble. Even though Jimmy Ashley was only flirting with her because he was drunk and in love with another woman, she couldn't help but like it, a lot.

Reapplying her lip gloss, Alison wiped away traces of eyeliner that had run around her lower lids with the edges of her thumb. She tossed her hair back over her shoulders and straightened her shoulders. This was her chance to show Cathy that she could be a good friend to her, even one of her best friends again. Jimmy needed to remind Cathy exactly what their relationship used to be like, and even though Alison had no idea how that was exactly, from the way Jimmy made her feel when he looked at her, she could hazard a pretty good guess. She knew exactly what he had to do to bring Cathy to her senses. And even if Cathy never knew that she'd given up the chance to get off with Jimmy Ashley for her, it wouldn't matter because Alison would know. And she'd know that she'd done the right thing. It was then she looked back up at the mirror and saw Jimmy reflected in it too.

"You and me, babe," Jimmy whispered in her ear as his arm encircled her waist. "How about it?"

"So," Catherine said, handing Marc a glass of wine. "How are things?"

"Difficult," Marc said, looking at her. "But I can't complain, I've brought it all on myself. I've got to start looking for a place to live but I can't quite bring myself to do it."

"Oh? Where do you think you might look?" Catherine asked him, desperate to make small talk, as if trivial conversation might fill in all the gaps between them and stop him from coming any closer to her. "Kirsty's boyfriend lives in this quite nice place up by the golf course, really excellent double-gazing . . ."

"I don't care, really," Marc said. "I don't care where I live."

"Oh, well it's good that you're flexible, they say often when people are looking for property they have expectations that are far too high . . ."

"You do know why I came here, don't you," Marc said. He put down his glass of wine. Catherine looked at it. She held on to hers as if it were a talisman that might protect her from what she knew was coming next.

"For a bit of a chat?" she said.

"Because the last time I was here we were interrupted," Marc said.

"Oh, right, that." Catherine heard herself laugh, conscious that mirth was the last thing she was feeling.

"I think," Marc said, leaning over and taking her glass out of her hands, "that I was just about to kiss you."

"Um, well," Catherine said, backing away. "You were, but in the meantime I've been having a think and I wonder if your kissing me is the most sensible thing for either of us to do because . . ."

And then his mouth covered hers and whatever she had been about to say was lost, engulfed by his kiss.

"Foxy lady," Jimmy muttered as he pushed Alison back against the tiled wall of the stall, forcing the door shut behind him and locking it. He kissed the curve of her neck, his hands in her hair, as his tongue flickered in her cleavage. "You are a very sexy woman," he told her.

"Oh God," Alison sighed, trying to find the will to push him away. "Jimmy."

"Baby," Jimmy said, running his hands over her shoulders and cupping a breast in his hand. "Need to get this top off, too many buttons, might have to rip it."

"Jimmy, wait," Alison said, planting the palms of her hands firmly on his chest and levering a few inches of space between their bodies.

"What's wrong," Jimmy said, looking around the stall as if he'd only just realized where he was. "You're right, not here. How about out the back? It's cold but I'll warm you up . . ."

"Jimmy!" Alison protested, looking down at Jimmy's hands, which still encased her bosom. She forced herself to concentrate. "Don't treat me like this, Jimmy. I'm trying to be a friend to you and to Catherine. Don't use me like this because you know how much I like you, it's not fair."

Pausing, Alison rather awkwardly removed Jimmy's hands from her chest and held his wrists down at her sides. "You know, you are a really great guy, and if you and Catherine were properly split up and you didn't still really love her and she didn't still probably love you, then I'd do it with you right here. I'd take my top off for you anywhere and I wouldn't care because I bloody fancy you a lot. I always have."

"So we're good to go, then." Jimmy smiled, dipping his head forward to kiss her.

"No, we are not," Alison said, turning her head at the last minute so that his lips grazed her ear. "I know you're drunk, Jimmy, but didn't you just hear what I said? Think about what you're doing, think about why you are doing it and how bad it is going to make you feel if it happens."

Jimmy took the one step back that the stall allowed and blinked at her. Without warning he sat down on the toilet and dropped his head in his hands.

"Okay," Alison said, feeling chilled now that the heat of his body was no longer pressed against hers. "A little less despair and misery, please."

After a moment's more hesitation Alison pulled her top back into place and crouched down in front of him. She put her hand on his shoulder and felt it shaking.

"I'm sorry," Jimmy told her, struggling to control his voice. "You're a nice person. You must think I'm a pig . . . I *am* a pig."

"You're not," Alison said. "You're just drunk and really, really stupid."

Jimmy covered his face with his hands and Alison crouched there with him, her hand on his shoulder, until finally the trembling stopped. Jimmy's face remained covered by his hands.

"I'm going outside," Alison said. "I'll ask the barman to make you a coffee. Then I'll walk you round to Catherine's and you can tell her you're going to Croatia. And I think I've got an idea that might make her sit up and think."

"Really?" Jimmy said eventually. "Look, I know I'm drunk as a bastard but I'm sorry for behaving so badly. Catherine's got a good friend in you."

"She has," Alison said as she straightened up with quite some difficulty.

The moment that Catherine closed her eyes it was summer again and she could feel the heat of that same sun radiate off of Marc's body as he pressed her back into the cushions, which yielded beneath her like the soft, long grass in the park. She felt the warm breeze caress her skin as his fingers deftly unbuttoned her shirt and ran lightly over her breasts and she was powerless in his arms.

More than that, she was seventeen again, fresh and new with no idea of what would happen next, and as long as she was in his arms, she didn't care.

His stubble grazed against the skin of her neck as his kisses traveled lower, and Catherine knew that if she kept her eyes closed it would always be summer, that summer long ago when for a few precious moments her life had shone like other people's always seemed to. Then she felt Marc's hands on her breasts, his teeth on her nipples, and she heard him groan. Opening her eyes just a little, she saw his dark head, his tawny complexion contrasting starkly against her own alabaster skin, and suddenly it wasn't summer anymore. Catherine wasn't in that park basking in the warmth of the sunlight, she was half naked on the sofa in her living room, her children asleep upstairs, and she was letting a man she barely knew now, had barely known then, and still had no reason to like or trust, undress her.

And Catherine realized that she didn't want to be that powerless seventeen-year-old anymore because her life had shone brighter after Marc had left her than it ever had done when she was with him.

"Stop, please," she said, stilling his hand and easing herself out from underneath him. His hair ruffled, Marc smiled at her.

"I'm sorry," he said, sitting up a little. "I'm going too fast. I wasn't prepared for how much I wanted you. There's still something between us, isn't there, Catherine? Still something really strong."

"Yes," Catherine said, quickly buttoning up her shirt, her fingers fumbling as Marc watched her.

"It's okay," he said. "I could unbutton that shirt all day long. All night long too."

"Marc," Catherine said steadily. "There is something between us but it's not real. It's the past. It's a moment in time where we both were once. A moment that meant a lot to us then, a time we've both often wished we could revisit, but I think maybe that's only because our lives now aren't going the way we want them to, not because we still have feelings for each other. It's that summer fifteen years ago that's between us and all the heat and passion we felt then. But it's not real, Marc. How can we feel anything real for each other when we don't know each other at all?"

Catherine could feel the heat in Marc's eyes as he looked at her. "Maybe you're right, but does it have to matter?" he asked.

"What do you mean?" Catherine asked, wide-eyed. "Of course it matters. We don't feel anything for each other. I don't love you, Marc."

For a second Marc looked stung, but then his expression became still and thoughtful.

"I loved you once a long time ago, but I don't suppose I love you now, I don't see how I can when I still love Alison," Marc said, looking up at Catherine. "I still want you, though, more than anything. Loving her isn't enough to stop me from wanting you."

He leaned forward again to kiss her but Catherine stood up.

"If you love Alison, then why do you do this? Why have you tried so hard to see me again if it wasn't because you thought that being with me again was going to somehow save you? You said you moved your whole family back to Farmington to find me when the only woman that can save you is the one you can't be faithful to."

"I do this, I say all of this because . . ." Marc sighed. "Because I wanted to have sex with you again, you're a very desirable woman. And because that time we had together back then when you were seventeen *was* special to me, it was a time when I kidded myself I could be just like any other man out there, happy and content. But even that memory is a deceit. After all, it wasn't so special that I didn't sleep with someone behind your back. Not so special that

I didn't leave town with a girl who I didn't know was pregnant and because I guessed that you were. Catherine, a lot of the time I like to think that I'm misunderstood, that my nonexistent childhood scarred me and made me into the kind of man I am. Sometimes I like to think that if only I'd met the right person, stayed with the right person, then I could be a decent man, the man I pretend to be. But I think it's time I stopped pretending to myself as well as everybody else. I'm the man who, loving his wife as much as he does, still pursues other women. I want you, Catherine. Even though I know it's wrong, right now I don't care, because I want you and I think you want me."

As Catherine looked at Marc, the sixteen intervening years since she had last kissed him settled quietly on his shoulders and he looked his age. Why Marc's saying everything that she already knew upset her quite so much she didn't know. Except that once she had carried his baby and cried for them both when they were taken from her. And because when she'd told Jimmy to leave, it was the thought of kissing Marc in the back of her mind that had partly spurred her on to end it, because she had to end it properly with Jimmy before she could explore any feelings she had for Marc. To discover so quickly that she didn't have any was quite a blow.

"I think you should go," she said.

Marc drank the remainder of his glass of wine in one swallow and stood up.

"That's a shame," he said. "I'd thought we could both help each other through this period of transition."

"That's just it," Catherine said. "For me this *is* a period of transition. For you it's your life, this is what your life will always be, moving from one woman you don't love to the next. I don't want to be one of them."

Marc nodded and shrugged on his coat.

"Funny," he said, "how people are always so keen to tell me how to live my life. It used to be Alison, then it was my son, then it was your *husband*, and now it's you. You're all the same."

"It's not the same," Catherine said. "Alison, Dominic, and even Jimmy tried to help you because they care. Because they want the people that love you to have a chance to be able to keep on loving you. But I don't care. I really don't care what you do next, Marc."

"You feel pretty good saying that to me, don't you?" Marc said with a hint of smile.

Catherine thought for moment and smiled at him.

"Damn right," she said.

"Hello, darling," Marc said to his wife as she appeared at the end of the path with Jimmy, whose shoulders were hunched against the chill of the evening despite the pint or so of hot coffee that was swilling around inside him.

"Hello, dear," Alison said, taking his appearance completely in her stride. "Pleasant evening?"

Marc hesitated and looked at Jimmy.

"Your wife despises me," he said. "She wouldn't have anything to do with me. So at least you know that."

Jimmy nodded and stood up straight. He looked down at the rectangle of light where Catherine was standing in the doorway.

"You are supposed to be in London," Catherine said.

"I know, but I needed to tell you something work-related," Jimmy said. "Don't worry, I'm not here to declare my undying love to you again. I got the message."

"Come in, Jimmy," Catherine said. "It's good to see you."

Both Alison and Marc looked back at the smile on Catherine's face as she let Jimmy in and closed the door behind him, narrowing the rectangle of light into oblivion. The pair of them stood at the end of the path looking at the shut door.

"So you didn't score, then?" Alison asked her husband.

"Nope, did you?" Marc asked, catching the wistful look on her face.

"No," Alison said. "If there's one thing I've learned it's that you can't stand in the way of your best friend and true love."

"And when did you learn that?" Marc asked. "Sixteen years ago this summer?"

"No," Alison said. "Just about an hour ago, as it happens."

Marc nodded. "Can I walk you home?"

Alison shook her head. "No, I think I'll stick around a bit longer in case I'm needed. If you could go back, though, that would be good, next door's au pair will be wondering where I've gone to."

"Leave her to me," Marc said.

"Croatia? On tour?" Catherine exclaimed. "Well . . . I mean, *wow*, Jimmy, that's great news! Of course we'll miss you, but you must go, eight weeks isn't forever, the girls and I will manage, they can always phone you and email. You do know how to use email, don't you?"

"I'll learn," Jimmy said without enthusiasm.

"Well, then," Catherine said. "Well done." She hugged him briefly and as she released him she briskly rubbed his upper arms. "Well done, you!"

"Thanks," Jimmy said, looking at her. "On tour at last with a fairly famous band. Dreams do come true."

"Yes they do," Catherine said, furious with herself that it was such an effort to be happy for him, because after all it was because of her he was leaving, because of her he couldn't stay. She could at least try to give him a good send-off.

"So can I go up and see the girls, I know it's late and a school night, but . . ."

"Go," Catherine said. "Go and wake them up. It's more important they see you."

Catherine sat on the top stair and listened as Jimmy talked to the girls, his voice low, theirs high and questioning.

"How long is eight weeks?" Leila asked him. "How many sleeps is it? Is it farther away than Christmas?"

"No darling," Jimmy told her. "I'll be back by the summer in time for your birthday. And it's not many sleeps, it's about . . . well it's a few sleeps."

"Is Croatia nice, Daddy?" Eloise asked him. "Are the people kind?"

"Croatian people are the nicest people you could hope to meet and it's a lovely country, with mountains and a seaside and lots of sunny weather," Jimmy said. "Not that I'll be seeing much of that what with being a creature of the night and all."

"Like an owl?" Leila asked.

"Pretty much," Jimmy said.

"I don't think I want you to go," Leila said eventually, her voice very small. "I think I'll miss you too much, Daddy."

"I'll miss you both too, darling," Jimmy said. "So much. But I sort of think I have to go."

There was a long silence and when Catherine peeped through the crack in the door she could see the three of them hugging one another desperately. As she watched the three of them together, it was as if the sun were already rising in the room.

"Okay, now," Jimmy said eventually. "You two had better get back to sleep, okay? I'll speak to you really soon and Mummy said I can even send emails to you. The time will fly by and when I get back I'll have about a million presents for each of you, okay?"

"Okay, Daddy," Leila said sleepily. "I'll pray for you. Love you, Daddy."

"And me, Daddy," Eloise added. "I love you too."

"Love you too, love both of you too," Jimmy said. "See you later."

Catherine had crept back downstairs before he came out of his children's bedroom. When he did emerge Jimmy stood outside the closed door for quite some time, waiting until he could hear them breathing steady and slow, as they drifted back to sleep.

"Right, then," Catherine said. "Got your passport? Because it would be awful if you got there and didn't have your passport and had to come home again . . ."

"Yep," Jimmy said. "I picked it up from the boat earlier, so no danger of that happening."

"Is it still valid?" Catherine asked.

"Amazingly enough yes." Jimmy chuckled. "I had to renew when we went to Spain with the kids and Mum, do you remember? That was the last holiday we had . . ."

"Travel insurance?" Catherine reminded him. "You need travel insurance, can't travel without it."

"The band takes care of that. They need it what with all the guillotines and swords. Turns out the undead are very safety conscious."

"And you're all packed?" Catherine said, aware that she was starting to sound like an overprotective parent.

"Two pairs of jeans, my jacket, a shirt, and a T-shirt," Jimmy said. "If I'm careful I won't have to do any laundry."

They smiled at each other and then, as they remembered what was happening, their smiles quickly faded.

"Is there anything else you wanted to say to me?" Jimmy said after a moment.

Catherine looked at him for a long time and thought of about one thousand things she wanted to say to him but didn't think she could, because she wasn't exactly sure why she wanted to say them and they were all things that had to be said for exactly the right reasons.

"No," she said.

"Okay, then," he said. "I think I'll go."

"There won't be a train for at least another half an hour this time of night," Catherine said. "Why don't you wait here for a bit longer?"

"Anything in particular you want to say to me in that half an hour?" Jimmy asked. Slowly Catherine shook her head once.

"Then I have to go now," he said.

"Right, then," Catherine said.

"After I've done this," Jimmy told her.

And then quite without warning he took her in his arms and kissed her. Not on the cheeks or quickly on the lips like he sometimes did. He kissed her properly, deeply, thoroughly, and passionately, his arms pulling her body into his as if for those few brief moments he might absorb her right inside of him. And just as Catherine found herself kissing him back he broke the embrace and walked out the back door.

"Jimmy, wait . . ." But before she could say anything else he was gone.

Twenty-nine

Catherine felt as if she should be dreaming, as if she should be having one of those dreams where you absolutely know you've got to be somewhere doing something that is completely vital but you can't remember what it is and the more you try to get there and the more you try to remember what it is the more you realize you are never going to make it. She felt like she should be having one of those dreams, only she was wide awake. All at once she was completely wide awake.

At the quiet knock on the back door she flew out of her chair, scrambling for her keys to unlock it.

"You came . . . Alison," Catherine said, her face falling. "Jimmy's gone to Croatia, he's gone."

"I know, that's why I've come," Alison said, and she smiled. "I was going to climb in through the window for old time's sake, but I thought that might push you over the edge."

"You know that he's gone to Croatia?" Catherine asked.

"Yes, he told me in the pub," Alison said. "How do you feel about that?"

"How do I feel?" Catherine said, a little dazed. "Oh, well I'm pleased for him, of course. And he certainly needs the money for a deposit on a flat."

"Catherine," Alison said, inviting herself in because Catherine clearly wasn't going to. "He's not here now. It's just you and me. So tell me, how do you really feel?"

"I want him to come back and stay here and not go to Croatia," Catherine said, desperately leaning against the counter. "I don't want him to go, but it's not fair, is it? What right have I to hold him back just because I don't want him to leave? I haven't got any right, have I?"

"No," Alison said. "Unless you happen to love him, for example? Because if you do, then he has the right to know."

Catherine stared at Alison opened mouthed, as if just for that moment she had been frozen in time.

Finally, she was able to speak. "How can I tell him one minute that I don't love him and then, just as his big dream is about to come true, tell him that actually now that he's about to leave me I might love him after all. I can't stand in the way of his dream again. He hated me for that before and he'll hate me for it again."

"He won't hate you for telling him the thing he most wants to hear," Alison said.

"But I'm over him," Catherine protested. "I don't care about Donna Clarke in the Goat anymore. If I think about it, I don't feel anything at all."

"That means you are over *that*," Alison said. "Not that you are over him. That means you have forgiven him, that you know that it didn't mean anything to him to be with her and that if he had you again he wouldn't ever, ever need anyone else. That means that you two have a chance to be together without any shadows of the past hanging over you, no bitterness or unfinished business. That means you should get your coat on and run after him right now. Because you love him and you finally have a chance to be happy."

Catherine looked at her. "Why are you helping me?"

Alison smiled at her. "Because you are my best friend. Look, his train is leaving in five minutes so it's decision time. If you want to go I'll wait with Leila and Eloise till you get back."

Catherine hesitated for a moment and then she grabbed her coat and ran.

Her chest heaved and her lungs screamed as they filled with the cold night air, and for the first time in her life Catherine wished that her legs were longer and that she was even lighter and thinner than she was, so that she could run just a little faster to find her husband.

And then suddenly Catherine stopped, as she gulped at the damp night air.

"What am I doing?" she asked herself. "What if it goes wrong? What if he doesn't love me? What if me chasing after him now is one big terrible mistake?"

She stood there frozen to the spot and she heard the blood pounding in her ears, the chill of the air against her skin, the water from the pavement soaking through her slippers, and in that one gloriously uncomfortable moment she felt utterly alive, as if all the energy in the world was for that briefest of times flowing solely through her. And Catherine knew she could only feel that way because she loved Jimmy, and if loving him was a risk, then this time, finally, it was one she was brave enough to take.

As she skidded into the station, she heard the rumble of the London train above her head pulling in.

"Jimmy, wait!" she yelled, her voice echoing down the empty underpass. "Wait!"

As she approached the steps that led up to the platform, she slipped in a puddle and lost her footing for a moment, falling to her knees for a few precious seconds. As she finally plummeted onto the platform, the train screeched to a halt.

"Jimmy!" Catherine looked up and down the length of the platform. It was empty. "Jimmy!" she called again.

Just then the alarm sounded as the doors were about to close. Making a split-second decision, Catherine leapt on board.

It was completely empty except for one boy in a hooded top, his head lolled against the window, his mouth open as he snored. For a split second Catherine wondered if Jimmy had gotten on the train at all, and then she realized that of course he had. He hadn't believed that he had any choice. Catherine had to find him and she didn't have much time, because in a few minutes the train would stop once more and then there would be no more stops until London.

He wasn't in the second or third carriage that she stalked through, her long coat flapping around her, her slippers slapping on the carriage floor. But he was in the fourth one, staring bleakly out the window, looking pale and tired.

"Jimmy," she said as she arrived in front of him, sitting down with a sway and a thump.

Jimmy looked at her.

"I'm still a little bit drunk," he said. "Are you actually there or am I hallucinating?"

"Jimmy, I'm so stupid," Catherine began, the words tumbling out of her. "And I know I don't have the right to ask you this, but please, can I talk to you?"

"Why?" Jimmy asked her, frowning. "What more is there to say?"

Catherine looked out the window at her own translucent reflection; now was the time to make her courage stick. Jimmy crossed his arms and raised an eyebrow.

She took a breath and looked him in the eye.

"Because I love you, I love you. I've only ever really loved you. Even when I hated you I loved you, even when I didn't love you I loved you, and I can't lose you now that I've come to my senses. I've wasted twelve years not letting you know how much you are loved and I don't want to waste another single second. I couldn't let you go without telling you that when you come back from Croatia, that if you want, me and the girls will be waiting for you. Waiting for you to come home to be with us again as a family. And I'm really sorry to rush you, but if you do want that you have to tell me right now because I've got to get off this train in about twenty seconds."

"Well, that's typical, you get ten years to make your mind up and I get twenty seconds." Jimmy looked at her with a tiny smile lightening his mouth. "What was it that brought you to your senses? Come on, tell me. Was it that kiss? That was one hell of a kiss, wasn't it?"

"Yes, it was," Catherine said, allowing herself to smile back at him. "It certainly was."

"I don't have to go," Jimmy said, leaning across and catching her hands. "Tell you what, I won't go. I'll come with you now. I want to, Cat, because all that stuff you just said? It's made me pretty much the happiest man alive on this planet."

"Oh, I want you to come back but you can't," Catherine told him, briefly pressing her cheek to the back of his hand. "You have to go—this is your big break! Go on tour and have fun, be brilliant and enjoy it, Jimmy. Because I'll be waiting for you when you get back, and anyway, missing you will be almost nice now that I know it won't be forever."

"They'll be the longest eight weeks of my life," Jimmy said, pulling her close to him and kissing her as the train pulled into the next station.

"This is the happiest good-bye I've ever had," Catherine told him, her fingers entwined in his as she stood up.

"This isn't a good-bye," Jimmy said, kissing her hand before he let it go. "This is the beginning."

As the train pulled out of the station, Catherine Ashley stood on the platform for a very long time, trying to understand exactly how her life had just changed. And then something occurred to her.

She had absolutely no idea how she was going to get home.

"Thank you," Catherine said to Alison as they sipped tea and watched the sunrise for the second time together. "And thanks for lending me the money to pay for that cab. I don't think any of this would have happened tonight if it hadn't been for you."

"It's my pleasure," Alison said. "Are you sad that he's gone for eight weeks?"

"I'm happy because I know that at last, maybe for the first time I've made him happy. And anyway, I've got the rest of my life to enjoy with him," Catherine said, smiling fondly. "Besides, I enjoy spending a sunrise with you, it's becoming a regular thing."

"Did you ever think we'd be like this again?" Alison said. "Friends, I mean?"

Catherine shook her head. "No," she said. "No, I never dreamt that we would be friends again, but now that we are I can't imagine a time when we won't be."

"And to think now our daughters are friends like we once were. Do you remember how we used to talk about that, how we said we'd always be together for all of our lives, how our children would be friends and we'd always have each other?"

"We were almost right," Catherine said with a smile. "In the great scheme of things it hasn't been that long that we've been apart. And now that the girls have found each other I suppose we'll be together a lot more." She turned and smiled at Alison. "It's good to have you back, Alison."

"You don't know how glad that makes me feel, hearing you say that," Alison said, her voice catching a little as she turned her face away from Catherine.

They sat in silence for a few minutes longer and then Catherine put her arm around Alison.

"Are you going to be okay?" Catherine asked her friend.

Alison looked into the rising sun so that the light drenched her face and she smiled.

"I'm going to be," she said. "I've got a funny feeling that I'm going to be."

Acknowledgments

More than anything this book is about female friendship and how important it is in a woman's life. So in that spirit I'd like to thank the incredible and brilliant women who are so crucial to my writing career. Lizzy Kremer, Kate Elton, Georgina Hawtrey-Woore, Jenny Matthews, Rosie Wooley, Sarah Darby, Catherine Carter, Kirstie Seaman, Margi Harris, Catherine Ashley, and finally an especially grateful and heartfelt thanks to Maggie Crawford, my editor and friend at Simon & Schuster. Maggie, thank you for being so wonderfully supportive and such an inspiration to work with.

Readers Club Guide

SYNOPSIS

For Alison James, moving with her family from London to her hometown of Farmington presents more than just a simple case of relocation jitters. The last time she saw Farmington, fifteen years ago, she was fleeing it—eloping with her best friend's boyfriend. Now, blessed with three children, but uneasy in her marriage, she wonders whether the decisions of her past have led her away from the life she was meant to lead.

Catherine Ashley, nearly divorced and a mother of two, can't help but wonder herself. Although she's contented with her children, and friendly with her almost-ex, she finds herself returning again and again to those few weeks fifteen years ago, in which she fell deeply in love, only to be betrayed and abandoned by her most trusted friend.

When the two women find themselves once more living in the same town, they must come to terms with the choices made and damage done in the past—in the process, healing the present and clearing the way for the right futures for both of them.

DISCUSSION QUESTIONS

1. Marc is first seen in the car, impatiently waiting for Alison. What is your first impression of him as a husband? What do you think are his real motivations for returning to Farmington?

2. When Alison returns to Farmington, she observes the changes the town has undergone, noting that it has evolved from "maiden aunt" to "trophy wife." How does the change in the town mirror the changes in Marc and Alison's lifestyle? Do you think any of Alison's observations are distorted, filtered through her own perspective? Do you think Catherine would describe the town the same way?

3. Both Marc and Alison acknowledge that she had a large hand in making him into the man he is today. Do you think she deserves credit for his outward success? Why? Is she then also to blame for the darker side of his personality?

4. Alison worries that Amy's anxiety comes from her own unhappiness at the time of Amy's conception. Do you think that children's personalities develop from the energy they pick up from their parents? Why do you think Gemma and Ellie gravitate to each other so quickly?

5. How much of Alison's decision to make a play for Marc was due to her attraction to him? How much of her motivation came from jealousy toward Cathy? Why do you think Alison was so threatened by the change in the social order of her

friendship with Cathy? Does hearing Alison's side of the story make you more sympathetic to her, or less?

6. Why do you think it makes such a difference to Alison to know that Marc had slept with Cathy? Why did she tolerate so much in her marriage to Marc prior to learning this? What did Alison gain from protecting her marriage?

7. Alison says that all along she's felt like a pretend adult, while Catherine feels the opposite, mature and grounded. Why do you think Alison feels stunted? What does it take for her to grow up? Does Catherine ultimately benefit from being a little less responsible and mature?

8. Describe Kirsty—how is her outlook on life different from those of the other characters? Why do you think she becomes such an effective bridge between Catherine and Alison?

9. Both Marc and Jimmy cheated on their wives. How are the situations different? Is Jimmy's cheating less of a betrayal? Why is he redeemed in the end, and not Marc?

10. Alison is continually drawn to the idea that she opted for the wrong life, stealing Catherine's instead of following her own path. What do you think constitutes the "right" life? What do you think the lives of the characters would be like today if Alison had never slept with Marc? What if Marc and Catherine had never met?

ENHANCE YOUR BOOK CLUB

- Feeling nostalgic? Bring in photos and share stories of your hometown with the group. How different is the town today?
- Are you still in touch with your childhood best friend? What would you want to ask her if you saw her today? Write a letter— share it with the group or send it off!

- For more about the author, check out her blog at rowancoleman.blogspot.com or on MySpace at www.myspace.com/ rowancoleman.

QUESTIONS FOR THE AUTHOR

1. I particularly enjoyed the parent-child interactions in *Another Mother's Life*. How do you write them so realistically?

I don't have a great memory, except for interesting conversations I've either had or heard. I have a six-year-old daughter and many small nephews and nieces as well as many friends with children of all ages. Conversations between parents and their children are often the most entertaining and I draw a lot from overhearing them!

2. How was this novel's process different from your other novels? Do you approach your adult novels differently from your books for teens?

With all my books I start from a central idea, then build the characters and finally plot it. Plot is crucial, of course, but for me believable characters that readers really care about are the most important element. *Another Mother's Life* differs from my other novels in that it is far more personal than almost any other book I've written. The only difference between the way I write books for adults and teens is really the length. Teen readers are just as sophisticated and demanding as my adult readers and deserve exactly the same kind of commitment and care from me. I do make adjustments in content and language, though. I think a lot about what I would want my daughter to read when she is older!

3. You center your story around a sharply drawn picture of childhood friendship. Was anything inspired by your own friendships or experiences as a teen?

The central friendship between Alison and Catherine is based on a friendship I had as a child and young adult, set in a version of the town I grew up in. There are elements of their relationship with Marc that did happen to me, the main one being that my best friend did run away with my boyfriend when we were seventeen.

4. You write from a number of different perspectives in *Another Mother's Life*. Was there a character you particularly identified with or enjoyed voicing?

I can honestly say that I really loved writing all the characters in this book, even Marc! There is a part of me in each of them, which is half the fun of writing—you get to disguise yourself in a multitude of costumes and characters. I loved writing Catherine's journey from hibernation back to life, and Alison's realization that her flawed life would never be fixable became really compelling. The character that was the most fun to write and the one that made me laugh out loud was Kirsty. One day I will give Kirsty her own book, or at least a short story—I think she deserves one!

5. You have a very entertaining web presence. What drew you to blogging and the online community?

I started blogging as a way to connect to my readers. It's always great to hear from them, to hear their thoughts and opinions. And I find it an awful lot of fun, although I am so busy writing books that I don't have time to blog as much as I'd like to.

6. Having begun your career on the publishing side, what inspired you to become a writer?

I always wanted to be a writer, but I didn't think it would ever happen, so I tried the next best thing and worked in bookselling and then publishing for several years. This just confirmed my belief that becoming a published writer was really, really difficult! But I kept on writing for pleasure, taking a master's degree in writing in my spare time, and one day I sent a story to a writing competition in a women's magazine. A few weeks later I discovered that I had won! Winning that prize opened a lot of doors for me, and within six months I had signed my first contract. It sounds corny, but I do believe that you have to keep dreaming for dreams to come true.

7. Who are some authors who have influenced your work?

I don't think that other writers "influence" my work as such, but I certainly am inspired by and enjoy the work of many writers. The Brontës, Austen, Dickens, and George Eliot are my classic heroes, and of contemporary writers I enjoy Sophie Kinsella, Marian Keyes, Kathy Reichs, Anne Tyler, Maya Angelou, Philippa Gregory, and about a million more!

8. How do the themes in *Another Mother's Life* relate to those you addressed in your earlier novel *The Accidental Mother*, which became a bestseller in the United States as well as the United Kingdom?

A central theme in both books is making sure that life doesn't pass you by when you aren't looking. It's easy to slip into a routine both personally and professionally and before you know it years and years have passed by and you've wasted the precious minutes of your life. I suppose I hope that, in some small way, I might encourage readers to reach out and grab life, to make things happen that will bring them the joy they deserve instead of waiting for life to happen to them.

9. Pocket Books has received a lot of mail from readers who want to know when you will return to the story of Sophie Mills, the heroine of *The Accidental Mother*. When can they expect a new Sophie Mills novel?

I am writing it at this very moment! It's fantastic fun to be back with Sophie, Louis and the girls again, although they have one or two problems to face along the way. Sophie has to decide if she is really able to commit to Louis, particularly as she finds out more about his past. *The Accidental Family* should be finished in late 2008 and I expect it will be published next year.

10. You've mentioned that you overcame dyslexia to become an avid reader and novelist. Do you have any advice for young readers who struggle with dyslexia?

My advice is to believe that you are just as clever and as capable as the next student and to treat dyslexia as a gift. Once you have overcome the technical problems associated with dyslexia then you come to realize that you are actually exceptionally lucky to be able to see the world in such a unique way. Dyslexic people tend to be exceptionally creative, imaginative, and adventurous and have a knack for solving problems and seeing around barriers. If you persist in learning to manage the condition and don't give up, then the whole world is your oyster.

11. How does motherhood affect your writing schedule? Does it feed your creativity at all?

I am very strict about my schedule because of my daughter. It's very important to me that I use the time she is at school effectively so that we can spend as much time together as possible when she is at home. I am very lucky to have a job that fits around her hours so well—many mothers don't have that option. As far as my creativity is concerned, my daughter inspires me probably more than anyone else I know. I write mainly for her, even though she is a good few years off of being able to read any of my books!

12. Can you tell us about any other writing projects on the horizon?

The next book coming out in the United States in spring 2009 is *Mommy By Mistake,* the story of Natalie Curzon, a busy and often capricious career woman who finds herself pregnant after a whirlwind affair in Venice. On leave from her glamorous job, Natalie has to forge a completely new life for herself—and her baby. Right now, I'm working on the next Sophie Mills novel, and also the sixth teen book featuring child star Ruby Parker. Also later in 2008 I will begin to write a series of supernatural thrillers that I've had planned for a long time for girls and boys, the first of which will be called *Welcome to Weirdsville,* which will be published in 2009.